HOW IT ALL BEGAN . . .

Fergus poured himself another glass of champagne. "Miss Barstow," he said, "I have the means to make you a movie star."

Her large eyes gazed at him over the rim of her glass. He was just a kid, even younger than she. But there was a potential under that cheap suit, a promise, too, in that attitude which had given him the drive to seek her out against such odds.

Deliberately she let her gown slip off one shoulder. She saw his amazement at several exposed inches of ivory flesh.

Later they lay together and he cradled her for a moment in his arms, his eyes closed. Then he stood up.

"Look, Miss Barstow," he said, "I hope you don't think–"

She looked up at him and smiled. "Don't you think under the circumstances you might call me Claudia. By the way, what is your name?"

THE BEGGARS ARE COMING
by Mary Loos

THE BEGGARS ARE COMING

Mary Loos

For
Edward Sale, my son—
a gentleman, a scholar, and an inspiration—
with love

THE BEGGARS ARE COMING
A Bantam Book / published September 1974

Published simultaneously in the United States and Canada

Bantam Books are published by Bantam Books, Inc. Its trademark, consisting of the words "Bantam Books" and the portrayal of a bantam, is registered in the United States Patent Office and in other countries. Marca Registrada. Bantam Books, Inc., 666 Fifth Avenue, New York, New York 10019.

PRINTED IN THE UNITED STATES OF AMERICA

CONTENTS

I

THE BRONX:
1913

1

The neighborhood would never be the same again. It was Saturday night and the East Bronx was astir.

The dazzling marquee of the new movie house, the Little Diamond, signaled that bright lights were coming to ordinary people. The first neighborhood nondenominational meeting place was opening.

Simon Moses fastened the blue satin ribbon that stretched across the lobby of his pristine theater. The brass fittings on his plate glass doors were polished to gold. Two potted palms rested in elegant jardinieres on the turkey-red carpeting. A fancy No Smoking sign stood on an easel in the lobby. Simon stepped back to admire the display sheets, then walked outside to make sure that all the light bulbs were on. The thought of the light bill made him a little sick.

He had come a long way in his thirty-eight years to own a three-hundred-seat palace like this. He had parlayed the profits from a secondhand furniture store and a furniture factory into four neighborhood movie houses. This newest one was a far reach from the first—a nickelodeon, created from an empty store and some repossessed funeral-parlor chairs.

The last workman had just left. It was incredible that the whole thing had come together. The auditorium still smelled of sawdust and paint; he'd barely had time to get his hair trimmed and his face steamed and shaved at Tony Cuneo's barbershop. Half the men there were dandying themselves up for the event and had congratulated him.

He had stopped at the tailors, picked up his tuxedo, rushed home, and dressed hurriedly, without even enough time to enjoy his reflection. He relished the fact that women said he was the handsomest man in the Bronx; he used his looks to bring glamour to his business, but now he seemed to present only a harassed face.

He had rushed from the apartment, leaving his two pretty daughters in the kitchen, excitedly pressing the flounces and sashes of their dresses. Esther, seventeen, was fair-haired like her mother; Martha, the youngest, had curly black hair like his.

His wife Rebecca was folding paper cuffs to protect her crushed-velvet sleeves while she handled the ticket booth. David, his son, the middle one, slender and scholarly, was brushing his Saturday jacket.

Simon took a gift box of cigars to hand out to dignitaries. After all, he figured, as he dashed around the corner to his new theater, tonight's the night. The sky's the limit! Eggs all in one basket! Sink or swim!

His brother, Abe, was in the auditorium smoking a cigar. He wore a checkered vest, and he looked rich. This burned Simon.

"Don't you believe in signs?" said Simon. "You know that film's in the booth already. You want to blow up the place? Why ain't you in front? It's about time for the trade."

"Why don't you relax?" said Abe. Twelve years younger, he was the smart aleck of the family. About to take his bar examination, he was also, naturally, the family snob, while being supported by his brother.

"So join up. The whole family's in on it. Why not you?" said Simon. "Esther's working the piano here along with Martha. Mother's handling the ticket booth, and David is helping your Uncle Sid run the film. Now, after you finish spieling in front, you'd better help at the door."

"You could hire some cheap help," said Abe. "How'm I gonna handle your legal problems if I don't get my degree?"

"Listen to me for a change," said Simon, "instead of thinking me, me, me like you always do. Even with this classy showhouse that's costing me my life's earnings, the Motion Picture Patent Company gives me rotten film. I gotta pay a fee each week for every one of my projectors. Rent, rent, rent, I never can buy, and half a cent a foot for lousy second-rate footage. And if I try to get a better class of picture from an independent maker, the Trust's goon squads come in and wreck my movie house. And if that happens, then who carries the whole family on their shoulders?"

"Well, if you have to make money, why do you play this trash? What's wrong with good movies like *Quo Vadis?*"

"I own the Astor?" said Simon. "Could I get a dollar fifty a ticket in this nebbish neighborhood? Fifteen cents will be tough enough, with kids free, and they all got six!"

Simon looked at his critical young brother. His nose quivered.

"These things *you* wouldn't remember. How our pappa who couldn't read struggled to keep us in school, with only a lousy barrow on Doyer Street to do it with. And how I worked to educate you better than me when he went. You know how much I've invested in your law education?"

"You'll get paid, you'll get paid, I'm not worried about *your* economy," said Abe wearily, having heard it a hundred times. "You know how to save a buck. You think I don't know about the bicycling of film between your picture houses?"

Simon clenched his teeth with rage and looked around to be sure no one heard.

"So ruin me!" he said. "That's gratitude!"

"Gratitude!" snorted Abe. "Who's been drawing up your contracts for free? Who works for you like a slave for nothing? I ought to give you a kick in the pants!"

"What?" said Simon, looking down at the kid's neatly shod feet, "with *my* shoes?"

He turned abruptly and strode away.

A fivesome stood staring through the elegant doors. Simon's anger choked in his throat, but he controlled himself. Martha was dressed in canary yellow, and her hair was curled up on her head above her snapping black eyes. David burst the door open and rushed in, full of enthusiasm. He knew why. A new projection machine to David was like every holiday in one.

Esther smiled, and he paused, as always, to smile back, for she was his favorite. Her pink dress cast a glow on her face. Her fair hair was folded in smooth plaits around her head, and she had pinned on a candy-striped ribbon which stood out on each side like wings. Her father knew how pretty she'd look sitting at the piano, her back straight as a rod, playing away at the action on the screen while the audience cheered and groaned.

He gestured, and the young people ducked under the barrier. Following the girls, Mike Cuneo, the barber's son, held open the door. His curly black hair was greased, and his broad face was wreathed in a grin.

Fergus Austin followed at the rear, ducking awkwardly under the ribbon. At seventeen, he was tall and skinny. He had red hair, pale skin, and blue eyes that seemed almost purple as he glanced through his thick red lashes. Like most boys of his age, he wore black-ribbed stockings and high shoes with knots in the laces. He had on thin pants and a tight-buttoned jacket, short in the sleeve and slick at the elbows. Simon remembered that when he came to visit, he always smelled of wool, urine, and cubebs.

Everything about Fergus rankled Simon Moses. He knew Fergus was enamored of his darling, Esther, and the idea revolted him. To him, the kid was a walking tract of righteous Catholic poverty. Simon detested the public drunkenness and misbehavior of Fergus's father, and the poor-mouth obsequiousness of his mother, who ran a boardinghouse.

If Simon had known that this night would link his destiny with Fergus, he probably wouldn't have opened his theater at all.

Fergus stuck out a bony hand and wrist. "Hi, Mr. Moses. Good luck."

Simon shook as brusquely as he could and pulled his hand away.

A man brought in a horseshoe of stock and asparagus fern from the office entrance. Gold letters on a ribbon read Good Luck.

"Nice," said Simon, reading the card. "It's from Bernie's Delicatessen across the street. They ought to. We'll do them nothing but good. Girls, you'd better go read the program and look at the posters, so you can decide what music to play."

They left, twittering about their project.

He turned to David. "You collect tickets, son. After they're all in, you can go to the projection booth. Can you handle splicing already?"

"Oh, sure, sure, pappa," said Dave, his face alight with pleasure.

"And check the signs," said Simon. "If they start to clap, check to see if the sprockets are off. And if a doctor is called, use the Dr. Blank Is Wanted at Once sign! Fill the doc's name in with grease pencil before you slide it. Okay?"

"Okay," said Dave. He rubbed his hands, testing their cleanliness.

Simon turned to Mike. "And now, neighbor, Eyetalians are supposed to be good at music. Live it up. Spiel. And run the Gramophone out front."

"Gee, me?" said Mike. "Me?" He clasped his head with pleasure.

"It's a snap," Simon said. "March up and down with your fingers in your vest like a big shot."

"I ain't got a vest," said Mike.

"Act like you got one," said Simon. "Throw out that golden voice of yours. Tell 'em it's the greatest laugh carnival in town. Yell, Mabel Normand, John Bunny, Bronco Billy Anderson."

"It says so out in front," said Mike.

"Since when can everybody read?" said Simon. "Wind up the machine. Sing a little. Laugh. Kid the goils. Big shots are gonna be here. Fifty cents okay?"

Mike looked delighted. In a minute he had his thumbs under his armpits, and he strode up and down grinning.

"And now," said Simon, "I left the hardest job for the smartest. Fergie, boy, this is very important. I'm gonna be busy with the honored guests. I got a bicycle with a basket on the handlebars out by the alley. When the *Bronco Billy* picture is finished, you take the can of film over to the Ruby. Pick up *Sailor's Honeymoon* and bring it back quick. Then as soon as you do that, you pop over to the Electric Theater and pick up *Gertie Learns to Swim*. Bring that back here, Fergie." Simon pulled out his turnip watch. "I'm depending on you, kid. The show must go on. Then you take *Bronco Billy* from the Ruby and take it to the Pearl—"

Fergus scratched his head. "Gee, Mr. Moses, I'm all mixed up. Why couldn't Dave—"

Simon waved his hand. "Dave understands splicing film. And they gave me such lousy, patched prints. I need him. Don't worry," he bent forward confidentially. "Don't tell Mike, but you're going to make a dollar. It's a higher class of work!"

Simon slapped his back. "You're a smart kid, this is a new business. You oughta go in it with me. I'll give you the card with the schedule."

When the first reel was finished, Fergus wheeled down the alley, and crossed the street, wobbling, as his bike skidded. Saturday night the whitewings couldn't keep up with the horses and buggies that thronged the streets.

Damned if I'll end up with horseshit on my good suit, Fergus thought, as he brought the bicycle under control. He began to wonder if Mr. Moses hadn't given him the dirty end of the stick. He stuck out his chin. I gotta be smarter than him, he thought. Seems something's fishy about jockeying these cans like this.

He got *Bronco Billy* to the Ruby. Esther's Aunt Hannah was just finishing playing "Alexander's Ragtime Band." A claque of ruffians was beginning to stomp and clap in unison. In the projection booth, the operator dimmed the lights, flashed on the No Stomping Please slide, and took the film from Fergus. He handed him *Sailor's Honeymoon*, and Fergus got it on the bike and raced back to the Little Diamond. Simon was standing nervously by the side door. He grabbed the film, slapping Fergus on the back.

"Great Fergie, just great, now get going to the Electric, pick up *Gertie Learns to Swim*, and haul it back fast."

Fergus, sweating, was about to complain, when he saw that Mr. Moses had slammed the door, which locked from the inside so no freeloaders could get in. He got on his machine, moved along the street in the wake of a Chinese laundry wagon, peeled off by the alley, and was surprised but pleased to see that old Uncle Irving Moses was standing by the door, one foot in the opening. Irving handed him *Gertie Learns to Swim* and slammed the door quickly. A little annoyed, Fergus moved down the street, got cussed at for splashing mud on a couple as he skidded to a halt, and then scooted down the alley.

Nobody was in sight. He must have been pretty fast. He bent over to unload the basket, and as he did so he was belted on the side of the head.

For a moment he was stunned. His teeth felt shaken loose; he almost felt the bones grate in his head. He slowly fell and heard his pants rip as his bony knee hit the ground.

This can't be happening to me, he thought. He pulled himself to his feet. Three toughs were staring at him. He'd never seen them before. Two moved forward, grabbed him.

"Bicycling, Bud?" the third one asked.

"Whata ya mean?" asked Fergus. He put his hand to his head which felt bigger than a balloon.

The man held the can of film up to the streetlight. Fergus tried to move, but the other two men held him.

"Now ain't that funny?" said the man. "This here can says, *Gertie Learns to Swim*. That ain't right, because it's not booked here at the Little Diamond. My boss says it's booked up the street at the Electric." His eyes were hard.

"Who you working for?"

"I don't know," said Fergus, surprised that he could even talk. "I'm just delivering."

"Just imagine, he don't know!" said the man. He reached forward and with calculated precision punched Fergus on the nose with a swift, hard jab.

Fergus felt a bone crack in his nose. After the flash of light, he felt the salt taste of blood on his lips.

"Memory better?" asked the man.

Fergus shook his head, trying to shake the pain away. He didn't know what to do. Suddenly he heard Esther playing *William Tell* on the piano inside. It meant that somebody had opened that door a crack. He cried out as loud as he could, "I don't know. And I won't ever know, because you'll kill me."

His stomach clenched in a knot of fear, for the door closed, and the piano was muffled.

The man hit him in the eye. Fergus hoped he'd pass out, but his torturer was too experienced.

"You won't be such a stupid mick next time," he

said, "workin' for these mocky bastards. And when I get through breaking your legs, you ain't gonna be able to bicycle illegal film no more."

The man moved forward to hit him again. Fergus thought for a moment he must have passed out and died, for a shower of flowers fell over the man's head and shoulders. The horseshoe of stock and fern, in its thick wire frame, sent to Mr. Moses from Bernie's Delicatessen, was being used as a weapon. The banner fell across the man's face, its Good Luck in gold letters bandaging his eyes.

The whole staff of the Little Diamond Theater erupted into the alley. Mr. Moses, Dave, Uncle Sid, Abe, and Mike were all wide-eyed scared, but they had every weapon they could get hold of, from pop bottles to the ceremonial scissors. Esther was still pounding away at the piano, and the movie was running.

Fergus's three assailants tore themselves free of the flowers and got out of the alley in a hurry.

When David Moses and Mike Cuneo brought Fergus home, mom put a beefsteak on his eye, packed his bruises with soda compresses, and tried to get him out of shock by giving him some hot broth. He threw up the broth.

His old man, alerted at Gertie's Parlor House that his son had been half killed in a brawl in an alley, got dressed, came home, and prescribed a medicinal shot of brandy. Fergus threw up the brandy.

A young intern from Germany, "Doc" Wolfrum, who lived in the Austin boardinghouse, gave him a sedative. He looked him over, checked his bones for breaks, his groin and belly for hernia, and then, violating all rules, looked at his nose, took hold of the swollen bridge, and gave it a pull, which caused it to snap. Fergus fainted.

"Otherwise he will a crooked nose have. The patient will live."

When Fergus came to, the doc gave him a pain-killer, taped his nose, and told everyone to clear out until the next day. "Let him sleep," said the doctor, "that is best."

David and Mike sat around. They wouldn't leave until he was resting easily.

"Who the heck hit me?" Fergus asked woozily, waiting for the pill to take effect.

"It was the film trust hoodlums," said David. "That Motion Picture Patent Company. Pappa says they're a rotten monopoly. If we don't pay them rent for every piece of equipment and every foot of film we show in every house, they strong-arm us. We can't operate, nobody can, without a license from them. They're robbers!"

"*Now* you tell me, you son of a—"

The pill was beginning to take effect. Fergus felt he was falling into a vortex. The shadowy face of David hung over him, a concerned look on his face.

"Jeez, Ferg, I'm sorry. They never raided us before. Pappa pays too much for his license the way it is. Why should he pay several times for the same film just because he has several movie houses? You can't even operate without paying the Trust off over and over."

Fergus closed his eyes and began to sink into oblivion. He heard his mother and the two boys whispering as they left. He tried to conjure up resentment against Mr. Moses, but he fell into sleep.

The morning was different. Fergus awoke in pain, sore, and seeing slightly double. The pain-killer made him feel thick, and his mouth tasted the way a chemistry set smells. He tried to figure out what had happened. Something was very screwy. And it all went back to Mr. Moses.

About ten o'clock, Mom opened the door. "Mr. Moses wants to see you, dear."

Fergus knew now something was fishy. His mother put another pillow behind him and straightened out the bedclothes.

"I don't feel so good," said Fergus. "My nose must

be busted, my ear hurts, and I can't see out of one eye."

"Oh, my God," said Simon, staring at him. Fergus knew he was scared. "I–I'm sorry, Fergie–"

He stopped. Fergus looked up out of his good eye. "My name is Fergus," he said.

"I'll do right by you, Ferg–Fergus." Simon took a handkerchief out of his pocket. "It's that movie trust. They hire bullies. It was the goon squad was after you. They should go to prison for beating up a kid."

"That won't fix my face or help my busted eardrum," said Fergus. "You didn't send Dave. You didn't send your brother Abe, or Mike. You didn't let me know you were trying to save money. I was the goat."

That made Mr. Moses more agitated.

"Look, boy, I had no idea. So everybody bicycles films back and forth. My four houses may be closed. The Trust may boycott me. Never rent me no more film. Take my cameras. Close me up!"

"Tough titty," said Fergus.

"Fergus!" said his mother.

Simon turned. "Look, Mrs. Austin, let me see the boy. You go out and talk to Abe."

As Mrs. Austin opened the door, Fergus saw Abe, all slicked up, standing by the door, bowing smartly to his mother. He wondered why the hell Abe should be so polite to his ma. Nobody was polite to ma.

"Fergie–Fergus–" Simon corrected, "I got problems." His eyes brimmed.

Fergus sat up. Nobody had ever put on a show like this for him. And he knew Mr. Moses had no use for him.

"Fergus," said Simon, "I need your help."

"Mine?" said Fergus. "What could I do? Get beat up again? Rip my other pants?"

He had Mr. Moses on a skewer. He winced. "I'll buy you a new suit, boy, even two pairs of pants. I'll do anything." He gave it a thought. "Reasonable," he added.

Fergus had never been one up on an adult before. It was a powerful feeling.

"Fergus," said Simon, "when you get better, you gotta help me. I need someone who can think big."

"What's wong with Dave and Abe?"

Simon looked hurt. "Could I ask you if I didn't need help. Me—who am to blame for you lying there, covered with blood."

Fergus put his hand up to his nose. Was he bleeding again? He decided it was a figure of speech. He shifted slightly in bed.

"Don't move," said Simon, leaning forward to straighten the blanket. "Don't move. Just get well. Do you know what a big world this is? The opportunity. Oh, I wish I had your youth." He put his hands out. "I'd grab it, and I'd eat it with both hands."

Fergus was puzzled.

"This film business," he went on, "they're gonna break that Moving Picture Patent Company. No more Trust. No more monopolies and backbreaking rentals. They've had us by the shorts. But they can't get away with it. Everybody's gonna look at more and more movies. And make more. Nobody can stop it. It's a gold rush, son, a gold rush all over again!"

"What has this got to do with me?" said Fergus.

"I need somebody can use his wits. We gotta find all the outlaw companies. We gotta find free-lance movies. We gotta get a product that doesn't break our back. Why, we might even make our own. Just think, Ferg—us, moviemakers. Actresses. Travel. You're gonna work for me."

"*With* you, Mr. Moses," said Fergus.

"With me," echoed Simon, surprised. "You gotta get around. Go to Fort Lee—Biograph. See how they work. I can't."

Of course he can't, thought Fergus, with a flash of

intuition. He's an exhibitor. He's known. But a kid could find out a lot about free-lance films and all.

"I'd have to be on a salary right away," said Fergus, "to spend the time. I'd have to give up my newspaper corner, and helping mom. That is, after my doctors get paid for."

Simon looked at him and grinned. "Say, Fergus," he said, "are you sure you're a goy? Are you sure we ain't related?"

Fergus managed a small grin. "How about it?"

"Well—how about two dollars a week?"

Fergus couldn't raise his eyebrows because his face hurt. It was a good thing.

"And I'll pay the doctors, and you get a new suit."

"I'll be in bed awhile," said Fergus. "You'd better have Dave or Esther or somebody bring me all the newspapers, reviews, and *Film Index* and *Motion Picture Story Magazine*. I'll study."

Simon looked at him with respect. "I'll have Esther bring them. We gotta think big."

He got up and took out his wallet. "Here's two dollars for the first week, partner."

"And a dollar you owe me for bicycling last night."

Simon didn't miss a beat. He took another dollar out and gave it to Fergus. "Think big," he said, flashing a false smile.

For a moment, Fergus lay back, trying to analyze his good fortune. His mother came in happily, disturbing his reverie.

"Did you have a nice visit?" she asked.

"Okay," said Fergus.

"You know," she said, pulling the curtains, "they're really nice people. Mr. Moses is so well mannered and handsome and open. I didn't know that Abe was such a nice young man."

"He ain't," said Fergus, looking at her suspiciously. "Why?"

She held up a paper. "Just for signing this little paper while you were visiting with Mr. Moses, he gave me a check for ten dollars. Imagine. That's quite a nest egg."

Fergus snatched the paper. She had signed a release on any injuries sustained by her son, Fergus Austin, in return for compensation. He looked at her with despair.

"We could have got a hundred dollars," he said. "Old man Moses never wanted any of this to be in court. He's in deep trouble with the film Trust. Why didn't you ask me?"

She looked at him, hurt. "Why, he's your friend."

That dirty old bastard, thought Fergus. Simon Moses is not my friend. He's my partner.

2

Sunday morning Esther, Martha, and David Moses came to see Fergus. Martha brought German chocolates, and Esther carried a plate of apple strudel, still warm, and some trade magazines. Dave had his camera.

Fergus was resting, wearing his horse-blanket robe. After they filed in and sat down, Fergus got up and went to the window. He pulled up the shade and turned around.

His nose was as thick as a sponge. His upper lip puffed out, and his eyes were slitted, both set in circles of purple. Esther let out a cry, Martha clutched the candy, and Dave let out a long whistle.

"Holy Kee-rist!" he said, "you look like a Chink baby!"

"Do me a favor, Dave," he said thickly through his split lip. "Take my picture."

Fergus stepped out on the fire escape in the glare of the sun while Dave snapped the camera.

"It's great!" said Dave happily. "Just horrible!"

Fergus really felt awful. He had a throbber. He was glad to get back into bed.

"We'll see you after school tomorrow," said Esther.

"Gosh," said Martha brightly, "I hope it doesn't keep you from graduating!"

"Nothing's gonna keep me from graduating," said Fergus. "Thanks for the magazines."

He turned toward the wall, resenting his headache. He had a lot to learn. Then he remembered something.

"And tell your pa, I want the new trade magazines, not just all the old cra–" he remembered the girls, "I mean junk he's through with. He promised."

When Fergus's face mended, there remained only a slight bump at the left side of his nose near his eye. He decided it gave him character. That Doc Wolfrum was pretty good, even if he was a foreigner.

Wolfrum peered through square steel-rimmed glasses at the stitches inside his lip and gave him salve to rub around his eyes.

"When you are a grown man," said Doc Wolfrum in his thick German accent, "you will remember how good is my work. You remember me, boy."

"Sure thing," said Fergus.

He had plenty of time to thumb through the pages of *Moving Picture World*, *Motion Picture Magazine*, and *New York Dramatic Mirror*. He was anxious to get into action.

There was a lot to learn, and he was going to do it. And the picture business was new enough so a young man with his wits about him could get to know it, could follow this flickering trail of excitement that was beginning to flow like a deep, widening stream not only through cities, but through towns and hamlets all over the land.

There wasn't enough on paper to fill his desire to learn. He snatched up every article and report, studied the overall picture, memorized the habits of the leading characters in the great new drama, and wondered how he could get to listen to them, as well as read about them.

He felt that destiny had kept him in his room at a

time when he could evaluate a new path, the first he had ever wanted to seek on his own.

One afternoon Mike Cuneo came in. His curly hair hung over his forehead, and he frowned, as he always did when he was in a temper.

"Son of a bitch," he said. "I'm movin' out the minute I get that passport from purgatory this June."

"Sit down," said Fergus. "What's eatin' on you?"

"My achin' ass," said Mike. "That old bastard took his strap to me. Me!" He laughed bitterly. "You should see his black eye."

"Who?" asked Fergus.

"My old man," said Mike.

"You hit your old man?"

Mike ran his fingers through his curls. "He shoulda thanked me. First, I get a job as a super, posing for pictures at Vitagraph."

"You did?" Fergus was impressed.

"They worked me three days," said Mike. "I made fifteen smackers. Fifteen! I posed for pictures with John Bunny and a kid named Norma. You know what?"

Fergus stared at him, a little jealous.

"I parlayed it in a crap game with the other supers. Acting is just a sideline, man. I cleaned up over a hundred bucks."

"How did you get so hot?" asked Fergus.

"Flats," said Mike. "A guy left some flats in pop's barbershop. He ditched them in a shaving mug when the coppers came by. I just borrowed them."

"Your old man caught you?"

"Hell, no," said Mike. "You think I'm stupid? I put some real dice back in the mug. If that character picks them up to play with he's gonna be surprised." He laughed. "You think I'm stupid or something? I just got whaled for playing hookey. The old bastard took away my fifteen dollars. I stowed the gambling money."

Mike sat down and unlaced a shoe. He poured a small pile of silver out of it and unfolded some greenbacks that were tucked in the toe.

"Godalmighty!" said Fergus.

Mike laughed. "I'm gonna get a joint of my own," he said, "as soon as I get sprung outa school. Lookathis. Four hundred haircuts to get this much money. I ain't gonna be a lousy barber!"

He emptied the other shoe.

"Jees!" said Fergus, "how did you walk?"

"I'm gonna work where the big mobs of actors are," said Mike. "Biograph's left the old house on Fourteenth Street, and they have a new factory in the Bronx. And this summer, I hear they're using a lotta folks out at Vitagraph in Flatbush. Ol' Mike Cuneo's gonna be smart and stick to the mob scenes. Did you ever think how many boobs are getting big money? They don't know what to do with it. Who wants to be a stinkin' actor? One actor gets five bucks. Ten actors have fifty bucks. Run a floating crap game. Get me?" He grinned.

"Take it easy," said Fergus. "I wouldn't fool around with flats, Mike. That's a good way to spend your summer at Sing-Sing."

"Do me a favor," said Mike, "don't be concerned about yours truly. You got a hiding place?"

"I got a tin box," said Fergus importantly, "with a few private papers and valuable things in it. I'm the only one has the key."

"Then you're my First National Bank," said Mike. He took two pairs of dice out of his pocket. "Maybe I'd better leave these babies," he said. "I can pick 'em up when I need 'em."

He tossed the dice on the bed. They all looked alike. He threw one pair on the floor. They came up sevens. He did it again. Then with a quick gesture he palmed them and threw the other pair. He was fast. Fergus shook his head.

"It's your life," he said. "Let's count the money and I'll give you a receipt."

They added up $113.15. Mike stuck $20.00 in his shoes, some change in his pocket, and Fergus banked the rest.

"Nobody knows," said Mike. "Not even Dave."

"Nobody knows," said Fergus. They shook hands. They heard the back door slam. Dave came in. Mike gave Fergus a meaningful look. Fergus nodded.

"Where ya been, Mike?" Dave asked.

"He's gonna be a movie actor," said Fergus quietly, "as soon as his backside heals. His old man just whaled him."

Dave looked at Mike with admiration. "You're not crappin'?" he asked.

"Three days," said Mike. "Fifteen bucks. And I coulda run four. Gotta go." He breezed out.

"We gotta work those movie factories," said Fergus. "When we were snots there were just a few nickelodeons and combination houses around. Now your old man can't get pictures to show, and he's gotta change his show several times a week, or the public can walk to another theater, they got so many."

"Pappa's scared of heisting films," said Dave. "The Trust is down every independent operator's neck. And they got plenty of head-breakers hangin' around."

Fergus looked at him and shook his head. "You're supposed to be the smart one," he said. "But I gotta break the big news, stupid. How much does it cost you to run a movie house for one month?"

"Well," said Dave, "what with rent, staff, film rental, tickets, and advertising, over five hundred bucks for one small house."

"So," said Fergus, looking wise and rubbing the new bump on his nose, "in one week you could make a movie for five hundred dollars. And you could make as much as—as ten thousand on it!"

"That's not our business," said Dave.

"Make it your business," said Fergus. "You'll save money in your own theaters; and a lot of guys will have to rent from you."

"Where are you gonna get the money, Mr. Astor?" asked Dave. "And the know-how?"

"We start learning," said Fergus. "It's a new business. Nobody but D. W. Griffith knows what he's doing, and since that Bible picture, people ain't so sure about him."

"Ya know," said Dave, "talking about know-how, I got a pal in Brooklyn; a real Frenchie, from France. This guy has a lab. Right around the corner from Vitagraph. His name's Jules Cadeaux. You needn't blab, but his lab's where we get the dupes we run. He's great, a real honest crook."

"Dupes?" asked Fergus.

"Dupes are copies of copies of original prints," said Dave. "Jules is from a French family that worked in film labs in Paris. He can make a negative or run a print off an original. It ain't so good as the real article, but who knows? And he's got some great connections. He knows a lot of operators in big theaters. They slip him the print after the night's show. Jules and his lab work all night. They get the print back before showtime the next day. There's lots of independents like my old man who can't afford to do business with the Trust."

"What if he got caught copying—uh—duping a film?"

Dave made a silent gesture like slitting his throat. "You gotta practically have a passport to even get in his lab. You know how we run now, we double up, or stick in a hot film from Jules's lab."

"How do you get the film back and forth?" asked Fergus. "I mean after what happened to me?"

"Uncle Abe worked that out," said Dave. "You know McNulty's undertaking parlor across the alley. We just rent his hearse and an empty coffin. You know something funny, nobody ever wants to look in a coffin. One or two even take off their hats as we go by, with Jules's dupes lying in state. It's a laugh. Even cops signal the traffic aside for us. It's hard to keep a straight face!"

"You mean your whole family is in on it?"

"It's dog-eat-dog in business," said Dave.

Fergus felt the old familiar twinge at the pit of his stomach. Always an outsider. He could just see the Moses family, all of them together, a rich, good-looking, powerful family.

◆◆◆◆◆◆◆◆

"The suit looks good," said Simon Moses, taking out his wallet tenderly as if he were saying farewell to a dear departing friend, "but I didn't mean you should look like J. Warren Kerrigan."

Fergus enjoyed his reflection in the three-way mirror in Horowitz's Haberdashery. He'd never seen himself from all angles except in mirrors at Coney Island. The new suit was dark blue. His Sunday shirt was a little yellow, but the vest hid most of that.

"Mr. Moses, believe me," said Fergus, using the low but precise tone he had practiced while his face was healing (he had decided that since he was taller than most people, the soft approach would be more impressive than the shouting of any runty street hawker), "I like the gray one better, but it's even more expensive."

Simon's faltering hand quickly drew out the bill.

Horowitz handed Fergus a bundle with his old suit in it.

Walking down the street with Mr. Moses, Fergus took his time. Not only did he have a captive adult for company, but for the first time in his life he enjoyed glancing at his reflection in store windows. Moses looked sideways at him. The suit was a link connecting him fatefully with this young goy. He shuddered, as indeed he might. Something warned him he had just bought not only a suit, but a millstone.

"You see," said Fergus, "you're too well known to go running around spotting trouble in your houses. I can scout around, looking for hoodlums. Now I look like a paying customer."

"I got plenty of family for that," said Simon.

"You know they're all working at showtime," said Fergus. "And who knows better than me your complications in finding dupes."

Simon put his index finger to his lips, as if the Trust was inside playing pool. "We'll discuss it later. Later."

"Don't forget," said Fergus, "I'm the biggest kid on the street. At these prices you got a good scout and a bouncer thrown in."

"Gotta get to work," said Simon. "See you later. And if you're gonna scout for me, Ferg—us—you'd better go pussyfoot, not be hanging around."

"I had no intention," said Fergus, standing very straight in his new suit. "I have plans. I'm going to get around town and see what's cooking in this business, Mr. Moses. It's all spread out, but everywhere people are talking. Some I'll hear on Fourteenth Street; I'll pick up news around the exchanges. And some around offices in Times Square. And around Elm Street out Vitagraph way."

"Good," said Simon going into the empty lobby. He wished this pest would leave him alone. "You run along, and report to me later."

"Not just yet," said Fergus, following him to his office, "but I will when you give me the three-weeks salary owed while my busted nose was healing."

Simon looked at him with pain, "You got false ideas," he said, "false. You were on sick leave."

"I was studying the business," said Fergus. "Why, Mr. Moses, even you don't know what's going on. Even the swells are lining up to see that wop movie, *Quo Vadis*. And it's as long as a play. They're paying a buck and a half a shot."

"I know, I know," said Simon sadly, "I gotta tell you and Davie and my whole family, I ain't a Vanderbilt."

"I'm trying to tell you something, Mr. Moses," said Fergus patiently. He had to pierce that fog of obsolescence. "You gotta think big, like you told me. From Fourteenth Street to the Bronx everybody's making movies. Long movies. No more two-reelers. Griffith is making movies in the winter in California. Mack Sennett has moved west. Even the Barrymores are posing for pictures. And the Barstows, why even Jeffrey Barstow might give up his stage play. Do you know what that means?"

"I'm not a patient man," said Simon, shuffling papers. "So what?"

"So," said Fergus, "movies are getting respectable. *Motion Picture Contest Magazine* had a national popularity contest, and Maurice Costello won it. Mr. Moses, over 430,000 people voted for him. He's so snooty he won't even help build his own sets out at Vitagraph, but they still sign him. And here's another thing. Wall Street is backing movies. That means so many films will be made by so many people that the Trust will go down the drain. No more ten cents a foot and two-buck assessments. No more sneaking films into your houses in coffins—"

Simon was horrified that Fergus knew. Dave would get it.

"So give me my back pay, plus the current week," said Fergus. "I gotta cover a lot of territory to keep up with things."

"I know too much already," said Simon, "like how a smart-ass mick kid tries to tell me how to run my business."

He reached in the cashbox and took out six dollars.

"I'm trying to tell you, Mr. Moses," said Fergus, with a firm grasp on the money, "that this is just chicken feed."

"So I'm a chicken," said Simon. "Give it back if it offends your nostrils."

Fergus took it.

"Someday you'll say, thank goodness you listened to the young generation and started making movies, instead of showing what somebody else is getting the profit out of. Why you suggested it yourself when I was getting over the beating the Trust gave me. You said we might even make our own, actresses and all, don't you remember?"

Simon slowly sat down at his desk and ran his fingers through his hair.

"So, you say things when you're upset. Look, I told you I'm not a patient man. Now I suggest you get out of here before I blow up! I ain't Laemmle. I ain't Zukor. I'm just a poor man trying to run four movie theaters and wasting time to listen to a nebbish kid. You said. I heard—I heard. Now beat it!"

Fergus pocketed the six dollars and left. Passing a trash can, he threw the bundle of his old clothes into it.

◆◆◆◆◆◆◆◆

Fergus's Morris High diploma went into the new strongbox under his bed. In it was a copy of the release Abe Moses had made his mom sign, giving up all responsibilities for any injuries incurred while under Simon Moses' employ. Clipped to it was the snapshot that Dave had taken of him with his nose a swollen blob. He looked more horrible than a payment of ten dollars indicated.

Fergus used his smaller tin box for Mike Cuneo's fluctuating gambling profits. One afternoon Mike came in and threw himself down on Fergus's bed.

"Son of a bitch, I'm peed off," he said, unlocking the tin box. Instead of taking money out of his pockets, he took money out of the box. He took off his new shoes and slipped the greenbacks in the soles.

"What happened?" asked Fergus.

"I was just into the crap game when the director called me for a scene. I got a part." He looked annoyed, "and when you got a part you got to be there to do the scene. So this girl Claudia can't remember what to do, and we have to take it about a dozen times. All the time I can hear the crap game going on, and I know from the noise that there's big action."

Fergus couldn't help smiling.

"In the scene I'm supposed to look surprised when the gunmen bust up the party. No wonder I did. I remembered in the middle of the scene that I had left my flats in the game."

"Did you get them back?"

"By the time the scene was ended, a big super named Pete Thompson took off with my flats and a roll that would choke a cow. And I got a call for tomorrow morning. Now how'm I gonna find my lucky flats? To cover this floating crap game ya gotta make Flatbush, the Bronx, Hoboken, Madison Square, Eleventh Street, Fifty-third, Twenty-first, all over Robin Hood's barn, wherever a company is shooting. There are too damn many movie companies!"

"How much money do you get for acting?"

"A stinking twenty-five dollars a week. I can't afford it!"

"I'll take your job," said Fergus.

"Wish you could," said Mike, "but you see, I tried to duck it. I'm in the middle of a scene. They explained, I can't just disappear."

"Maybe you better not pose any more," said Fergus.

"You gotta have a job," said Mike, "or they throw ya off the stage."

"Could you get me in?" asked Fergus.

"Sure," said Mike. "I gotta work tomorrow. Meet you in front at half-past five."

"In the afternoon?"

"Naw, stupe. We get there early in the morning to be made up. I'm telling ya, it's no sleigh ride."

After an hour on the Third Avenue el and the trolley car, Fergus and Mike joined the crowd in front of the Vitagraph factory.

"My gosh," said Fergus, "there must be a hundred people!"

"Two hundred," said Mike. "Half of 'em are inside already."

A man standing by the door selected the supers, pointing a finger at the ones he wanted; Fergus wasn't sure he pointed at him, but Mike grabbed him by the sleeve, and they moved on to a brightly lighted room. A white oilcloth-covered table was loaded with cans and jars. Mike patted Spud, an elderly makeup man, on the back, and picked up a thick stick of greasepaint. Mike plastered a stiff pink mask on his face, greased his hair, and Spud drew his eyebrows, circled his eyes, put a touch of brown paint on his lips, and powdered his face.

Fergus was next. He looked in the mirror.

"Kee-rist," said Mike, "you look like a bad corpse!"

And he did. Where Mike's handsome dark face took to the outlining, Fergus's blue eyes stared out of the black arches and lined eyes that were painted on him. His red hair looked like a dye job in contrast.

"You haven't got a makeup kindly face, son," said Spud, "but don't worry, it all looks different in black and white."

They moved onto the set, a hotel lobby decorated with potted plants and gold chairs. An orchestra tuned up, and a cluster of men were standing around a camera. Behind a painted flat some supers had already gathered to play cards and gossip, and a man with a pushcart was selling coffee and sinkers.

A group of girls filtered in from the women's wardrobe room. They gathered giggling around the coffee wagon.

A girl entered from another door. Fergus and every other male turned to watch her. She made all the others seem like supers. She seemed to be in a world of her own. Every gesture was unique. There were other young girls in the room equally pretty; some had more perfect features. But she was the one everybody watched. She carried built-in drama in her every movement.

A cloud of black hair curled around her heart-shaped face. She walked with a swinging motion, moving little tassels that hung all over her puce satin frock. She twirled a beaded bag in little arcs as her lithe body undulated. She sat on a small golden chair and threw her slender arms up as if she were going to topple over. Fergus almost moved forward to help her, when Mike caught his arm.

"Leave her be," said Mike, disgusted, "she always does that act when she sits down."

"Who is she?" he asked.

"That's Claudia Barstow. You know, from the big-shot acting family. And she's a pain," said Mike. "That's the dame who didn't know her ass from a hole in the ground. She's the one held us up an hour yesterday while my money went down the drain."

Claudia Barstow turned, aware that she was being watched. She smiled at Mike, giving him a little wave of her calcimined hand, and blinked her luminous eyes, heavily made up with mascara. Her painted lips parted in a warm smile, and she deliberately arched her neck as she turned to reveal an uptilted nose.

"A Barstow!" said Fergus. "That's class. Boy, is she pretty!"

He stared at her, transfixed.

"She thinks!" said Mike. "Say, are you in a trance?"

Fergus flushed and looked away.

There was a sudden flash and sizzling as the mercury vapor arc lights were turned on and an acrid smell made Fergus taste the fillings in his mouth. He flinched.

"It's just the carbon lights," said Mike. "They're getting ready. Don't look into them or your eyes'll get bloodshot."

A man wearing his cap backward looked in the camera. Next to him the director, Joe Compton, in puttees and a horse-blanket jacket, blew a whistle, and then shouted through a megaphone. It took a moment for the chatter to simmer down.

"Now folks," he said, "this is supposed to be a fancy society party. Everybody must be gay. You're having a swell time. Can anybody do the turkey trot?"

A few people raised their hands, mostly girls.

"Ragtime?" he asked. "One step. Fox-trot. Grizzly bear?" Hands went up. "Bunny hug? Anybody who dances well gets two bucks extra. We have to have about six partners for Miss Barstow."

"Barstow!" said Fergus softly, staring at her again. Jeffrey Barstow's young sister. The daughter of Chauncey and Belinda Barstow.

She smiled, waving at the director.

"The royal Barstows," said Fergus. He automatically raised his arm. "You know who the Barstows *are?* I didn't know they were acting here. I read about 'em in the trade papers. I thought they were in Europe, or on Broadway."

"She's on her back most of the time," said Mike, "from what I hear."

"You," said Compton, pointing to a handsome gray-haired man, "and you." He looked at Fergus, who stood a head above most of the people around him with his hand raised, "and you there, Stilts—"

Some people grinned. Fergus flushed.

"*You* can do the bunny hug?" asked Mike.

"I've practiced some," said Fergus. "You just sort of bend back and forth. I can catch on."

An assistant rounded them up, Miss Barstow was called, and the action was set. Fergus was to cut in on the gray-haired man, whirl Claudia around twice, and then relinquish her to a silly-looking fellow with popeyes and a waxed moustache. Claudia was to flirt with all of them.

"Now Stilts," said the director to Fergus, "try to

bend back and forth, that's right, and look annoyed when the next fellow cuts in."

Fergus rehearsed. When he caught Claudia Barstow in his arms and twirled her around, the pressure of her slim waist against his hand and the grasp of her slender hand was gone before he had time to be scared. It was as quick as catching a fly in a sandlot ball game.

But when he stood aside and realized that he had made contact with her in front of all those people, his pulse began to quicken. After several rehearsals, Compton called action, and the cameraman began to grind. The orchestra played away, and, in his excitement, Fergus rushed in and met Claudia's inviting, warm smile, face to face. It hadn't been that way in the rehearsal. He floundered making a turn, and his heel ground into her instep. She let out a screech of pain, and the action stopped.

Joe Compton rushed in. She limped to a chair and sat down.

"My foot!" she said. The director bent down. Fergus had ripped her silk stocking, and her instep was bleeding.

"Oh, I'm so sorry!" he said.

She lifted her face. The tears were flowing, along with streams of mascara, which fell down in black spatters on her satin frock.

"You stupid idiot!" she said.

The makeup woman rushed in with a towel, mopped the wet mascara off her face, and Compton and the gray-haired super helped her limp into the ladies' dressing room for first aid.

"No more amachoors!" said the director.

Fergus stayed cautiously in the background and managed to get through the day in a cloud of humiliation. To his surprise, no one paid any attention to him.

On the way home on the el, he knew that he didn't want to be an actor. Maybe he'd take his five dollars that he really hadn't earned and send Claudia Barstow more red roses than she'd ever seen in her life.

There was something about her—the gestures of her expressive hands, the magical way she moved, the wide-spaced eyes that seemed to hold so much promise. He felt a chill that clenched at his heart and traveled down his body. It was as if he yearned for something he hadn't known about before, yet wasn't sure what it was. She was a mystery woman; haunting. She made him dream.

In the shabby sanctorum of his room Fergus lay on his bed and thought about the movie company and all the people he had watched. Out of all that confusion a permanent record had been put on film. Someone took that product and rented it over and over again, until the money multiplied like blowflies on a dead alley cat.

It didn't matter if the actors got drunk, broke their legs, got old, or died. What they did was captured. Not like the stage where you had to do it every night. Holy mackerel! The thought was enough to scare you. You were stuck with it, once it was on film.

And those jobs. Being any kind of technician was crap. That was for slaves. He wasn't cut out to be an actor. Running a camera was for people like Dave Moses, you had to be in love with machinery. A director is a show-off. He likes to tell people how to act. How the hell does *he* know? If he was handsomer he'd be an actor. Now that supervisor was everywhere. He put the company together. But even he worked for someone.

Take even a big-shot like Mr. D. W. Griffith. He went to California when someone sent him. The papers said he was in trouble for making a long movie, *Judith of Bethulia*. Biograph told him to make short movies. Even Mr. Griffith had to do what someone told him to do. Who were these someones, and how did you get to be one?

Fergus couldn't hang around Luchow's and the Astor Grill to know the men in control. Damn being young and poor.

Simon Moses had everything—a bankroll in his pocket; an intelligent face; even ma said he was handsome; and he owned movie houses. Why, he could talk to newcomers like Laemmle and Zukor and the independent operators and learn a thing or two. But he didn't have enough moxie to move into a bigger world. He was yellow.

Fergus sat up, his pulse quickening. He thought, *I'm not yellow. I'll get my foot in the door somehow. I'll be someone. This is a new business, everything is up for grabs. The Moses family is the way. They're in the movie business. And I'm in business with Mr. Moses whether he likes it or not.*

His mind was whirling. He listened to the familiar boardinghouse sounds, and he was ashamed that he was so poor, that he didn't have a chance to live in a high-class way as the Moses family was beginning to do.

There was no question about what he had to do. He had the opening, and he was going to be in business with the smartest man in the neighborhood and somehow work at the studio where Claudia Barstow, the most beautiful woman in the world, was acting. He flushed at how he had stepped on her foot in front of all those people. But that new movie world was *his* world, or it was going to be, and, somehow, he was going to make contact under better conditions.

He got up and looked at himself in the mirror. His hair was on end, his shirt crumpled. Hating his looks, he slicked down his hair with oil. He wished it was black and curly like Mr. Moses'. But at least oil made it look less red. He put on his best tie, dressed in his new suit, and gave himself a final glance. He practiced moving slowly, holding his arm carefully folded, stroking an imaginary moustache.

The lights were sparkling in front of the Little Diamond. Dave came out into the lobby.

"Where ya been?" he asked.

"I've been acting. Company was shooting a scene with me and Claudia Barstow doing the turkey trot."

"In a pig's ass," said Dave. "You are the limit, Ferg!"

"Ask Mike," said Fergus. "He was there. She just couldn't get the step, so I had to do it over and over."

Fergus knew he was safe; Mike would say anything, as long as no reference was made to a crap game.

Dave said, "You gonna be an actor?"

"Nope," said Fergus. "Not enough money in it."

"Aw, come off it, Francis X. Bushman. This is your old friend Dave. I guess two thousand a week wouldn't be good enough for you, if you get to be a star. Which, by the way, I doubt."

"You know something," said Fergus, swallowing his anger, "if you don't look out, you'll end up being a jockey to a can of film all your life. You're always talking. How come *you* don't get behind a camera?"

"How can I?" said Dave hotly. "You know I'm learning the theater business. I got to work for my pa."

"Well," said Fergus, "I'm sorry you're not interested in my idea. It may surprise you, however, to know that I have other backing. I can go elsewhere. It's just this idea. With a camera."

The magic word triggered Dave.

"What idea with a camera?"

"I'd have to go to that lab in Brooklyn you mentioned to work it out," said Fergus.

He could tell by the way Dave's eyes flickered that old man Moses had told him to keep Fergus away from their theater activities.

"You wouldn't want to go," said Dave. "It's way out near Vitagraph."

"So, I never been to Brooklyn?" asked Fergus.

"I gotta go there later and get the—" he looked around cautiously, "You know what, in a wicker hamper. Then I go get McNulty's hearse at the stable and bring it into the alley behind the Little Diamond."

"I got a feeling," said Fergus, tapping his head. He saw Dave look at him with respect for the Irish instinct. "Ya know, you gotta be smart. For Christ's sake, Dave, have I gotta be the only Jew in our company?" He grinned.

"What company?"

"Jeez but you're stupid." Fergus lapsed into silence. He could almost hear the wheels grinding as Dave's mind began to grasp the implications.

"Don't tell my old man I took you with me," Dave said, "or I'll get it. You gotta know a lot of angles to get by, and this undercover film market is dynamite."

"Dave, when we get through in this business, we'll *teach* 'em."

3

♦♦♦♦♦♦♦♦

The two boys stopped at a loft on Elm Street. Dave rang the bell at the side of a locked door.

"What's so secret?" asked Fergus.

"Listen," whispered Dave, "if the Trust knew about this place, it'd go up in smoke. This is where the independents rent film when the Trust blacklists them. And this is where all the indie movie companies get their cameras and film and developing. Man, this is a factory. Wait until you see. Stick with me, kid!"

They heard shuffling footsteps coming down stairs. A man peeked through the grill, and Fergus heard the rattle of keys.

"Hey, Jules, it's me and Fergus Austin, my partner," said Dave. "He's okay."

The keys rattled again, and they were let in, while the man bolted the doors. Then he turned and grinned and gave Fergus a strong handshake.

"Hi," he said. "Come on up. We're busy today."

He led them up the stairs.

Jules Cadeaux was not exactly what Fergus had expected. He was in his mid-twenties, scholarly, blond, his squinting pale blue eyes framed with steel-rimmed glasses, and he had a wide smile. His shoulders and long arms were powerful. But his body seemed strangely short. He had a gentleness about him that came from his slow, careful speech, something new to Fergus.

"Pleased to meet the genius's friend," he said, smiling and gesturing toward David as he unlocked another stout door at the head of the stairs.

They entered a loft. The air smelled of acetate and chemicals. No Smoking signs were pasted all over.

Fergus looked over the factory with curiosity. At one end of the laboratory, the rafters were hung with strips of celluloid on rollers. Cans of film were stacked on trestle tables and in corners. Camera parts were racked, some on tripods leaning at insane angles. A desk held reams of papers, more on hooks studded the wall around it, and a stack of gray ledgers and boxes of papers filled open cabinets.

Along a corridor was a row of smaller cubicles, darkrooms, splicing rooms, and a sign, Projection Room, above an opened, dark doorway.

Several girls in smocks were working amidst the confusion, oblivious to anything but their mechanical chores.

Jules pulled out a can of film and unwound the reel on a spindle. He took a title from another, put on his white cutter's glove, and started splicing it. Fergus wondered how the spaghetti strip of film that fell into a receptacle could be put together again, but Jules seemed to know what he was doing.

"Here's your product for tonight," he said.

Dave looked. "*In the Sultan's Palace*," he read. "Mabel Normand! How did you get that?"

Jules set his razor by the pot of fish glue. "Now Dave," he said, "I told you. Quiet."

Jules turned to Fergus, shaking his head. "Oh, well—trade secrets. You know you can print fifty feet of Mabel Normand from *In the Sultan's Palace*, splice it on to any old early comedy of hers, and everybody's satisfied." He grinned conspiratorially.

"Don't he beat all?" said Dave.

"Here's *another* lulu," said Jules. "Broken box. Lens

intact. Some strong-arm men tried to wind it around a director's head. Some poor innocents trying to shoot an independent on the street in front of the Trust's front door. Idiots."

He and Dave bent their heads over the injured camera. Fergus was forgotten. He meandered.

Film was running in the projection room. The door was open, and he stepped in cautiously, adjusting his eyes.

Pennant-waving women on parade flashed on the screen. They were dressed in flowered and feathered hats, summer suits and dusters. A German band marched by, doing a goose step, then several grinning politicians in a polished Stanley steamer motorcar, tipping their top hats.

Two women carrying a banner, Votes for Women, led a group of college suffragettes, marching with steps that seemed short and waddling because the camera was oversped.

"For God's sake, what's this?" asked a man with a cigar.

"That's last year's suffragette parade at Washington Square. I thought if there was enough, we might hire this girl, and with a coupla shots put out a new picture—"

"It's a year old. Who wants it?" said the smoker.

"Look. There's Mrs. Oliver Belmont with her fancy hat," said the first voice.

"Who needs her?"

A hatchet-faced girl with a Wellesley button on her jacket carried a banner, Suffrage for Woman; there was a gap in the ranks, and behind her skipped a girl in a middy blouse and blue serge skirt. She wore a boater hat with fluttering ribbons and carried a poster that read I Will Vote as if it were a fashionable umbrella.

She happily waved at the camera, blew it a kiss, and shrugged her shoulders. It was apparent the cameraman had been taken with her and had followed her movements.

"And that," said the man, "is Claudia Barstow."

Fergus started. Her dark hair was puffed about her face, and her wide eyes crinkled in a smile. It was Claudia . . . His heart pounded.

"Who?" asked the man with the cigar.

"Jeffrey Barstow's kid sister. Look, there's Mrs. Otis Skinner. Must be the actresses' branch."

"That Barstow's a peach," said the cigar smoker.

Look at her, thought Fergus. Look at her *move!*

"A fresh peach," said the man.

"How come she isn't on the stage?"

"She's played stock and a little Shakespeare with the Barstows in England. But I hear she's a wild one. They can't tie her down. Even Jeffrey Barstow won't take her along on tour. He says he has too much trouble with his own habits to take on those of his sister."

"Too bad," said the man with the cigar, "she sure is a looker."

There were more shots of the parade. The vivacious Claudia had the camera full on her. A woman, obviously a society matron, bird wings on her hat, stepped in the front ranks.

As the reel continued, all hell broke loose. A couple of young boys began pelting tomatoes at the parade. Claudia picked one up and threw it back. It was pitched into the ranks again, and went splat! into the feathered hat of the lady. The kid ran; Claudia chased him, caught him, and belted him with her pole. Several policemen moved in. The society woman tried to straighten her hat, slipped on the tomato, and, just as she did a pratfall, the policeman grabbed her arms. She thought she was being arrested, fought them off with her hat over her face, and Claudia moved in and swung on the cop.

At that moment the camera ran out of film.

"Mack Sennett ought to use this brannigan," said

the man with the cigar, "but we certainly can't. But I might use that Barstow dish sometime."

The houselights suddenly turned on. Before Fergus could move, a figure dashed out of the projection booth, hurtled toward the man with the cigar, snatched it, and stomped it on the floor.

"Get out!" he said in a thick guttural voice. "Did you not see the signs? No smoking. No smoking! Must I show you what can happen!"

He stood in the harsh light. His face was a mask of seared flesh, twisted, contorted out of normal expression. It had been burned and had healed in thick scar tissues, streaked with red and white blotches. There was no hair at all on the eyebrows or forehead, and he stared with almost lidless eyes. His upper teeth were exposed by his shrunken lip. He was a living skull.

The two men retreated.

Fergus stood by the door, afraid to move. He was almost bowled over by Jules, who had come running into the room.

"Papa!" he said. *"Papa! Doucement! Doucement!"* He turned to the men. "Get the hell out of my lab!" he cried.

The door slammed, and Jules took his father by the arm.

Jules gestured to Fergus to follow and led the old man to a room marked Private.

"They were smoking! They were smoking!" he kept repeating.

"It won't happen again, papa," said Jules.

He carefully closed the door.

"He'll rest on a cot in there," he said. "The dark soothes him. Let's have coffee. He gets so excited. Smoking is dangerous. This whole place could go—pouf!"

They went to a small kitchen. Jules poured coffee from a pot on a small stove. His hands were shaking.

"I'll be all right in a moment. And I'll tell you."

Jules took a bottle of cognac out of a cupboard and laced both coffee cups. He struggled to calm himself.

"It goes back fifteen years," he said, "a long time ago, in Paris, and it almost ruined the whole motion-picture business in its infancy. I was just a kid. Papa had brought a reel of our experimental film from our laboratory in Saint Cloud to be projected at a great society affair at the Bazaar Charité. He said it was my chance to see the elegance of Paris. My father, carrying the precious film in one hand, led me by the other. The building was flimsy, a temporary housing, but it was decorated with flowers, bunting, and flags.

Papa as usual filled the little projection lamp with ether. There was a flash as the match touched the lamp; the ether exploded. In a moment flames had ripped through the hall."

Jules paused, his head bent. When he continued, his voice was so low Fergus had to bend forward to hear.

"Somehow he carried me out and we escaped, but 185 people died in that fire. Papa's face and my body were almost destroyed—ah, here I go, talking too much, sorry. Papa is a fine craftsman. We thought this would be a better world for us."

He laughed bitterly. "Some world! With your whole stupid industry tied up by the patent company. If you don't sign up with their company and pay their duties, you don't make pictures. Jeremiah Kennedy's secret service has made us move three times. Well, this loft is safe enough—so far. And you know something? I get my film stock from the Lumière Laboratories in Paris, that's why I don't have to deal with Eastman, who ask too many questions. It's a big business, and anyone who wants to make films or show them ought to be free to do it."

"I'm going to do it—somehow," said Fergus.

"So? You like this business?" asked the Frenchman.

Fergus nodded.

"Papa always says, you have to love what you do.

So much that nothing can stop you. Cinematography is my life."

Jules stood up, and they walked into the main room of the loft. "What's your company intending to do?" he asked.

"Right now," said Fergus, "we're firming up. I think I can get some backing. Maybe we could take some of your film, shoot some scenes to tie it up, and make up a picture. I got an idea with your suffragette stock. I know this actress, Claudia Barstow."

"We have plenty of stock," said Jules. "Just don't say where it comes from. I can rent you a camera, do your developing, and help you with cutting. Also, if you need business letterheads, I can print them. Money in advance. You can check my developing and printing costs with any in town. My advisory fee will be 10 percent of your gross. My transactions are strictly confidential. Any discussion about Cadeaux and Son outside the premises will result in complete confiscation of any of your property in our hands."

Jules started splicing film. His efficiency and skill seemed to soothe him. Fergus had come up against a Gallic personality which could change from emotion to practicality in the turn of a sentence.

Fergus's mind buzzed with the possibilities within this treasure trove. Somehow he would work it out. First he had to contact his bankroll. And then, as if fate had dealt him a hand with the face of Claudia on each card, this might be the way—the only way he knew—to see her heart-shaped face again, to watch her arms and hands and her supple body moving against the restraint of her garments as she seemed to weave a magic path by her very existence.

◆◆◆◆◆◆◆◆

"I'll pay you 3 percent interest on your money," Fergus said to Mike, "or cut you in on the stock of FEDA productions."

"The hell with your dumb stock. I'll take the interest," said Mike. "And I want my three hundred back soon. It's my working capital. Matter of fact, I've got a pretty big stake to be sitting around a boarding-house in a tin box."

"I agree," said Fergus, "but you can't have a bank account without your folks signing for it; you're only seventeen."

"Okay, okay!" said Mike testily. "I trust you. Anyway, I'll be eighteen pretty soon. How much have I got?"

Fergus glanced at the papers on his desk. He had to so his eyes wouldn't blink.

"It's $2,420."

Because Mike came in and out in such a hurry, he had never counted his fluctuating capital. Fists full of money disgorged from his pockets and shoes or were taken from the box again with an equal rush. So Fergus had managed to personally stash about two hundred, a little at a time. He'd written an IOU on it to soothe his conscience, but that was locked in his own strongbox.

"Gimme five hundred," said Mike, taking his shoes off. "I'm working a big set tomorrow. By the way, your girl friend Claudia is through with the picture."

"That reminds me," said Fergus, "could you get her address for me? I might use her in our picture."

"Are you loco?" asked Mike.

"I got reasons," said Fergus. He took out his new stationery, fresh off the press at Jules's lab. In sloping Gothic script, the letterhead read.

FEDA FEATURE FILM PRODUCTIONS

President, Fergus Austin Vice-President, David Moses
Treasurer, Abraham Moses

P.O. Box 432
New York Central Post Office.

"FEDA?" asked Mike.

"The first letters of my name and Dave's," Fergus said. "We got use of a two-hundred-foot Ernaman camera, laboratories in Brooklyn, a great deal of exclusive footage, and our own editing facilities. I'll write you a legal IOU."

"Does old man Moses know about it?"

"He'll find out," said Fergus. "Our plan is to finish our first feature, rent it to him amongst others, and then let him know we made it."

"And Abe's secretly in on it? His own brother?"

"Abe's going to be our salesman. As soon as we have our negative, Abe's going on the road, sell states rights, and Mr. Moses can whinny."

"Abe'd make a snake," said Mike.

"Snake makers are very valuable," said Fergus, "aside from the fact that we gotta have one adult. He's great on contracts."

"He's gonna look nifty in a striped convict's suit."

"Listen to who's talking," said Fergus. "Get me Claudia Barstow's address. Where does she live?"

"Her and another actress have some kind of flat on East Forty-fifth Street. The other dame works super when she ain't modeling dresses."

After Mike left, Fergus extracted three hundred dollars from his wad, took twenty-five and put it in his pocket, and, in a flourishing hand, wrote on a piece of the corporation stationery, "Continuity for *The Day of a Suffragette*. An original by Fergus Austin. Purchase price, $15.00. Rewrite expenses, $5.00. Typing, $2.00. Travel to and from laboratories, $2.00. Mail and stationery—" he paused, wrote down $6.00 and took another five bucks from the three hundred.

His personal bankroll was growing.

◆◆◆◆◆◆◆◆

Fergus looked at the lineup of mail drops and read, Claudia Barstow, Lilly Hansen, Apartment 3A.

He rang the buzzer, shifting his dozen long-stemmed roses and his script to his left hand. No one answered. He found the door was open. He pushed it so eagerly that he decapitated one of the buds. He picked it up and stuck it in his lapel.

The lobby of the walk-up looked pretty classy. He put his hand protectively on the wad of cash that was his matrix of security, cleared his throat, and looked up the stairs.

As he did, two voices yelled at each other on the landing above. He paused.

"And that's it," said a ringing male voice. "No more handouts. Get one of your lays to take care of it. Fool me once, shame on you, fool me twice, shame on me."

"And when did you get so frigging moral?" shouted a female voice Fergus recognized as Claudia's. "How many dames have you knocked up?"

This comment was ignored by the recipient.

"Get the money where you picked up the packet. That is, if you know who it was," said the male voice.

"Listen, you lousy son of a bitch. I merely asked you as a family courtesy. I don't need your help. I just did a movie out at Vitagraph."

"Your speed, my dear, your speed."

"And an important executive is calling to see me about another picture. A lead. So go screw yourself."

"If I could, I would," said the man. "It's a higher class of person."

His footsteps clomped down the stairs.

Fergus stood, paralyzed. There was no way to avoid a meeting. The door slammed upstairs. By the time the man came down one flight Fergus had figured out who it was. It had to be Jeffrey Barstow, Claudia's famous brother.

He ducked out the front door and reentered, closing it with a slam. He stood at the entrance as Jeffrey came into the foyer.

Jeffrey Barstow wore a natty single-breasted suit, a cravat that spoke of Bond Street, and a homburg, his trademark, perched jauntily on his classic head, giving his features an air of aristocratic breeding.

"Pardon me," said Fergus, his voice sounding to himself as if it came from another person, "could you direct me to the apartment of Miss Claudia Barstow?"

Fergus, balancing his script, his flowers, and the cap, which he unfortunately chose to take off in a flourish of worldliness, was muddled. He dropped the script.

Barstow gaped at him. Fergus set down the roses and picked up the script. Then his cap slid out of his grasp and he retrieved it and put it on again.

Barstow let out a snort and broke into braying laughter.

"Oh shit!" he said. He brayed again. "The important executive!"

Fergus, burning with embarrassment, stood his ground.

"I—I do have a business appointment with Miss Barstow," he said haughtily, clutching at flowers, script, and straightening his cap.

"I beg your pardon," said Jeffrey, "I thought you were a juggling act."

Fergus walked stiffly to the stairs.

He heard one more bray. Barstow left. Fergus had never hated anyone more.

He glimpsed himself in the foyer mirror. He looked like a peeled grape. He looked sixteen. Even the new suit was cheap and wrong. How could he compete in a world with slick, handsome Jeffrey Barstow in it? It wasn't too late. He could run.

He put his hand in his pocket. He had over five hundred dollars. It was a wad to impress anyone. Money talks. You can't be yellow in business. Piss on Jeffrey Barstow.

He rang the bell to apartment 3A. He heard steps and the clank of bracelets, and the door opened.

He fought his intense self-consciousness. Those wide-set eyes with almost too many eyelashes, the mocking lips, the slender neck, and oh, the way the clothes seemed to reveal her body instead of covering it! What did she do that was so different? What made her move like that?

She wore a clinging blue and gold harem gown. Even Fergus could tell that she didn't wear anything under it. A scent of sandalwood came from the apartment. She had a warm, musky smile on her face, which froze as she looked at him.

"Flowers?" she said. "Oh, I'll take them. Thank you."

Even her voice . . . all Barstow . . . and husky . . . elegant undertones from her English background.

She took the flowers and started to close the door.

My God, she thinks I'm a delivery boy! He swallowed quickly and remembered the low, authoritative voice he had tried on Mr. Moses.

"Miss Barstow," he said, "I am the executive director of FEDA Productions."

For a moment her face was blank, and then she seemed to go limp.

"Well," she said, "today's sure my day."

At least she didn't slam the door.

"You mustn't be taken in like your—your brother was, by my youth," he said quickly. "I assure you, I have backing and a continuity to show you. And a bankroll—"

He reached in his pocket and pulled out the roll of bills, which he had put together with a rubber band.

"Well, I'll be goddamned," she said. The money seemed to amuse her. "I've often heard of bankrolls. This is the first time I've met one. All right. Come in."

He came into a room that was like a movie vamp's lair. A low sofa in front of a fireplace was draped with a Spanish shawl. A large kewpie doll with a light under its skirts was on a table. In the corner was a Gramophone on a French table strewn with records. Oriental plaques studded the walls. It was all too opulent for him to see at once. He just had to feel the atmosphere.

"So Jeff, the bastard, saw you," she said, sighing.

"Yes'm."

Although he was wary, her piquant face, the luminous eyes, and that long swan neck, got to him. She gave him a sharp glance.

"Say, I know you. You're—you're Stilts. The fellow who tromped on my arch at Vitagraph." She looked annoyed.

"I'm sorry," he said. "I didn't come to take you dancing. I have the means to make you a movie star."

She sat on the sofa, falling back on the cushions, and put her hand on her forehead.

"I have a bitching headache," she said.

"I'd like to take you to dinner at Luchow's," he said.

"No, thank you, mister," said Claudia. She looked at him. "What bank did you rob, Stilts?"

Fergus reached in his pocket. He handed her an envelope. The flashy FEDA stationery unfolded. Attached to it was a fifty-dollar bill.

"That," he said, "is a bonus when you sign my contract. My partners and I are prepared to pay you a hundred dollars for four days' work. And this is no two-reeler. It is a real, bonafide feature. Here is the continuity."

"Oh, the hell with that," she said. "Four days' work, huh? It sounds interesting, but I can't."

"You've got to," said Fergus. "I'll give you an option for two more, at—two hundred a picture. You're the only one can do this picture."

"Why?"

"Because," said Fergus, "we're using the stock from the suffragette parade. That's how we can make it."

He wanted to bite out his tongue. He just couldn't help talking too much.

"Boy," she said, "you're so dumb, you've got to be honest. Well, okay. I'll level, too. I got a problem. I'm sitting on the nest and I've got to get out of it."

Fergus looked puzzled.

"You know, I got to have an abortion."

She looked as if she had just said close the window.

"Oh, what the heck," she said. She went to the kitchen and brought back a tray with champagne on it. "Let's get a bun on."

She handed the bottle to Fergus, and he managed to open it without disgracing himself. It gave him something to do while he recovered from his shock.

"Bottoms up," he said as they drank. This was more than dreams were made of. Dave should see him.

"I think maybe I know someone can help you," he said.

"If you throw the abortion in, I'll do your movie," said Claudia.

"It's a deal," said Fergus.

She looked at him. "You're quite a kid. You know, in this ridiculous business, you might make it. You've got enough gall."

Fergus poured himself another glass of champagne. It didn't taste as good as beer. But here he was, alone with a beautiful woman.

"You sure you can handle that doctor?" she asked.

He nodded. "I think I can. I'll call him. He lives in my boardinghouse."

"Well, that makes it easy." She held out her glass.

There was a ringing sound. She reached for the kewpie doll, opened its skirt, and to Fergus's surprise, lifted out the earphone of a French telephone.

"Hello—Hi," she said, her voice dropping, so Fergus knew instinctively she wasn't delighted. "Oh, Christ, not again—Well, give me an hour. But listen, if this guy's going to live here, get yourself a new roommate. So he pays the rent. So he gave you another present. Tell him to take it home to his wife. Why can't he take you to a hotel?"

There was quite a pause.

"To you he's well known, to him he's well known, to

me he's a pain in the ass—Okay, okay. I'll be out in an hour."

She hung up. Fergus's imagination was making little sallies into the future. He felt more secure.

"Miss Barstow," he said, "if you do three pictures with FEDA, you won't need a roommate."

She sipped her wine and looked at him.

"Could you get that little plumbing job done for me tonight?" she said. "I have no place to stay, anyway."

"I can work it out. My doctor friend can use money. But why not let me take you to dinner first?"

Her large eyes gazed at him over the rim of her glass; she stood up. She was little, she only came to his shoulder, and looking at her was heady stuff.

She studied him. He was just a kid, even younger than she. She saw such blind admiration, such excitement in his eyes that it intrigued her.

She'd observed that look when the females fawned over Jeffrey backstage. But she, the young sister, usually got glances of appraisal, as people wondered why she wasn't in some production, or stares of lechery from the men. She had never rated such a star-worshiping look.

What is this, she wondered? It isn't just to bed with me, he's too innocent. And after what I've gone through with that lousy man who dropped me, I need it.

She let her gown slip off one shoulder. She saw his amazement. How different from the pawing of the men she had known.

She liked the straight set of this boy's shoulders, the piercing blue eyes under the wide forehead and thatch of red hair. He was clean, and—and new—new to everything; no tricks. What she could show him. There was potential under that cheap suit—promise, too, in the attitude that had given him the drive to seek her out against such odds.

"Well," she said, "as long as I must go through it, why not have one for the road?"

"Sure," he said, reaching for the champagne.

She put her hand on his.

"That's not what I had in mind, although it helps."

She put one arm around his neck, caressed his ear, and with the other hand she opened his shirt, and he felt her delicate hands expertly fondling him, unbuttoning.

He was shocked. It all happened so fast, and it was all new to him. Of course he had fantasized and knew what it was all about. But this—this incredibly beautiful creature, what if he couldn't do it!

But she showed him, with passion in her face and voice, as well as the magic of her perfect body. It was incredible. To be caressed, to see this loveliness, to feel the body he had watched with fascination. The fragrance, the mystery of this woman, Claudia Barstow, who wanted him.

In a moment he was on the sofa with her, and she had maneuvered so that she lay on him, exposed him, and there was no problem. He was ready, hard and hot, and it was the most natural thing in the world for him to follow her expert movements. He felt he would perish with sensation, looking up at her face and her breasts pressing over him.

"Now, now," she whispered, "that was too soon, too soon. How about one for Claudia?"

She moved him slowly over her, massaging his buttocks with her hands, so that in a moment he felt himself growing hard.

"Easy, easy," she said in her low, passionate voice, "oh, it's so good—"

Her smile of pleasure grew. Later they lay together, and her heavy breathing suggested that he move aside. He cradled her for a moment in his arms, his eyes closed, and then he stood up and pulled on his pants. He knew by the hot sensation in his ears that he was flushing. She pulled her dress on, giggled, and put her face against his shoulder.

"You know, Stilts, I think I took your cherry."

He didn't know what she meant, but he poured her a drink. His hand was shaking. Nobody would believe him, just nobody.

She took the drink and looked up at him. His passion had moved her strangely, and she liked him. She patted his cheek without a word, for his innocence touched her. Imagine that she would think he was dear; but she did!

She sipped her drink and then went to the bedroom. He sat waiting, not believing what had happened. She came out, dressed in a pretty green frock and a fur cape dangling with tails. She wore a pungent perfume, and her flawless face was powdered.

"May I use your bathroom?" he asked.

She smiled. "Of course, silly. I thought you had."

The bathroom was a welter of towels, powder, silk chemises, and scattered makeup. He cleaned himself off, washed his hands, rinsed his mouth, and looked in the mirror. To his surprise he looked the same.

He picked up a dainty tortoiseshell comb and smoothed down his hair. It had never entered his mind that a man-about-town would have his hair ruffled in a boudoir. From now on, he'd better carry a comb. He straightened his tie and decided that, in spite of Jeffrey Barstow, he didn't look so bad. Considering what had just happened, he must look pretty good to Claudia.

As he came into the living room, he gave her a smile. She was sipping the last of the champagne.

"Where shall we go?" he asked.

"Luchow's will be fine," she said. He picked up his cap and started for the door.

"Wait a minute," she said. "How about that contract?"

"Oh," he smiled. "And the continuity."

She sat down on the rumpled sofa. He gave her the fountain pen that Esther Moses had given him for graduation, and she signed the document. She unclipped the fifty-dollar bill and put it in her purse.

"Look, Miss Barstow," he said, "I hope you don't think—"

She put a hand to his mouth.

"Don't you think, under the circumstances," she smiled, "you might call me Claudia. By the way, what is your name?"

◆◆◆◆◆◆◆◆

The call to Wolfrum had worked more easily than Fergus would have believed. Fergus held the lamp with the naked light bulb as Doc Wolfrum directed. Wolfrum was a strange bird, a German medical student. Fergus had spotted several women sneaking up to his cheap quarters in the attic bedroom and had found him seeing one out one morning. Now he wondered about it; they must have been patients. But he didn't have time to ponder about the doc's private life. Claudia lay on a cot that had been covered with a rubber sheet, and paper bags were at hand for the bloody refuse. Fergus's stomach churned, and he turned away.

Claudia moaned, her legs spraddled as the doctor probed the inner recesses of her body, shocking Fergus as he thought of what passion he had felt there so recently.

"For Gott's sake," Wolfrum whispered, "you want someone should hear?"

He turned to Fergus. "If she keeps up this noise, it is necessary you hold a towel over her mouth."

"I won't cry," she whispered. The sweat was pouring over her face. "Oh, God, how much longer?"

"You should have had this done sooner," Wolfrum whispered. "All you women are alike. You think of the pleasure. Just one more time. One more time—" he made a face. "Now take it easy, we're almost through."

Claudia clenched her teeth. The doctor removed more matter and threw gauze into the paper bag.

Fergus thought he was going to faint. Part of his semen might be coming out of her. Could the doctor tell she had sex only a couple of hours ago? Is that why he made that crack?

Wolfrum looked at Fergus.

"Stop looking green," he said. "You should have thought of this when you got her in this condition."

"Me?" said Fergus. "Me?" He realized there was no use to explain.

The doc continued. Claudia lifted her head, and, rolling her eyes, fainted.

"My God!" whispered Fergus. "Is she dead?"

Her legs slipped sideways.

"Of course not," said Wolfrum. "Hold her legs. Wide apart."

He threw down his forceps and turned to Fergus angrily.

"*Gott in himmel!*" he said, "I am risking my life and my career. Now spread her legs and hold them up. It is just as well she has fainted."

Fergus set the lamp on the floor, held up her legs, and Doc Wolfrum quickly probed, scraped, cleaned, and finally said, "You may straighten her out."

Fergus straightened her legs, saw a trickle of blood pour over the rubber sheet. Wolfrum caught it quickly with a towel.

When he finished, Wolfrum handed him the bloody towel and he put it in the bag.

"Now, get the trash out of here, where your mutter won't find it."

He took her pulse.

Fergus tiptoed down the stairs. His head was throbbing.

When he returned to Wolfrum's room, Claudia was asleep, covered with a blanket. The shade was on the lamp, and Wolfrum was boiling his instruments in a steamer with a long tube attached to the gas jet. It was all done with Teutonic thoroughness. A carefully organized system.

"She will have to stay here," said Wolfrum. He rubbed his eyes. "Oh, Gott. I have an examination tomorrow. I have got to rest."

"Don't you have to watch her?"

Wolfrum shrugged his shoulders philosophically.

"She will sleep. She is not bleeding badly. I gave her a pill. In the morning you can walk her downstairs and get her in a carriage. Go out the back door. At nine o'clock everyone is at work, your mother is in the kitchen, Ermingarde is in the basement with the laundry. It is the proper time to get someone out. And now you can give me a hundred dollars."

"A hundred dollars!" said Fergus.

"Now," said Wolfrum, in more than a whisper.

Fergus reached in his pocket, turned from the doc's curious eyes, and peeled the money off his diminishing roll.

"Perhaps," said Wolfrum, "I can sleep in your room."

"Why sure," said Fergus. He was so tired that he didn't care what happened. He looked at Claudia. How could she be so beautiful. Her skin was paled to ivory, and her lips seemed bloodless. The thick lashes fell against her cheek, and her hair hung in damp tendrils against her milk-white neck. But Fergus was washed clean of any desire for her. He could hardly believe, as he smelled the antiseptic odors of the room, that he had this evening performed his first act of sex with the same creature who lay here, scraped and bleeding.

Doc Wolfrum followed him quietly to his room. Fergus got into his nightshirt and fell onto the bed. In a few moments, Wolfrum had shed his pants and shirt. Fergus not only saw the dirty drop-seat union suit, he smelled it. Well, what the hell, it was only a minor irritation.

The real problem was upstairs. He was filled with misgivings. Never in his wildest fancy could he have thought that the beautiful Claudia Barstow would be in his mother's boardinghouse, near death. If anything happened to her not only would he lose her, but he might even go to prison. What was it, accessory to manslaughter? And, if everything was all right, he had to figure how to get her out of there without being seen. How could he ever explain the situation to his mother?

To compound his problems, he felt that Wolfrum seemed to be touching him too much as he tossed and turned. He moved miserably toward the edge of the bed and braced himself to keep from falling out.

Finally Wolfrum turned and said testily, "For Gott's sake, lie still. I have to get some rest!"

"Sorry," said Fergus, "I was just thinking about getting her out of the house tomorrow morning."

"That's easy," said Wolfrum. "Remember, I told you. At nine o'clock everybody is at work. Walk her down the back stairs. Nothing to it."

Fergus realized his instinct was right. This was no new experience for the doc, who must have been paying his rent with money from this abortion mill. He lay awake, wondering at the complications in life that had never before entered his mind. No wonder he felt queasy. How many things could a man go through in one night!

His first experience in sex . . . the glamour of Luchow's, abetted by Claudia's popularity . . . his first taste of elegant company and fine food. Who could believe how much it cost. Even the tip was more than he dreamed a dinner would cost! But the stakes were high. The glorious Claudia Barstow across from him at a candlelit table . . . the dreadful stark reality of Claudia on a makeshift operating table . . . and now, this queer bird in his bed.

Youth and exhaustion took over. Hanging precariously on the edge of the bed, he fell asleep.

4

Fergus and David sneaked every waking hour to be in the Brooklyn laboratory. Fergus told his mother he had a job in a lab and gave her two dollars a week from his filched money, and Dave provided his father with a product and spun long tales of how difficult it was to scavenge.

Fergus took notes of entrances and exits, rights to lefts, lefts to rights. He woke up sweating in the night, fearing he would ruin their effort, and wrote descriptions of the costumes in the suffragette parade to match up when they interviewed supers.

He made notes of potential gags and routines from the Mabel Normand and Ford Sterling comedies to fill in their picture, which was to be called *Day of a Suffragette.*

Jules ticked off the footage from his stock. "You will have to shoot three days, with the continuity you have written," he analyzed. "If the conditions are satisfactory, you will have a feature-length picture. You might make as much as five thousand dollars."

It was heady, a daring project.

"I wish the Professor could be with me when we shoot," Dave said to Jules.

"No chance," sighed Jules. "It is his fate to be locked in darkness, away from anyone who can see his face."

"I'd like to use your English Prestwich camera," said Dave, examining the machine. "Four hundred feet would sure be easier on our schedule, working in the street."

"No," said Jules. "You must use an Ernaman. I know it only carries two hundred feet. But I have two. In case of accident, you can replace parts. You must always think of that time emergency when you have a company working. You will have at least twelve people on daily payroll."

"My God!" said Fergus. "Twelve?"

The incidentals were mounting up beyond belief. The money he had cadged was almost gone. There was no way he could figure the horrible expense of Claudia's abortion into the budget. A hundred dollars!

"And where will you store your film and cameras at night?" asked Jules. "It's too far to get back and forth every day. And I don't want any obtrusive trips made to this address."

"I don't dare leave it at the Little Diamond," said Dave. "Pop's nosy. Why hell, he'd open it up to see what feature I brought to show, and there we'd be with our raw film ruined."

"You must keep it in a dark place," said Jules.

"If the Trust was on our tail," said Dave, "they'd sure nail you marching into your boardinghouse with that stuff."

"I know," said Fergus gloomily. "After that bicycling, I'm a marked man."

He began to pace. "I've got it!"

"What?" asked Dave. "Not my place. Even Uncle Abe couldn't sneak a bagel in without my old man catching him."

"Horace McNulty," said Fergus.

"Horace!" said Dave. "The funeral parlor!"

"Well, that's where you stash your theater film," said Fergus.

"Not exactly," said Dave. "We just use his hearse, and take it out from the alley to our theater."

"Well, it's five steps in the other direction to leave it in his mortuary. We could use the same stunt, carry it in a hearse. Late afternoon, early morning. They'd just think he was bringing in a stiff. We'll borrow some of his space in the back room. We'll stash the two Ernamans and some cans of film at night. What difference does it make?"

"It's gruesome," said Jules, "but practical. A cool quiet place."

"You know that darky kid, Buck Green, went to Morris High with us? We'll hire him as an actor. Dress him up in livery and a tall hat," said Fergus. "He can pick up the hearse at the stable, get the stuff at McNulty's, take the hearse back the hours they use it, and do the same at night. We'll run him through the scene a couple of times. He'll think he's a big movie actor."

"That's pretty hot stuff," said Dave. "How do you know Horace will let you use his mortuary?"

"He and my pa are great pals at the Chowder and Whist club."

"What the heck is that?" asked Dave.

"It's the secret name for the guys who hang out at Gertie's Parlor on Saturday night."

"That's blackmail," said Dave, grinning.

"That's life," said Fergus.

◆◆◆◆◆◆◆◆

The summer week was bright and hot, perfect, if uncomfortable, for shooting on the streets.

The night before, Fergus tossed sleeplessly, jumping up a dozen times to check his notes and add to his file of index cards that would guide him in his plans.

Fergus got an unemployed makeup man to join up; they rented a bakery wagon for their street headquarters.

Claudia was in good spirits. As the center of attention, she was animated; a set was her natural home. She wore the same middy blouse and navy skirt she had worn in the suffragette parade, and her boater hat, the ribbons refurbished.

A stout woman was hired who was dressed like the society woman in the original parade. Girls who were college types, two top-hatted politicians, and three little boys to hurl tomatoes were easily cast.

While the dew was still on the hedges, Buck Green drove the hearse to location, took it all the way back to 154th Street, caught a trolley to whatever street corner had been designated, worked all day, and at four o'clock went uptown to the stable again to bring it back, convinced that when he got there he would act again.

Mike took a couple of days off to help Fergus through the problems of flushing the supers out of curbside card games or free lunch counters and into action where it mattered.

"You gotta watch 'em," Mike said, "they're always full of monkeyshines. Excepting in front of the camera. I know. Why over at Griffith's set one day they found three guys asleep at pay-time after a beer lunch. They hadn't been in front of the camera all day. It's a game they play."

"What about your game?" asked Fergus.

"Got a little hot up at Vitagraph," said Mike. "I gotta find a new studio. Couple of sorehead losers who worked in the office hollered. You could of heard them to Canarsie."

"What are you going to do? Quit?"

"Nah. I got a guy on my payroll carryin' the game up there now. And a spotter of course, to check him. I may go to Chicago for a little. Essanay got a big company there. I can always get in actin' and then work around."

"Why don't you stay and get in the company," said Fergus. "We'll double your investment."

"Chicken feed," he said, "chicken feed. Listen, I got

in a crap game yesterday when your actors got their first paycheck." He made a face. "Fourteen lousy bucks."

Fergus was a natural supervisor. He cased every location before the company assembled and had at least three exits worked out in case of attack by Trust thugs.

Each morning, he met Buck on location, transferred the camera and new film from the hearse to the bakery truck, after peering through the curtains.

He had worked out a system of giving each super a ticket from the Little Diamond Theater which they turned in at the end of the day and were paid a quarter apiece. While this commotion was paramount, Dave would approach the waiting hearse, quickly getting the camera from Fergus. If there was any sign of hoodlums loitering about, the hearse would go around the block and return with caution.

Esther and Martha both appeared on the first early morning in lacy summer frocks, their hair piled into a tower of curls.

"What the hell did you tell them for?" Fergus asked Dave. He was very nervous, watching both of them on the street talking to Claudia, a real, live actress.

"Well, they deserve to get in on it," said Dave. "Geez, Ferg, the old man leans on them just like he does me. They have to run their tails off at the show every night. Just let 'em be part of the crowd. Martha thinks she's Mabel Normand anyway, and this week Esther is Florence Lawrence."

Both girls thought they were featured players. Dave gave them a thrill by pointing the empty camera at them and cranking. They smiled and mugged, making all the self-conscious gestures of amateurs, which would have disbarred them from any career in movies had they actually been recorded on celluloid.

"Crise," said Dave, "everybody from Buck Green to my sisters are hams at heart. It makes you sick."

"They haven't the faintest idea of what we are doing," said Fergus.

"Do you?" asked Dave, smiling.

Fergus flushed and pulled out his filing cards.

"I do," he answered. "Left to right. Right to left. How many times I wrote this stuff down! This is the scene where that society lady slips on the tomato."

"Left to right," said Dave. "Right to left, okay old pal."

"Check," said Fergus. "Now, Rosemary, you walk over toward Claudia, then topple."

David focused the camera. The show was on.

There was so much to do Fergus didn't have time to be scared. They chased sunlight all day long. If the crowd got too thick, they moved a block or two.

Just before the sun got too yellow for Dave, Fergus leaned against the bakery truck. Claudia was sitting in the front seat powdering her nose. Funny, he thought, that we did that thing together. He still folowed her as she moved and listened as she spoke, enchanted.

"Say," said Claudia, "your friend Wolfrum sure is a great doctor."

"He ain't my friend," said Fergus.

"Hardly a drop of blood, afterwards," said Claudia. "Hardly a drop."

"Did you ever tell the—the fellow?" asked Fergus.

Claudia looked at him.

"I mean," said Fergus, "the man that was responsible."

Claudia glanced down a moment, and the Barstow gall took over. No use to let this kid know that it was a wandering minstrel, a handsome actor that her brother wouldn't have let play super in one of his plays. Her mother would have batted her for even talking to him. It just happened this man had appealed to her. Lonely, after bouts with older, pushy men whom she rejected, she had let him into her bed several times. But when she had begun to think of him romantically, he was not available. Ah, well—brazen it. Hoping she wasn't flushing, she smiled at Fergus archly.

"Oh, Stilts," she said, "you're so funny."

"What's so funny?"

"How do I know who it was?"

As she picked up her mirror and fluffed out her wealth of dark hair, Fergus tried not to look shocked. In his imagination, a glittering crowd of millionaires, playboys, and great people of the stage and business world pursued her and won her favors. He was amazed that she was slumming to do this picture with him.

"Don't look like that!" Claudia said. "Come on now, honey. You can't be Buster Brown all your life. Claudia knows you're a big boy. And there's a lot to learn. Any time you want to do more research, just let me know. It gets better all the time."

"How can you talk like that?" Fergus gasped. "Just as if it was—it was—" Words failed him.

"What's wrong with it?" she asked. "Wasn't it good? Didn't you like it? I loved it."

She closed her eyes a moment, recollecting.

"You smell a flower. You taste good food. You look at a beautiful sunset and carry on about it. So what's wrong with feeling the most delicious, wonderful exploding sensation the human body can experience?"

"I—I don't know," said Fergus, "only I—"

"Listen," she said, slapping his arm, "I could tell you what to know in one minute if we were alone. Now don't get me thinking that way, you bad boy."

He was thinking that way as a matter of fact. This was a terrible time to find himself getting hard. And he was afraid of this wanton, beautiful woman.

Dave broke it up. "The sun's getting too low. One scene crossing the street and then we'll wrap it up."

"Okay," said Fergus. "Now folks, step along. One more shot. You all work tomorrow."

Esther Moses stared in the direction of Claudia,

who as usual was the center of attraction. Fergus saw the irrational anger a pretty woman gets when she looks at an incredible, natural beauty. And no matter what you thought of her, Claudia sure was that.

◆◆◆◆◆◆◆◆

"You know," said Fergus ruefully to David, as they lounged in his bedroom, which had become FEDA offices, "I'm beginning to think this world is a very complicated place."

He fingered his depleted bankroll.

"I don't see how we're going to pay for prints."

Mike was beginning to separate his gambling winnings into numbered bundles in rubber-banded packets. Fergus couldn't tell David that Mike's funds had been bled anemic earlier. A stack of IOUs revealed a skim-off of over $350. Laboratory expenses, camera rentals, and even Abe Moses' expense account would be staggering as he peddled the prints to the New York, New Jersey, and Connecticut areas and the western and southern markets.

The wise states rights boys smelled a shoestring operation outside the Trust, made cheap offers, and held out for print delivery. And Jules wouldn't deliver film without a large down payment.

Jules was getting testy, and if Mike called in his loan, as he threatened, there would be panic. Soon Mike would be eighteen, and then there was no way of blackmailing him anymore; the money would be in his keeping.

"How are we going to go on with this?" asked David. "We can't even get a money partner without showing the film, and Jules wouldn't let *nobody* in the lab."

"This you ask," said Fergus, "you with four grand picture houses. We could have a showing in the Little Diamond."

"Are you out of your mind?" said David. "Geez,

Ferg, I don't know how we're gonna let my old man know what we've been doing. He'd knock my block off. The Trust would use his picture houses for kindling if they found out."

"But the money," said Fergus, "the money! It makes the picture house business look like peanuts. As I said, since when has he been against money? I guess that's about the only thing he's interested in."

"I ain't so sure," said David. He grinned.

Fergus looked at him. That sort of leer always had to do with alley talk.

"Meaning what?"

"You know that girl Junie," he said.

"Junie," said Fergus. "Your Uncle Abe's friend—once in a while."

"Yeah, the one who hangs around outside the Garibaldi Pool Hall. Well, I saw my old man trip over the curb dropping her a word or two the other day. And she answered, too. And smiled, cozylike."

"Well, I'll be damned!" said Fergus.

"This world is a very corrupt place."

Fergus felt as if veils of ignorance were being stripped from his mind. When Dave left he lay back on his bed. They were all growing up. He'd had sex. They'd made a movie. He began to think about the grown-up world. Even his mother had noticed old man Moses was handsome. Claudia was an education in herself. Even the terrible night of her abortion couldn't make him forget her.

Thinking about Claudia made him uncomfortable. It just wasn't good enough now to do what he'd done alone for a long time. He wanted the feel of Claudia's hands on him, he wanted her breasts and smooth womanskin. And that wonderful face . . . and eyes looking up at him. Imagination moved him. He hadn't really done it right yet with Claudia . . . with his clothes off.

He hated things she said and suffered at what she

did. But she was Claudia, beautiful, mysterious, and unknown; he felt he'd never be free of her.

Maybe he'd better call her. His excuse was the next picture. Already he had a notion for the next scenario, *Saturday at Coney Island.* He fought off the growing heat in his groin and turned practical.

He called her from the dubious privacy of the hall phone in his mother's boardinghouse. The phone rang a long time, and then as his heart was beating a tattoo, she answered.

"Yes?" she said testily.

"Hi," he said lamely.

"Hi, who?"

"This is me. Fergus Austin."

"Who?"

"The—the bankroll. You know, FEDA Productions."

"Oh," she said. Even Fergus knew it was a letdown to her.

"I just thought maybe you'd like to have dinner. And we'll talk about the next picture—"

"I'm tied up right now," she said. "Call me some other time."

"I might leave my number—" he said breathlessly. "You know, to talk about the movie. I have a notion."

"Okay," said Claudia. "I'll jot it down."

She took the number. He heard a Gramophone in the background. He hung up and sat dejectedly by the phone, thinking that he'd never hear her voice again, that she was making passionate love to some handsome son of a bitch, and that even knowing him—Fergus Austin—had been a big social and sexual error on her part.

He went to his room and sat on the bed, hating the smell of frying fish and the poverty that seemed to smother him. He wondered if his clothes smelled of it, warning anybody that he was a faker, an Irish boardinghouse keeper's kid, trying be a big shot.

Days passed. Claudia loomed in his imagination, more beautiful, more seductive, more desirable each time he thought of her. It seemed an incredible dream that he had ever possessed her, and his longing made him ache in the night or turn weak, even as he walked along a street.

He didn't have to look up her number in the directory. As he called, he felt he could hear his heartbeat. He could always hang up if a roommate or a fellow answered, or if she sounded angry or busy. No answer. After it rang twelve times he hung up. At least he had heard a bell ring in the place where she lived. He remembered every detail of the room. He could just see her, the halo of dark hair, the teasing smile. He felt sick with desire.

He waited. Then about nine o'clock one evening, hitting the depths of despair, he tried again. Leaden air promised a storm and stifled his spirits. Of course she wouldn't be in, and he'd torture himself again, but he could hear the sound of her phone ringing.

"Hello," she said cheerily.

"Hello, Miss–uh, Claudia, this is Fergus. You know, Fergus Austin. I just, just thought you might like to step out for–for a late supper."

Obviously she had expected someone else. "Listen Fergus, it's nine o'clock. What makes you think I wouldn't have a date?"

"I didn't," he said. "I just thought–"

"Well, think again."

She was at the point of hanging up. He gathered his forces. "Well, I just wanted to remind you of my number in case you lost it. You know, to do an errand, or anything."

"Thanks, I've got it," she said. "I'll call you. But you'll have to excuse me now. I'm getting ready to go out. So long."

Well, that did it, he thought, who would ever talk to a dummy like me again?

Flushing at his social inadequacies he went to his room and miserably thumbed over some old movie magazines. The hall phone rang. To his amazement, Ermingarde, mop in hand, informed him that some girl wanted him on the phone. It couldn't be Esther, she'd be at the Little Diamond.

He rushed to pick it up.

"Hello, Fergus," she said.

"Yes?"

"This is Claudia Barstow. I've changed my mind. Why don't you come over for a little nightcap?"

I must be out of my mind, Claudia thought, as she waited for Fergus. What was she doing, looking forward to a visit from a kid? It wasn't just that she'd been stood up again by the handsome actor. She couldn't bear the agony of loneliness and humiliation after a man had rejected her. She had to have an audience to realize that she was pretty and desirable.

She'd be glad to see him. He made her feel like a real person, not just a fake, as her brother Jeffrey had told her she was, tossing her curls through each day, using the handle of the Barstow name. She hadn't ever really belonged to the theater; she had been a fringe artist, a pet, and forgotten like one when it came to the honest work and sweat of production. And she had often been dropped for her peccadilloes.

But Fergus made her feel she could do anything. To him she was magic.

She set up the drink tray, lit a stick of incense, and when there was a knock on the door she opened it so enthusiastically that for a moment she wanted to laugh when she saw the surprised look on his face.

It hadn't taken long for him to respond, for in turn, she had made him feel like a man.

◆◆◆◆◆◆◆◆

"Oh, Fergie," she said, leaning on one elbow in her bed, "you are really getting the knack."

He caressed her breast and kissed it gently, savoring it with his tongue.

"Ooh, that's good. Don't stop." She fell back, and Fergus knew that she was looking on him for the first time as a vehicle of pleasure.

At first she had told him to do this and that, and he had followed her command. With some instinct, although he set the pace, he held back. Afterwards, when she shuddered and lay abject and limp, he surprised her, and himself, too, although he didn't let her know that. But he brought her alive again. He knew now where to caress, tease and titillate her, doing it his way, slowly, waiting for her frenzy, and then pinioning her in a burst of passion.

He became aware of several things. However it had happened, he was not an awkward boy. He was a man in her bed. He could give, or he could hold back.

He decided to hold back and see what happened. She snuggled against him, took his hand, and put it on her breast. He took his hand gently away. She lifted her head and peered into his face.

He looked into her eyes, brushed back her random locks, and smiled gently. It was all he could do not to explode, but this was his moment.

"What's the matter," she asked, "are you all worn out?"

He ran his fingers through her hair and produced an enigmatic smile. "Oh, no. Not at all. I could go on all night. It's just that I have some things on my mind."

He turned his head away. She reached for his chin, moved his face to her, and kissed his lips.

"It's our picture," he said. "I have to get more backing. I know how, but I'm going to need your help."

"What did you have in mind?"

"Well, I know a theater owner. We could start by having you meet him at, say, Luchow's, for dinner, and show the picture afterwards at one of his theaters. He might be interested in making you a movie star."

Claudia sat up in bed.

"Well, damn, Fergie," she said, "you're not so stupid for a kid. Okay, get it off your mind. Meanwhile you said something about going on all night."

They did.

◆◆◆◆◆◆◆◆

At 8:15 P.M. on August first, Simon Moses fell in love for the first time in his life. He thought he loved his wife, Rebecca, and his daughters, especially Esther, but this was different.

He had been invited to dinner by, of all people, Fergus, who came to see him in his office, through the back door, as always. At first he had been reluctant, and on second thought, suspicious, afraid he'd get stuck with a dinner check for some tomfoolery. And the thought of going to dinner at Luchow's was insane.

"Mr. Moses," said Fergus, "you may think I'm sticking my neck out, but I've found a way for you to own your own pictures and at the same time meet a famous actress. You couldn't ask a lady to Bernie's Delicatessen on a business appointment. And if you don't believe she's an important personality, ask your brother Abe."

"What would Abe know about an important personality?" said Simon. "He ain't even got one himself."

Abe had been alerted. He revealed without revealing. A combine of bright young talent had bested the Trust and made a very sharp, commercial little flicker, and the young woman involved was none other than a Barstow, and she might even, if persuaded, get her brother, Jeffrey Barstow, to throw in with her on the next one. Abe was not at liberty to reveal the name of the filmmakers, but they had unsold film to show it was no pipe dream. They were in a slight money bind over print costs, and if Miss Barstow liked his looks he might get in on it cheap.

"Where did anybody give Fergus Austin enough money to invite anyone to Luchow's to supper?"

"You'd be surprised," said Abe. "That mick's smart. So go. What have you got to lose?"

So Simon Moses put on his best suit and a foulard tie, had a shoeshine and a shave and trim, and met Fergus at eight o'clock at Luchow's. He was also beset with indigestion. It was two hours past his usual dinnertime.

He was more rattled than he revealed when a captain asked him, as he fumbled at the entrance, if he were the gentleman Miss Barstow expected. He was ushered into a wonderland of music, elegant people, and conviviality. He felt insignificant and poorly dressed as he approached a table, recognizing Fergus's red hair. For once he was glad to see him.

Claudia sat like a queen, spectacular in a gown of shimmering pale lilac. She had a tasseled gold purse on the table, and when she moved it to make room for him, a dizzying scent of gardenia wafted into the air.

Fergus jumped up to introduce them.

Claudia extended her slim hand, and it seemed to fold like flowers as he held it. He stared, dazzled, into the most beautiful face he had ever seen. He bowed low and sat down dumbly.

A waiter poured champagne. This was also a first for him.

"Fergus has been telling me about you, Mr. Moses," said Claudia, "but I must say, if I had met you all by myself, I would have thought you were a poet, instead of the owner of a theater chain."

Simon leaned back. He suddenly felt adequate.

Fergus observed him. Was this the man he had known as Esther's father? Perhaps the shaded candlelight, the flowers on the table, the music, and Claudia's admiring glance transformed him. His parchment skin seemed turned to ivory, his dark eyes were limpid, his hair shone, and, as he held the champagne glass, even his hand seemed elegant to Fergus.

"Well, I don't exactly have a theater chain," said Simon, "just four neighborhood houses."

He glanced down. He seemed charmingly modest, thought Claudia.

"Don't believe it," said Fergus. "He's a comer."

"I can believe you," said Claudia. "Well, here's to futures. You don't mind if I call you Simon? That's an interesting name."

They both sipped, looking at each other over their glasses.

Fergus glanced at them with a twinge of jealousy. At the same time he exulted that he was really in business with Mr. Moses this time. And he was proud of Claudia.

Simon was flushed with wine and excitement.

"I'm sorry my brother Jeffrey couldn't be here," said Claudia, "I'd like him to meet you."

In a pig's eye, thought Fergus.

"But you know," she said, "he's playing in *Brigade* and of course had to be at the theater."

"Of course," said Simon, figuring he'd better look it up in the papers. "Maybe we could go see it sometime."

"Oh, yes, and meet him later backstage."

Simon's world was whirling, it was expanding so rapidly. A cloak-and-suit man passed by to greet Claudia and kiss her hand. He moved on, casting an amused eye at Moses and winking at Claudia behind his back.

"Friend of my family," said Claudia.

Simon felt better. But he felt a strange new twinge in his gut when anyone touched this delicate morsel of a woman. He had never felt like this before. What a lovely little thing. She made him feel virile, all male, and expansive as she looked up at him.

"Now what shall we order?" asked Claudia. "I'll leave it to you. Fergie said we might run my film for you at your theater later, after your show. I just can't wait."

"Neither can I," he said. He turned to Fergus. "Fergus, I insist on being host to this lovely lady. This is a big occasion."

Fergus put up a polite hand, "Oh, no sir."

"But I insist."

Fergus could not believe it. But he accepted.

Simon was panicked. What could he order? He'd never seen a menu like this. He plunged, and he won her.

"You know I'm a poor schlemiel," he said, "and you know your way around here better than me. So you do it, lovely lady. The sky's the limit."

"You'll learn," she said. "I'll be your teacher."

The captain stepped up and suggested. Claudia augmented. Simon noted with some astonishment and chagrin that Fergus seemed to know his way around to a degree.

"See that man, Mr. Moses," he said, "that little man over there. He's Carl Laemmle, and they say he's doing everything he can to break the Trust."

"It's the only way we'll ever be able to make our own pictures," said Claudia. "And look, over there coming in to meet Adolph Zukor is Dan Frohman. That shows that movies are really getting some respect from the legitimate theater."

"I hope so," said Simon. "My theaters were hard to come by, partly because the rental of film and equipment costs so much. And sometimes the Trust gives me lousy film. Lousy. You know, I wish I had better pictures to show my neighborhood audiences. They're poor people. And movies could open up the world to people who have to live in one room."

Claudia reached forward and patted his hand. As he looked down at the smooth young hand on his he could not believe it. This beautiful woman . . . this glittering world. He felt a new desire gnawing at him, to be greater, more important, more involved in it all.

"You don't know me—and you may think I'm crazy," he said, "but good pictures, not jumping junk, could be so important to—" he gestured expansively, "to the world!"

"I don't know you, Simon Moses," said Claudia, "but already I like you."

"You're right," echoed Fergus, "Mr. Moses. Movies are a real escape hatch; you forget yourself when you see them."

"True," said Claudia. "I want to make people laugh and cry and love and enjoy the lives of the people up there on that screen."

Glowing with their nobility of purpose in freeing people from problems of the world, releasing the slaves, each of them secretly considered the wealth and prestige that might be his along with it.

As the elaborate dinner was served, Claudia commented on the personalities who seemed to enter and exit as if they were on stage in full flower. They stared in awe at handsome Francis X. Bushman who joined Adolph Zukor's table. A young director, Cecil B. de Mille, came in with Jesse Lasky, his partner. Claudia commented that they were going west to make pictures where the weather was good all year-round.

Between bites of oysters, terrapin, pheasant, and peach melba, Simon and Fergus gaped at the great, near great, and next to great.

By the time the meal was ended, Simon was corrupted. Having broken all dietary laws, he was now eager for the rest. A vainglorious desire for power, prestige, wealth, and love grew, festering under his beating heart, and with it a turmoil in his nether regions.

With brandy they chatted on about pictures. Claudia and Fergus knew enough gossip to spin yarns. Simon listened while he actually observed the participants. They left in a whirl, he guiding Claudia preciously by the gloved elbow, while diners watched him, Simon Moses, escorting a beautiful woman, a Barstow yet! He already felt like a big shot as she bowed at several acquaintances.

"I'll just run the picture and let you analyze it, Mr. Moses," said Fergus, "and afterwards, if you'll excuse me, I'll just pop out the alley and get it back to the vault."

He thought that sounded classy, and anyway they paid him little heed. Mr. Moses told him not to worry. He'd escort the lady home.

Fergus had David stashed in the projection booth. They put on *The Day of a Suffragette* and peered out to watch their masterpiece. Claudia and Mr. Moses sat alone in the theater. "It looks pretty good," said David. "Look at that Billy Bitzer backlight. I think the old man is enjoying it."

"You just bet," said Fergus.

He could see Claudia's curls brush against Simon's ear as she pointed out various incidents on the screen.

After the houselights were on, they felt it wise to disappear. Obviously the best salesman was out in front. They stashed the film in the mortuary. As they had planned, the night watchman had been paid off with a bottle of Irish whiskey, and was asleep on a chair.

They crossed the street to Bernie's Delicatessen for a sandwich, feeling like men of the world.

Fergus was sad, wondering if Claudia would do the same thing with Mr. Moses that she had done with him. What a strange and marvelous woman! In her apartment she had been so wild, had talked in such a shocking way that it had staggered his imagination. And now, with Mr. Moses, she had been so knowledgeable about the picture business; she seemed to have filed every bit of information there was to know in that room of famous people. She had seemed an important lady, and he felt he didn't know her at all, never could.

In bed, he thrashed about, clenching his hands, thinking of Claudia. He hated Simon Moses: he was in that apartment, he was rich, he was handsome. Of course they were together on that sofa. She was pulling that lilac dress off her shoulders and offering him those pink-tipped white breasts and, after that, her dark, mysterious place of pleasure. Why should he kid himself? It was all his own fault, he had offered her to Mr. Moses on a platter.

◆◆◆◆◆◆◆◆

But he was wrong.

Claudia had set up the champagne tray, gotten her roommate out of the way, and was prepared to entertain Mr. Moses.

"How would you like some champagne?"

Simon held up his hand.

"Oh no. My dear young lady, I couldn't possibly handle anything, except maybe a cup of coffee. My head's dizzy now, from so much food and drink, and—and you."

She looked at him and smiled. He was staring at her in such an openhearted way, not disguising his admiration, that she was overwhelmed. A man shouldn't wear his heart on his sleeve like this. She felt like she was blushing. What was the matter with her?

"Well, of course, I'll put the coffee on, and we can talk."

As she bustled about the kitchen, and he heard the sound of tap water, the shaking of a coffee canister, the rattle of spoon against metal, he felt he had never heard such wonderful sounds in his life. She was doing this for him!

"I don't want to be any trouble," he said apologetically as she came back.

She dismissed the trouble with a wave of her hand and offered him a cloisonné cigarette box. "Would you like to smoke?"

He took a cigar out of his jacket pocket. "Okay?"

"Of course," she said.

To his amazement she took it from him, bit off the end, spat it delicately into an ashtray, and lit it.

As she handed it to him she smiled. "I used to do this for my father. My brother Jeffrey only smokes a pipe or cigarettes. Do you smoke a pipe?"

Recovering from putting the cigar in his mouth after it had touched her incredible lips, he shook his head.

"That's beyond me. It's only for handsome actors. I guess I have a lot to learn."

"Simon, you don't have to learn anything."

His head spun. "Would you mind calling me Si? Somehow Simon seems formal-like, you know?"

She smiled. "Okay, Si. Now. What did you think of the picture?"

"I think you are wonderful. Every time you're on that film I can't look at nobody else. You know, don't get me wrong. I know I don't belong here. I know I never could have dreamed of meeting a beautiful lady like you. I'm just a plain, hardworking man. If it wasn't for movies, I'd be juggling furniture in a secondhand furniture store and making cheap chairs in a little factory in New Jersey. Look, Claudia, I'm a fake. I don't belong in Luchow's, I can't even talk good English. God knows, I try! If I was around you, you'd have to correct me."

"Not correct you, Si, teach you."

She left him and went to the kitchen. She stowed the glasses, set up the champagne tray for coffee, and stood there for a moment. How could anyone be so honest, bare his soul this way! The man was so vulnerable.

The coffee wasn't ready. She went back to the living room. He was meticulously tapping his cigar on a little ashtray, concerned that it might soil this elegant room.

She smiled. "Don't worry, Si, just relax. You know,

you mustn't think my life is all Luchow's and luxury. I've barnstormed as a kid with my family, I have to get up at five and take the streetcar to the studio just like everyone else. I'm not rich, Si, and I've had a few bumps myself."

He stared at her. "I can't believe it. Anybody who looks like you and belongs to the Barstow family has got to have everything."

She laughed.

"You've been honest with me. Okay, I'll be honest with you."

She reached for a cigarette, and he fumbled to light it; he'd never dreamed of a woman smoking in front of him. She inhaled, leaned back, and looked at him. What a handsome man, how alert he was to every move she made.

"You know, I'm the blackest of a black-sheep family. Barstows are always in trouble. I've messed up my start—lost jobs because I drank, got mixed up with the wrong men, or forgotten my lines because I was too busy living. The family won't even subsidize me any more, Si, and they're right. Why do you think I'm so crazy about movies? Because that's the only chance I have. One performance, one picture at a time I can manage. I just can't cope with the night-after-night grind of the stage. I'm too much of a slob for that."

Simon shook his head. "It can't be, it can't be."

"It can be," she said. "I'll get your coffee."

He stood politely as she got up.

She turned. "Look, please, don't do that. Don't stare at me like that. Don't be so tense. Don't put me on a pedestal. You know the main reason I did that funny movie you just saw? Because I needed an abortion. So now you know."

She went to the kitchen. What in hell was wrong with her? Why did she have to tell a stranger her personal affairs? Why give Si Moses her moment of truth? She took her time arranging the tray, got out some sweet biscuits, and came back, annoyed with herself.

He was gone.

Well, I've done it, she thought. Here I was about to talk to someone who really listened and might even have made movies with me. That kid, Fergus, who tried so hard to get going, will hate me, and I deserve it.

What had happened? She had let a good-looking man who really appealed to her run the other way. She poured herself a cup of black coffee, but she let it sit. Simon's cigar had been left burning. She sat looking at it. What was the matter with her? On an impulse, she picked up the cigar, put it to her lips, and took a puff. His lips had touched it, but never had touched hers. It seemed very personal. Then, annoyed at herself, she snuffed it out.

◆◆◆◆◆◆◆◆

It was Thursday afternoon. Claudia was playing her newest Irving Berlin record and humming "When the Midnight Choo Choo Leaves for Alabam," when the doorbell rang.

There stood Simon. A raincoat was hung over his shoulders, and he had a suitcase in one hand.

"Si!" she said lightly, "What are you doing here? What's the matter, did you run away from home?"

He didn't smile. She backed up, and he moved into the room. He put down his suitcase and looked at her. His eyes filled with tears. He felt foolish, but he didn't care.

"What's happened?" she said.

"I was an idiot to run away the other night. I was just—scared. I'm in love with you," he said.

She stood staring at him.

He put his arms around her and held her.

"I know I shouldn't throw myself at your feet. It's not smart. But I can't help myself. I'm going to a theater owners' convention in Atlantic City," he said. "I want you to go with me. If you don't, I don't know what I'll do."

She lifted her face, and he kissed her, gently, with a lingering excitement. He was quivering inside, his trembling hands touched her cheeks tenderly. She waited a moment to see how she felt. Her heart melted at his vulnerability. Then her arms went up to him, and she surrendered herself to a feeling of enfoldment, of protection, and of incredible tenderness—to be loved for the first time in her life in such a way.

She pulled away and looked into his eyes. He was crying. He sat down on the sofa, racked with sobs.

She felt tears in her own eyes. She bent over and wiped his with the palm of her hand.

"I'll go with you, Si," she said.

◆◆◆◆◆◆◆◆

Simon returned home from Atlantic City with a sunburn and sand in his shoes. He complained testily about being tired and asked to be left alone when Rebecca asked him if he was coming down with something.

Fergus called Claudia, and she told him to leave her alone. She had a bad sunburn.

At first he was hurt. But there was nothing he could do. From the first he had known Claudia was faithless.

He met Esther in front of the Little Diamond after a matinee. She wore a new blue dress and had her blond hair tied in a stiff white taffeta bow.

"Fergus," she said, "where have you been?"

"Making a fortune," he said.

She smiled at him, and he melted. Maybe he was still in love with her. It was different. It had nothing to do with rolling in bed with a hot dame. His heart lightened.

They had strawberry ice-cream sodas, larked and joked about friends and graduation. David and Martha joined them, they talked about the new movie and their plans, and Fergus went home elated. He was in business. Mr. Moses was going to be their partner, arrange to distribute their picture, and forgive them their duplicity in making a movie behind his back. As a matter of fact, he would damn well have to forgive them anything. Talking about duplicity.

But at night Fergus still lay in bed, staring at the ceiling, unable to sleep when he thought of the things Claudia had been doing, with, of all people, Mr. Moses.

It was a crazy world, but if that's what money and power did to people, then he'd better have money and power, so he could do it too.

◆◆◆◆◆◆◆◆

These days Simon wore starched shirts with real collars and French cuffs. His suits were custom-made; somewhere he had picked up good taste and was sporting an elegance that caused comment in the neighborhood.

His business interests had burgeoned, everyone said. The Little Diamond and his name appeared in the borough papers, and politicians now crossed the street or paused in the lobby to shake *his* hand.

Fergus worked at hiding his envy. He knew he could only bide his time, and he hid his hatred in each little payoff that found its way into the strongbox under his bed.

The worst had happened when Abe visited his room. With his mother in the kitchen nearby, the visit was quick and furtive. And what Abe had said was so fast and complicated that Fergus couldn't figure it out. All he knew was that triumph had turned into disaster.

"Look, kid, I'm sorry but we've got trouble. To begin with, our product is a risk. You shot the stuff with an unlicensed camera and imported French film, instead of Eastman film. You know what the Trust will do if any of them catch that. They'll bust our heads. And also, your title of ownership is cloudy."

"No such thing," said Fergus. "We've paid all down the line."

"Listen, smart aleck," said Abe, "there's big money tied up here. A producer only gets 50 percent of a sale if he's riding high and is legal, and we're bastards. On top of that, you ought to know the states rights boys who distribute get the cream. And you've got a crappy product with no star for a puny advance against a low percentage as a starter. You smart-ass kids think making a movie is it. Who pays to make thirty or forty prints? How the hell do you think it sees an audience?"

"A Barstow isn't chopped liver."

"Wrong Barstow," said Abe. "Jeffrey Barstow, chicken liver—Claudia Barstow, chicken shit."

"She's going to be a star," said Fergus. "Just ask Mr. Moses."

Fergus noted the flicker of his eyelid and knew he had him on that point.

"And the quality of your picture. It looks like your grandma's patchwork quilt. It's been an uphill fight trying to sell it. I've shown it everyplace but the toilet at the Astor."

"I didn't think it was *Quo Vadis*," said Fergus testily, "but if it hadn't been for Dave and me, you wouldn't have a percentage of anything."

"You've got a percentage of very little," said Abe, deflating him, "you and that smart-ass nephew of mine. You and Dave are in debt to that crooked lab in Brooklyn; don't think Simon and I didn't investigate. We could be in some real rough legal action, old boy. Neither of you is an adult. You can't go around signing papers. Now Simon and I have to take over and get you out of the soup before you go to juvenile court."

"What for?" said Fergus. "The picture's made. You've been out selling the product."

"Without portfolio," said Abe. "Now I discover it doesn't even belong to us. A lot belongs to a joker named Jules Cadeaux and his father. Two illegal con men running a questionable film lab."

"Oh my God!" said Fergus. He'd forgotten about his obligation.

"But we'll haul you out. You just hand over all that stupid FEDA material, your printed stationery, tell me everything you signed without my okay, because it's all illegal, of course, and we'll protect you kids and even cut you in."

"Cut us in!" said Fergus. "What do you mean, cut us in? We made it."

"Listen, stupid, I ought to let you fry. But I've got to protect David. You could both be arrested right now. Put that in your pipe and smoke it."

So Fergus had dragged out his hope chest from under the bed, handed out his precious packet of FEDA stationery, his contract with Claudia, his agreement with Jules Cadeaux and the lab, and his signed deal with Mike Cuneo.

"My God!" he said, "I've opened up another kettle of beans. Where the hell did this kid get this kind of money to loan at 3 percent?"

Fergus hung his head. Abe could hardly hear his voice.

"A kind of floating studio crap game," he said.

Abe looked at him, astonished.

"If you guys manage to stay out of prison, you are sure in line for Tammany Hall."

But once he had the papers in his hand, he was more conciliatory.

"Look," he said, "Simon Moses doesn't want to cause you any trouble. We'll start a company and absorb FEDA for the time being, so you and Dave won't be juvenile delinquents."

"You knew we had this going," said Fergus. "Your name's on it!"

"I didn't know how far you would go," said Abe, "and you cosigned a few things you didn't bring up, old boy. You'll get a profit. You're just beginning. We'll pay you a decent part of the profits on *Suffragette*, we'll put you on a salary of fifteen dollars a week, and you'll get 2 percent of the Moses stock in the new company. That's pretty good for an underage kid who has his ass in a sling. Oh, and one more thing. Simon will take over Claudia's contract and negotiate a new one."

As he made the last remark, Fergus knew in a flash. *Day of a Suffragette* had sold, and sold well. Simon Moses wanted to sign Claudia and have control of her future. That meant there would be pictures made. While his face burned and he felt the tips of his ears get hot, he smothered his rising Irish temper. You couldn't get sore at people in business. It made your reason go out the window. And so he swallowed the bile.

"For now," he said. "But wait until I'm of age!"

Abe patted him on the back.

"Attaboy!" he said. "Keep up your dander."

As he left, Fergus knew Simon Moses could not have come to see him. But he also began to realize his position. He was needed. Funny he, Fergus Austin, should be the key to Claudia.

He knew damned well that Mr. Moses could not ask his brother Abe to pick up Claudia and bring her to the restaurants they now frequented. Even Dave did not know where he went when most kids his age were in bed. He led a double life, and he was in a position to ask favors, getting little dribs and drabs of money which he stashed away. It gave him gooseflesh to think of his power.

There were times when he felt he couldn't go on

with the charade. He looked at Claudia and wanted her and was chagrined to see her glow when Simon joined them. But somehow when he got out into the world a little more, he might just work it out so this man could not have the exclusive on this wonderful, glorious creature. She was too damn good for him, even if he was good looking, the dirty old man. He was at least thirty-eight!

Without the thin thread of adult Moses support and authority, Fergus could not be in the picture business. He could not get fifty dollars for "shooting scenarios." He could not be supervisor of any picture Claudia was making and skim off the top of the budget, and he could not meander around the high spots of New York being cover-up for Claudia and Mr. Moses. Although his pride hurt, his dignity was upheld by the fact that he looked better; he had filled out on good freeloading food, he had better clothes, and, among other advantages, quite a few people were led to believe he was Claudia's lover.

He had carefully tucked away some of the stationery that had the hopeful FEDA name on it. He began to wonder what the name of the new Moses company, Titan, stood for.

One evening while his father was out drinking, he looked it up in the thumb-worn dictionary on his rolltop desk. Titan meant gigantic, colossal, but Fergus gloated over the classic definition: "The Titans were the earliest children of the earth . . . a massive dim-featured race, but with an earthly rather than celestial grandeur, embodiments of mighty force dull to beauty, intelligence, light."

He chuckled to himself. Serves 'em right. Quite an epitaph. At least FEDA had meant Fergus and David, two friends who had high ideals.

He read on about the Titan, Prometheus, who defied Zeus and brought fire to mankind and in punishment was chained to a rock, vultures gnawing at his liver. Someday, the legend said, he would be freed. Fergus dreamed about how he, too, would break his chains and rise up.

So he sketched a clenched, defiant fist, with links of broken chain held in a tight grasp, flames leaping skyward between each finger. That would be the Titan logo, and he alone would know what it signified.

It would be his way of saying *fuck Simon Moses.*

5

◆◆◆◆◆◆◆◆

"You know," Claudia said, as they drove to Sherry's, "I love this Simon Moses; he is honest, very generous, and he lays it on the line with me, Fergus. I mean he asks *me* what I like to do, for a change. And you know, Jews are very passionate lovers."

Fergus looked at her, hurt.

She patted his hand.

"No offense," she said. "It isn't just money, presents, having an apartment by myself, and him wanting to make me a movie star. Though I like that, too. I kind of think pictures are the real thing with me. I get a big kick out of walking on *that* set and being *that* person. And then afterwards, it's kind of cozy, curling up with a nice, hot Jew, who's crazy for me."

"That's a rotten way to put it," said Fergus. "Why don't you say you're in love with him?"

Claudia looked at him and gave a bray of laughter, which seemed typical of herself and her brother Jeffrey.

"Oh, for God's sake, Fergie. Of course, I love him while we're in bed. Otherwise, it wouldn't be any good, would it? But he really gets to me. I never liked anyone this much before. This time I'm going to mind my manners. You know, all the Barstows are good actors. It's in our blood. I messed it up pretty good the first couple of years. They threw me out of the academy for never showing up. I got scared and got smashed on my first Broadway show, and they sacked me. The next one I fought with the pansy director, and he fired me. The third one I got an abortion and just couldn't continue. And Jeffrey got sore at me, oh, so sore! So then I went for movie jobs."

"Your brother drinks a little bit himself," said Fergus.

"True—true, but he always shows up."

"Well, there's nothing wrong with the movies," said Fergus. "More and more stage people are joining up. Look at Bernhardt in *Queen Elizabeth* and Lou Tellegan and James O'Neill. Do you think we'll ever get your brother?"

"If he gets offered enough money," said Claudia.

They pulled up in front of Sherry's before Simon arrived.

Fergus escorted her to their table. A few people nodded, and the captain smiled, for Claudia had alerted Simon that a little money crossing palms would help him have a favored table.

"You have to help me, Claudia," Fergus said, "it's time to get a new project going. All respect due to Mr. Moses, he has to be pushed. I've been working on a new scenario, *Saturday at Coney Island.* I want to show how funny people are on a day off, how they do goofy things they wouldn't do at home, and how they get serious or sad just before they pack up and go home."

"That sounds cute," said Claudia.

"Of course it's written for you," said Fergus. "You're a society girl taking a day off to play with a lifeguard and meet people."

Claudia's eyes sparkled. Fergus delved into facets of proposed action. In a moment, Claudia galloped away in imagination with him. They topped each other, laughed at ridiculous situations, and admired each other's fantasy. It was the first actual story conference Fergus ever had, and he soon realized there is no common ground greater than that of two people, one admiring the other, and both of them needing a job.

By the time Simon joined them, they were gushing with enthusiasm. And as Claudia put her hand on Simon's wrist, patting it, as she explained story points, he happily fell into their mood.

◆◆◆◆◆◆◆◆

Claudia was made for the new medium. She liked to work among people, to joke, to laugh, to run through quick scenes. There was, she said, thank God, no dialogue to be stuck with; you could do your scene over if you messed it up, and there was always the fun of going to a new place, working with new people. And she loved to improvise; it was fun and games.

David followed every offering of David Wark Griffith, not so interested in Biograph, which had invaded the West, as he was an ardent follower of Arthur Marvin and Billy Bitzer and the new freedom of their cameras. To David, the camera was the magic of moviemaking and the actor a necessary evil to be fitted into composition.

Simon got on speaking acquaintance with the men who were moviemakers and learned about distribution and sale of franchises. He learned a great deal from the sales boys who talked the most; he realized they were only peddlers. As a theater operator he could hold forth himself. Many a johnny-come-lately asked the handsome theater owner, with beautiful Claudia Barstow by his side, what he thought of certain properties, and he glowed, knowing his world was ready to expand.

"Abe," he said to his brother, "I'm jumping the fence. I'm putting up money for another movie from scratch. What do you say?"

"I'd say," said Abe, whose hair was getting prematurely thin, "that I ain't got enough hair to take a chance on getting my skull bashed in."

"Everybody's doing it," said Simon. "You keep telling me a producer now is getting 50 percent, minus advances of course, and the distributor gets 30 percent. I'm only realizing 20 percent on my movie houses, with all our sweat going into the daily grind."

"It's a steady sweat," said Abe. "You sure you aren't being influenced?"

Simon rustled papers.

"It's all settled. After all, it's my money. Get that bakery wagon lined up for Coney Island," he said. "The boys plan to have film and camera stashed in the back room I rented in Bernie's Delicatessen. Sun comes up early; we'll hit the water about ten if we're lucky. Better take along a little brandy in case the kids get cold in the water."

He means Claudia, thought Abe. He shrugged. At least it might have a future, and it was better than running errands for four movie houses or peddling product with the Trust on his neck. So—what the hell. He went along with it. Just the same, Simon was pretty sneaky. You sure could bet it hadn't been mentioned at home in front of Rebecca!

◆◆◆◆◆◆◆◆

Claudia thought it would be wise to see her brother backstage before she introduced Simon Moses to him. Once in a great while, mostly in dressing rooms or during rehearsals, the Barstows managed to find a moment of truth, for time was precious then, and they got to the point. Also, there was an unspoken feeling among them that no one else in the world was like the Barstows; therefore, between fights, they had to glue themselves together with loyalty and interest in each other's affairs.

Their careening careers, either aflame with smothering success or on the brink of some disaster, called for concentration when there was a conference. And such moments usually were signaled with a direct approach. Like Indians, they never bothered with hellos, good-byes, or social trivia.

"Simon Moses is out front," said Claudia, "I want you to see him."

Jeffrey, pulling each inch of his body hose into perfect placement, stood in front of a pier glass and checked the splendor of his famous legs. He shifted his codpiece a little to the right. His dresser handed him a velvet doublet.

"Any reason?" asked Jeffrey. He looked at her and pinched her cheek. "You look blooming, and off the sauce."

"I am," she said. "It's revolting. But the camera shows if you've had a few the night before. Even at twenty-one."

He looked at her.

"Twenty-one," he said. "Christ, is that all you are? You were a tramp at fourteen. Well, that means you're on your own. I don't have to drag you out of the soup any more. And it looks as if dear mummy and daddy are tied down to Drury Lane and Brighton for the season. What are your plans?"

"You're not going to like them," said Claudia. "That's why I came."

He buttoned his doublet and sat at his dressing table. His eyes pierced into hers. God . . . my brother's handsome, she thought. Not a flaw, at thirty-four.

"Well? Speak on, at least you're alerting me."

"I'm signing on with a new motion-picture company."

Jeffrey turned on his swivel makeup chair.

"I hope," he said, "your reason is not between your legs."

"Not completely," she said, "but, jesting aside, Jeffrey, it's the new thing. What I like is, when you do a movie, it's done. No endless repeat of one's guts and heart each night. God, I couldn't bear to do what you do, one thousand echoes of the same thing. In pictures, you *image* yourself forever, and people can see you at your peak. Look at Bernhardt. An old lady. Yet everyone will be able to see her act even after she's dead."

Jeffrey smoothed his hair.

"At her age, I think the film's embarrassing."

"Anyway, I have lots of time to go along with it and see where it's going. And, at least it's better to be working with a movie company than to just sit. Do you know how lousy it is in this city to sit at home, or go out with some fright just to keep from being alone? It's different with you. You can pick and choose. You're a man. *You* can prowl, and it's considered attractive."

"*You've* done your prowling," said Jeffrey. "Now, my dear little sister, blessings on you, try talent. Long ago, a very attractive and famous lady, older, I may add, who taught me a few things, said, 'Jeffrey, always remember, when an important man falls in love with a talented woman, he should sponsor her art. That way, while he is bedding her, he can say that he is a patron of the arts. This gets them both off the hook with dignity.' So find an important man, make him your patron, and stop fucking around with the standard city studs who will only sample you and move on. Or keep it underground, if you must have your jollies."

"I see what you mean," said Claudia, "but I *have* to have companions. I wonder why I dread being alone?"

"Because you don't like yourself," said Jeffrey, "and after all, luv, you are a Barstow, and we can't help needing an audience. This new picture business is made for an egomaniac like you—you can watch yourself act *ad infinitum*."

Ignoring his crack, she plunged on. "Well, the flickers are getting quite an audience. I really think it's for me. It's improvisation, it's fluid, it is a lively art, you know. And as Uncle Billy Jeff used to ding at us when he thought he'd continue the Drury Lane strain in us, relate to the moment, realize each experience is unique, and most of all, relate to the person who shares the scene of the moment, as if that person was the only living creature who shares your life . . . for in theater that must be true, or you have cheated your audience, and they have paid to watch you. So satisfy them or they won't come back."

There was a knock at the door.

"Five, Mr. Barstow."

"This is the first sense you've made, ever," said Jeffrey. "My God, you really listened to the old fart. I've never heard such an undisjointed speech from you. Perhaps you have more in your noggin than I thought."

"I'm glad you feel that way. By the way, we're shooting at Coney Island tomorrow. I'm delighted you approve of pictures."

"I loathe pictures," said Jeffrey. "They're a long, thin strip of shit."

"Give them time," she said. "Why don't you meander down to the location. You know, we really work hard. It might amuse you."

"Hardly," he said, "but you seem quite set up. Perhaps I'd better investigate."

She kissed him.

"Later?"

"Oh, later," he said, "at least it's keeping you in condition. You look quite decent. Bring your patsy to my dressing room after the performance."

"Don't expect too much of Si Moses," she said. "He's a nice, hardworking man who owns four movie houses and is learning to be smart enough to jump from exhibitor to moviemaker. Likely tomorrow's millionaire. Just like a lot of 'em you see all over town at night, living it up by candlelight for the first time. And don't forget, even Daniel Frohman is joining up with some of them. Who knows, maybe you will someday—as I said to Fergus Austin—when they offer you enough money, or you have to get out of town."

Jeffrey cocked an eyebrow.

"Practical thinking. Are you still seeing that kid, the juggler?"

"He'll be along."

She left him in the wings.

For once Jeffrey was wrong. Simon Moses, he thought, must be the patsy, and that Irish kid, God knows why, was the boyfriend, otherwise she wouldn't have dragged him along.

At least my sister's interested in something at last, he thought. Of course it would have to be the galloping tintypes. His family in toto would froth at the mouth at such a thought. But he cast the random thought of vulgar films aside and set his face for his entrance.

The curtain rose, and twelve hundred people waited for him to carry them on wings of fancy. Which he did, spurred somehow by the fact that Claudia was in the fourth row center with a moviemaker who had better see a little acting done right.

◆◆◆◆◆◆◆◆

"I'm gettin' outa here," said Mike Cuneo. "The town's too hot for me just now."

"What happened?" asked Fergus.

"Well, I told you about Biograph. Seems they've got a couple of cops on my trail. And someone told my pop about the flats. So you know what? I'm gonna blow out the candles on my eighteenth birthday cake, and lam out with my bankroll in my knickers before the candles get cold."

"What will your pop say?"

Mike snorted. "Anybody who lays a leather strap to me ain't got a right to say nothin'. Essanay's doin' fine in Chicago. They got J. Warren Kerrigan and Francis

X. Bushman and Billy Anderson, and that means lots of people workin'. So *good-bye pal.*"

Fergus looked distressed.

"I was counting on you for bankroll."

"Uncount," said Mike. "I can do better than 3 percent, old pal. I'll keep in touch. Soon as I settle I'll get a mailbox so you can reach me without nobody tracking down my address."

Fergus wondered if he'd get the next word from Mike in jail. But he was too busy with his own plans to give it much thought. When the enormity of a picture company—with Mr. Moses shelling out the money—hit him, he got nervous indigestion, and even his mother couldn't make him eat.

At night he slaved over his plans. David worked with him devising camera setups and figuring out how to match scenes. They worked for hours at the Brooklyn lab with Jules, who gave them pointers or ran film while they studied it.

"You see," said Jules, "if you have a chance you can use a gauze, like Billy Bitzer learned from that German, Leezer. That will make Claudia Barstow look like an angel, even in that harsh beach light. You can't control your shade like you do in a studio with overhead linen on slides. So try gauze. Here, I loan you these."

David held one lens up and admired it as though a jewel was in his hand.

"Now use your reflectors right, practice between the shots with anybody who's around, before the actors get in place. See?" he moved his hands, tilting the fingers. "Remember, on this orthochromatic film Claudia's blue eyes could come out like fish eyes, so be careful. And Fergus, group some people or an object in the foreground to give depth. Don't worry. Just be natural, don't try to be fancy. You're not Mr. Griffith—yet."

"Geez," said David, "I'm scared."

Jules smiled at him. "Everything you do is experience. When you see the film you will learn something you didn't know before. Just take good care of my camera."

He patted it and rubbed it with a soft cloth, for it was the glistening tool of his trade, his magic eye.

David caressed it as fondly as Jules had. And Jules patted him on the back.

"I know you," he said. "You'll bring it back better than when I sent it out."

"You can just bet," said David. "After all, didn't I help you put it together?"

Fergus took out the memo cards filed in his pocket. He scanned them.

"Lay off," said David, digging his finger in Fergus's ribs, "you'll wear 'em out. And you know them by heart anyway."

"I hope, I hope!" said Fergus, crossing himself.

◆◆◆◆◆◆◆◆

Simon Moses looked at the beehive of activity on the beach. This is the biggest payroll in the history of Moses Enterprises. Even four theaters were buttons compared to this. Where did they all come from?

He wore a straw hat, gaudily announcing Souvenir of Coney Island, purchased at a stall when the sun beat down. He had shed his coat and undone his necktie.

Fergus, in a big hat and goggles, his nose painted with zinc ointment, wore a flapping white shirt and tennis shoes, along with a striped bathing suit, for he was in the water and out directing the splashing scenes with Claudia, two kids, and an old man with a walrus moustache.

Pete Bingham, from the stage, played a brawny lifeguard. To Simon he seemed a little run-to-gut, but when the camera was on he sucked it in, and he was handsome in an overbearing way. Claudia said he was a phony, and she didn't like him at all, and Simon was relieved.

To Fergus and the crew, Claudia was pure gold as a comedienne. As soon as the focus was on her, she seemed to glow from within. She was the silly, petulant rich girl who set her foot down on the plebeian sand so the audience could imagine how hot the sand must be. She looked with outrage at the homely men who flirted with her, her aristocratic nose uptilted. And when a handsome man crossed her path, she simpered, the way anyone might imagine a rich, sheltered girl would do. She made a hundred little gestures with her flexible hands. She ate a Coney Island hot dog like it was pheasant, peeling back the roll with the éclat of a Chaplin. Mustard fell on her suit, and she mopped it up with an expensive lace handkerchief, to the dismay of two fat lady supers.

Fergus was busy getting props together to keep up with her fertile imagination. At one point he jollied a little old lady into loaning her French poodle for a bit Claudia dreamed up of using its fluffy ruff for a napkin.

Some moccasin telegraph, which always seems to be in action when a movie company appears, had alerted the seaside that a picture was being made. Three men had to be hired to hold back the gaping mob.

David, his cap backwards so he could look in the camera, hopped about with his bare feet in the hot sand.

The actors huddled under rented beach umbrellas, resting in folding chairs, among soggy towels, lotions, bottles of soft drinks, and orange peels.

Claudia wore a pretty bloomer suit and a bathing cap with ruffles, her curls peeking out on each side. The property man had set up a little canvas-sided shelter against the wind, where she could retreat to peel off her wet suit and put on a duplicate dry one. Inside was a wicker chair and a little makeup table.

She beckoned Simon into it, as she left the scene in her dripping suit.

She discussed bits of action with him. It made him feel she depended on his decisions.

"Oh, Si," she said, kissing his ear, "this will be a good one, because it tells a human story—and by the way, my brother Jeffrey liked you last night. He said you were handsome and vital. How about that!"

He stared at her with delight.

"A Barstow says *I'm* handsome! Me, Simon Moses!"

"This Barstow says you're handsome. Don't get any ideas just now, though. I have to put on a dry suit."

She had just stripped the wet suit off when the tent was ripped asunder. She screamed. Simon turned; flash powder flared in his face.

For a moment he blinked, stunned by the fierce light. When his vision cleared, he saw Claudia holding the suit in front of her naked body, also blinking. And then he looked at a crazy world. Every man in the company was fighting. David was battling two men who pulled the camera and tripod from him and, before his horrified eyes, flung it into the ocean.

Fergus struggled with two other men who wrestled a film can away from him. One swung on him, knocking him down, and he fell back with his nose bleeding.

"What is it? Who are they?" Simon cried. "Call the cops!"

David rushed to him. "It's the Trust, pappa!" he said. "My camera! My camera!"

"Oh, my God!" said Simon, turning to Claudia, "get over to that hot-dog stand!"

Fergus stumbled up, holding his nose.

"Fergie, get her clothes!" said Simon. "Bring them in that hot-dog stand!"

Fergus groped into the reaches of the canvas, came up with a suitcase and a handful of garments, and started for the sidewalk, leading Claudia and blocking her bare behind. There was another flash as a picture was taken.

Into this disorder stepped a dapper man. It was Jeffrey Barstow, out of context, standing near his cream Stutz Bearcat. He stared at his naked sister.

"For God's sake, Claudia, what kind of movie is this?"

"Oh, Jeffrey," she said, starting to cry, "it's that lousy Trust. They're beating up the whole company!"

"The hell they are! How do you tell the good ones from the bad ones?" he asked.

"The good ones have a sunburn," said Claudia.

Jeffrey threw his hat and his tweed jacket on the sand.

"Mr. Moses," he said, "form your troops. We can't let hooligans do this to the arts."

Several bystanders, two lifeguards, the owner of the hot-dog stand that sheltered Claudia, and a drunk carrying a beer joined the fray as soon as they saw Jeffrey Barstow was in it.

In a few moments several newspapermen arrived. A photographer who had a stand nearby had covered the scene in full detail.

It was a draw until the riot squad came and hustled both sides into two Black Marias.

All the contestants were exhausted and glad to end the melee, even if it meant being booked at the Coney Island precinct.

Jeffrey's lawyer arrived and got him out for the evening performance. Before he left, Jeffrey asked Fergus to step out in the hall.

"Listen, you little son of a bitch," he said, "I don't know what this is all about, but you stay away from my sister."

"But it isn't my fault," said Fergus, "the Trust—"

"I loathe weasels," said Jeffrey. He socked him in the eye. "That's to remind you. Lay off."

Fergus leaned weakly against the wall for a moment, then went back inside, holding a hand over his eye.

"You could have protected us better than this," said Simon. "Oh, God, what's going to happen now!"

He had in mind the picture of himself with Claudia, bare-assed naked as the tent fell in.

Mr. Moses, Dave, and Abe left together.

Fergus found himself standing in the hall.

Here he was, outside again. His nose hurt. His eye was puffing up. His shirt was torn. It was a long haul by public carrier back to where he lived and a longer way, he felt, to making pictures.

◆◆◆◆◆◆◆◆

Simon Moses feared he faced complete ruin.

His second picture was incomplete. He had signed so many notes the interest was compounding beyond belief. In his hand was a scribbled warning that if he messed with independent picture making any more, the seats of the Little Diamond would be ripped to shreds. The Trust didn't fool around with cheapflints who used unlicensed cameras and smuggled French Pathé film.

When he came home from the office, Esther and Aunt Yetta met him in the parlor. His wife Rebecca was nowhere to be seen.

It was the first time his beloved daughter Esther had ever looked at him with flashing anger.

"Where's mamma?" he asked.

"She's in bed," said Esther.

"She's sick?"

"She sure is," said Esther, "and Martha and I are taking turns holding her hand. The doctor just gave her a sedative."

"The doctor!" said Simon.

A doctor hadn't been in the house since Martha was born.

"What's the matter?"

He started to rush toward the bedroom.

"I wouldn't be going," said Aunt Yetta.

The sere little woman hadn't discussed anything for years but kreplach and what went into gefilte fish.

"This is what's wrong," said Esther. "It came in the mail today, pappa."

She handed him a photograph—Claudia, posing like *September Morn*, looking startled, and right behind her, himself, shirt open, a surprised miscreant.

"Oh my God!" said Simon.

He looked at Esther and Yetta. They stared at him like strangers.

"It was all a mistake," he said. "We were making a movie."

"You sure were," said Esther. "It's all over the newspapers. Well, you'd better not see that—that woman again. And explain it was just a movie to mamma."

Simon went into the darkened bedroom. He gestured to Martha to leave.

"Becky," he whispered. "Becky, it's me. I—I don't know what to say. I've been a pischer. I just wanted to make money in movies."

She turned her head to the wall. He noticed with a pang the gnarled hands, the hands that had worked so hard in the early days at a sewing machine, and so deftly, even in the affluent days, reeling out the tickets and watching his money, to see it was counted right. And all the time keeping his house and his children, his clothes and his life in order, so he could go on with his busy world.

"Oh, Simon," she said, "how could you!"

He saw her throat constrict as she swallowed. She still kept her face toward the wall.

"I'm sorry if I gave you hurt," he said. "I didn't mean to do it, Becky. It was just a movie, just a moving picture."

She didn't turn her head.

He started to weep.

"I'm in deep trouble, Becky, deep trouble!"

At this, she turned and looked at him. His hands were over his face. She sat up, slowly, drugged.

"Oh, Simon," she said, "Simon–"

She put her hands out to him, and he put his head against her thin shoulder. She tried to comfort him.

"Why didn't you tell me. You've been a stranger."

"It's my first bad business deal," he said. "That idiot Fergus got me into a movie. And now the Trust is on my neck."

"Well," said Rebecca, "let's talk it over, Simon. We can make out. Have Yetta give you some chicken soup, and I'll have some, too, with nice matzo balls, and you'll feel better. I just can't face anybody tonight–I'm staying in bed." Her eyes brimmed with tears.

She had her soup on a tray in bed. This was as shattering to Simon as anything that had happened.

"I'll handle the ticket booth, pappa," said Martha, "and Yetta can spell me. You and ma stay home and straighten it out."

The family left for the Little Diamond.

It was the first time in years Rebecca and Simon had been alone in the apartment. He felt uncomfortable and strange.

When he went into the bedroom Rebecca had put on her pink silk nightgown, a birthday present from the girls, never worn before, and she had brushed her ash-blonde hair over her shoulders.

Simon dressed for bed, lingering in the bathroom.

He put on his pongee pajamas and a flannel robe. He looked in the mirror. With another twinge, he realized that he and Claudia had shopped for them in Atlantic City and had fun at the madness of buying such personal things together, those wonderful first days.

He got into bed with Rebecca.

She turned out the light and reached over to caress his cheek. He fondled her, but it was no good.

After a while he said, "I'm sorry, Becky, I guess I'm just tired. Maybe we'll talk tomorrow. Nuh?"

Becky softly turned her back to him, and he lay awake, guilty and miserable. He could tell by her breathing that she was not sleeping, but waiting for his own breathing to let her know he had fallen asleep.

He dared not move, for if he did, she would wonder why he didn't talk.

And Claudia, his lovely Claudia. She might be awake, too, wondering why he didn't call.

Finally, he sat up.

"I have to call the Little Diamond," he said.

He went into the hall, muffling his voice as he gave Claudia's number to the operator so that Becky could not hear. The phone rang and rang. Maybe the operator was wrong. He called once more, risking everything again. There was no answer.

He went back to bed.

"How do you like it, when the storekeeper's away nobody answers the phone," he said, trying to laugh.

He settled down to a miserable night, resenting Becky in the bed, resenting the itchy heat, resenting the absence of Claudia, and wondering miserably where she was and who she might be with. And that gave him an erection, so he had to turn away from Rebecca and hide his turmoil. What was he going to do to keep Claudia in his life? That seemed the only thing that mattered.

6

♦♦♦♦♦♦♦♦

Fergus played the waiting game.

There wasn't much else he could do. Again his mother put beefsteak on his eye.

"It seems to me every time you get mixed up with that movie crowd, you get in trouble," she said.

He was a celebrity. Along with Claudia and Jeffrey Barstow and Mr. Moses he was in pictures of the brawl at Coney Island. He was also mentioned in one paper as being an official of Titan Films.

Of course, Mr. Moses was responsible for the Ernaman camera. They had gone back and hunted for it, but it was at the bottom of the sea, covered with sand from the big breakers. Nobody would ever find it. There was too much metal holding it down. And Jules would be on their tails any minute.

The best thing was to hide out.

And so he was surprised when Mr. Moses came to see him.

"I just wanted to see how your eye was, boy," he said.

"It's okay," said Fergus, fearing he was going to ask for his money back.

"I wonder if you could do me a favor?" said Simon.

"*Me* do you a favor?" said Fergus.

Then he thought, there I go, so he abridged it.

"Every time I do you a favor I end up with my face bashed in. What do you want this time?"

"Fergie—Fergus," said Simon, "I want you to pick up Claudia and bring her to Luchow's tonight. We got to talk business."

Funny business, thought Fergus. Simon Moses couldn't move alone with her. He had to have him.

"Well, Mr. Moses," he said, "I don't know."

Simon put out his hand.

"Fergus, I have that letter in my pocket guaranteeing you 2 percent of my Titan stock."

"Not yours," said Fergus, "2 percent of *the* stock."

Simon looked at him with malevolent eyes.

"For this I helped you," he said.

"For this," said Fergus.

Simon went to the door. "It's a deal," he said, "if I see you at Luchow's with Claudia Barstow at eight o'clock."

◆◆◆◆◆◆◆◆

"And so, to be together, we must be apart."

Simon leaned across the table and whispered to Claudia, while Fergus ordered.

He had come into Luchow's to find he was a celebrity.

From a nobody, everyone knew, now, he was a moviemaker. The scandalous fight at Coney Island had won him a place in the evolving motion-picture society. And he realized, as did Fergus, that the Barstow name had given him glamour. It was big-time.

Six men stepped up to him and congratulated him for helping to break the Trust. Even Mr. Laemmle greeted him with clasped hands as he passed by.

An exchange man from Boston sent wine to his table with his business card and a note: "If you're going into production, contact me."

"So there's only one thing to do," said Simon. "We have to gamble for keeps."

"How?" said Claudia.

"I'm going to send you and Fergus to California," said Simon, "and set up out there. You can stay at a classy hotel while Fergus gets the company organized. David gave me a great idea. We'll finish *Saturday at Coney Island*, only we'll make it *Saturday at Santa Monica*. I will come west in a couple of weeks, and we'll be in business away from the Trust. Everybody's doing it. And, lovely lady, I'm going to make you a big star if it takes my last dollar."

Claudia put her hand on his.

"Oh, Si, I can't let you do this!"

"Don't be silly, my dear," said Simon. "I can't let all these smart Jews beat me out, can I?"

He laughed, along with Claudia.

Oysters Rockefeller were served. Wine was poured.

Fergus looked at Simon. How he had changed! He seemed to be in control. Even Claudia was emotional.

"Nobody ever cared for me like this before," she said.

"This is just the beginning," said Simon. "Enjoy."

He lifted his wineglass and toasted her.

Fergus could hardly eat. California! Setting up Titan.

"Mr. Moses," he said, "we'll have to talk a deal. I had other plans."

"Don't be a nudnick," said Simon. "Who else is taking Claudia to California?"

"Well, we might wait a little," said Fergus, "and get some of the business settled."

"Don't be silly," said Simon, "you're going right away. We'll talk business, don't worry."

◆◆◆◆◆◆◆◆

The night before he left, Mrs. Austin packed Fergus's carpetbag.

His father was out, and Fergus was glad to get

away from his weeping mother. Her concern about his new job was a pain in the ass.

"I don't like to think of you among those strangers."

"Mother, they won't be strangers. Mr. Moses will be out there, and later the whole Moses family. And if I hit it big you can come out and spend your old age in the middle of an orange grove."

"What would I do with all my boarders?"

"We'll take care of that when the time comes," he said, "but I'm going to make you rich, you just see!"

He knew he would be invited out to dinner, and sure enough, he picked up Claudia as usual. Her apartment was a shambles.

As they left to meet Simon. Claudia handed him a little bag.

"Check this for me," she said.

"Why?" he asked.

"I'm going home with you."

"Are you crazy?" said Fergus. "Have you and Mr. Moses had a fight?"

"Don't be silly," said Claudia, "I have to see Dr. Wolfrum before I go. I'm on the nest."

"Not again!" said Fergus.

"Just shut up," said Claudia as they got in the hansom cab, "and let's have a pleasant evening."

"Well, one thing," said Fergus, "I'm not going through *that* again."

"What's the matter," said Claudia, "a little abortion upset you?"

"No," said Fergus, "it's just the nightmare I keep having about running into my mother and having her ask me who you are and what you are doing there. And having to share my bed with that queer bird, Doc Wolfrum. But I'll work it out."

He grinned, feeling very sophisticated.

"I'll tippietoe," laughed Claudia as they drove off.

◆◆◆◆◆◆◆◆◆

Fergus's hegira to California was a nightmare from the beginning. He had lied to his mother about the train departure, saying he had to pick up extra luggage. He put Claudia in a cab, a block away, sitting in discomfort, while he said good-bye to his mother, got into another cab, paid him off, and switched to the waiting cab, feeling like the Black Crook, and hoping no one would see him with a pale woman leaning against the window looking like she was going to faint.

At Grand Central Station, Claudia's maid was waiting, grumbling and worrying over piles of luggage at the Twentieth Century Limited.

Fergus had to learn the necessity of bribing porters to handle the overabundant cargo.

Simon Moses was no help. He rushed to the station to see them off, distressed at Claudia's pale face as well as upset over her departure.

"You shouldn't go," he said, "you should rest. I had no idea it would be like this—"

"Forget it," said Claudia. "I'll be okay. It never bothered me like this before."

He flinched.

"Sorry," she said. "Just let me get to my compartment."

He helped her on the train, looking foolish carrying a massive bouquet of roses.

What a help, thought Fergus.

Seeing how they were staring at each other, Fergus was embarrassed. "I'll go check the luggage," he said.

"Oh, Claudia," said Simon, "how can I do without you?"

He blew his nose noisily.

"Now, Si," said Claudia, "let's not have any waterworks. It's good I'm going to Hollywood. It's good for *us*. I know you're putting yourself in hock, and I'll work hard, sweetheart."

He said, "Just stay. Stay with me. I don't give a damn. I love you. We'll work it out."

She leaned back, feeling faint.

"It's too late," she said. "We're on our way, and we can't make movies here. The Trust would wreck your houses. I'll write you, Si. Be good, and come out soon."

Fergus appeared in the doorway.

"Can you believe it, I had to tip three bucks for all that luggage!"

Simon looked at him with extreme dislike. This young whippersnapper getting to take Claudia, his woman, to California on his money!

"All aboard!" yelled a conductor.

Simon bent over and kissed her cheek.

"Run along," said Claudia.

Simon stepped off the train just before it pulled out, and Fergus waved at him.

"Take care of her—take good care of her!" said Simon.

"Don't worry, Mr. Moses. She'll be all right."

As the train jerked and pulled away, Fergus saw him blow his nose and wipe his eyes, a forlorn man, waving helplessly with his limp handkerchief.

◆◆◆◆◆◆◆◆

Fergus went to his berth to check his luggage. The poor bastard, he thought, what a mess Moses has himself in. A real one, knowing him, to hand me such a bankroll . . . and he can't even face his family.

He sat musing, as the ugly outskirts of the city passed by, until the porter disturbed him.

"That lady in compartment C wants to see you, mister."

He found Claudia curled up in the berth that the porter had made up. She looked pitifully small in the bed, her dark-circled eyes enormous in her small face.

"Oh, Fergie," she said, "I just feel lousy, and I'm bleeding. I hate to do this, but I can't open my luggage. Could you get out my small case, and get me a wrapper and a nightgown, and some pills that Wolfrum gave me, and I'm sorry, Fergie, say I'm your wife or something, and have somebody get me some sanitary napkins."

"Maybe we'd better get off the train," he said.

"We can't," she said. "You'll just have to help me out. And get me some gin and that thermometer in my makeup bag."

Fergus assorted the luggage, got her nightclothes and the pills, poured her some gin, and bribed the porter to get the necessaries. In a few moments he came back to find her half asleep. He picked up the thermometer she'd left on the ledge by the window. It registered 102°.

"Holy mother!" he whispered.

He wondered what would happen if she died on the train. They'd probably have him up for murder or manslaughter.

In the evening he had the porter bring her soup and orange juice. She sat up and sipped some gin with the juice, and then couldn't keep down the broth.

All night he stayed in his clothes and made vigils to her bedside. He got the porter to get a bowl of cracked ice and made her put chips between her lips.

In the morning he was able to sit her up. The compartment smelled of sour blood, and he put the refuse in a paper bag and sprayed her perfume around. He bathed her face and arms, neck and breast, using the scented soap in her kit.

Oh Claudia . . . my beautiful, sick Claudia.

Her face was waxen, and there were purple shadows around her pale eyes. Somehow he felt he loved her in a different, deeper way than when she was just a beautiful, wanton girl, for she was defenseless. In the train, hurtling through the land, each of them was dependent on the well-being of the other.

Before they got to Chicago, he propped her up, let her make up her face, brushed her hair for her, put a scarf over her hair and knotted it clumsily, helped her into her clothes, and packed all her gear.

"There now," he said, "just think of California. You're going to get on that Santa Fe Deluxe train and live like a queen the 2,267 miles to Los Angeles. In sixty-three hours, think of it, you'll be among the orange blossoms!"

"The way I feel, I may be among the lilies," she said with a sickly smile. "Oh, Fergie, I'm scared."

So was he.

They left the compartment, the sicksweet-smelling faded flowers from Simon, and Fergus told the porter she was recovering from an operation. They got a wheelchair and lifted her into it.

After endless waits, tips, loads of luggage, redcaps, cabs, and another wheelchair at the Dearborn Station, he got her on the Santa Fe Deluxe in one of the six through cars, carrying her in his arms into a drawing-room pullman. He posed as her husband and took the sofa berth, settling her in the double berth as soon as they boarded.

At Kansas City, Fergus took her temperature, for she was very still during the night. It was 103°. He debated taking her off at the station, and getting her to a hospital.

"Claudia," he said, when she opened her eyes to take some juice, "your temperature's gone up. I think I ought to take you off the train and get a doctor."

"No, Fergus," she said, "you can't. They'll get my name, and I'll be in the papers. And then it'll be a worse mess. And you're with me. It'll fall on your head, and Doc Wolfrum's. Not to mention the mess for Si. Just forget it. I'll be okay. Where are those pills?"

He gave her another one.

As the train rumbled through the night, and he heard the clang of the signals, the oncoming roar of other trains, and saw the flash of semaphores and lights as they passed towns and hamlets, he felt he was on a train going to hell, rushing too fast, with a woman who might be dead. Sometimes he got up to see if she were still breathing. Once, as he looked, her eyes opened and she reached her hot hand to his.

"Thank you, Fergus," she said. "Is it all worth it?"

"It is, Claudia," he said.

He patted her hand, realizing that twice she had called him Fergus. He felt sorry for her—a little, lonely woman who had reached out for a touch, who couldn't bear to be alone, and who had paid for it with this wracked body.

"Take it easy, Claudia," he said. "Tomorrow we'll start to get into the beautiful country. And if you're better we can sit in the observation parlor and look for Indians."

And maybe take you off at Albuquerque, feet first . . .

Damn Simon Moses. He passed the buck to me with a pocket full of money. If anything happens, I'm the patsy. I'm crossing state lines traveling with someone else's very sick woman. And don't I love her, too?

The next morning Claudia awoke with the bright sunlight striking her eyes. The blind had been left up. For a moment she listened to the click-clack of wheels on rails, and she leaned up on one elbow, startled to discover where she was.

She shook her head with disbelief as she looked out at the burning landscape. A Navajo woman with two bright-eyed children was waiting at the crossing in a buckboard. She was handsome and brown and waved as the train slowed down. A vast land of red earth, mesas, green mesquite, and piñon stretched endlessly to a backdrop of roiling thunderclouds, pasted low against a blue, blue sky.

For the first time in days, Claudia's body seemed free of the burden of sickness. Her forehead felt cool, and she savored the pleasure of being able to stretch and to breathe deeply.

She turned, to see Fergus asleep on the sofa bed.

He looked dusty and hot, his white shirt plastered against his sweaty body, his mouth open. What in hell, she thought, is this lanky, redheaded kid doing on this crazy train ride?

She looked out again, as the train came to a creaking stop. The landscape looked fragrant, and the compartment was stale. She sat up and tried to wrench open the window. She couldn't; she was weak.

"Fergus, hey, Fergus, open up this window, let's get a whiff of fresh air."

Fergus struggled out of the pit of deep, fatigued sleep and threw his arm over his eyes to shut out the blinding sun.

"Come on!" said Claudia.

Fergus sat upright. He stared at her. She nodded.

"Yes, I'm fine. I'm just fine."

How could she look so radiant?

"You may be fine," he said, "but I'm a wreck."

He wrenched open the window. The hot desert air blew a little whirlwind of dust into the compartment. Fergus forced it down quickly.

"Look out," he said, "you'll get cinders in your eyes!"

"It's better than dying of suffocation."

She looked at him as he yawned and pushed his thick hair back from his forehead.

"Where are we?"

"Someplace around Devil's Canyon," he said.

She peered out and made a face.

"It figures."

How was she going to share the rest of this endless trip with this kid staring at her?

"Look, Fergus," she said, "I'm just filthy. How about getting out my bottle bag, and then clearing out. I'm going to take a sponge bath and get on some clean duds. Go have breakfast, go to the observation platform—or something."

When he left, she stripped and filled the folding silver washbasin with water. She soaped, sponged, and rubbed cologne over her body, looking at her ribs showing against her pale skin and at her flat stomach.

Although she was weak, it was wonderful to feel alive again, and clean. Oh, if only Si were there, to be with her and coddle her and look at her with devotion. She felt a need for him, for his affection, and for the security his presence gave her. No one had ever loved her before, day in, day out, no matter what she did.

She sat up with a start. For the first time she realized how much she loved him. She wanted this one man to be with her; a man much older, uneducated, yet he had caught her with his care and interest in her, in Claudia, for no other reason but that she was Claudia.

Well, he would join her soon, and somehow they'd work it out. It would be better without his feeling of guilt about stolen moments, with his family in the same town. Just get through this endless journey. How had the pioneer women ever stuck it out along these endless horizons, when it seemed too much for her on a luxury train? She hated the clack-clack of the wheels on the track.

Well, it would end, and there would be new work, a new world, and she was protected. That stinking Jeffrey would see what she could do. This was one comfort; if she made good in movies, her parents and relatives would see it. Even if they were in England. They couldn't beg off and say sorry, they couldn't get over for an opening. That was the good of movies, they were a portable art.

She looked at the circles under her eyes, applied makeup and rouge, so she wouldn't be a fright. As she finished her ablutions and combed her hair, she thought she looked fairly well, and loss of weight was not so bad after all; everyone knew those tricky cameras added weight, even to small people.

Fergus, half dozing, was sitting with a cup of cold coffee when Claudia entered the dining car. She was lovely in a lavender silk dress, and as always he saw all eyes follow her as she sat down at the table.

She ordered orange juice, oatmeal, two eggs, two lamb chops, and some toast and jam and devoured them all with relish. Fergus watched her make friends with the steward, a traveling man, a railroad official, and the brakeman passing through.

That's an actress. She had to have an audience. She just isn't real unless she's showing off.

Claudia moved on to the observation car. Exhausted, Fergus went back to the drawing room. The porter had made up her berth, and he settled his head against the dusty rough velour of the sofa bed. The porter sympathetically brought him a pillow and plumped it up. As he fell asleep, his thoughts were of Claudia. He'd had it. She worried him to death, tore his heart out with unconcern, and then drifted off to intrigue anybody around, while he was left a limp rag.

Claudia stayed as long as she could in the club car talking to strangers, looking at magazines, and watching the landscape. Of course she was grateful to Fergus, he was a dear and she liked him, but it was going to be hell sitting out this trip with him staring at her.

If they had known what a gentle valentine this adventure was, compared to the kaleidoscope ahead of them, they might have stepped off at the next dusty station and taken the next rattler back.

II

HOLLYWOOD: 1913—1934

1

◆◆◆◆◆◆◆◆

The brick red Santa Fe station at Los Angeles was of bastard Moorish architecture, surrounded by webs of tracks; one side leaned toward the sluggish Los Angeles River, Boyle Heights, and factories that were beginning to spew their evil smells and vapors over the landscape. On the other side the station faced the old Los Angeles Plaza, with a small sleepy adobe church, soup kitchens, midnight missions, and the outskirts of a ramshackle Chinatown. Farther down the streets, pawnshops, secondhand stores, flophouses, and business offices rubbed elbows with newer stores and more opulent offices and restaurants.

Not far away was the Alexandria Hotel, grandly styled in florid false Louis Phillipe fashion, with an elegant presidential suite, and a conglomoration of rooms, banquet halls, dining rooms, and marbled foyers.

As Fergus ushered Claudia to the registration desk at the Alexandria Hotel in Los Angeles, he was agape. It was far from anything he had seen in the East; there was a babble of excitement, spawned out of a bubbling broth of cultures.

Wealthy Californians, new oil tycoons, snobbish Los Angeles merchant society, mostly from Iowa, trying to be blue bloods, walked past the gregarious newcomers as if avoiding the pox.

There were sea captains and shipowners from the seven seas; visiting merchant princes, peddling their wares to equally prosperous buyers. There were tourists in search of orange groves, youth, and sunshine. New motion-picture personalities, gaudy and eccentric, pushed through the crowds, preening. New Yorkers and Europeans who had come west for adventure studied the whole panorama and decided on their objective.

Fergus recognized some of the men he had seen on Fourteenth Street, and Claudia greeted acquaintances from Sherry's and Delmonico's—people like themselves who had come on the new treasure hunt.

Scattered among them were silk-clad girls of Claudia's world, wafting perfume, fortune seekers with bodies or talents as their wares.

Claudia signed the register with a flourish. The Barstow name caused the clerk to summon an official who effusively greeted her and promised a nice airy room with a view.

Claudia looked at the crowd. The hotel official gestured disparagingly.

"We can only apologize that this movie riffraff is taking advantage of our hospitality," he said, "but I can assure you, we will not allow you to be bothered, Miss Barstow."

He turned to Fergus.

"And you, sir—are you staying here?"

"I shall have to stay farther west," he said, grandly, "I have business interests in Hollywood."

Claudia thanked the manager.

"I think I see some friends," she said, "excuse me," and she moved into the hubbub, ignoring the proffered respectability, Fergus following.

The unofficial casting office of the infant film business was in the lobby.

A large oriental rug had been sunk into a shallow recess in the floor, padded thickly, so it was flush with the rest of the floor. It was standard practice for the ambitious unemployed to gather by it in the afternoon. Those who were superstitious strolled cautiously to the edge of the rug and touched it with a foot for good luck.

Some sat in carved chairs around the perimeter, posing, trying to look attractive or bright, hoping to be offered a job. They were all young, and they were establishing a new life-style. They gathered in a fraternally obsessive cluster, sharing information and plans; it was movies, movies, movies, night and day, and some of them would be involved the rest of their lives. It took nothing but one's presence to be told all the news of the industry, and anyone who listened could take pieces of the jigsaw puzzle and try to make a pattern.

Soon Claudia and Fergus were involved with a sprightly group. Most of the young people lived in nearby boardinghouses. Pretty young women would gather in the lobby in their best dresses, saunter to the dining room for a cup of tea, and, if fortunate, check into the hotel, where they could be part of the group when the best jobs were handed out.

Fergus learned that the smartest thing a young man could do would be to appear at a location in the morning. An actor might be needed, or he could hold the reflectors, help tote cameras, or do any odd job in order to become a member of a group. There were at least several dozen companies at work, and many more on the way. Studios were burgeoning in many a loft and barn.

One fellow, Stuart Plimpton, a nervous man with nicotined fingers and a waxed black moustache, who had once directed a play in Chicago, told Fergus that sometimes the Trust still got their brutes west and latched onto an unlicensed camera, but if you were in trouble, you always headed for Tijuana, Mexico, a few hours away, and hid out with your film negatives until the danger was over.

"Stick around," said Plimpton, "there's a lot of angles, kid. There's no telephone line to New York yet, and if you can just get the raw stock and a machine you can make a picture with rubber checks before they catch up with you. And the minute you've got film, baby, you've got a bankroll."

"I'd better get out and find space," said Fergus. "Where are you staying?"

"I'm at Blondeau's Tavern at Gower and Sunset," he said. "It's a roadhouse, but they've rented the backyard for moviemaking. Look me up."

Plimpton spotted a man who had a clipboard and was signing up people, and he sauntered off.

Fergus caught up to Claudia. He could see she was going to be in the middle of a group any minute, whether she knew them or not. Who could help wanting to talk to her, with her beauty and her vivacity. No doubt, he thought, in half an hour she'd be telling them.

"Claudia," he said, "I've got to get settled. You know how Mr. Moses is. Time is money. Give me about two weeks. As soon as I get all the gear together and find space, we'll get cracking and wind up *A Day at Santa Monica*. You know, camera, flats, equipment, props, that stuff."

"Fergus," said Claudia, "don't bother me with all that junk. Just get it together, and you know Claudia will light up. See you."

She melded into the crowd, as he had anticipated, causing considerable attention.

Fergus had been so absorbed with Claudia's problems on the train that he hadn't realized all he must do. Camera, film, space, equipment, a crew. How do you do it in a new town when you don't even know anybody? He wished David were there. He was so smart ferreting out things.

He took the trolley out to Hollywood, with his baggage. On the advice of the conductor, he got out at Vine Street and walked down a lane that was trimmed with pepper trees and eucalyptus.

There, as if waiting for him, was a big red barn. Across the front it said Webber's Stables.

He walked in. At first it seemed empty. Then he saw an old man asleep in a swivel chair.

"Hello," said Fergus.

The man awoke with a snort.

"They're all out," he said, "all rented. No more horses."

"I didn't come for a horse," said Fergus.

He looked around. Sliding doors opened on a field, and, beyond it, wild oats, purple lupine, and orange poppies waved in a slight breeze that seemed to sweep down from Cahuenga Pass.

"You wouldn't want to rent some of this space, would you?" he asked.

The man stood up, scooting his chair away. He was a red-faced, Iowa expatriate, and he glowed at the sound of money.

"Might just," he said. "My horses are out during the day. But they gotta sleep nights."

"Well, I only need the barn during the day," said Fergus, "but I need space to put up some scenery. Maybe we could make a deal."

"You movie people?" asked the man suspiciously.

"I sure am," said Fergus.

"Let's see the color of your money."

"What's the deal first?" asked Fergus.

"Maybe forty dollars a month. Providin' the horses sleep in."

"Seems fair enough," said Fergus.

"Color of money, I said."

Fergus pulled out his roll, a secret he had learned.

"Advance after the deal's on paper," said Fergus. "Where can I bunk around here?"

"Well, you might go over to see Kathleen Martinez across the street. She dishes up grub for a lot of them movie cowboys."

"I'll get the contract written tonight, Mr. —?"

"Mr. Webber," said the man. "Pleased to make your

acquaintance. Now mind, no whorin', finaglin', nor gamblin' in these quarters. I'm a hard-shell Baptist."

They shook hands, and Fergus left his luggage while he checked the restaurant across the street. It was a two-story red and white wooden building that had started as a chuck wagon and had gradually enlarged. The pepper trees were a shelter in the hot California sun, and cowboy actors tied their horses beneath the feathery branches and sat gabbing and picking their teeth.

A sign announced in scrolled elegance that the restaurant was Kathleen's Café, but it was referred to among the film elite as the front office, ptomaine tower, belch gulch, or, simply, the place.

From breakfast on, which began at six o'clock, the restaurant was a mass of activity. Kathleen, her Mexican husband Tony, a Greek dishwasher, Xerxes, and two Mexican girls put up box lunches of ham sandwiches, hard-boiled eggs, potato salad, pound cake, and an orange.

When the executive branches of any company returned to jerry-built quarters from location or finished a day's work and gathered to prepare the continuity for the next day's shooting, Kathleen had the hot table set up for dinner, and the men could come into the kitchen and have an unofficial beer or even a quick tot of whiskey before they went back to their evening stint.

Casting, staff meetings, and sometimes writing and rehearsing occurred at the oilcloth-covered tables. Trestle tables were laden with thick mugs and glasses, bottles of ketchup and Tabasco, dishes of a Mexican hot sauce, referred to as hellbroth by the customers, who were often so busted that they spread it on the free sourdough bread to keep their stomachs from rumbling until the end of the day, when they got paid, and then bought themselves a real meal.

Behind a railing was a line of steam tables to handle the mob when shooting was held at the nearby mushrooming studios. Rich soups, savory stews, spicy chili con carne, frijoles, Spanish rice, franks and sauerkraut, pot roast, and well-buttered whipped potatoes were always heating, and, when the company was flush, chicken and spareribs, turkey and steak were cooked in the kitchen at the rear, where there was also an oven, perpetually disgorging a cargo of homemade juicy fruit pies and big square pans of thickly frosted cake. It was exceptionally good grub for such a primitive setting.

Kathleen was the personality every successful café must have. When Fergus came in, there were a few cowboys, from the stable studio Lasky and de Mille had set up down the street, and a clutter of white-collar men, who only differed from the actors in the fact that they didn't wear greasepaint or blue or pink shirts to protect the camera from glare.

Before he realized he was in a self-service cafeteria, Fergus sat down and waited a while, tearing up a piece of bread. He saw someone spoon some of the hot sauce on bread. Thinking it was ketchup, he did the same, took a bite, and stood up, gasping for breath. As he choked, several cowboys turned around, and one began to laugh. A hand suddenly reached toward him and a woman's voice said, "Eat this, quick." He grabbed the plain bread she handed him and shook his head, his voice paralyzed.

"Eat this!" she urged. "Do what I say. Then you can drink something."

He took the bread and chewed it, struggling for breath. His mouth still burned like hellfire, but breathing became possible. He sat down, dared to inhale, chewed another piece, which lowered the flame in his mouth, and then looked up, tears still in his eyes, at a red-haired woman. She was a blur, but she handed him a cup of coffee pale with milk.

"Drink this slowly, kid." Her voice was soft, and as he sipped the coffee and recovered, he turned to focus on her.

Kathleen was in her early twenties. She had prominent blue eyes and a short freckled nose. Her curly hair was pinned back in a knot on her long neck. She was slim, with slender arms and long fingers and blue veins that showed at her temples, in the cleft between her full breasts, and in the almost skim-milk sheen of her inner arms. She wore a white blouse and skirt, and a clean kitchen apron was tied at her small waist.

"I'm Kathleen Martinez," she said. "You must be new here. Just get off the train?"

Fergus nodded. He felt like the original greenhorn in his dark city clothes. They had set so smartly on him a moment ago.

"I just came out to see about some studio space," he said. "Took the Webber Stables for my company."

The hot sauce made his voice uneven.

"Well, if you're going to make your pictures here in Hollywood you ought to get a room. You don't want to have to commute every day. Unless you've got an automobile, you'll have to leave Los Angeles in the middle of the night."

"Where should I stay?" he asked.

"We got a room for rent. It ain't very much, but it's sure easy to roll out of bed to your work. Unless you're very rich and want to stay at that resort, the Hollywood Hotel."

A short, heavyset, handsome, olive-skinned man in his early thirties came to the table. He wiped his hands on his apron as he approached.

"Another casualty?" he asked. "*Salsa picante* ain't Yankee food."

"This is my husband, Tony Martinez," said Kathleen.

"Saludos," said Tony. "Now you been initiated."

He spoke with a soft, Mexican inflection. They shook hands.

"Hey, Tony," said Kathleen, "this kid's getting up another picture outfit at the Webber Stable." A quick look seemed to flash between them, as if there was a hooker in the deal somehow. "Maybe we could rent him a room."

"Sure thing," said Tony. "Five bucks a week. Sheets and towels once a week. Payment in advance. Breakfast thrown in."

"Okay," said Fergus, getting out his wallet with a flourish. "My name's Fergus Austin."

He handed Tony five dollars.

"Well, glory be," said Kathleen, "a countryman of course!"

"There's no use trying to butt in when two Irishers get together," said Tony. "I'll get back to my peach pies. Welcome."

Fergus wondered how this pretty woman had gotten mixed up with a Mexican guy.

Kathleen sensed the question in his eyes.

"Tony's a hardworking fella," she said, "and a good cook. I came from New York, too. My acting career lasted about two weeks. I worked at Mack Sennett's idiot mill out in the valley. All I wanted to do was laugh every time I saw the fool antics goin' on, and they didn't want me to laugh all the time. And every traveling salesman in the U.S. headed for us cuties every time they hit town. It was either a wrestling match or eat in some beanery alone. As a matter of fact, that's how I met Tony. It was a fiesta down at the church near Olvera Street. He was barbecuing ribs, and he was so polite. He took me to church Sundays and introduced me to his folks—nice quiet people, but we couldn't talk much, they only talked Spanish. He courted me with flowers and candy and took a long time to ask me to marry him. So of course, I said yes."

She looked down with a sadness her words denied. Then up at Fergus and at his suit.

"Well, it'll be a pleasure to have a gentleman around that don't look like his pants will stand up by themselves when he takes 'em off."

"My luggage is at the stable," he said.

"I'll get Xerxes to fetch it," she said.

She set her lips, and a shrill whistle, like a doorman calling a cab, came from them.

Xerxes came running from the kitchen. He looked at her as if the sun was rising.

"Xerxes," she said, "this is Fergus Austin. He'll have the front room. Go get his bags over to Webber's Stable."

Xerxes gestured with the tip of his finger to a lock of his curly hair and dashed out the front door.

"He's a nice fella," she said, "but these Greeks aren't very good at our language. Now you just settle down. Let me know if you want for somethin', and be our guest to dinner the first night. Better eat early before those Cahuenga Pass cowpokes get in and gobble up all Tony's best barbecued ribs."

Fergus's room at the top of the staircase was small. It was dominated by a double bed with a knobby iron headboard. Under it was a thunder mug. On a bureau was a basin and pitcher, and a whatnot cabinet on the wall had a rack for towels, a soap dish, and a plaster statue of the Holy Virgin, Mexican style, dark, with stars on her blue robes. There was a curling calendar on another wall with the controversial nude, *September Morn*, on it. Fergus smiled, for it made him think of Claudia at Coney Island.

There was a bentwood chair at the desk. Fergus discovered that he looked over Vine Street and the Webber Stable, and by leaning out the window he also could look up toward Hollywood Boulevard where the riders came down to the studio by horseback and buckboard at sunrise from Cahuenga Pass.

Fergus stowed his clothes and his gear and took out his *Webster's Dictionary;* his gift copy of *Riders of the Purple Sage* that Esther had given him to read on the train; the thin-papered Bible his mother had put in his hands; and the Oxford Press *Complete Works of*

William Shakespeare his father had handed him as his legacy, saying that if he understood what was in this book, he wouldn't need to know anything else.

He put them all on the desk, along with a notepad and his fountain pen. He took off his coat and looked out on the roof of Webber's Stable.

Upward drifted the comfortable fragrance of peach pies, the sizzle of frying chicken, and the sounds of vegetables being chopped on a board.

Garbage cans were being dragged outside by Xerxes.

It all made him think of the boardinghouse at home, and he was comfortable. And also, a very pretty colleen whose lilting voice he could occasionally hear was running this whole show.

Outside, the sound of several auto motors stirred the silence. He leaned out again. Fords, Appersons, Marmons—rich merchants going home to their comfortable gardens and houses down near Adams Street and Alvarado where he heard the old Angelenos lived.

A Duesenberg came by, moving slowly. Fergus almost fell out the window. It was the same kind Eddie Rickenbacker was racing in Sioux City. Fergus saw the slick head of Dustin Farnum and another man with a cap on, maybe Mr. de Mille, coming up from their barn down the street.

Fergus settled back, enjoying the last rays of the sun. He didn't long for the gossip of Fourteenth Street or the evening chatter at Luchow's.

This was it. This was where movies were being born. And he was in it and had a lot to do.

He grubbed about in the bottom of his duffel, took out his strongbox, and set it carefully under the mattress.

He got out his notebook.

"Schedule:" he wrote, "buy workpants, cowboy shirt, boots. Find out where de Mille got that cap. Ink. Notepads. Pencils. Erasers. Get somebody to slip us copies of de Mille and Griffith continuities. Find typewriter or typist. Thought: meet janitor who empties wastebaskets at different studios. Make deal for typewritten pages or notes. Find out rates for Mr. Moses at Hollywood Hotel. Price of car rental. Rent horse from Webber. On second thought, find prices of rooms at Alexandria Hotel. Keep Moses downtown."

Kathleen knocked on his door.

"Time for grub," she said. "You like your room? Do you need anything?"

"It's great!" said Fergus. "Great! I don't need a thing."

And he didn't.

After a good dinner, he sat listening to the movie cowboys talking about their day's work and the eccentricities of various directors and actors. He went to bed when they locked up at nine. Before he could list the day's events he fell asleep. The scent of coffee awoke him before the sun was up. He heard the sound of dozens of horses as they came clomping down the dawn-lit street from Cahuenga Pass and the foothills.

He arose, relishing it all, for it was going to be his, all his.

2

◆◆◆◆◆◆◆◆

Fergus soon learned that the plans he scribbled at night were not the answer to his problems. He had to move his campaign fast to make it come off. These were the times of being a winter soldier.

He found an unemployed sign painter who made him some reflectors out of gold foil on hinged boards. An old man sold him a broken prop box and repaired it for five dollars. Some lights from a busted movie company were discovered in a storeroom at Blondeau's Tavern, and Fergus and Plimpton borrowed a wagon from Kathleen's Café for a quarter and hauled them over to Webber's Stable.

Fergus decided he had to put in a cement floor at the stable so equipment could be rolled around. That meant building a drainage system, so the crew wouldn't be electrocuted with water from stable cleaning, or stumble around in horse droppings. The flooring cost him an unexpected ninety dollars. Framework had to be built outdoors, for the muslin diffusers would have to be moved about during the harsh sunshine—the most important source of light for shooting.

He wished he knew more about making pictures; what he saw on the streets was not enough. What he needed was the wise organization of someone who had already been blooded. Then he realized that he was near Mr. de Mille's barn.

That was it! And after dark it was deserted. He would just have to try his luck some moonlit night and mosey around. A sprawling yellow barn, surrounded by eucalyptus and blending into an orange orchard, it did not seem in any way a repository for cinematic dreams. The backyard was partially platformed with jerry-built flooring, level enough and stout enough for a camera. Above, flimsy scaffoldings held fabric strips on wire slides. They had been shoved back for the night and lay in limp pleats. To Fergus, it all looked miserable, sordid, and impossible. Somehow he had to make the same thing, imbue it with life, and send the product on celluloid strips to Mr. Moses. Fergus's heart sank. He drew crude sketches of the setup, noticing how the electric cables were situated and how the props and settings were rolled through a barn door on roller platforms and dollies for protection at night—and how everything was padlocked tight, although he could peer in through small windows.

He walked by an old man sitting in a creaking chair, reading by the light of a street lamp, and wondered if he was a caretaker, or just somebody who had nothing else to do. There were plenty of those here. Everybody seemed to want to come to California—for the weather, for the oranges, or for some taste of lotus land.

Fergus knew he had to be a jump ahead of anyone who carried out his plans. Fortunately, at Kathleen's, craftsmen of all sorts discussed their work in technical terms. He was amazed at the acceptance he received from people who surmised he knew what he was doing. He learned to listen and nod his head. This usually made him seem sage, especially to anyone who believed he had a bankroll and could put them to work.

Old man Webber was a skinflint, Kathleen warned him, and was getting his building fixed up free. She also advised a contract so there could be no shenanigans.

Webber told him he would have to pay to get the manure cleared away each day. But one of Tony's brothers was a gardener and would pay a dollar a week for the harvest. So Fergus would get his stable cleaned and hosed, once a day, free. The old man only glowered when he found out, and Fergus felt good about putting one over on him.

He decided early that he would not direct again. There were too many things that could go wrong behind the scenes when he had to stand near that camera box. If he had been patrolling when the Trust crept up on him at Coney Island, he might have saved Jules's expensive camera. It would be wise to get somebody like Stuart Plimpton to pose the people, and he would be supervisor.

Like most workers in Hollywood with a limited income, he took the little jitney bus down to Los Angeles to bank the money in the affluent Farmers and Merchants Bank.

One day the little red bus was so full of young people rushing to cash their paychecks in this new bonanza, that in spite of the fact that he had on his good suit, he had to sit on a fender and hang onto a strap. But everyone was in a good mood and made jokes about being in movies, and he picked up some important information while the warm wind blew his tie into his face.

As usual, everyone in the jitney talked about the Trust. Most of them thought of themselves as members of Robin Hood's merry band, hiding in the Hollywood forests.

The Motion Picture Patent Company was the sheriff of Nottingham, trying to mow down the people with violence, tithes, and taxes, while they were fighting to survive for a just and fruitful way of life.

Now there was hope that Jeremiah J. Kennedy, head of the Trust, and his elaborate spy system, which had even seeped out west, were having their own troubles.

Not satisfied with granting licenses only to motion-picture cameras rented from the Trust, and to film of Eastman derivation, J. J. Kennedy had realized that the exchange men were beginning to be the new rich of the growing motion-picture business.

The wealthy Trust now offered licenses only to exchange men who sold licensed film to their licensed theaters; but they were having trouble with exchange men who had subexchanges, where they sold maverick film rights right under the counter, so to speak, along with their licensed product.

The Trust had planned to control the whole motion-picture business from the making right through exchanges and on to the box office.

Raids still continued, with busted heads and burned celluloid. If de Mille, an independent, hadn't taken home an extra reel of film in his saddlebag up Cahuenga Pass the other day, his picture would have been destroyed. But he'd been smart enough to film everything twice on separate reels, and sure enough, his lab was vandalized, the negative spread all over the floor like spaghetti and stomped on. The Trust had expected his whole fortune to go with it.

Fergus shuddered. He knew the Trust behavior as well as anyone, but he thought it wise not to reveal he'd had a previous record. Nobody could tell what side anybody was on. It was like a war, but there were no uniforms to tell who was who.

Anyway, the gossip continued, Kennedy and his cohorts, under the name of General Film Company, had bought up almost all the exchanges with money they'd gotten from license fees, taxes on film and cameras, and film rentals. One big exchange, owned by a man named Fox who was protected by owning his own theater chain, had refused to join up, and his strongest ally was a political group—Tammany.

But the hot news was that the Trust was brought to court; the Motion Picture Patent Company was accused of an unlawful conspiracy in restraint of trade.

As slow as this legal battle was, with millions of dollars at stake, movie theaters were growing like mushrooms, and many of them were going independent. The Trust was losing its muscle.

A Pathé film salesman, Brulatour, had made a deal with Eastman to sell to independents, at the rate of a million feet a week. And if you couldn't get that, you could still get by with French Pathé film, if you could get it.

Fergus thought of Jules Cadeaux and the Professor, and he wondered if there were any way to get in touch with them.

There was more exciting news. An exchange man named Hodkinson had decided it was time to cancel out the business of states rights, that dreary taking of each film on a laborious trek to the various sectional representatives for purchase. He started a distribution company, so films didn't have to be smuggled back East by fearful independent operators on that long, soot-filled train ride, to be sold to the independent states rights boys.

Fergus put the fragments together. Doors were opening. The Trust had weakened its position by going along with short movies. They still thought of pictures in terms of twelve-minute vaudeville turns, and now everyone was after stories and three-reelers of consequence. He knew that with Claudia and a camera (God, he wished David were here!) he could be in business. And someday, he and Dave would break away and be FEDA again and make movies their own way.

The last bit of gossip, more immediate to most of those on the jitney, was that if you bought a drink at the Alexandria bar, for twelve cents, they had a free lunch that could sustain Diamond Jim Brady. And you could nurse your drink and snack to your heart's content. Everybody did it.

He deposited his check from Simon Moses and walked over to the Alexandria. Somewhere around the million-dollar carpet, among the marble pillars, he knew he would find Claudia or hear news of her.

If she wasn't around, he imagined her under the most romantic conditions, with the richest, most attractive men, and he would stand at the bar among shouting, enthusiastic strangers, feeling more isolated and lonely than he ever did in his room above Kathleen's Café.

But this early evening he found Claudia a little dispirited. To him, it only meant that her vivacity was diminished, her lovely face in repose, which made him feel protective, and, for the moment, as if she were in focus for him alone.

"Let's get out," she said.

He was delighted he didn't have to propose it. They strolled a few blocks to a Chinese restaurant. They ordered won-ton soup and chow mein, and they drank countless bowls of steaming yellow tea.

Claudia leaned back. "I'm revived," she said. "Now, let's get down to brass tacks. Honey, if there's anything to know about movies, I've heard it all. Every unemployed four-flusher on the streets is an authority."

She'd heard Lasky had over forty thousand dollars advance for *The Squaw Man.* She'd also heard of a man named Hodkinson who handled the film exchange for Los Angeles, San Francisco, and the Pacific Slope as far east as Denver. He was a big-time buyer of independent product. This was something new in the West, his organization in merchandising and distribution—of course they charged 35 percent. But what alternative was there?

"I know all about that," said Fergus knowledgeably, not mentioning that he'd heard it while desperately clinging to the fender of the jitney bus. "There's a new breed taking over, no more finagling with those robbers in the East, and, by the way, we're going to be ready to start any day. All I need is to find a camera."

"They're as rare as hens' teeth," said Claudia.

"I'll get one," said Fergus, wondering if she could sense his uncertainty. "You'd better be prepared to get out of this rat race and move to the Hollywood Hotel nearer the studio. Stand by, now."

"You know, Fergus," said Claudia, her eyes wide over her bowl of tea, "this is the new gold rush. Mary Pickford's coming out to make a movie at a thousand dollars a week."

"None of my affair," said Fergus, "but what is Mr. Moses paying you?"

"None of your affair, as you said," her eyes narrowed in a smile, "but it's going to be more, and there's going to be more and more things going on out here, all the way from Keystone to Griffith. So let's get on it. Is daddy sending you the money to start?"

"He has," said Fergus.

She laughed, and he flushed, remembering how they had gotten together the first time. He was stirred, and he put his hand on hers.

She pulled her hand away gently and then patted his.

"Oh, no, Fergus," she said. "Not just now, anyway."

"Why not?" he said.

"Because I'm kind of peculiar," she said. "I didn't mind having you when there was nobody important in my life. But I'm still hooked on that man. Don't ask me why."

"What man?" he asked stupidly, thinking of her sorties away from the hotel.

"Si Moses, you idiot. I don't know why. He just seems to make me go. I miss him so much! Imagine me, with all the oil and land boys after me, and I'm still waiting for that man to get his ass out of the Bronx and come out here."

She sighed.

"Well, maybe sometime—" said Fergus.

"Maybe sometime," said Claudia. "Fergus, if I get unhooked, I'll sure let you know, because we could have some good times together—that is, if you wouldn't be too serious. Meanwhile, you get our company going."

"Right," said Fergus. "After all, Mr. Moses isn't Mr. Astor. Let's make some money instead of spending it."

He had a sudden image of himself being thrown out by an irate Moses and going back to New York in disgrace, back to his old room in his mother's boarding-house.

Never!

Claudia crunched a lichee nut between her fingers, took out the little dried black fruit, and put it in his mouth, then prepared another for herself.

"Now don't get sore at me, honey, because I won't go to bed with you. You're my true friend. I know what you did for me on that train. And Claudia won't forget."

He snapped back from his business worries to the immediacies of his body.

"I don't want to be just your friend."

She took his hand again.

"Look, Fergus, you've got to understand me. I could go to bed with you right now. But I won't. Not till I get that old son of a bitch out of my system. Maybe I'm just dreaming of Si because he isn't here. But if it doesn't work forever, and honey, I have a hunch it won't, then I'll welcome you, with open arms and legs. So stick around, but don't keep it on ice, because the more you learn, the better you'll be, and it may come in very handy."

Fergus tried not to reveal his shock.

"You'll have to get used to me," she said. "Some of us are pretty rough in our family. Jeffrey's no lily. I'm no rose. Now, let's go. I'm tired."

They walked through the streets to Fifth and

Spring, where the hotel was disgorging a group of Angelenos in stiff dinner clothes, the ladies, even in the warm evening, in ermine and mink, their hands encased in the kid gloves of a very new social aristocracy. Claudia and Fergus entered the lobby.

"Aren't they a case?" said Claudia, smiling at him.

His heart congealed. She was so beautiful. Out of the corner of his eye he saw several men look at the glory of her face and smile. One greeted her, and she returned a wave. He wondered if she were really true to Mr. Moses and was just dusting him off, but he smothered the apostasy.

"Maybe tomorrow," he said, "we could get a car, and Plimpton, and go down to the beach and look around for some locations."

"I'd like it," she said. "I know some kids from Mack Sennett. They're shooting at Castle Rock. We might see how they operate. I'll get the hotel to put up some sandwiches."

"Never mind," said Fergus. "I have friends, I'll take care of it."

She reached up and pecked him on the cheek.

"You think of everything, Fergus," she said. "Let's get cracking. Hike your tights and light the torches!"

She whirled away, and he went out into the street, feeling lonely in a strange land. He had to walk, to clear his brain and the swelling in his groin, and think of what he had to do instead of what he wanted to do.

Maybe the Trust really was beginning to crumble. As long as movies could be made out here, and somebody was finding a way to sell them without the Motion Picture Patent Company making everybody smugglers, there was no way to stop making money.

Why, Claudia was prettier and livelier than anybody he'd seen but Mary Pickford, and Pickford was raking in the money.

Of course, Mr. Moses had handed him a hot rock,

sending him out here without any contacts or experience, but he was lucky; he was here.

This was where it was beginning, like a gold rush, or a land grab, and with Claudia as an asset, he'd better have a picture going before Mr. Moses arrived.

Riding on the bus, he tried to disentangle his visions of Claudia and his ambition. If he could be involved with her career, he would be close to her. Success didn't mean only money or power, success meant being part of Claudia's orbit and being with her again as he had before. To achieve this, he had to be realistic. He had to be in control. Disliking his youth and his poverty, he got off the bus and walked down Vine Street, the echo of his footsteps the only sound in the shuttered-down neighborhood.

The yellow light shone on the stairs of Kathleen's Café. Looking up, Fergus saw a square of light and the ruffled curtains of Kathleen and Tony's bedroom.

He walked upstairs, unlocking the door at the landing. As he passed their door, he heard a faint, low sound. It was almost as if someone were sobbing. It couldn't be.

He entered his room, enjoying, as always, the patch that fell like moonlight from a street lamp on the other side of a pepper tree. It filtered in a lacy pattern which made his plain room seem decorated.

He walked to the window, relishing the liquid complaint of a mockingbird, but feeling very sad, for it was a sound that would have been wonderful to share.

He remembered he must order the picnic lunches. He went back to Kathleen's door and knocked gently.

There was silence and then a small voice.

"Who is it?"

"It's Fergus—could you fix me up three lunches tomorrow? I'm taking two people to look at locations."

More silence, then a nose blowing.

"Oh—" she said, "of course—of course—"

There was a pause.

"Have you got a cold?" he said.

"Oh, goodness—no. Okay, Fergus. I'll take care of it."

"Hope I didn't bother you," said Fergus. "Goodnight."

He went back to his room. She must be crying. He felt sadder than ever that Kathleen should have troubles. She seemed so strong.

He returned to the window. A soft breeze wafted in. He'd like to go to sleep with his cheek on the windowsill, just watching the waving fronds of the tree and hearing the faint plop of little peppercorns dislodging and falling on the roof. He thought of Claudia. Was she in her nightgown, or was she naked? Was she sliding into those sheets in that hotel, her beautiful body lying in that big bed alone, unused, when it could be so wonderfully alive . . . oh, beautiful Claudia, with her breasts, and thighs . . .

There was a soft knock at his door.

"Come in," he said. He didn't even lift his head.

"Fergus," said Kathleen, "do you want chicken for your lunch box?"

He turned his head.

She wore a soft blue dressing gown, and her red hair was hanging in plaits over her shoulder.

He stood up slowly.

"Oh, my dear," she said, seeing the sadness in his face. "You, too?"

He sat on his bed.

She moved to him.

He looked up and saw that her eyes were red and her face was wet with tears.

"It's just no good," she said. "My husband won't love me. He feels guilty. His Mexican family prays for forgiveness because he married me. I'm a foreigner to them, Fergus. And he prays instead of loving me and runs away to them. He's gone again."

Fergus stood up and put his arms around her. She

hid her face in his shoulder, and he felt the warm tears against his neck.

"Kathleen," he said, "don't cry. You're so beautiful, you mustn't."

He kissed her wet cheek, and their mouths met, and the salty sadness of her tears went away as their lips parted and their longing tongues touched.

Slowly, she unfastened his tie and shirt, and he her sash and robe, and when they were naked, they settled on his bed. Once her body shook against him as she sobbed, but as he touched her she forgot her sorrow. He discovered the blue-veined whiteness of her breasts and caressed them, and she stroked his shoulders and his arms and chest, and when they fell together in a gentle and loving comfort, the sharp sound of the mockingbird was forgotten.

◆◆◆◆◆◆◆◆

Fergus awoke with a feeling of lightness. At first he wondered why, and then he remembered—the woman who had gratefully lain in his arms and who had responded to every overture. The soft body, the long plaits of hair, and the fragrance in his seekings. And the warmth and joy of tender words that had encouraged his manhood.

He arose, feeling strong and ready to face the onslaughts of Claudia and the day.

In the kitchen Kathleen handed him the box lunches with a strong, warm hand, and a quick, flickering glance of gratitude. He saw Tony putting pies in the oven, wiping the sweat off his face, waving a busy hand in his direction.

Fergus felt sorry for him, amazed that he could face him coolly, after what had happened and, most likely, would happen again while Tony went off on some unknown penance, denying himself what should have been his.

Fergus was surprised that he could take it so

lightly. His greeting to Kathleen was a touch of his thumb against her breast as he took the lunches from her and looked into her eyes.

He went out into the morning, met the man with the car he had hired, stowed the lunch boxes, and looked across the street.

Two men stood in front of Webber's barn staring at him. They seemed familiar. One was stooped and wore a wide-brimmed hat, dark glasses, and a dark, square-shouldered coat. He had a rabbinical beard. The other raised a greeting arm in his direction.

It couldn't be!

He crossed the street slowly, and the shorter man made a gesture for him to be cautious.

"My God!" he said, "Jules! Professor! What are you doing here!"

"*Doucement!*" said the Cadeauxs, both at the same time.

"The Trust is after us. We got smashed up," said Jules. "They broke in our laboratory and wrecked it. All film, all equipment, everything, up in flames. But we got some cameras out, and I had some film vaults at another place. We're here now. David Moses told us where you were, so here we are."

He gestured at the outrageous false beard covering his father's scarred face.

"It was necessary for papa to wear this wretched thing on the train. I think he is smothering. Where can we stay? David said you would help us."

"I have a stable here," said Fergus. "You can use the loft. I'll tell old man Webber you're my staff."

Everything was falling into place. Of all the people he ever could have needed, Cadeaux *fils* and *père* were the ones. With their skills, their camera and raw film stock, he was in business. And with Claudia, and Mr. Moses, he would play it as if he had arranged to have them appear at the right moment all the time and had geared everything to fit his master plan.

Once the film was in the can and passed on to a

middleman, everything would be great. He had dreaded the idea of long train rides back to New York; stifling heat, open windows, blinding cinders; sleeping with the negative film hidden in a wicker basket, clutched between legs while dozing, or shackled to an ankle while eating at Harvey Houses along the line. He knew a man's hopes and dreams and fortunes could be destroyed by one hired brute with a match or a bludgeon.

The Trust, that monster that had held an entire growing business in a tight fist, was now threatened in its turn. Fergus felt he had only to stick tight, grind out a reel a week, and watch what happened.

He got the Cadeauxs settled, made arrangements for Kate to feed them, and rushed off to pick up Claudia and Plimpton at the hotel. Knowing that he was in control of his picture company, he met Claudia. And he could look at her in a different way, possessed of a certain peace, knowing that last night a woman with milk-white skin and soft voice had loved him, needed him, and found him a man.

◆◆◆◆◆◆◆◆

The only thing that saved Fergus in these first, crude days was the fact that Hollywood was a testing ground for any sort of filmmaking operation. Many of the men he hired were his age or younger, and even the older men had little experience in this new field.

He arose now at predawn, long before the cowboys came down the pass to have breakfast. At the barn, he loaded a rented truck with his camera equipment, reflectors, flats, a prop box that carried everything from whiskey and gin to plaster of Paris for making breakaway props for fight scenes. Folding chairs and tables, towels, bottled water, body makeup, crepe hair, beards, and moustaches juggled about with paint, nails, tools, wardrobe, and several toilet-seat covers for outhouses thrown together at exterior locations. Last loaded on was a carton of Kathleen's lunches. Thirty-five cents apiece including a pint of milk for each. But it was a necessary expense.

He soon learned that to save money he must save time. He must be prepared to be first-aid nurse, makeup man, pay clerk, hairdresser, carpenter, and walk-on actor.

Often he had to build a shelter for Claudia, hook up her dress, help with her hair, and surreptitiously pour her a tot of whiskey if she got cold or a glass of gin if she got menstrual cramp and had to be active.

Once the truck was loaded, he turned it over to the cameraman, Ned Glover, and the crew. Then he would drive the old Packard limousine he also rented, pick up Plimpy, who always came rushing out of his boardinghouse in the dawn, bundled up, looking sleepy, a cigarette in one hand and a fist of production notes in the other. He would immediately rush into a spate of discussion. Right to lefts, left to rights, symbols to use to save time, ideas for inserts, subtitles he had jotted down while studying the scenario he and Fergus had written the night before, and gimmicks for the various actors, to improve their characters.

They would pick up the actors, as far afield as old hotels on South Grand, to the vine-covered cottages that were beginning to dot the orange groves of Hollywood.

The last stop, at 6:30 A.M. would be Claudia's new residence, the Hollywood Hotel. Fergus would have to roust the night clerk out of the dining room to open up the switchboard and ring Claudia's room.

In about ten minutes she'd come running downstairs, bundled in a great English tweed cape, carrying her wardrobe. She did her makeup in her room, and her porcelain-smooth painted face, with her large heavily mascaraed eyes, always looked strange to Fergus in the morning light. Her hair would be swathed in pink tulle to hold it down.

"Nice morning," Fergus would usually say.

"Drop dead," she'd answer.

He'd take her makeup kit, a large bag packed with a change of clothes, scarfs, dark glasses, oddments, and a car rug.

She'd get into the rear seat of the Packard, throw the robe over her lap, and curl up and sleep until they arrived at location.

Thus the day began. It was a constant revelation of improvisations. As the sun climbed higher, Claudia rose out of her lethargy and came alive.

She and Plimpy dovetailed their skills, she taking the lead in improvisation, he leading her into ideas. Then, her personal whims erased, Fergus really loved her. Sometimes he would get gooseflesh as he saw her in motion, the precision of her timing, the beauty of her body as she took on the character and moods of the person she portrayed. Fergus realized what it meant to be a Barstow. With honesty, he could write his daily report to Simon Moses and say the filming was coming along well.

At the end of the day, when she was fatigued, it was a different story.

"Don't think I'm going along with this forever," she would say. "I want a maid to take care of me. I want my own car and driver. I want my own tent on location, with a table and makeup mirror, a chair, and a cot or something I can rest on. How long do you think I'm going to take this shit!"

"Now, Claudia," said Fergus, "you know as soon as we get some money into this company, you'll have the best of everything."

"Promises, promises," said Claudia. "And more ham and less bread in those goddamn sandwiches. What are you doing, cutting the meat with a razor blade to make five cents apiece on the deal?"

Fergus flushed; he was getting a kickback of three.

And that was not all. He soon realized that there were a great many trucks and secondhand cars for sale; fly-by-night people were forever moving. Figuring what he would pay for rental, and the possible resale value of rolling stock, he dipped into his meager money and bought a truck. He immediately founded a rental company, named it elegantly Elite Rentals, added a Packard touring car, and, after the down payment on credit in the name of the Moses company and assets that Simon had given him, siphoned off a profit against the monthly payments. This he salted away, feeling more secure with each penny added to his savings account. He felt no guilt. The sky was the limit for Claudia's expenses, and Moses paid the same rental money he would have paid anywhere else. If Fergus could make a profit, that was his own shrewd business. He was delighted to be getting a little edge on Simon Moses. After all, he, Fergus, was taking all the risks.

Busy with production and the filming of the first picture, Fergus discovered that the Cadeauxs were moving as swiftly in their little loft as he was about town.

They had brought an old Pathé camera with them. They had contacts in Tijuana for all the Pathé film they needed. So in this time of peril from the Trust he did not have to deal with black-market Edison stock or reveal the whereabouts of his operation to an unknown middleman.

Jules built a complete laboratory with developing and fixing tanks. Fergus learned through the grapevine that de Mille was selling his "hypo" fixing fluid to a trucking agent, who was paying five dollars a load for the silver that could be processed out of the waste material. So he made a similar deal, and put the profit in his pocket.

Jules and Fergus worked out a system of unrolling and rolling reels on spindles, so the old-fashioned rewinding was finished. After the negative was meticulously cut, the titles scratched onto bits of film to be printed properly later, the locked cans were turned over to the Wells Fargo Express, which had muscle of its own to protect against the scavenging Trust.

"Someday," said Jules, "we will have our own complete laboratory."

"Don't rush," grinned Fergus. "I insured our last picture for thirty thousand. Since it cost ten we'd make quite a heap if they lost it."

But Wells Fargo, having had experience from earlier days of train robbers, never did.

At night when they worked, the Professor hung his fake beard on a hook. Whenever they went out, mostly to Kathleen's restaurant or to walk up to the silent Hollywood Boulevard in the warm anonymity of the California night, the old man put on his disguise. In a town of eccentrics, nobody seemed to notice. He just looked like an old Hasidic scholar.

Father and son slept on cots in the loft, used the crude bathroom for their ablutions, and guarded the property at night.

One evening, while Fergus, Jules, and the Professor were looking at film through a makeshift cigar-box viewing machine, they heard the horses nickering softly below.

They motioned to each other and silently waited.

They heard steps coming up the ladder. Jules picked up a heavy reel of film, and Fergus a brick doorstop, and they stood poised.

There had been rumors that several men from the Trust had hopped off the Santa Fe and were cruising about town.

But the Professor was the one who signaled the alert. He moved forward, picked up a lamp, and shone it on his own face, revealing the lidless eyes and the bare-fanged drooling mouth shimmering in the light. He swung open the door, and let out a growl.

There was a howl of terror at the apparition, and two men fell headlong down the steps and slammed out of the stable.

Fergus felt his heart beating against his side and looked at his two friends.

Jules began to laugh and slapped his father on the shoulder. The three men embraced, thumping each other on the back. Then they sat down at the crude pine table, laughed until they cried, and toasted each other with a slug of cognac.

When Fergus returned to his room, he buried his face in his pillow. He wished Kathleen could have come to him, but he heard the drone of Tony mumbling his prayers. He knew that she, too, would turn her face to the wall and wait for a blessed moment when Tony fled to his family, and they could enjoy the rare moments that life gave them, to assure each other that there was love and sympathy and tenderness in a hard world.

♦♦♦♦♦♦♦♦

Simon Moses was finding the first year most difficult, both in New York and Hollywood. And the traveling was worse than hell, it was purgatory. Sometimes he felt he lived in a world of shunting trains, with the smell of live steam and pin grease, and perpetual cinders in his eyes. He was jarred awake by water and fuel stops. The Raton Pass with groaning halts for engine changing was always the worst, for if he was on his way to see Claudia, he felt the trip would never end. He also loathed facing Fergus, discussing minute details of production, and then having to leave things in his hands. On his way to New York, the train seemed to be carrying him back to uncomfortable, guilty family responsibilities, quarrels with his brother Abe, and business problems that proliferated in his absence.

He'd thrash about on the train, sweating, thinking of the new debts he had just learned he was running up. A picture could be made in January and not receive adequate returns until the summer. Meanwhile the interest on his loans went on and on.

In New York, trouble was no exception.

"Look," said Abe, "if we go on, we've got to move into bigger offices and get new furniture. Do you realize I have to play chess with dozens of buyers, each with their own grubby little states and territorial franchises, to make this whole thing come off. They all stick together like a pack of bandits. The minute the word gets around that I'm accepting low bids, they know I'm hustling for that scratch-up company gobbling us alive on the Coast."

"Well, you won't have to deal with states rights long," said Simon. "We can get this new distributor out West to take us on, and all that load will be off your back. We're negotiating. How about that?"

"Thirty-five percent," said Abe. "On your borrowed money you pay him 35 percent *gross*. You pay the interest, it makes me sick. They get the whipped cream. You're expanding too fast, you're gambling on capital."

"What can I do?" said Simon. "If I don't keep Claudia on salary, and producing, someone else will grab her."

You just bet, thought Abe.

"And Fergus had to rent two automobiles to move our gear and cast. The equipment rental boys are getting smart."

"Maybe Fergus is getting smart. That son of a bitch isn't renting them—he probably owns them," said Abe, not realizing his hunch was correct, "and is making a fortune off of us. Buy your own. And borrow—borrow on your theaters, borrow on the furniture factory, borrow on your reputation. If you're determined to go this way, I'll get the wheels in motion. Because, if I have to make these cockamamy deals, they'll know we can't meet our payroll."

"Okay," said Simon, irritated.

"You want to be a big movie shot," said Abe, "that's the way it's got to be."

Simon knew it was true. Although cars and simple equipment were on the cost sheets as being leased, he suspected Fergus was siphoning off penny-ante profits. This was a big poker game, and he was shrewd enough to know he held the winning cards. Every time he saw new invoices, he immediately arranged to purchase similar equipment and cancel rentals.

This infuriated Fergus, who had to sell his equipment without letting anyone know it was his personal property. It took some doing, and often a slight loss.

The whole game became a running competition, and of course Simon was the winner. However, these petty skirmishes were only a part of Simon's problems.

His wife was looking at him askance these days. Now he had to force himself to get in bed with her; being away from Claudia was the only thing that made it possible. Sometimes he wondered if Rebecca had any way of knowing that he tried to conjure up Claudia's lovely body and beguiling ways, and to remember snatches of her exciting bed talk, to have sex with his wife.

Until recently, he had functioned in a world of new affluence; now he realized it was only a pittance, considering his goal. He was in a confusion of hopes and guilts.

The Moses family had always clung together, protecting each other's interests, even if they were vocally critical.

In the expanding Jewish society it was now possible to have a lawyer and a doctor, as well as merchants, and, if there was enough manpower, a cantor or a rabbi to enrich the family. That way, one or another of everything was taken care of.

All of this was a far cry in one generation from the ragpicking desperation of the impoverished emigrés who had come from Europe to find religious freedom, food, and shelter.

Under these new conditions, there was even room to forgive one eccentric in the family—a scholar, a musician, an artist, or even an actor.

But now something bewildering had come into the culture. Many kinfolk in the big cities were beginning to realize that the theater and movie business was taking a gigantic shape over the land.

When the men became obsessed with this new octopus business, they would get out of hand. They had money and time; they traveled without their families to outlandish places; they rubbed elbows with all sorts of strange people. And that was not all.

Like Solomon, they embraced women of many faiths, who used every enticement to snare them, for they were valuable. They worshiped strange gods and lost their covenant with Jehovah.

The men pandered to their many guests, making lasting treaties with strangers. They built larger temples called movie theaters, and they housed Mammon.

And so, the women chose a life of increasing richness. They spent more time in fashionable pursuit, for they were lonely.

The men learned new luxuries as their time became more valuable. Mammon and Jehovah somehow merged. The new God symbol was the picture and the legend painted on various studio water towers.

When Rebecca first saw the Titan logo, she went into her room and wept. The large fist with the broken chain and the flames sprouting out of each knuckle seemed sacrilegious to her, and terrifying, a symbol of dreadful things to come.

The priests of this new cult were the representatives of the vested interests. They delegated the funds that moved the puppets.

The actors, actresses, and creative staff were the

vestal virgins and acolytes who brought about the miracle of endless millions of feet of celluloid.

Thousands of humans were in thrall to this new force throughout the world. Temples were scattered afar, and disciples were becoming as numerous as leaves in a forest.

Long gone were the days when Chaplin had said, "We used to go into a park with a stepladder, a bucket of whitewash, Mabel Normand, and come out with a picture."

Stars were making fortunes. And all the young women of the land were imitating the actresses and passionately worshiping the actors, to the despair of their elders.

◆◆◆◆◆◆◆◆

Fergus was still only an employee, but, having been on the job since the beginning, his knowledge was essential. Simon suspected his holdings had grown like those of many unit managers and supervisors.

Although it was traditional for men who handled picture finances on the field to steal pennies, the larceny was minuscule compared to the thousands in legal loot the Moses interests siphoned off their corporations.

Fergus's shrewd little take would only make it possible for him to live in more luxury than his salary allowed. He could have better lodgings, if he wanted, own a Ford; and frequent the better restaurants where he could meet people in the picture business on a footing of apparent affluence—which made his connections with the Moses interests seem more valuable than Simon would admit.

He started to salt a little away in gilt-edged bonds for what he hoped would be a better future position in the industry. However, he learned the ever-constant rule of success. Along with his increasing economy he had expanding financial responsibilities. His father always seemed to be in and out of doctors' offices and hospitals with threats of pneumonia. His mother suffered from the maladies of old age which had come upon her early—arthritis, rheumatism, and a bad back. She was ever finding new and expensive quick-cure quacks.

The boardinghouse in the Bronx became more and more decrepit. It took a larger staff to run the place; there was insurance, new furnaces, new plumbing, and paint for the old wreck, so his parents could hold their heads up and say they made their own way. Fergus figured he could have bought a fine mission-style California bungalow for the expenses that went east.

Simon's greatest problem was personal. Even if he was almost a millionaire, and the most enchanting woman in pictures was his mistress, he had to settle in one place, to try to be a whole man, or his life would be a nightmare. And that place, both because of Claudia and the business, had to be Hollywood.

He remembered his first trip with misgivings. He, Simon Moses, who had hardly been farther than his furniture factory and recent sorties into the glamour of New York, was traveling first-class; an enormous United States he had never realized was leading him to an established business in an unknown land of adventure with a beautiful woman awaiting him. These realities were more incredible than any dream. He had splurged on a diamond bracelet with money hoarded from holiday theater receipts that even Becky knew nothing about. These guilty dollars squandered so fecklessly added to his excitement.

When he checked into the Hollywood Hotel, there was a message that the company was working at Webber's barn, he should come right over.

He'd bathed quickly, changed his clothes, hired a taxi, put the bracelet in his pocket, and rushed to the studio. There he had walked into a busy backyard setup. An electrician asked him to please move, he was in the way.

Fergus spotted him and led him through a maze of fake walls. Claudia threaded her way to him, gave him a quick platonic peck on the cheek in front of the company, and told him she'd be right back, the light was going to change fast, and they had to finish.

For a half hour he watched, and finally he drove her back to the Hollywood Hotel in a taxi.

"I'm sorry, Simon," she said, "but once you start a routine you have to stay with the pace. And we finish with the actor we hired for this sequence tomorrow, we have to wind it up."

"You look beautiful," said Simon. "I'm going to take you out, you tell me the best place, and buy you champagne, and just look at you."

"Oh, honey," she said, "I'd love it, but I have to be up at half-past five to go on location."

He looked disappointed.

"Now," she said, patting his hand, "that doesn't mean you can't have dinner in my sitting room, and a visit. Oh, I'm glad to see you!"

"You look a little thin," he said.

"The camera adds ten pounds," she said. "I have to be super thin."

He sat watching, absorbing her beauty, while she creamed her face and bathed, all the time telling him amusing incidents about the work and her world, which made him feel even more of an outsider.

Later they dined frugally in her sitting room. Over a cup of coffee, wishing for the champagne and candlelight of more festive moments, he handed her the fine moroccan leather box.

She opened it, took out the bracelet, and, with a wide-eyed glance, went to him and kissed him.

"It's lovely!" she exclaimed. "Oh, Si, you're going to be so rich, and so am I. Wait until you see our next scenario. Fergus is doing a good job. It's one of the best."

She patted the bracelet as an afterthought.

He tried to be utterly pleased. This moment of splendid giving. A hotel suite with his beloved. No home to have to go back to, with a lame excuse. But somehow scenarios and Fergus had taken the romance out of the moment.

"It's so pretty! I can wear it in one of the new sequences. I can see it right now!"

After dinner she dimmed the lights, and they went into the bedroom.

As always, he had waited to see her slim, beautiful body, the high proud breasts, and the perfumed mystery of her which was the reason for his long journey and the chances he had taken with his life and his money. She was more lovely and more desirable than even his imagination could conjure, perhaps not as wild as those first days, but more tender, more settled, he thought. But as he loved her, a gush of passion overcame him, and in spite of the desire he had to pleasure her, his excitement overtook him. He knew it was too fast.

But she hid her disappointment, for she was weary. He needn't know how unfulfilled she was. It really wasn't worth it, she thought, to try so hard for orgasm tonight.

She turned to him.

"Simon, my darling, I really love you. It's so wonderful to have your arms around me. To know you love me. And when the company doesn't work so hard—well, maybe next weekend it will be better all the way around."

He looked at her lush beauty and realized that she had waited, and what had he given her? But what could he do? She nuzzled sleepily against him.

"Honey, you'll have to go. I'm just bone weary. You must be tired, too."

As he got into his clothes in the dark, he could tell she had already fallen sleep. He peered out into the garden and looked at the palm trees. He decided they were quite ugly.

On his way back to New York, he thought, well, that's what you wanted, to have a successful movie company, and Claudia wanted to be a star. Who was it said, watch out what you ask for, you may get it.

3

◆◆◆◆◆◆◆◆

Three years had passed.

In 1917, Titan Films made fifteen pictures a year. A studio had been set up surrounding the red barn, which now was a corporate shrine. Jules and the Professor still used it as a lab, but the horses and Mr. Webber were long since gone.

It seemed incredible to Fergus, but the Trust was gone. The Motion Picture Patent Company had been destroyed by the United States government, which ordered the group to desist from their unlawful acts, as well as by the vitality of such film companies as Titan, which insisted on longer pictures and bigger budgets.

It was strange to discover that the beast in the forest no longer existed. There were so many growing production problems and so much competition that the Trúst, which had triggered the whole move to Hollywood, was almost forgotten.

Fergus found a need for better quarters. He moved away from Kathleen's, without misgivings, but with memories and a friendship. Perhaps her guilt at their love affair had kindled a kindness and understanding for Tony's problems. And Fergus soon discovered there were lots of pretty and ambitious young women who were as free as the breeze and just as accessible. It became easy and natural for the two Irish people to become friends and confidants; and once Tony got used to Fergus, he joined up, and they all became close companions.

Fergus rented a little bungalow on Fountain Avenue, and sometimes, after the cafeteria shut down for the night, they'd come by, breaking up his midnight paper work. Over hot coffee and sandwiches that Kathleen brought, they would plan new moves. Fergus started a studio lunch catering business with them, grandly named Elite Caterers. He would in every sense be a silent partner because one of their major clients was Titan studio. They bought an old Model T truck and built a special body on it with panels that opened up for a steam table and coffee percolators. It was the most up-to-date location lunch wagon the picture industry had seen, and they planned, when it was all paid for (mostly by the Moses interests), to add another and eventually have a fleet. Everybody had been complaining about the perils of location. The standard lunch bores had become anathema to picture people. After a few hours in the sun, the very smell of hot cardboard, stale tuna sandwiches, and a leaky dill pickle was enough to make anyone queasy. Now, with a portable icebox to keep milk cold, Tony's wagon became a luxury of a favored company.

One Sunday, Tony suggested they drive out in the Titan Packard towards Calabasas. Tony had a cousin who owned a truck garden. All his good tomatoes and lettuce and onions for the restaurant came from there.

"That land's a comer," he said, "now that we got water from the Owens Valley. You ought to see it."

They wound through Cahuenga Pass.

"Like my second cousin Leo Carillo says," Tony remarked, "the battle of Cahuenga Pass was memorable. The Mexicans and the gringos met, one man was killed, two wounded, and they stopped and had a barbecue."

Tony's cousin Pancho, a tall, skinny youth, worked

twenty acres of sweet farmland along the skirts of the rolling yellow hills near Calabasas. He lived in a small shack, planning to marry his girl, who lived with Tony's family, as soon as he had five hundred dollars in the bank. Already, thanks to Tony, he had over four hundred. He was delighted to see the hamper of food Kathleen brought along.

"Amigo, that looks good! I'm sure sick of beans and tortillas," he said.

They sat under a grape arbor, drank sweet wine, and feasted on barbecued ribs, fresh sweet corn, and Tony's specialty, chocolate sour-cream cake.

"Where'd you learn to cook like this?" asked Fergus.

"I worked as a kid in the kitchens of the old Pico house, and the Alexandria. Boy, they had good chefs and good food in those places!" said Tony.

Fergus rinsed his hands in the watercress-choked stream bordering the picnic ground. He looked past the windbreak of eucalyptus trees. Beyond was a vast expanse of yellow-brown foothills, and higher, greener peaks. Sycamore, manzanita, occasional yucca, and stately live oak studded the landscape. In the distance, a canyon cut a deep shadow in the sunlight.

"What a place to shoot a chase!" he said.

Kathleen laughed. "That's all he ever thinks about. If he went to heaven he'd ask Saint Peter if he could shoot the pearly gates! Look out, Pancho, or your house will be a western sheriff's ranch house in the next one he makes."

"I was thinking about that," grinned Fergus, "but my western heroes can't wade their way through neat rows of lettuce. Is that land over there for sale?"

"Everything's for sale," said Pancho. "That is a Spanish land grant like most everything. Every other family in Sonoratown has a scrap of paper with swell names on them, grants from the King of Spain. All a man had to do in the days of our great grandfathers was to have a horse, ride around from one point to another between sunrise and sunset, and claim it. But now with taxes and no big cattle industry, everybody's busted. I think this land belongs to the Eduardo Castillos. Ours is the last remnant from the Martinez's onetime wealth."

"What's the name of the ranch?" asked Fergus.

"They all had grand names. That big one was La Finca de Nuestra Señora de Guadalupe; the country place of our Lady of Guadalupe."

Fergus wrote it down, along with the name of the family who owned it. He breathed deeply, savoring the smell. What a country, and most of all, what a location ranch!

"And wouldn't you bet, Pancho," said Tony, "the lot that Kathleen and I are lookin' at on Hollywood Boulevard for a new restaurant costs almost as much as our twenty acres here. Good thing we got classy gringo friends like Fergus, or we couldn't get a loan at the bank."

"It's going to be grand," said Kathleen.

"And I can show off some of the things I learned for high-class people, instead of just handing out chow to cowpokes," said Tony.

"There were no complaints," said Fergus. "I had to let out my belt two notches."

As time passed, Kathleen and Tony had three children in rapid Catholic succession. The youngest boy was named, at Tony's suggestion, Fergus Ysidro, and Fergus was the godfather. Sometimes, when Kathleen and Fergus sat in the new café, the fact that there was a Fergus Martinez at home in his crib would make them glance affectionately at each other; both grateful that things had turned out the way they did. The only thing that bothered her was whether or not the girls Fergus brought in were good enough for him.

Fergus and his friends often came to dine at Kathleen's Tavern, which was a new social center for the more affluent picture people and merchant society.

Soon people called in for reservations. The food was exceptional. Choice Kansas City beef, mussels from the local shore, oysters and crab brought down in iced barrels from the North, Mexican lobster and shrimp, fancy sandwiches, and fanciful pastries, made by of all people, Xerxes, the Greek handyman, who studied as assistant pastry cook down at the Alexandria with a countryman who had come in from Paris.

Kathleen and Tony bought a pseudo-Spanish hacienda up in the hills above Highland Avenue. They had an Irish nanny for the children, a Chinese cook, and Tony's family produced a sere duenna, an elderly aunt, Lola, who supervised the household, a chain of keys at her waist to lock up everything. She reminded Fergus of Aunt Yetta, who had done the same thing for the Moses family.

Hollywood people dearly loved characters, and the pretty colleen and her gifted Mexican husband were popular figures, along with their children—the red-haired black-eyed girl, the black-haired blue-eyed boy, and the baby with ginger ringlets and blue eyes.

"Wait until you meet Esther," said Fergus to Kathleen, "that's the girl you'll approve of."

"And where," said Tony, "is Simon Moses going to hide Claudia Barstow when his family comes out?"

"That's to be seen," said Fergus.

"You'll probably be the patsy like you were before," said Kathleen. "I hope you can handle *that* kettle of fish along with Esther."

Fergus grinned, but he wondered, too, for things were different now. This was *his* town.

◆◆◆◆◆◆◆◆

The Moses family settled into a nice gabled California house on Alvarado Street. It gave them all kudos, writing back to New York, for they had several lemon trees, an orange, a fig, an avocado and a sycamore tree, gardenias, geraniums, and a fishpond to brag about.

After recovering from the shock of living in a roomy house with a large garden, having a Japanese gardener to care for it, a Mexican girl to clean, and Yetta to continue her kosher kitchen, Rebecca set about attending to Hadassah and her husband's social affairs.

It was a new world. She got her hair bobbed and indulged in her first manicure, to go with her new diamond rings.

At first Esther and Martha felt marooned. They overshopped, bought new clothes, took tennis lessons, and slowly made a few friends, mostly from the circles of exiled theater people who were also from the East. They met some young folks through B'nai B'rith, saw movies, attended studio previews, and occasionally went to see Titan's pictures being made.

Fergus took Esther to a few parties and sometimes on Sundays Martha went with them to the beach down in Santa Monica, where all sorts of ball games and water sports were in progress, and people of the same age got to know each other, no matter what their social background. Yet Esther complained that Fergus had less time for her by far than they had in New York.

As time passed, she learned how to dress her blond hair more effectively and how to wear smart, fashionable clothes. Because of her father and Titan Films, she was pushed forward on various charity committees, sometimes even being invited to events with the denizens of Gramercy Place, where a tribe of mainly blue-eyed pale-haired people, many migrated from Illinois and Kansas, were establishing a second generation of taller, less snobbish citizens. Providing "picture people" behaved properly, and did not step too far out of their place, they were allowed to add luster, excitement, and money to some of the charity festivities.

Fergus, with a good wardrobe, a decent salary, and a new Ford touring car, was now a suitable escort for the Thursday-night dances at the Hollywood Hotel, where the movie society felt more at home. He began to take Esther out more often, even though he saw the cold eye of Simon watching him. It was a difficult situation, for he still acted as cover-up for Simon's meetings with Claudia. Beach restaurants, clubs, and roadhouses were their meeting places. Also, Claudia took a posh apartment on Sunset, managed by a silent Japanese cook and a French maid, where Simon could visit, entering from the basement steps.

Several times Fergus tried to date attractive Los Angeles girls of good family, but the equally cold eye of their fathers and brothers made him realize that there was a barrier between Los Angeles society and anyone connected with the picture colony. So he stayed within the comfortable film group.

One great bonus to Fergus when the Moses family moved west was the companionship of David, who had grown into an enthusiastic, volatile young man. Sometimes he and Fergus went catting in the lower reaches of Venice and Santa Monica, or along the assorted perimeters of the Plaza and Broadway, but they soon realized it was a shoddy escape. The young hopefuls of the film industry offered more enthusiasms because their interests and ambitions were similar. However, this area narrowed as their companions had an unfortunate habit of trying to take advantage of potential connections with the Moses organization.

Fergus was delighted to have David handle the camera on the new western pictures that had been added to the Titan program. He was a practical craftsman, doing more with key light, full light, and kicker than many of his more experienced confreres.

Fergus had his own struggles in the expanding company. He worked night and day preparing the elaborate transportation system. Equipment, props, personnel, and food had to be moved to and fro with military precision. Often when he leased ranch or farmland, the ranchers had a habit of driving trucks and livestock through scenes, spoiling them. He hoped David would be his ally in purchasing the ranchland he had always dreamed about for Titan.

One Saturday he made a suggestion. "There's a rodeo out Calabasas way near the Martinez truck farm. Why don't we go out and see what's going on?"

"Sure," said David, "let's take a camera. Maybe I can grab a little stock footage, and why not take Martha and Esther?"

It was a day as beautiful as the one Fergus remembered when he first saw the ranch, its golden hills reaching up into a glorious cloud-flecked blue sky.

"Believe it or not," said Fergus, "Tony told me that when the bandit Joaquin Murietta got this far out of Los Angeles Pueblo, they gave up trying to catch him, and here we are making it on an automobile road."

"I can understand it," said Esther, as the car negotiated a sharp turn. She enjoyed being thrown against Fergus and holding onto his arm for security.

He smiled at her, "It won't be long, we're almost there. But keep hanging on, I like it!"

She flushed, but still hung on.

"Glad I brought my sky filter," said David. "Jules and the Professor wanted me to try it out."

A group of rodeo riders, hangers-on, and countryfolk were sitting on a split-rail fence. Fergus paid the admission fee.

They had barely settled when a young saddle-bronc rider came out of the chute. His spurs were correctly above the point of his mount's shoulder, and as the horse tried to throw him and went wild, he rocked to and fro. His free hand was held high.

"Lookathat!" yelled a bystander, "boy that kid sure stays away from the apple. He's gonna make it!"

A whistle blew after a whirlwind eight seconds; he

stuck on, and a horse came alongside to lift him off while his steed went on sunfishing, going crazy. The bronc rider swung agilely onto the rear end of the horse alongside, slid off, and walked nonchalantly to the fence among the cheers of his peers. He settled casually alongside Fergus. David, excitedly holding the portable camera, focused in on his face, as he came up, and Martha jumped up to shake his hand.

"You were wonderful!" she bubbled.

"Martha!" said Esther, but she was lost in the noise.

The young man grinned. He had slim hips, wide shoulders, and the swelling muscles of a man who had kept himself in prime condition all his twenty-five years. He had the face of a cameo, a cleft chin, wide-set blue eyes, and, when he took his hat off, his sandy hair tousled itself into curls.

He casually left, walking to a pickup truck rigged with a ramp to carry his horse. A little Mexican kid stood by, wiping the dust off the ornate sideboard which read: PUNCH WESTON, RODEO RIDER. STAR RANCH, STOCKTON, CALIFORNIA.

The Mexican boy reached into the front seat and handed him a beer. David moved in with his camera, catching the slouch of the bronc rider as he drank deeply, wiped his mouth with his sleeve, cast a careless wave at some of his fans, and turned again to Martha who still stood staring at him.

"So long, sugar," he said. "Boy, you got lips as pretty as a bing cherry."

He got in his truck, the Mexican kid jumped in, and he drove off toward the judges' stand.

"You know," said David, "I think I've just made a film test."

◆◆◆◆◆◆◆◆

"Let's see what the girls think," said Simon.

Whenever Simon had anything exceptional on film, he always liked to ask a few secretaries, a couple of wardrobe women, and a script girl or two to come in, so he could get their reaction. This was referred to privately as Mr. Moses' kitchen cabinet.

The girls were thrilled.

"He's more handsome than Wally Reid!"

"If that isn't a western star, I've never seen one."

"You can buy him for me, Mr. Moses," giggled a mail-room girl.

Fortunately, Punch Weston's wagon carried his address. When he came to Hollywood for an interview, he was in complete control. He carried a pack of Bull Durham in the left-hand pocket of his ranch jacket, wore a Stetson on the back of his head, which made a curl fall over his brow. He crossed his boot-clad feet on a low table, rolled himself a cigarette, and said he didn't much mind working for a picture company if he could do the Calgary stampede when it was time, and if he could use his own pony. He was such a star in his own right that neither tycoon nor camera fazed him. He merely struck a match on his pants, while Fergus and Simon Moses stood by spellbound, and smoked his hand-rolled cigarette, holding it in the corner of his mouth.

He was immediately put into a western, then another. On the strength of this success, Fergus tried his ploy.

He drove Simon out to the Guadalupe ranch. They stopped at a ruined adobe house, nestled by a stream, the usual lane of olive trees leading up to it, sign of Spanish colonial days.

"Look at it," said Fergus. "What a set! And all that land. No more messing around with dirt farmers. We can fix up that dilapidated barn for storage. Think of all the hauling we've had to do with our equipment and props. We can even take that old tack room and those stalls and put up temporary dressing rooms and a small office. This land's valuable, Mr. Moses. We could have some Mexican family live on an acre or two and grow vegetables. Imagine home-grown vegetables for your table, courtesy of Titan. Even your own little hideaway if you want to build a cottage by that pond up there in those peaceful hills."

Simon's eyes widened. This would be a wonderful place for Claudia, away from—everyone.

"Privacy," said Fergus, realizing his thoughts.

"And a lot of money," said Simon. "You're asking me to put out at least fifty thousand dollars. That ain't growing on any trees I've seen around here yet."

"How do you know?" said Fergus. "It just may be, you know. Would you like a breakdown of our transportation and storage costs?"

"I'll think about it," said Simon.

Back at the studio Fergus immediately went to the property department, now expanded to a row of rooms that housed, among others, a sketch artist, Phil Grey.

"Phil," he said, "I want you to sketch me a California dream house, on the Spanish style, with a fireplace not only in the living room, but in a large bedroom that looks out over the hills to a pond. And make it look like—well, a kind of love nest."

"Say," said Phil, "that sounds good. We making a love story? Who for?"

"We might just," said Fergus, "if you can put a little, uh—sex, into it. It would undoubtedly star Claudia Barstow."

The next day Fergus took the sketch to Simon.

"Well," he said, "this is the sort of little place that would be awfully nice out there in God's country."

He left without saying a word.

In due time, the four-thousand-acre ranch was bought so that a small house with an adobe wall surrounding four acres of it could be built for privacy.

Punch Weston became the pet of the town, got himself a rustic house in Laurel Canyon, drove a specially made Pierce Arrow around Hollywood, and took to stardom with more pleasure and less concern than anyone who had hit town. Glamour just came naturally to him.

Martha, lost in this strange new world, fell in love with him.

"Keep that cowboy bum away from Martha!" said Simon to Fergus. "It's bad enough he made a pass at Claudia right in front of me at Kathleen's Tavern the other night. I don't want to see him around my home, too."

"I'll try," said Fergus.

He still wondered how Rebecca could be so naïve about the other life of her husband, and how Simon could command the behavior of others, considering the life he was leading with Claudia.

"I want Martha to mind her manners and remember who she is," said Simon. "Don't you know one nice boy she can double-date with you and Esther?"

"There's the new cutter," said Fergus, "that nice kid from L.A. high."

"That sissy!" said Simon. "Not my daughter. What am I going to do?"

"Keep her away from the studio."

"Easy said! Maybe Dr. Wolfrum should talk to her about the facts of life."

Fergus stared at him.

The fact that he had sent for Wolfrum to be the doctor at Titan studio had outraged Fergus. The old man had called the only abortionist he had ever known, just in case, and set him up for his license to practice under the guise of respectability.

All I need, thought Fergus, aside from running the physical side of the studio, is to have to keep Martha away from Weston when she hangs around the studio.

He still looked at Esther with affection; she was the girl of his school days. He did not have to pretend with her or be afraid she'd find the chinks in his armor. She always found his company to her liking, even if she sometimes complained she did not see him enough. But that was flattering. Occasionally, after a night with some little actress, he would look at Esther's clean loveliness and be ashamed. He would wonder if he could live a life of happiness and family security with her, without complications. The only stumbling block was the fact that her father was Simon Moses.

Sometimes he would look up at the studio water tower and smile wryly to himself, recollecting that he alone knew that the Titans were earth creatures of a low order.

◆◆◆◆◆◆◆◆

Time came for a yacht. All the tycoons had them, and Simon had to have status. Along the shores and coves of California, a man was as good as his vessel, even if he and other newcomers, non-Protestant, could not belong to any of the posh Los Angeles clubs.

Simon bought a 125-foot motor yacht, the *Gypsy*, from a Pasadena estate. Rebecca sailed with him off the Long Beach breakwater into a choppy southwesterly, and it did not agree with her, so henceforth she stayed home, while he went off with his staff, enjoying relief, he said, from the busy life of the studio.

The girls and their friends often took it out, for Simon trusted the captain, Wheeler, and his wife who ran the galley and acted as stewardess.

But usually the *Gypsy* anchored in Emerald Bay at Catalina. Fergus, Claudia, Plimpton, several writers, and sometimes a trusted actor, actress, or staff member joined in on what were loosely called story conferences or production meetings. It was the safest and most usual way in which a man could have protected leisure time with his mistress and still work with his staff.

Claudia chose these times to sleep, read, discuss new scenes, and treat Simon with the traditional affection expected of their relationship. However, close quarters, and the personalities of some of the hard-nosed writers, piqued her. In his cabin, Fergus would hear her, as they moored in the quiet nights of the Catalina Isthmus, arguing endlessly, and he knew she was tilting the glass. Late the next day she would appear, contrite and lethargic.

At these times Fergus was glad he was not the target of Claudia's whims. He was sorry for Simon, who was always so concerned about her comforts and pleasures. And often the cruise was shortened so she could return to town to some event, if things did not go the way she wanted. The yacht was obviously not the answer to privacy.

The little casita at the Guadalupe ranch was the place where Simon and Claudia went when there were no conferences, and there was a moment of peace and quiet between them. Deliberately, there was no telephone, servants were housed off the property, and only a few privileged visitors were invited.

Sometimes when Simon had to attend meetings in New York, and Claudia was getting in condition for a picture, she would stay at the ranch, ride horseback and swim, and these were the only truly peaceful days she had.

Occasionally, Fergus knew, she would have a quick romance with an actor who caught her fancy, or a director who held her interest as he told her how to live her current character. This particular situation was prevalent in Hollywood. These fantasy romances usually ended with the picture, and if used properly sometimes gave a spark to her performance and made a better movie. Of course, this was never mentioned where it might be heard by Simon. And he was so engrossed in his studio life, his devotion to Claudia, and the responsibilities of holding up his dignity as a married man and a father, that he was blissfully ignorant and protected. Nobody ever wanted to bear bad tidings to an emperor; slaves had been known to die that way. And death in Hollywood was exile from a favored high-salaried spot.

One hot summer afternoon Fergus was at the Guadalupe ranch. The iron gates to the casita were ajar, and he recognized Claudia's silver Hispano Suiza parked in the drive.

As he entered the patio, she called out to him. She had been swimming in the lake and wore a Chinese robe over her suit.

"Come inside and have a drink," she said. "That's one good thing about adobe, Fergus, it's cool. Those Mexicans knew what they were doing in a hot climate."

He came into the pleasant room. Large picture windows set in iron grills framed the distant beauty of the lake and the rolling hills a mile away.

"How peaceful this is, after the rat race of production down below," said Fergus, falling into a comfortable chair. "This really is an escape hatch."

"Yes, it is," she said, "too much. Especially when Simon's away so much. When will he be back from New York?"

"Next week," said Fergus. "I guess he's just as anxious to get back as you are to have him."

There was a pause. He looked up. She was smiling at him.

"Not so anxious as you might think, Fergus," she said. "You've always been such an idealist."

"He's been very good for you," said Fergus.

"Oh, good," said Claudia wistfully.

She smiled again, that piquant personal smile that always made him think of her as she had been before stardom and his own success had separated them.

"For the love of God," she said, "you don't think that there's excitement any more with Simon. You know you can be devoted to a man and still not enjoy fucking him. Oh, Fergus, how I long to have a young man throw me on a bed and give me a real, wild time—use me up—exhaust me, fill me deep and make me cry out like—well, like he was a wild stallion. I'm a woman, you know, and a very passionate one."

Fergus felt a growing in his groin. As always she shocked him even while she excited him. He sipped his drink and stared at the frosted glass.

"Look, Fergus," she whispered, coming closer to him. "Stop staring at your damned drink. I want you to make love to me. Right now. I need it. Isn't it better if it's you? We know each other; you love to love me, that's been proven, and as I remember you were damned good in bed as a kid and are probably much better now."

"But Claudia—" he said, "how could I?"

"How could you!" she said. "You know you're longing to be in me right now. What's to be lost? Simon isn't missing anything. He can't have me, he's away, and there's too much of me for him anyway. Why sometimes he can't even get it up anymore, and I want sex. Do I have to throw myself at you, for God's sake?"

She pulled him up by his hands and stood looking at him, then pressed close.

"Please," she whispered, "Claudia wants you on her bed right now. Oh, what I want to do to you!"

She reached her hand along his body under his coat.

He was lost.

They went to the cool bedroom, ruffled white curtains blowing faintly in a warm wind, and she ripped the coverlet from the bed, soft and inviting with its ruffled pillows. She peeled off her wet suit, and as he stripped off his clothes and came to her, he felt the delicious coldness of her wet body against the heat in him, and they fell together on Simon Moses' great Spanish bed, fusing in a passion that was half angry and punishing because of what they were doing.

Later, spent, they arose from bed. She threw him a bathrobe. As he put it on, he flushed, for the initials on it were S.M. It seemed more of an intrusion than using her body.

They walked out into the secluded patio, through the garden, dropped their robes, and swam in the private inlet of the lake.

"Claudia–" he said, "it was wonderful. But it mustn't happen again."

She threw water in his face.

"What's the matter, you dummy," she said, "didn't you like it? I did, and I'm going to say, thank you, Fergie, I needed that. Very, very much. And don't say what's going to happen, you never can tell."

He drove back to town, feeling both guilty and fulfilled, recalling Claudia's ripe beauty and remembering how much he had wanted her so many times. This time he had been prepared to do everything a woman could ever want of a man. Maybe she was right in her pagan views. He had taken nothing from Simon Moses, and he and Claudia had given each other incredible pleasure. He could not help feeling vainglorious. He knew he was far, far ahead of Simon in pleasuring his woman.

Ah, that Claudia. Still the same wanton. She had crystallized into the town's glorious extrovert pet, ravishing everyone with her beauty, chaining everyone with her foibles, and she had thanked him, Fergus Austin, for giving her pleasure. It was his dream come true. Poor Simon. Imagine him pitying Moses!

Strangely, his triumph in her bed eased his longing for her. He had proven himself, and he felt liberated from the nagging hurt of his youthful pride, so disturbed when Simon Moses had become the man in Claudia's life. Now he felt he could face her eye to eye. And likely, yes, likely, it would happen again. Carrying this secret rendezvous smugly in his mind, he went about his work.

◆◆◆◆◆◆◆◆

The European war seemed far from the busy life in Hollywood. American films had become more important. There was a booming money market. So what if costs zoomed? So did prosperity. Urban laborers sought recreation at night after work. More picture houses and a larger turnover of films was the answer.

Picture companies flourished in the West. Additional studio space was added. Out in the valleys, deserts, and foothills, land was purchased. Fergus was delighted that he had already tied up the Guadalupe property, where strange false-fronted western streets and tenements were already being used in the burgeoning production.

Simon lorded it over his studio in a large suite of offices overlooking Vine Street. Fergus, as supervisor, handled the physical problems of filmmaking, with a production staff, secretaries, and accountants. According to protocol, his business offices had a fine view of an alley.

Los Angeles, once a temporary campsite for the celluloid gypsies, suddenly found itself nurturing a very rich and growing infant industry.

Then, in April 1917, Wilson asked for war. It was a matter of flag-waving—"The World Must Be Made Safe for Democracy."

Claudia insisted on doing a war picture. It was a huge success. Picture magazines and rotogravures were full of her in Red Cross uniform passing out doughnuts, kissing doughboys, waving flags, and teaching a class in first aid.

Chaplin, Mary Pickford, Bill Hart, and Marie Dressler were called "soldiers of happiness" on Liberty-loan tours, selling war bonds, leading rallies, being photographed in newsreels, pepping up the democratic way of giving.

One afternoon, at a Liberty-loan rally in downtown Los Angeles, Simon stood in the front row. He liked the excitement of rallies with his stars. The prop department had manufactured all sorts of gimmicks to surround Claudia.

With the Elks' band behind her, she was enticing a crowd of buyers. She danced back and forth and sang through a megaphone which had the Titan logo on it.

> Oui oui Marie,
> If I'll do this for you,
> Then you'll do that for me. . . .

David pushed through the crowd to his father. Fergus followed him.

"Well, pappa," he said, "I didn't want you to know until I finished the picture. But I'm going."

"Going where?" said Simon, smiling. "I guess you're due a little vacation, so okay. Let's talk about it later."

"You don't understand," said David. His father's eyes were back on the stage. Claudia was bending over, pinning a little flag on a man who had bought a fifty-dollar bond. She threw him a kiss and came to Simon. He smiled and pulled a bill out of his pocket, as prearranged. She pinned a little flag on him and bent over and pecked his cheek.

He smiled, embarrassed in front of David, but she moved on to another victim. It seemed to him that his son's voice pierced his consciousness from a distance.

"I mean I've enlisted." David grinned, attempting to make it seem like a lark. "Uncle Sam has nabbed me."

Simon fingered the little flag at his lapel.

"That's ridiculous!" he said. "I'll straighten it out. You're too important to the company."

"I'm important to Pershing," said David, "me and thousands like me."

Simon looked over his shoulder at Fergus.

"Well, you usually get in things together," he said, "I suppose you two buddies will both be leaving."

Fergus looked away.

"What's the matter," said Simon, "you got out of it?"

"They won't take him," said David. "He tried."

"What do you mean, won't take you!" said Simon, already resenting him.

"It's my ear," said Fergus. "You remember when I got hit by that Trust goon when I was bicycling for you—I got a punctured eardrum. I'm deaf in one ear."

Simon's world had changed. Titan studio could help raise money for bonds, but it couldn't stop his son David from going away to war.

"You're not going," he said to his son.

But in April 1918 David was part of Pershing's AEF.

Far from Hollywood, one cold and rainy afternoon, he slugged through the mud and slush of Ypres trying to recall the brightness of the rally. He wished he'd asked his father to let him run the camera department when he came home; he'd write him. But it was impossible for him to concentrate on anything but trying to keep warm. He put one weary foot in front of the other on the slatted path over the rainpools of the desolate death pits and peered through the dusk at the stumps of splintered trees that stood like wounded bodies all about him.

He wished he had a camera.

But, he reflected, it would be too dark to get a picture of the wasted land. He'd just have to remember how ghostly and miserable it was.

All he really wanted, he thought, was to get rid of the cooties and wear dry clothes. As he thought of how great it would be, he felt hot, and his head began to thump. In a moment he saw a glimmer in the trees, and a burst of fire scattered all about him. He hit the mud, feeling ashamed. My God, what was wrong with him? Couldn't he take it? He felt sick to his stomach, but he remembered that lots of his buddies had told him they felt the same thing. It was a buck fever you got over when you got used to it.

After about an hour, his sergeant and several men came through.

"Get up, old buddy," one of his pals said, "it's quiet for the moment, and we're going to get some chow."

The boy looked at David strangely.

"You okay?" he said. "Did you pick up some shrapnel?"

David shook his head and tried to smile.

"I'm okay," he said, "just got scared, I guess."

As he spoke, he keeled over.

"Oh, Christ," said the sergeant, "another one."

Four days later, David was dead of influenza in a small field hospital, along with twenty-four other youths who had come to France to make the world safe for democracy.

◆◆◆◆◆◆◆◆

Hermosa Beach, some twenty miles south of Los Angeles, was a settlement of comfortable summer houses scattered along the sandy beach. It was a good place for Rebecca and the girls to get away from the pressures of Hollywood and the summer heat, and it was convenient for Simon to have them there. He could be with them on weekends occasionally.

A Pacific Electric trolley car left the station at Sixth and Main and transported help and lesser luminaries to weekends and casual summer evening get-togethers at the Moses house.

Fergus passed it, grateful he didn't have to take trolleys any more.

The old-fashioned brown gabled house rented from Easter until August nestled on the edge of the wide beach, a promenade in front of it. A raft was anchored beyond the breakers.

Esther greeted him in her bathing suit, eager to swim.

"Hurry up!" she said. "It's gorgeous!"

He looked at her trim body and the happiness in her blue eyes as she looked at him, and again he realized how pretty she was and how much a part of him.

"I'll rush!" he said. "Won't waste a minute!"

He headed for the simple outdoor bathhouse, stripped the city off him, and got into his new striped bathing suit. He felt wonderful. Life was beautiful, here with his girl. That's the way it should be. He thought of how different this was from his swim with Claudia; there was no guilt, only joy.

They rushed over the hot sand, dropping their towels, splashed into the pounding surf, and swam to the solid, comforting float. They climbed up, panting, happy to be in their private seagirt world.

They lay there, their bodies dripping after a swim. He pulled off her fancy flowered rubber bathing cap, and her damp blond curls fell about her shoulders. She turned her head, her cheek flat against the cocoa matting, peering up at him.

"You look pretty enough to paint," he said. "Whatever happened to that Bronx schoolgirl?"

He sat up and touched her golden arm.

"That Bronx schoolgirl is bored." She frowned and sat up, tossing a parabola of drops from her hand as she waved angrily.

"You're always working, pappa's always working. God knows where Martha is half the time. You know mamma, she won't complain to pappa because when she does, he just slams the door and goes out again. He says if he can't have peace in his own home, he isn't coming home."

Fergus was grateful that women couldn't read minds. He knew how Simon maneuvered to bring about a quarrel so he could flee. If Rebecca's behavior could be termed guilty, he could squeeze in one more evening with Claudia, who had a much prettier and gayer bungalow in Santa Monica, below the palm-lined cliffs of the public park. It was more accessible to everyone in Titan studio than her Vine Street apartment. She kept her French maid and her Chinese cook, and a coterie of friends were always swimming, playing cards, eating, and drinking on the comfortable glassed-in terrace facing the ocean.

"Well, I'm here," Fergus said, "so don't pick on me. I practically had to walk out on a production meeting to spend this weekend with you."

"With me," snorted Esther. "With the whole family, worse luck!"

He bent over and kissed her cheek.

"You sure take a golden tan."

"Work," she said, turning over on her back, "and lots of vinegar and oil. I'm a traveling salad."

He kissed her, this time on the mouth.

"Well," he said, pulling back, "this is the way I'll take my salad from now on."

She embraced his wet shoulders and pulled him down. She kissed him, her lips slightly open. It was the first time she had shown him that she had desire, and he pursued her invitation, finding her exciting and wanting more of her.

He felt himself harden against the raft, and he pulled away, looking around. There was no privacy; this was a hell of a place to be falling passionately in love with her.

"You know," he said, "I'm afraid this raft is a billboard, and I'm getting hot and bothered by you. Maybe we'd better swim over on the other side."

She looked into his eyes and then looked toward the house.

"Oh, Lord," she said, "here we go again!"

Aunt Yetta was out on the balcony, waving a red blanket at them, then hanging it on the railing. This was a signal that there was some important message, usually from the studio.

"Let's get it over with," he said, "and then maybe I'll drive you down the coast. We'll find some romantic candlelit tavern and have dinner."

She pulled on her bathing cap and they dove off the raft, surfacing in time to race for a large swell. She swam a little ahead of him.

"Hey, wait!" he said. "You're supposed to be with me!"

As she waited, treading water, he smiled at her. What a healthy young woman! What children she would have! As he had in the Bronx, he looked at her with delight and wondered if he really weren't truly in love with her.

Aunt Yetta was jumping up and down and waving her arms.

"Look at her," said Esther. "She certainly seems excited."

"You know," said Fergus, "she always lives somebody else's life, carrying somebody else's messages. Why didn't she ever get married?"

"We were all so busy working as a family, in furniture stores and in pappa's movie houses, somebody had to stay home," said Esther. "So I guess she was the sacrifice."

Aunt Yetta had rushed down the stairs, and she met them on the porch. Her hands were clasped, and she began to keen, bending over, until her head seemed to touch her apron.

"What is it?" said Esther. "Aunt Yetta, what is it?"

Fergus took her by the shoulders and lifted her.

She gestured upstairs.

Fergus looked up, and then he faintly heard the deep, low sound of what could have been an animal in pain.

Yetta's lips parted.

"David," she whispered.

When they reached Rebecca's room, they found her sitting on the edge of the bed, the telegram clenched in her hands. They had to pry her fingers loose to read it. She was shaking.

Esther stretched her mother out on the chintz coverlet, and Yetta put a throw over her.

"Don't worry, mamma," she said, "we'll find pappa."

Later they stood foolishly in the living room, awkward in the face of death, staring at each other.

"Where's pappa?" whispered Esther.

"I'll find him," said Fergus.

"I'll go with you," said Esther.

"No," said Fergus. "You'd better stay with your mother. I'll get hold of Doc Wolfrum and have him phone in a prescription. She'll need sedation. You'd better give her a slug of brandy."

Aunt Yetta went to fetch it, tears streaming down her sallow cheeks.

Esther walked out to the garage in the alley with Fergus.

"Don't think I don't know where you'll find pappa," she said. "Oh, Fergus, poor David!"

He put his arms around her.

"Bear up, honey," he said. "I'll take care of you. You know that."

He got into his car and started up the coast highway, the "regret" telegram in his pocket. A scrap of paper seemed to be the only way anyone could realize David was dead. Bright David; David the genius; David, whose skilled hands and agile mind would never put together a fractured Ernaman camera or splice a film. David, who had loved movies so much that he had found a way to make pictures when they were playing hooky, who liked to look through a strip of film in a lab the way some people enjoyed seeing an art exhibit.

Fergus had always taken it for granted that someday he and David would be partners. They would have spun the dreams into a tapestry; they would have made giant steps. Now he was stuck with the pedestrian imagination of a man whose real interest in pictures was money and his passion for a faithless woman.

He found himself hating the thought of Claudia. She was a user and an abuser. Everyone fell in love with her instant charm. On film she was gossamer, gathering all the dreams others had written and invented as if they were a shower of her own attributes. Right now she and Simon were probably in bed. What did he care about that family in Hermosa Beach going through their travail?

At Claudia's beach house, he recognized the flashy cars of various actors, and Simon's Packard. He pushed open the gate and walked in. By God, if they were in bed in that private suite, where they often retired in the afternoon, pretending to go for a walk along the strand, he would pull them apart and shove the death notice right up Moses' backside.

Instead, he found a group of the usual Sunday sycophants sitting on the sand, drinks in hand. Claudia and Simon were at a card table idly involved in watching her director, Plimpton, playing himself a cheating hand of solitaire. Fergus resented the triviality of the moment more than if he'd found them in bed.

Simon's usual look of annoyance at Fergus revealed itself for a second. "What do *you* want?"

"Hi, honeybun," said Claudia.

She pecked him on the cheek. "I'll get you a drink, big boy. Come on, what's the funeral?"

"This," said Fergus.

He set the telegram down in front of Simon.

"You'd better come home."

As Simon's chair scraped on the flagstone, Fergus noticed that everyone there was silent. They knew they were watching a drama.

For a brief moment, as the enormity of David's death hit Fergus like a blow in the stomach, he thought, my God, I've got fifty yellowing sheets of FEDA stationery. Now we'll never get to use it. There won't be FEDA—Fergus and David. I'll tear it up. No, I'll burn it page by page, old Dave, old buddy . . .

◆◆◆◆◆◆◆◆

Fergus, with the entire Titan complement, paused for the traditional moment of silence. It seemed incredibly sad that the sprightly friend of his childhood should have only this to represent the memory of his life.

He sat through a memorial service at the old Temple B'nai B'rith on Wilshire Boulevard, wishing in a way that the body of David could be there, the casket draped with a flag, to be buried, to make a period of his being, a curtain to descend so other lives could go on.

Two weeks later he came home to find his day maid had left a letter by his bed. He looked at it in shock. It was from David.

He sat down and stared at the familiar writing on the thin gray paper, afraid to open it. Finally he did, as carefully as if he felt he might hurt it. It was written in pencil and mailed by Red Cross ladies who had taken it from him at a mobile canteen.

Dear Fergus,

Well, you'd better get your good ear ready, because I'm going to talk it off when I get home. This has been a great experience. I sure wish I had the old Ernaman and some film. It's about time we shoot what's real, and have I seen plenty of that! Let's stop crapping around, and get FEDA started again, and make some honest to God stories about real people, and what people want, and what we're fighting for. Although I'm not quite sure what is right now. All I want is to be warm and dry and have no cooties and sleep in a good bed as long as I want to. I can't say I wish you was here. You're lucky. Kiss all the girls for me, and write, old buddy, and tell 'em all not to send sweaters, we haven't got the time or place for that junk. Anyway, when I get home let's make good movies, our way!

Your pal,
Dave

For the first time that he could remember, Fergus put his head down and wept.

The next day at the studio he decided he must tell Mr. Moses about it. He walked through the plush offices to the inner sanctum. The secretary, Miss Mosby, looked up, distressed.

"Mr. Austin," she said, "he just isn't seeing anybody. He just sits in his office most of the time."

"I'd better see him," said Fergus.

Fergus walked in before he saw that Simon was sitting at the desk, bent over.

"I wanted to talk to you, Mr. Moses," said Fergus. "It's about—David."

Moses stood up.

"Haven't you got any sense," said Simon, "or any feeling? How dare you mention *his* name to me when you stand here, and my boy died for his country on Flanders Fields."

Fergus stood, pale and shaken.

"I—I'm sorry."

Simon sat down. He seemed to crumple.

"I—I'm sorry too," he said. "It's just that—just that—"

He stopped, choking on his words.

"I'll leave," said Fergus.

"What did you want?"

Fergus put his hand to the letter in his pocket. But he knew it would hurt Simon in more than one way.

"Nothing," said Fergus.

As time passed, he sometimes thought that David would come walking in, saying that someone had messed up the dog tags and it was all a joke.

As months passed, and when he saw the ravaged face of Rebecca Moses, he realized it was true. Her carefully peroxided hair was allowed to turn white, and her silhouette drooped into that of an old woman, as sere and unloved as Aunt Yetta.

Simon Moses, also, seemed to take the turn that befalls a man when an only son, an heir, dies. Thus the dynasty of the father perishes, too. For a year he would say Kaddish every morning and would die again with his son.

Over 116,000 men lost their sons before the AEF came home. Flu had ravaged the world, and many thousands had died of it, but for Simon, his son was the only one who was lost.

Simon never overcame his guilt that he was with Claudia when the news reached him. One more thing was held against Fergus—he had humiliated him publicly, by throwing the death notice in front of him at Claudia's house.

Every time Simon looked at him, Fergus saw the outrage in his face, that it was Fergus who lived and was in business with him when it should have been David.

The family moved back into town.

When Fergus came to see Esther, he would find Simon fussing with his scripts and papers in the study, glancing up to scowl, his world cut off from what little life there was in the house.

Fergus saw Esther more and more, taking her away from the sadness of the house. It took a while before they could discuss David, but a bond united them, and through that came some minor lovemaking.

Fergus comforted her, and there were kisses. Then he caressed her breasts, and held her close, and she would cling to him, body to body, but he would go no farther.

"We will wait," he said. "This is not the time, Esther. I won't start with sadness."

She was angry.

"You just won't start, period!" she said. "What do you want me to do, have an affair with someone else, and then say, okay, I'm damaged, now you can go to bed with me, nobody can say *you* did it."

"Esther!" he said, shocked, "don't talk like a Hollywood tramp. You know I love you. When it's right, I'll ask your father. You should know that!"

"You know what *he'll* say," she said. "Fergus, we have our life to live. Let's elope."

"No *sir,*" said Fergus. "I intend to keep on working at Titan. As it is, I'll have a tough time supporting you in style. And I won't live a second-rate life in this town. You'll just have to be patient. I'll work it out."

Meanwhile, he knew, the word was out at Titan to watch his every action. If there were any way Moses could get him out, he'd go.

So he did his work, kept honest books, supervised everything with as much efficiency as he could muster, looking out for traps.

Claudia went on a shopping trip to New York. Jeffrey was opening in a play. Before she left, Fergus drove down to her beach house and took her a book—a new historical novel.

"This is a good picture for your brother," he said. "It's about the Norman Conquest; you know, all the things we live by. He would play William, and if you don't mind a little incest, you can play his wife, Matilda. You're tiny like she was. She's the one who embroidered the whole Norman Conquest in a tapestry. It would be a special, big money. What do you think?"

"I'll read it on the train," she said. "Wouldn't mind getting away from modern things. Are you all right? You seem a little nervous."

"I am nervous," he said. "The old man's on my back."

"So I know," she said. "I don't see him as much as I used to. I guess he's had to stay closer to home since David died. I hear Rebecca looks a million years old."

"It's very hard for all of them," said Fergus. "I'll never have another buddy like Dave."

"You know," said Claudia, "it's pretty lonesome sometimes. Of course I always knew Simon had a wife, and marriage was never in the cards for us. But

Fergus, we've been together five years! You get awfully used to someone, and, when it comes to family holidays and festivals, a mistress always comes out at the small end of the horn."

"He loves you," said Fergus, "you know that."

"It doesn't do me much good long-distance," she said. "I'd better get out of town for a spell. You know, Fergus, I've discovered that you can love someone and still find sex aside from him if things don't work out the way you thought. I don't really think it makes any difference—as long as it doesn't hurt him, and I wouldn't do that. So, I'll charge my batteries instead of being depressed."

"If I know you," said Fergus, "you'll do it in New York."

She smiled.

"You wouldn't like to give me a little charge up before I go?"

He patted her hand and laughed.

"Not just now."

"Well, how about that!" said Claudia. "Now I guess it is true about Esther. You two do it yet?"

"She's a virgin," said Fergus.

Claudia laughed.

"You're taking a big risk if you hitch up to a virgin. You ought to try her out first, you dope."

Fergus flushed.

"Well, well," said Claudia, "I wouldn't want to be in your shoes. You know Simon's a tough old buzzard when it comes to his family. Incidentally, someone ought to tell him his daughter Martha's shacking up with Punch Weston up in Laurel Canyon."

"God forbid he finds out," said Fergus. "We've got the biggest western yet going. Anyway, bring Jeffrey back and tell him if he comes it won't be so easy to black my eye as it was when I was a green kid. Confidentially, see how he feels about fifty thousand dollars and wire me."

"My God!" said Claudia, "for that he'd play Roget's *Thesaurus*."

4

♦♦♦♦♦♦♦♦

It seemed as if 1919, the year following David's death, triggered a bad time for Fergus, the Moses family, and Titan, along with the picture industry.

The flu epidemic and the tragedy in Europe emptied theaters. Claudia's second war picture, along with the rest of the flag-waving propaganda films, fell into the postarmistice doldrums. Titan's economy had shrunk to less than 10 percent of its usual fat profits.

Fergus was forced to lay off old regulars and was warned by Simon that everyone might have to take a cut in salary.

And what does armistice mean when a son will never come home?

The parades, the newsreels, the rotogravures of the return of the AEF, freedom for women, cigarettes, bobbed hair, Emma Goldman and free love all passed by as Simon plunged into work with a vengeance born of emptiness, and Fergus, with a vengeance to prove himself.

♦♦♦♦♦♦♦♦

"You look beautiful," said Fergus, as he held Esther in his arms.

She was dressed in a pink tulle gown, and he felt it

was right that the Alexandria orchestra was playing "A Pretty Girl Is Like a Melody."

She rested her head against his cheek. He was pleased. She knew when not to speak.

It was time, he thought, to say his piece. There would never be a way to get around Simon Moses; they would just have to take it into their own hands when the time came.

On the way home he drove with his arm around her and felt that, come what may, he would talk to her father. Maybe tomorrow at the office.

Simon was sitting up, waiting for them, reading a newspaper. He stood up.

"Esther," he said, "you can go upstairs."

Fergus was irritated. What right had he to sit up when they were both adult and had known each other always?

Esther stuck her chin out.

"I'll stay," she said, pulling off her long white kid gloves.

Simon looked at his daughter, surprised. Fergus noted how his bifocals slid down on his nose. It made him seem older and disturbed the handsome face that, until recently, women had admired.

"All right, if you insist," said Simon. "You asked for it. Sit down both of you. I think we'd better talk."

They both sat, Esther straightening the flounces of her gown.

"Fergus," said Simon, "you have been deeply involved in my studio. You have learned a great deal. But that does not mean I intend to have you get any ideas of being one of my family."

"I think that's my choice," Esther said quietly.

"I will not have you get mixed up with a man who is not of my choosing," said Simon.

"I said *I'll* make my choice," said Esther.

Fergus stood up. "Now just a minute, both of you. Nobody has asked me what I choose. Mr. Moses, I went to work for you as a raw kid. I've got pictures of how my face looked after the Trust made mincemeat out of me. I'm half deaf. I did some pretty good errands for you across the country in my time. I took risks—"

He watched the panicked look on Simon's face, followed by a glance of hatred. He held up his hand.

"You still think I'm a kid. Well, sir, I am now twenty-three. I am one of the best supervisors in town. I can get a job anyplace. Even with business in the doldrums. I know what profits you've made because I'm partly responsible for them. We can weather it. I have a future with Titan because I choose to. I helped start it, before I was even legally able. You and Abe took over from Dave and me. Dave's not here to protect me."

He noticed the quick flicker of Moses' eyes. He felt briefly ashamed of himself, but this was a fight for life. Fergus had mentioned Dave deliberately. He continued. "I am not going to quit. And when I am ready, sir, and you are ready, I will discuss whether I want to become a member of your family. And until then, neither you nor Esther, as much as I care for her, will decide for me."

He turned to Esther, who had put her hands to her cheeks in shock.

"I've told you, Esther, before. Wait for me. I'll make the decisions. Good-night to you both."

He bowed, he hoped, in a dignified manner, and left.

Both of them looked after him, speechless with surprise.

Finally, Esther said, "Now, see what you've done!" She burst into tears and ran out of the room.

Simon knew he had faced a defeat for which he had not prepared himself.

Upstairs, Esther slammed her bedroom door and, as she undressed, she looked at her body in the pier glass. She was young, slim, and pretty.

Why didn't Fergus really want her? Why didn't he

want to love her passionately, right now, as she wanted to love him?

She thought of him as he had said, "Neither you nor Esther, as much as I care for her, will decide for me," and the impact of him as a man made her want him more than ever. Oh, God, she had to have him. Rumors about Claudia and others had come to her ears, and more than ever she wanted to be his wife, to have him love her, alone.

Martha came in. She wore a cherry red robe, was creaming her face, and had pinned back her hair. She looked very much the daughter of Simon Moses, with her poetic, heart-shaped face.

"Where have you been?" asked Esther. "When I want to do things with you, you're not around, and when I need a little privacy, here you are."

"That's just darling!" said Martha. "Maybe I need you and you're not around. Did you ever think of that?"

She wiped her face in a fluffy towel and for a moment hid her eyes.

Esther slipped into her nightgown.

"Pappa just had it out with Fergus, and he walked out."

"It's your own fault," said Martha, her voice muffled in the towel.

"Why do you say that?" asked Esther.

"Never bring your lovers home. Don't you know, parents can never face the idea we're women. Especially pappa."

"Fergus isn't my lover," said Esther. "Worse luck!"

Her tears began to flow again.

"Who knows who's right," said Martha. "So if you love, you get hurt. If you don't, you hurt anyway."

She buried her face in the towel again.

"Esther—" she said, looking up.

"What?" Esther said, blowing her nose.

Martha looked at her.

"Oh, skip it for now," she said.

She left the room slowly.

Esther, preoccupied, cold-creamed her face, and wondered how Fergus could ever come to the house again, or how she could drop in to see him at his office, as she often did.

◆◆◆◆◆◆◆◆

Jeffrey Barstow, at forty, was not exactly a white knight in shining armor, but he saved Titan single-handed.

The Norman Conquest was handled by a new, young, witty woman scenarist, Tilly Robards, as the story of an adventurous romancer, with many a gay ambuscade and several fierce battles featuring William's physical prowess and swordsmanship. Jeffrey's romantic manner and handsomeness promised innate cocksmanship, which enchanted the women. *William the Conqueror* saved Titan in the same way Valentino's *Four Horsemen* was to save Metro.

Jeffrey settled down with the elite bachelors of the town at the Los Angeles Athletic Club, where he could have his drinking bouts and not be pestered by the multitude of unsolicited women who tried to get into his bed.

He always preferred to select his own bedmates, and their name was legion. When he was bored, he drove his Stutz Bearcat, shipped west as part of his incredible fringe-benefit contract, to the rendezvous of his choice, where he could leave when it pleased him.

Life seemed to be set up for him to enjoy the fruits of his work, his talents, and his enthusiasms.

With his agent, Seymour Sewell, he prowled about with the San Diego and Santa Barbara yachting society. Seymour had a diesel cruiser, the *Empress*, stately and slow moving, a traveling bedroom and bar for successful miscreants and peripatetic females. The women aboard were never ladies, but young, untried actresses and semiprofessionals who could get to be a bore after the third hangover.

Seymour, a heavy drinker but light fornicator, was content with them, for every cat was gray in the dark to him.

Jeffrey, with his inborn romanticism, in spite of his scoffing, wanted a woman of substance—someone who could be gay, make love, enjoy sunsets, yet lie abed half the day if he wanted, a woman who would listen while a man read aloud. Yet she must be a woman who could, after her pattern was fathomed, be returned to shore without an unpleasant aftermath while his ship of conquest sailed on to another port.

And so it was necessary for him to have his own yacht. Of course, it would have to be romantic, a sailboat, with practical auxiliary diesel engines. There would have to be a master cabin with a large bed, dressing room elegancies to befit a queen, and, above all, crews' quarters away from the private lives of owner and guests.

He found the *Zahma*, a gaff-rigged schooner. He docked her in San Pedro, and as often as possible dropped anchor at Catalina Island in Cat Harbor, away from the Boy Scouts and merchants who chose the east side of the little strip of peninsula at Emerald Bay for their rendezvous.

Olsen, his captain, was a taciturn Swede. He picked up a crew—one Italian, two Mexicans, one Irish boy, and the customary Chinese cook, all trained not to speak unless spoken to. The *Zahma* became Jeffrey's spiritual home. Here, he could make love privately or be alone, read, study scripts, and indulge in the gaieties of drinking and the athletic euphoria of getting in shape after a bout and preparing himself to once more admire the reclaimed beauty of his person. There was something of the phoenix in Jeffrey—he relished rising anew out of the disasters of his debauches.

Occasionally, like any luminary, he was forced to

attend festivities connected with the motion-picture world.

One such affair, which even Seymour Sewell said was a necessity, was a party at the Moses house. Simon and his family had moved into a stucco colonnaded house on upper Hollywood Boulevard, complete with indoor pool, tennis courts, and a grand solarium filled with marble statuary and ferns, interspersed with wicker furniture.

Ignoring New York banking dignitaries, Jeffrey wandered toward Moses' two pretty daughters. Martha detached herself from the side of Punch Weston, whom Jeffrey considered a dimple-chinned vulgarian, and talked to him about theater, but Jeffrey, expert at such matters, saw that she was talking with her profile turned and her voice a little loud, for Weston's benefit. Jeffrey's hackles rose. He was used to women who used their wiles on him to prove their worth to another man.

He cut her short and moved to the other daughter. She was different. There was a softness about her, her fair hair clustered in ringlets against the cameo sharpness of her profile. Her blue eyes seemed to hold a warm innocence, and she neither beguiled nor rejected, but spoke to him as one person to another.

"Do you really like it here, Mr. Barstow?" Esther said. "I should think you'd be much happier in New York or London. I get so tired of listening to shoptalk. Sometimes I feel I'm bound hand and foot in strips of celluloid."

He was amused.

"Then you're not such a golden princess as I've heard."

"Mr. Barstow," said Esther, "how can a Jewish girl be a golden princess in Los Angeles society?"

He was enchanted.

"No doubt as a young matron you'll run the town. Just wait. Of course, with my maverick family, my background is so scrambled that I am most fortunate. I don't have social pretensions at all."

Esther flushed.

"I beg your pardon," she said, "I may not have made myself clear. I don't have social pretensions either. It's just that I think maybe I was happier playing the piano at the Little Diamond Theater in the East Bronx."

"Well, obviously you are not spending your time well," he said. "You need a few lessons, my dear, in being a free soul. Why don't you come down to San Pedro on Sunday, and I'll take you sailing on my *Zahma.* She is lovely and sleek and poetry on the sea. Like you, she's a lady."

"It would be daring," she said.

She neither bridled nor denied, but stood thinking it over.

"I'd be honored," he smiled. "Tea, and I mean tea."

"How would I ever find it?"

He fished in his pocket and brought out a printed card, with waterfront directions to the *Zahma*'s dock, among the commercial fishing boats.

"Always prepared," he said. "I think three o'clock would be perfect, if it is for you. I can't make it earlier because I have to be in town for a meeting with my agent."

"I really don't know," she said, "and don't expect me if I'm not there at three. But thank you, and I'm glad we met at last. Excuse me, I have to talk to my Uncle Abe. He's just in from New York."

She tucked the card into the cuff of her blouse and moved over to a group with her mother and Fergus, greeting her Uncle Abe with a kiss.

Jeffrey looked after her, a bit piqued at her abrupt departure. She was not sophisticated enough to be leading him on, so she intrigued him. He saw the baldish head of Seymour Sewell, happily launched on anecdotes and his fifth bourbon. He joined him.

"Let's spin out of here," Jeffrey said. "I've done my duty."

"Well," said Fergus to Esther, "you didn't waste much time on Jeffrey Barstow. I was watching every move."

Esther put her hand on his arm.

"Jealous, I hope. What are you doing Sunday?" she said. "Would you like to go sailing?"

"Don't make me laugh," said Fergus. "With these vested interests here? Why do you think your father had to invite me to this party? I have to finish our production breakdown on the last six months. Wall Street's our overseer now, honey, didn't you know, and they've got out the bullwhip. Your father isn't handing out bootlegged French champagne for nothing. The only way we can control our production is through exhibition. And we're starting our own theater chain. It's sink or swim, Esther."

"Look," said Esther, "I merely asked you if you'd like to go sailing, not the whole history of Titan Films."

◆◆◆◆◆◆◆◆

Sunday at half-past three Esther appeared on the dock. Jeffrey, sitting in his favorite perch on the fantail with a rum collins in hand, pretended not to have expected her. He peered down at her, his sunglasses low on the bridge of his nose, as if he were trying to recall her to mind. Then he gave her his dazzling smile.

She wore a white pleated skirt and a sweater to match. Her hair was tied back in a blue ribbon. She paused to look at the *Zahma*'s sleek hull, taken by the beauty of it.

Jeffrey watched her. She was different from most of the other women who boarded in a mincing way. It might as well be a hotel room for all of them.

"Well," he said, "I gave you up."

"I was so disgracefully early," she said, smiling up at him, "that I drove all along the waterfront, and now I'm disgracefully late."

"Come aboard," he said. "I disgracefully let the crew go, but let's have tea."

She swung up the landing ladder and paused to feel the polish of the varnished handrail.

"I'll bring our tea on deck," he said. "There's always a kettle aboilin' on the stove."

He returned so quickly that she knew the tea tray had been set up ahead of time.

He set the tray on a wicker table.

"Perform the ceremony," he said, "while I fetch the rum."

She poured the tea, admiring the pewter and china and the delicate array of sandwiches and cakes. He returned with a squat crystal captain's decanter.

"If you keep house like this," she said, "I pity any woman who gets mixed up with you."

"Oh, no," he said, "I'm really a great slob. But my slave-driving captain's a Swede, my Chinese cook likes to show off, and this craft is as near Nirvana as I may ever attain in life."

"I like this," she said. "My father's yacht isn't so—so sleek and functional somehow. My sister and I take our crowd out—but you know he uses it a lot—privately!"

He saw her flush.

"Yes," he said, "I know—we all know it, so why pretend. Rum?"

"I don't think so," she said.

"The afternoon becomes chilly," he said, flashing his famous sidelong glance at her. "Perhaps it would be better if you joined me in a tot."

"If you insist," she said.

He poured a measure, and then another, and they settled down, drinking slowly.

It crossed his mind that if he became involved with

her, it would also include the responsibility of facing Simon Moses. But since her father was in so deep with his sister, there would be little he could do about it.

He touched her shoulder.

"Why don't we go below? It's getting cold."

A brisk wind was moving in from the sea, and a heavy pall of gray was scudding overhead.

He seated her on a comfortable lounge in front of a glowing Franklin stove. The salon was warm with mahogany bookcases, lined with colorful books. A few Currier and Ives seascapes lined the walls, and the brass lamps and portholes shone richly in the dusk.

"It's glorious," she said.

He stood watching her a moment, enjoying her fresh beauty.

This may be deeper than it looks, he thought. There was something delicious about warming up a cool woman.

"Forgive me a moment," he said.

He stepped into the master cabin, threw back the coverlets on the carved Venetian bed, exposing silk sheets. He discarded his clothes, putting them in a locker.

He glanced at himself in a full-length mirror bolted to the wall. He approved. He was in his prime, and as always under such conditions, ready for action.

He walked naked into the salon. She sat, her profile against the dark background, hardly seeming to realize he had returned. As he waited, commanding her to find him, it seemed to him an infinity. Slowly she turned and her eyes kindled as she looked at his naked body, his penis enlarged and erect.

As he came toward her, she slowly stood and looked not at his naked body, but at his face. This excited him.

"Mr. Barstow—" she said.

"Ah, my dear," he said in a low voice, "one does not

address an amorous and naked man by his surname. Jeffrey would be better."

"Mr. Barstow," she insisted, "I'm afraid you've made a terrible mistake."

She moved away from him, stepped lightly up the stairs, and opened the door, slamming it after her.

He heard her footsteps on deck and on the landing ladder, and then along the dock. He heard her start her sports car and speed away, gears shifting.

He could not believe it. Such a thing had never happened to him.

He sat down, his buttocks cold on the leather sofa. He finished the bottle of rum and sat until twilight became dark.

He took a fresh bottle on the way to his stateroom where he fell into bed, realizing for the first time that he was more than halfway through life, and it might be a downhill road a great deal of the rest of the way.

He lit a silk-shaded light and examined himself in the mirror. His body looked all right to him. There might be a bit of paunch. He pulled it in and lifted his chin slightly, so the Barstow profile in all its beauty seemed flawless again.

What in hell was wrong with her?

He settled into the bed, drinking straight from the bottle.

◆◆◆◆◆◆◆◆

Fergus's secretary, Harriet Foster, rushed into his office. She was pale and her hands were up to her face.

"Oh, Mr. Austin!" she cried, her voice quivering.

"For God's sake, Harriet," he said, "calm down. What is it?"

"It's Martha Moses," she said. "She's dead."

"What!" said Fergus. "What the hell are you talking about?"

"Captain Wheeler on the yacht called from Long Beach. She's dead in her cabin."

"Oh, my God! Did they call the police?"

"I don't know. Shall I get him back, or call Mr. Moses?"

"Get Captain Wheeler," said Fergus, "on this phone. *Don't* call Mr. Moses."

He talked to the captain and listened, then he called Dr. Wolfrum in the infirmary.

Fergus and Wolfrum ran down the dock in the hot morning. The *Gypsy* was shuttered tight. The frightened face of Captain Wheeler peered out. He let them aboard and gestured toward Martha's cabin as they hurried down the corridor.

"Nobody's aboard, not even my wife. Nobody knows. Miss Martha came aboard last night," he said, "and just said she was tired and wanted to rest, that someone might join her later. But he didn't."

"Who?" asked Fergus.

The captain glanced away.

"Listen," said Fergus, "we know who it is. They've been here together before, haven't they?"

Wheeler nodded. "That cowboy star. Punch Weston. Anyway, he didn't show up. I waited until after ten this morning and knocked on her door. There was no answer, and it was locked from the inside. I had to push the key out and use a duplicate. Oh, God!"

Fergus peered in, and the horror of the room sickened him. Martha lay naked on the bed. By her side a knitting needle. She had tried to abort herself. Her body and the bed were red with blood. Her swelling stomach was white against the gore.

"My Gott! She must have been five months pregnant. Why didn't anyone notice!" said Wolfrum. He drew the bloody sheets up over her. "Poor liebchen, why didn't she come to me?"

Fergus looked at the shrouded figure, thinking of his trip across the country with Claudia. That same sour smell of blood hit him, and he recalled his fear.

"What are we going to do?" said Wolfrum.

"We're going to call Mr. Moses," said Fergus. "We'll pick him up by dinghy at the Venice pier, and we'll head for Catalina."

"Catalina!" said Wheeler. "I can't do that without informing the police."

"You'll do no such thing," said Fergus. "Dr. Wolfrum is here. Miss Moses is not well, and he prescribes some sea air."

Wolfrum, white with terror, shook his head. "Don't get me involved with this."

Fergus turned on him.

"Since when," he said. "Listen, you butcher, we protected you with a fake Swiss citizenship during the war, we bought your criminal record in the Reeperbahn, and you'll damn well sign the death certificate as we choose."

Simon was picked up in a dinghy off the Venice pier and Fergus took him to the cabin without a word.

He pulled back the sheets, and Simon let out a cry of anguish.

"That's enough," said Fergus. "For five months you didn't bother to look at her. So shape up. Now, go sit in the salon. Doc, give him a sedative, and we'll talk later."

Wolfrum took Simon's arm and led him to the salon. He sat, the effects of the drug gradually taking hold, looking blindly out of the porthole as they moved in an uncomfortable chop past the fourteen-mile bank toward the rough waters to the far side of Catalina.

Past Church Rock they moved southwest. It was a cold, windy morning. The sheet-covered, trussed-up body of Martha, heavily weighted, slid with a small plop into the sea. Simon stood weeping, as the waters closed over his daughter's body.

There was not a ship nor small craft in sight. A flock of scavenging gulls and a prowling pelican skimming the waves on his eternal search for food were the only witnesses.

A mile farther out, the bloody mattress and sheets, also heavily weighted, were jettisoned.

Later the captain ran up the owner's flag. Martha Moses and her father were logged aboard.

Wolfrum and Fergus signed the log dated the previous day.

The yacht was moored off Emerald Bay in the cover of darkness. In the morning, a report was made, twenty-four hours late, of Martha's disappearance. The captain had put a spare mattress and bedclothes in her cabin, the bed was rumpled, and her possessions were left near her bunk, a book of poems face down on the bunk, as if she had casually risen.

The Coast Guard clipper came alongside. In respect for Mr. Moses' grief, and because he was under sedation, the authorities questioned Dr. Wolfrum, whose distress at the loss of such a lovely young girl, whom he had known for years, was respected.

"Miss Moses had been complaining of a migraine," he said sadly. "I prescribed a sleeping pill and left two by her bedside. Undoubtedly in pain, she took one, as one was left, as you can see."

He gestured toward the bedside table, where the pill had been set next to her slim gold wristwatch, and shook his head.

"She must have gone topside for a breath of air," said Fergus, standing in the corridor, "and lost her balance and fallen overboard. If only her sister had been here—they were very close, always shared the same cabin—I'm sure it wouldn't have happened. But unfortunately Esther and Mrs. Moses had to stay in town for a charity event."

The Coast Guard lieutenant arranged for Wolfrum to take a speedboat to the mainland and break the news to Esther and Rebecca before the *Gypsy* returned to its berth.

Fergus thanked the lieutenant and gave him several bottles of cognac.

"Please let us know immediately if there's any news," Fergus said, sincerely, as he shook the young man's hand.

As the cutter left, he breathed a sigh that no one had noticed they were short of crew. Likely they thought the crew was below. Anyway, he could help the captain moor, as he had helped cast off.

And it was a good thing he was aboard, to steer Simon Moses through any ordeal ahead.

◆◆◆◆◆◆◆◆

There on the mainland slip were Clarissa Pennock, dean of women movie columnists, in her usual flowered hat, and a sharp, elegant young entertainment reporter, Andrew Reed, out from New York. A photographer stood by. Fergus knew he was up against the pros. He turned to Simon, who stood at the salon doors, unsteady, but still on his feet.

"Take it easy, Mr. Moses, and stay here," he said. "I'll take care of them."

How, he had no idea.

He walked down the boarding ladder and shook hands with Clarissa Pennock. Her eyes widened.

"Well, Fergus," she said, "this is just too, too terrible. I just felt I had to be here personally to convey my sympathies."

Fergus put his hand on her arm.

"Miss Pennock, it's like you to be so kind to this wonderful family. You know how we all feel about them."

He felt Andrew Reed's sour glance and turned to shake his hand, too.

"Thank you both for coming," he said. "Mr. Reed, I'm glad a man of your caliber is here, too."

"Stop the bullshit, Austin," said Andrew. "I smell a story, even out here in the fresh air."

"Andy!" said Clarissa Pennock. "Really, at a time like this! Now Fergus, tell us all about it."

"There's nothing to say now," said Fergus. "The Coast Guard is searching for her body. We pray they find it."

Oh, Christ . . . if they find it!

"Where and when did it happen?" asked Andrew. "Wasn't there any other yacht nearby?"

"None, unfortunately," said Fergus.

If one boat had spotted the *Gypsy* coming in from the other side of the island!

"I've got to get Mr. Moses home to his family," he said. "You'll have to excuse us under this tragic circumstance. He is in a state of shock. You know—especially after losing his son in the war."

Andrew blinked. This ploy made it a bit difficult for him to take a rude offensive. However . . .

Fergus turned to Clarissa Pennock.

"Miss Pennock," he said, "I'll see that you get to talk to Mr. Moses as soon as possible. You know how they feel about you. I can assure you, he'll be grateful in *every* way."

She smiled brightly. This was a rich promise. Simon Moses was becoming a powerful man.

"Of course, dear boy," she said, "and you might as well call me Clarissa. The rest of Hollywood does. Give my love to dear Mr. Moses."

He walked her to her old Pierce Arrow open touring car. The black driver in black alpaca livery was sweating it out in the heat.

"Poor Paul," she said, smiling brightly at Fergus, "I do wish I could afford a limousine so he could be more comfortable. But you know how expenses are on a poor newswoman's salary."

Fergus handed her in, figuring how much a new car was going to cost Titan. She waved, and the car pulled away.

He saw Andrew trying to peer through portholes of the yacht and was glad he had thought to close the interior curtains before they docked. But he was anxious to get Andrew Reed away, and he moved quickly, standing between Andrew and the yacht.

"Now," said Andrew, "was lover boy aboard?"

"What are you talking about?" said Fergus.

"You know. The cowboy. Punch Weston. Everybody knows she was meeting him at his cabin in Laurel Canyon."

"Ridiculous," said Fergus. "She happened to be going around with a very nice young cutter at Titan, a kid named Horace Ingram."

"Don't ask me to believe that bushwa," said Andrew. "I've met him around *my* set in town. However, I'll respect your privacy for now. By the way, I have a young friend, handsome chap, did very well in the theater in New York—everyone says he's one of the best-looking young men in America. He should be in pictures. I'd appreciate it if you'd take a look at him. Titan should sign him up. He happens to be in town at the moment."

Fergus looked at him and was outstared.

"Tomorrow," said Andrew. It was not a question.

"I'll see to it," said Fergus.

"Leslie Charles is his name," said Andrew. He gestured to the photographer to leave with him.

In the week that followed, Punch Weston abruptly left town. He was dropped from the star roster at Titan, owing to health problems, the press was informed. Titan took a half-million-dollar loss on their spectacular new western. Weston retired to the healthy reaches of his ranch with his Mexican wife and three children.

Simon Moses was known to turn more and more of the operation of Titan Films over to his brilliant young supervising director, Fergus Austin.

Clarissa Pennock was given exclusive news on Titan stars and properties, and, on the strength and the prestige it gave her, she became a widely syndicated columnist. She rode about Hollywood in a new custom-built Rolls Royce. The car had been given her, she said, by a secret admirer.

Leslie Charles was added to the acting roster of Titan. He was a slender, sensitive young man with theatrical experience. He had an elegance that pictures needed; there was an innuendo, suggested by the publicity department, that people like Punch Weston were too crude for the growing sophistication that films were giving to the people of America.

5

◆◆◆◆◆◆◆◆

The bitterest day of Simon Moses' life was the day he gave his daughter Esther in marriage to Fergus Austin.

Because of the tragedies in the family, it was a quiet wedding. It was held in the morning, amidst the camellias and bougainvillea of the Moses garden.

Fergus's father had passed out in a snowdrift and died of pneumonia the preceding winter, and it seemed propitious to bring his mother out to the Coast for the wedding. She sold the boardinghouse and planned to remain in California.

For the wedding, she was dressed in the best that money and a discerning wardrobe woman could buy.

Esther, as pretty as she was, was not the one Mrs. Austin would have chosen for her son. The fact that Mayor Woodman performed the ceremony was lost on her. She grieved that a priest was not performing the sacraments.

At the same time, Rebecca and Simon Moses were wishing that a rabbi was promising their nice Jewish girl eternal blessings with a fine Jewish groom, at Temple B'nai B'rith.

The young couple left for Santa Barbara in their new Cadillac V8 touring car.

"We'd better take Mrs. Austin back to the hotel,"

said Rebecca. "Remember, Simon, she's lonesome, too."

"The hell with her," said Simon. "She's caused me enough trouble by whelping Fergus Austin."

"Now, Simon," said Rebecca, "we only have one child, and she's always been crazy about him. Let him be."

So Simon, Rebecca, and Mary Frances pulled up to the Hollywood Hotel in their Packard limousine.

"I'll take you for a nice ride to Pasadena this weekend," said Rebecca. "Meanwhile, you get settled, dear."

The chauffeur opened the door.

Simon looked toward the lobby doors and sat, paralyzed.

Out of the door came Claudia and Jeffrey Barstow with several friends. They were laughing and had obviously been drinking.

"Well, anyway," screamed Claudia to her brother, "this is one wedding gift I won't have to buy. I wasn't asked, naturally. I could have given away the groom, though. Actually, he's not bad in bed."

"You could give me the bride and I wouldn't complain," said Jeffrey. "She was on my yacht once."

As they laughed, they both saw the limousine—Rebecca, eyes wide; Simon, frozen in motion; and Mary Frances Austin, enthusiastically thanking them for a lovely time. The moment passed. Claudia and Jeffrey got into the Stutz Bearcat and sped away, the brass gas tank flashing in the sun.

Simon sank back into the dove-colored upholstery of the limousine. The car pulled out, heading west on Hollywood Boulevard.

He felt as if he were riding in a coffin. He was crucified after all he had given Claudia all these years. He could never be finished with her, not only in his heart, but in business. Those bastard Barstows were the keystone to his fortune. He hated while he loved, and his hatred turned again on Fergus.

He glanced at Rebecca. Her face was almost as white as her hair.

"Oh, Becky!" he said.

She put out her hand.

"It's all right, Simon," she said. "Now maybe you know."

Know what, he thought. She's known all along. There aren't secrets in this town. What has she heard that I don't know? He swallowed and looked out the window, holding her hand so that her fingers hurt, even with gloves on them.

In the few blocks to his house he thought of his bright son, David; of his winsome daughter, Martha; and of his beautiful daughter, Esther, the only one left. He had delivered her into the arms of his enemy.

⬩⬩⬩⬩⬩⬩⬩⬩

Claudia sat in a speakeasy off Sunset Boulevard with her brother. She was crying.

"Oh, God," she said, "somebody should put me on a leash and lock me up when I've been drinking. What have I done to Si! He'll never forgive me!"

"My dear," said Jeffrey, pouring himself a drink from the table bottle, "you are a member of the Barstow clan. Nobody forgives us. We forgive them. What does he expect you to do when he's not around? After all, this isn't the Victorian age, it's almost 1920! We're modern. You're a vital, attractive young woman. You should have been at Fergus's wedding. After all, you saved his skin, and vice versa, a thousand times."

"Under the conditions, it would be impossible for me to be in the Moses house." She blew her nose.

"You seem to be coming down with a cold," said Jeffrey. "I prescribe another large shot of whiskey."

"Right," said Claudia.

He poured it.

"It's so lonesome sometimes, Jeff. It began when

David died. First it was shivah. For a week, Si told me, they cover all the mirrors, sit on the floor or hard benches, and friends and relatives fill the house with their mourning. And then the next year it was poor little Martha. And they went through it all again. The only time I could be with him was at the little casita at the Guadalupe ranch, and then only when he was supposed to be working. He tried to make it up with gifts and affection. My God, I've got half of Brock's jewelry in a safe-deposit box. But it turned him off as a man with me. Guilt, you know. But he's been good to me, Jeff, and he's the only one who really ever cared. In my way I love him more than I thought I'd ever love anyone."

"That matters," said Jeffrey, sighing. "It doesn't come often in life. Sex is as close as the nearest bar-stool. But love—"

Claudia continued, losing herself in her own problem.

"The Moses family's always having those depressing religious ceremonials. Even when they're celebrating, they do weird things like tasting bitter food and sitting on a matzo. And they all cling together like ants."

"Don't forget our own family," said Jeffrey. "The Catholics do pretty good on holidays, too. That's what you get for mixing with a Jew. They beat us hollow on religious festivals. You should have picked on a nice Protestant man. All they celebrate is Christmas, Thanksgiving, and a sort of half-assed Easter."

"Oh, shut up," said Claudia. "Don't try to cheer me up with your sillies. Just let me suffer. I deserve it."

"So suffer," said Jeffrey, "but in that case I'm getting my ass out of here. I have an appointment with a most enticing young lady who is anxious to suffer in another way. Come on, I'll take you home where you can fall down in comfort. Besides, it's very incestuous to get drunk with your sister."

"What a comfort *you* are!" said Claudia haughtily. "Oh, how could I have done that to that dear man!"

"He'll get over it," said Jeffrey. "They always do when you rub against them. But Fergus, good God, what you've done to him!"

He winced.

"Poor Fergus," said Claudia. "And now I won't even have him anymore."

"You need a new cast of characters," said Jeffrey as he helped her out.

◆◆◆◆◆◆◆◆

Right off Hollywood Boulevard on Laurel Avenue, a roomy bungalow nestled among eucalyptus trees and a lush California garden.

It was perfect for the newlyweds. Esther decorated the spacious rooms with English furniture, crystal chandeliers, and bright chintzes. A tennis court was built, and the long veranda at the back was furnished with comfortable wicker furniture.

An expert Viennese cook took over the kitchen; a Polish maid did the cleaning and waited on table; a Japanese chauffeur took care of the three cars and butlered at parties.

Esther was inundated with all the linens her Belgian laundress could care for. Crystal, china, and silver poured in as tribute to the Titan heiress.

Esther settled her house, arranged for the usual Sunday parties for studio people, called on her many new friends, and learned to call her husband at required hours. She would meet girl friends for lunch, shop or have her hair done, take a tennis or golf lesson, and return home for a nap, a tub, and change of clothes. She found time heavy on her hands. It was hours before Fergus came home. It was not a good time to call other people. Dutifully, she would wait until seven o'clock, and then call Fergus's executive secretary—homely, enthusiastic Harriet Foster, who was her pipeline.

Usually Harriet would give her the day's rundown;

all the petty production problems were of vast importance in Miss Foster's mind. Fergus was usually in conference, in a projection room, or meeting with some department head; he would get back to her. He would call, long after the irate cook had announced a ruined meal. He would be home soon. Something had come up. Would she be patient and have one little drink; he'd get there when he could.

Esther would take a little drink. Then another. Then thumb through a magazine or try to read a book. Then take another little drink. She was ashamed to call her mother or friends and admit that Fergus wasn't home.

In desperation, she suggested a projection room be built on one wing. It could have all the best equipment. Fergus explained that it would be fine to look at the product of other studios, to see what was going on, maybe weekends, but he couldn't bring cutters, unassembled film, or department people into the house. Most of his work must be done at the studio.

Often he came home to find her petulant, under the depressing influence of too many drinks, or languorously sexual, wearing an elegant hostess gown and wondering why he didn't immediately fall into her arms, for she had been thinking of him amorously all afternoon.

"Honey," he'd say, kissing her, "I can't come home from a hard-hitting business office smack-dab into a harem. You look gorgeous, but just give me a moment to simmer down and have a drink."

But by the time that happened, some studio crisis would likely break their mood. When they did take a few hours off, urgent phone calls would come, and any hope she had for their intimacy was shattered. Sometimes she had to dig her nails into her palms to keep from ripping the telephone line out of the wall. She smothered her anger, but it smoldered in her.

Fergus was not the ardent lover she had dreamed he would be. She was beginning to realize that his super executive personality could not allow him to commit himself to a sustaining romantic relationship with a woman. His career was too absorbing to spend time on courtship as she had expected. He accepted her sweetly when she was sweet, testily when she was testy, performed his conjugal rights, and moved on to business affairs as if a switch had been turned on or off.

Her next thought was to have a child. It would be none of his affair. Something of her own to love. If it were a boy, she'd name him David, after her dead brother, and that would make her mother and father happy. But each month she was disappointed, and she wondered if the tensions and disillusions she was facing had kept her from the pregnancy she wanted.

One July evening Fergus came home and put his arms around her as she met him at the door.

"I have good news for you, honey," he said. "We're going on location to Arrowhead Springs tomorrow. We're staying at the hotel, and you're going. Won't that be great? We'll mix business and pleasure for a while."

"That's wonderful!" she said. "I won't get in your way, I'll take loads of books and riding clothes, and I can take those steam baths—"

"Hold it down!" he said. "We're not going to settle there, sweetheart, it's only for four days, and there's always something to do. Pack my riding clothes, too."

"Who's going?"

"Well, Plimpton, a camera crew of course, wardrobe people, the still man, Jeffrey Barstow and Claudia, about four actors, six extras, and some wranglers. We're doing *The Reapers*, that western novel. It's a perfect property for the Barstows. They're going to be stupendous. You know, post-Civil War in the West."

"Spare me the plot," said Esther. "I'll pack. What time do we leave?"

"I'll leave around five in the morning," he said, "in the studio car with Plimpy. You follow in the touring car with Hori driving, I don't want you to take that mountain road yourself. You'll get up there in time for dinner—with me!"

She threw her arms about him and kissed him.

"Now," he said, "let's have a bite. I have to bear down on that script and talk to the writer on the phone after dinner."

She packed. A few days away even with the company might have the excitement of a holiday. After all, he didn't have to take her; he wanted to.

In the morning it was raining. Fergus was long gone, but she closed the suitcases and happily saw the rain turn to drizzle, and the drizzle fade. She walked into the garden in a burst of sunshine. The roses were awash with moisture. She picked a few to take along as a sentimental token. Their sweet scent would be lovely in the hotel room.

She rearranged her hairdress, a coronet of curls tied up with little white ribbons, and put on a fleecy white coat over her silk dress.

She added her rain cape and an umbrella and boots for security, but the weather turned so fair as they started out that she didn't even have Hori put up the side curtains of the car.

Near Riverside, a stinging wind began to blow. Hori parked.

"We have to put up curtains, Mrs. Austin, and this wind so bad, it may mark up paint."

"Oh, who cares!" she said. "It's so beautiful out!"

She stepped out of the car. Rows of vines stretched toward the purpling foothills and snowcapped San Jacinto. The whole earth smelled of the perfume of living things. What a beautiful land; a land of promise. Nearby was an adobe building. She walked toward it and saw that it belonged to the vineyard. A shy Italian woman greeted her and sold her a bottle of red wine.

She bought it happily. She and Fergus would drink it together, maybe in bed. She had heard of the exciting practice of taking cold wine in your mouth and kissing your lover, pressing the wine with kisses into his warm mouth. That would be something that would surprise Fergus.

She got in the back seat, settling back for the trip into San Bernardino, and the short climb up the hill. She knew the hotel site would be marked by the ancient Indian sign on the mountain. A vast earth-barren arrowhead had been made in some mysterious way by the Indians, long dead, who, it was rumored, had poisoned the earth, destroying any foliage. Thus the giant symbol could forever be seen, pointing to a medicinal spring.

When they passed the outskirts of the town, a blasting rain began. Hori maneuvered the car through the slippery roads. They finally came upon a flood that undermined the road. Hori got out.

"It's no use, Mrs. Austin," he said. "We can't get by. The car is too wide."

She looked out. Even through the sheets of rain she thought she saw the immense earth-barren arrowhead against the green foliage of the steep hill. It was pointing to where Fergus would be, and she was going to get there.

"How far is it?" she asked a man who was setting up red lanterns in the washout for the approaching night.

"At least two miles, ma'am."

"Well, that's not so far," she said. "Hori, you take the car to San Bernardino and arrange to get my things in tomorrow one way or another. The company's already at the hotel. I'll walk in."

"You gonna walk in that rain?" asked the workman.

"I don't melt," she said, "And my husband's waiting for me."

She pulled on her boots, put on the silk rain cape over her coat, and carried her purse, her bottle of wine, and her bouquet of roses, all protected by the umbrella.

She felt adventurous walking into the storm armed with a flashlight.

The laborer watched her.

"She sure must like that guy," he said.

◆◆◆◆◆◆◆◆

The greatest demoralizer of motion-picture personnel on location was leisure time. Men and women had gathered in a strange environment away from home and family. They were herded into little cubicles, and their only meeting place was a bar or restaurant, unless they were allowed temporarily into the supervisor's, director's, or star's plush suite, which was only a respite that made them more dissatisfied when they got back to their own modest digs.

Unless they came armed with books or innocent diversions, they gambled, drank too much, quarreled, and as often as not, slept with someone they really didn't find particularly right for further association.

This limbo embraced *The Reaper* company as the rains continued. Word was soon out that there had been a washout down the road. Fergus was informed that his wife would be unable to get through, and the phones were temporarily out of order.

Claudia called at his suite.

"This rain is a hell of a thing," she said. "I'm going crazy, Fergus; come on, let's have a drink."

He spotted the nervous energy that triggered her when she felt boxed.

"Good," he said, "let's all have a drink and go over the script."

"What do you mean, all?" she said.

"I mean your brother. It's a good time to have a reading."

"Don't you ever think of anything but work?" she said. "My God, but you're getting dry and dull."

She gestured at the champagne bottle in a cooler on the coffee table.

"Come on, honey, I had it sent up, and you didn't even notice it. You must have opened quite a few since that first one you did for me. Remember?"

He looked at her and smiled. Seven years . . . seven years. You were supposed to change completely every seven years. He certainly had.

He opened the bottle and poured two glasses. "You're even more beautiful now."

"That's my Fergus." She held the glass to him and sipped. "We've been lucky for each other."

"We have," he said.

"I know you had to marry that schlumpf," she said.

"Now wait," said Fergus, "she's a very lovely girl. And I was always stuck on her."

"Not to too great a degree," said Claudia. "Your memory isn't that bad."

"You're a goddess," said Fergus, drinking, "and no one can help worshiping a goddess—from time to time."

"Then worship me," she said. "I feel in the mood."

"Come on, Claudia!"

"Listen," she said, pouring two more drinks, "I'm lonesome. You know Si's been out of my life since—well, since your wedding. I won't go into it. But remember when I told you at Guadalupe that you weren't robbing Simon of anything when he wasn't around. Well, the same goes for Esther. She isn't here. What's to lose? And Fergie, you know what's to gain."

The wind and the rain blew a gusty drumbeat against the window. Claudia turned off the lights. Not a word was said for a moment, then she came to him.

"This moment—Fergus—" she whispered, "this moment. A rainy evening. Just us. You know how our bodies fit together. I want you, and you do want me, don't you?"

"I do," he said.

"Right now, and here."

She dropped the gown from her shoulders and

pulled the sash. It fell in a heap on the floor. She was naked.

The desk clerk gave Esther Austin the key to her husband's suite. She turned the lock quietly, juggling her roses and wine.

She stood in the dark, watching them together on the floor, unseen.

It took a moment to register.

She slowly closed the door and stood in the sterile hall. She put the key in her purse, moved the wine bottle into the cradle of her arm, still carrying the roses, and walked along the corridor. She stopped to lean against the wall. She dropped the wine and it smashed noisily on the floor.

She stood terrified, trying not to cry, wondering where she could go.

A square of light fell against her as the door opposite was flung open.

It was Jeffrey Barstow.

"What the hell?" he said. "What was *that?*"

She didn't answer.

He saw she was in shock.

"The wine—" she said, "I broke the wine."

She began to weep soundlessly.

"Esther!" he said. "Come in."

He led her into his sitting room and took off her wet rain cape. He took the soggy flowers.

"Pretty," said Jeffrey, cocking an eyebrow, "but you really didn't have to—"

He lifted her chin and smiled at her.

"Now, it can't be that bad when you're with me. Do you want champagne, wine, scotch, bourbon, tea—rum?"

She smiled faintly, remembering.

"That's prettier," he said. "The hell with wine. You're dripping wet. That calls for brandy."

He took off her coat, sat her down, and untied her

coronet of ribbons. While she sipped brandy he took a bath towel and dried her hair.

"Look here, my dear, if it's what I think it is, you're much too lovely and desirable to let it bother you."

He flashed his blue-eyed glance.

"If you'd let me, I'd make you forget about Claudia and Fergus in five minutes. Want to bet?"

"I don't think you could," she said.

He poured more brandy.

"Now drink it fast. We wouldn't want you to get pneumonia. Why don't you let me try—"

She shook her head.

"I'll stop any time you say."

The curtains were drawn. He threw more wood on the fire and with tenderness and attention to every button and lace he slowly undressed her, caressing her, kissing her breasts, stroking the tender inside of her arms and thighs.

She never told him to stop.

He loved her gently and deeply; and when they were finished, he poured more brandy, and they stayed in front of the fire, talking. He marveled at the beauty of sensation, as it comes in the quickening moment. What a gift!

Then he caressed her again and possessed her more fiercely, now that she was ready.

She responded and was not ashamed.

"You see," he said, "the second time is to prove to you that it was not just a necessity. You are lovely, Esther, and I wanted you very much that time on my boat."

"I guess I was stupid," she said.

"Ah, no, this was the ripe time for us."

She stood up to get her clothes.

"No," he said. "You can't go. You are going to stay with me tonight. You and I will have one beautiful, uninterrupted memory, and you will go to your husband sweetly, not in anger. Because, you know, my dear, you and I have had the best of the bargain."

He made her smile.

Later he ordered a large dinner for himself, served in the sitting room. She stayed in the bedroom, and when the waiter had left they dined royally, sharing the meal, laughing at their prank.

And that night he took her to his bed. In his arms, she knew she had never been properly loved before. He waited until he felt the growing excitement moving her into joyous submission, then he moved deeply and swiftly, finally feeling the tightening pulse of her ecstasy, binding them together in a rush of fierce mutual fulfillment.

He held her tenderly and thanked her for giving him such joy. She fell asleep in his arms feeling beautiful and complete as a woman, as she never had before.

In the morning Jeffrey was gone. On her pillow was a yellow rose and a little note on a piece of hotel stationery: "Thank you forever, J.B."

No one seemed interested in the fact that Esther had spent an evening and a night away from her room. The desk clerk had given her the key and expected she was with her husband.

Fergus was so occupied that when she appeared at noon and said she had just walked in over the road, no questions were asked.

She had a brandy hangover, she felt chilled, and guilt hung on her. But when she looked at Fergus and thought of him rolling on the floor, naked on top of Claudia, her guilt fled.

She was relieved to discover that she had a fever. She stayed in the bedroom, and Fergus had a bed set up in the sitting room, so she avoided him. The road was repaired, and she went back to town in a studio car before the company left, for their schedule was delayed by the intermittent rain.

All the way home she kept taking the little note out of her purse. If it had not existed, she would have wondered that she had been given such an experience, but she smiled as she put it away.

At home she avoided Fergus, saying it would be terrible for him to catch cold during this expensive picture, there was so much at stake.

Titan had taken a terrible drubbing in not releasing Punch Weston's half-finished western after Martha's death. Claudia's second war picture had been a dud, because of armistice, and the lifeblood of Moses' money was going into glossy picture palaces, essential for showing the Titan product. Block booking was also the only way to get rid of some of the slighter pictures that were ground out to keep the stages busy and the overhead in line.

Esther discovered she was pregnant. At first she was panicked, then she thought Jeffrey Barstow would be a wonderful man to father a child, so long as it did not have to be reared by him. He was intelligent, and the famed Barstow beauty and charm would be a great heritage. Also, she was not ashamed, for they had loved each other that brief night.

As she thought of Claudia and her father, and Claudia and Fergus, it became a bitter joke, which she clung to in the growing dislike she had for Fergus. But she knew she had to lure him into her bed once, to make certain he could never suspect that the child was not his.

She prepared his scotch and soda with a heavy hand when he came home one evening, and she dressed in a silk hostess gown.

After his favorite dinner, she told him some amusing tales she'd heard about town. She was so lighthearted and such a gay companion that he relaxed, and after a brandy and soda he went to bed with her and performed the duty that would put her at ease the next few months. As he lay with her, she could not help but compare his swift selfishness with the tender, encompassing love Jeffrey had given her, out of the joy of their bodies and the imagination of his poetic, passionate mind.

Her mother and father were delighted with the pregnancy, and Aunt Yetta and Mary Frances Austin both started to crochet monstrosities.

Fergus accepted her pregnancy as a natural conclusion of their marriage. And they drifted further apart.

It wasn't that he was cruel, or that he deserted her. He was there in body at night, tired and nervous, grinding his teeth until a dentist had to relocate his bite. He was up at dawn if he had a picture shooting, and he read late into the night when he was preparing.

Because of his hours, Esther told him they would be better off with separate bedrooms. His irregular habits raised hob with the servants who all had to be highly overpaid. They added a night butler to the staff and built a steam table in the kitchen which kept food ready at any hour.

Once Fergus came in late, took his dinner out, and began to thank it, laughingly saying it was much more understanding than his wife, who had been sleeping for hours and rarely seemed to know, or care, whether he was in the house or not. Well, he mused, perhaps that was what pregnancy did to a woman; attention to the fetus rather than the former lover was dominant. He smiled wryly, for once he had been irked at Esther's constant, amorous attentions. Now he missed at least the comfort of candelight and food served on fine china. He made up his mind to eat more often at Kathleen's new tavern. At least a smiling face would always greet him.

A new wing was added to the house, with a nursery upstairs and an office downstairs. Phones rang from various key theaters throughout the country at any hour of the day or night. Fergus had to know comparative grosses by the hour, and his mood was dictated by the messages he received.

Esther vowed she was not going to have her child exposed to these midnight interruptions. They would just have to work out a way to divide their lives from this encroaching monster of business.

She tried to come to grips with herself as she lay in the night, feeling Jeffrey's child growing in her. The bitter joke that she and her mother had both been crucified by Claudia Barstow made her long, heavy hours lighter. Oh, if all the people who had known about Claudia and Fergus could only know that the handsome, talented Jeffrey Barstow was the father of her child! That would pale any of the standard, overt actions of Fergus and that bitch! Sometime, somehow, she would tell someone. She had to do it, it was such a classically funny situation.

She thought about Jeffrey constantly, maneuvered conversations to what he was doing, and, when she was in beauty parlors, snatched up the growing piles of popular movie magazines. Sometimes when she saw his picture with beautiful women, she became depressed. Then she had to argue with herself that she had no right to be jealous. It had only been a fling, and thank God no one knew how she felt. And she should be guilty about this child she carried in her.

One day toward the end of her pregnancy she was taking a late afternoon walk along lower Laurel Canyon. She plucked a sprig of honeysuckle, enjoying its fragrance.

A familiar Stutz Bearcat pulled up. Her heart beat fast.

For a moment Jeffrey stood staring at her. The sun painted her complexion like an apricot and gilded the tendrils of hair over each ear. He took her hand, kissed it, and took the honeysuckle spray from her.

Esther looked down, flushing.

"Lovely Esther," he said, in that unforgettable Barstow voice, which even now sounded like a caress, "please look at me."

He had given her a glance of such affection that it

stunned her. Gazing on his handsomeness and remembering, she felt at peace with him. She smiled.

"I love you, too," he said. "Oh, Esther, where can we meet? How can I see you?"

"It's useless," she said.

"Sometime. Somehow!"

Several cars passed. It was impossible for them to continue standing there.

Jeffrey put his hand out and gently touched her stomach. There was a question in his eyes. She nodded and smiled at him, trying not to let the tears fill her eyes, for she wanted to see the look of growing wonder and joy on his face.

"Yes—" she said, "and thank you, Jeffrey."

He swallowed, for a moment unable to speak. Then he whispered, "I am very proud."

He looked at her, not moving, as if he were memorizing the moment. He inhaled the fragrance of the honeysuckle and stepped into his car and was gone.

◆◆◆◆◆◆◆◆

When Esther held her son in her arms and looked upon his face, she was lost to the flowers that filled her room. She longed to tell Jeffrey, but it was impossible. And her heart was wrenched when she received a large basket of white orchids, an incongruous little pot of honeysuckle and a note tucked in it: "I share your happiness. J.B."

She hid the note under her pillow and eventually put it away with the note he had scribbled the one glorious night they had together. She longed for him and had the nurse bring her all the movie magazines she could get. When no one was around, she looked at his pictures, and once when the baby was brought in, and the nurse left, she held a picture up to him and whispered.

"There he is. There is your father. Isn't he beautiful!"

She wished she could have named the baby Jeffrey, but that, too, was impossible.

She quickly hid the magazine as the door swung for visitors. It was the two happy grandmothers, Rebecca and Mary Frances, each aglow that Esther had presented a son to the family.

"I just love girls," said Mrs. Austin, "but I'm so glad the first one is a boy."

"What are you going to call him?" said Rebecca.

"Mother," said Esther, "we've gone over it a dozen times. You know there's no name for him but David."

Rebecca wept.

"My Davie would have liked that," she said, dabbing at her eyes.

"Only if you won't cry," said Esther. "I can't have the waterworks every time you call your grandson, now, can I?"

"I'm sorry," said Rebecca. "I'll try."

She touched the swaddling blanket. "I think he looks like his Uncle David," she said.

"Nonsense," said Esther, "he looks like a very red, new baby. And I love him."

The grandmothers weren't even allowed to touch him with gloves on. So they sat in straight-backed chairs and oohed and ahed about the flowers, and Esther was only sorry she couldn't have a drink because she was going to nurse her son.

At home, Fergus saw the baby on Sundays and sometimes looked in early in the morning before he went to the studio. He occasionally promised Esther that they were going to have lots of fun with David when he was older—trips, hunting, fishing, and swimming—but Esther knew it was a pipe dream, like the ones they had once had of going to Europe or taking a motor trip up the coast to Canada. It just wouldn't happen.

After the baby was installed comfortably with the English nanny, and Esther had stopped nursing him because the doctor said she was too nervous, she settled into a postpartum depression.

She felt she had nothing to do in life. Experts seemed to do everything better than she could. Her social position was difficult, for Fergus rarely went out, save on affairs of business protocol. She was a wife who rarely saw her husband, yet she had to bear her loneliness secretly because of her pride. Her parents were no help. Her father spent most of his time shuttling back and forth to New York; and her mother, gnarled fingers laden with too many diamonds, and Mrs. Austin, work-red hands encased in white kid gloves, visited like two harpies, snatching for some crumb of security through the grandchild, a totem of what they had missed in life. They were capable of sitting around for hours, building towers of clichés, admiring all her privileges in this new affluent life. They drove her mad.

She developed a devouring interest in the Barstow family and constantly asked Fergus about properties for them.

"Why are you so interested in them?" asked Fergus. "You know Claudia and Jeffrey are the studio problem children. Always getting in some scrape or another and getting bailed out."

"Since when do motion-picture stars have to be Sunday-school teachers?" she said. "Maybe I'm thinking of some good property for you. That ought to make you happy."

She had the idea of reading books that might be good for Jeffrey. Every time she read one that might suit him, she imagined herself as the heroine, and this fantasy was a comfort to her. At the moment, he was having a hot romance with a beautiful Viennese star the studio had just imported, and, although that disturbed her, she was glad in a way that she could not try to see him, for it would have been impossible. Everyone knew what everyone did in this town. She knew well from many sources that not only her father, but Fergus, had been intimate with Claudia. But she didn't care anymore.

As time passed, her depression deepened.

She developed frequent headaches, and one day she awoke in tears, sobbing uncontrollably. This continued for two days.

Even Fergus was disturbed.

"The blues often happen, honey, after a baby. I wish I could take you away, but you don't know how difficult it is just now. We took a loss of $380,000 between Punch Weston's unreleased picture and Claudia's war film, and that was just the beginning. The stars are pricing us out of business. Every time Mary Pickford goes to a new studio and makes a new deal, we have to raise the ante to keep our own stars happy. The other day Rowland at Metro was saying the lunatics have taken charge of the asylum. Fairbanks, Pickford, Chaplin, and Griffith are killing us with their new company. Those dirty huns have brought in a crazy modern movie, *Cabinet of Dr. Caligari*, and a director named Lubitsch did a spectacular picture called *Passion*. So now everybody wants to be extravagant and European. Stars want to be directors or supervisors, everybody's paying a fortune for stories, and the whole economy of Titan's spoiled stars is on my shoulders. Your father's New York office sets up our budgets, now, what do you think of that! They don't seem to realize everything has doubled. I have to function out here on brain waves from people across the continent who don't know a damn thing about a studio's problems."

He saw she was still crying into her handkerchief.

"I'm sorry about the speech," he said, "but Esther, you've got to realize the responsibility that's been put on me. If I don't make things go, your father will replace me. No doubt with a Moses relative."

"He wouldn't dare do that!" she said. "Not with you married to me!"

As soon as she had said it, she knew it was a mistake.

"I made it without you," he said angrily. "Don't you forget that for one minute."

"I didn't mean it that way," she said, crying, "I just meant, I love you, and pappa knows it."

"Well, prove your love then by snapping out of it," Fergus said. "I have too much trouble at work to come home to a wailing wife. You've got it soft. Why don't you read, or play golf, or get out. Don't be such a recluse. Look at you!"

He gestured toward the disordered bed.

"You've been in bed since I left this morning. No wonder you feel sick."

"I am sick," she said.

"Then I'll call a doctor," he said. "It's too much for me. I'm no specialist. I'll have Wolfrum come see you tomorrow."

Good God, he thought, why did I say Wolfrum? Of all people. But Wolfrum knew all the secrets of the Moses family, so it was just as well. After all, it wouldn't be good business for the gossips to get any inkling that Simon Moses' daughter, Fergus Austin's wife, looked like she might be heading for a nervous breakdown. People would wonder. Things were bad enough at the studio without anyone imagining that Esther knew things about Titan that were distressing her.

Wolfrum . . . that bastard was the right doctor for this private problem. He wouldn't dare open his mouth.

He walked out of the bedroom and closed the door quietly, but, Esther felt, with anger.

Later she heard his car drive away, and she lay awake trying to read. When she heard him return, she quickly snapped out her light, so he would think she was asleep and not have words again. She waited, her heart beating, for him to come up the stairs and peek in to see if she was all right. But he passed without checking her and went into his room. She heard his voice as he made telephone calls.

She fought a migraine and finally, after pills, she slept uneasily until late the next morning.

Dr. Wolfrum was concerned.

"Migraine headaches run in your family," he said. "Your father would be much better off if he took medication, but he thinks aspirin and codeine are a sin."

"All that stuff does me no good," said Esther. "Please, give me anything to relieve me. I just can't go on this way, or I'll die!"

He gave her a hypodermic.

She felt an exhilaration that ended with her feeling wrapped in a cocoon of comfort and well-being.

Three months later, Fergus's overprotective secretary, Harriet Foster, bustled in importantly with a sheaf of bills in her hand. Annoyed, he looked up, but in a moment his disturbance was much deeper.

"I know Dr. Wolfrum is awfully expensive, Mr. Austin," she said, "but my goodness, these drugstore bills are way, way out of line. Mrs. Austin must be very ill."

After one look, he dismissed her as casually as possible and sat staring at them, a sick feeling in the pit of his stomach.

He came home early, at a normal dinnertime. The downstairs was darkened, for the servants apparently expected him hours later. Esther lay on a chaise in the cave of her jade-green bedroom, an unopened book beside her. She was still in her nightgown and a wrapper. She had been there, the stiff taffeta drapes closed against the light, since morning.

Cautiously, he bent to kiss her. Lifting the lace sleeve of her wrapper he saw the little red needle pricks on her pale arm.

"Esther," he said, "Esther, this isn't like you."

"I'm fine, Fergus," she said, "just fine. Anything wrong?"

Her words seemed out of focus, as if a foreigner were pronouncing them very correctly.

"Nothing," he said. "I just thought, well, it's been rather dull for you. Maybe we ought to take a little vacation. Go up to Pebble Beach; practice up on a little golf."

She looked alarmed. "Oh, no!" she said. "No!"

"Why not?"

"I—I couldn't leave David."

"We'll take him. It's time to get him out of the goddamned nursery."

"But—the studio." She was panicked.

"Now just put on something, Esther, come on down to dinner, and we'll talk about it."

Fergus went downstairs, poured himself a stiff scotch, rang for the butler, ordered fires lit, lights turned on, steaks on the grill.

She's really hooked, he thought, she's afraid to get away from the source of supply. I'll be damned if I tell Simon Moses. This is my problem. I'll handle it.

Half an hour later, Esther came downstairs. Her Florentine hostess gown and her hair, wound in a rope around her head, were set off by her glittering eyes and the enameled fixity within their depths.

Fergus was appalled. This imitation Claudia Barstow was his wife; this sick woman his product. He'd been so busy he hadn't given her any life at all. He went along with the enforced gaiety, realizing that a new needle hole on her arm was creating it. The trip to Pebble Beach was planned, and he informed her that the baby's nurse, Miss MacDonald, was having a holiday, they were going to take someone more easygoing.

Esther packed her things. The new nurse took over. As soon as they were on the golf course at Pebble Beach, the nurse efficiently frisked Mrs. Austin's luggage, took out the narcotic kit, and locked it in her own overnight case as ordered.

The second day, Mrs. Austin was equally vivacious. The nurse found another kit, craftily concealed in a douche bag.

The third day, Mrs. Austin was locked in her room.

The fourth day, an ambulance drove her, sweating and in agony, with a doctor aboard to control her, to Las Cruces Sanatorium in Pasadena.

Fergus proceeded to the studio, where production was starting on the new film, *Goldstruck.* He set to work with a force that was even startling to his staff.

Wolfrum entered Fergus's office.

"I ought to kill you," said Fergus.

Wolfrum sat down and lit a cigarette.

"I don't think you'd do that," he said, "after the services I have performed for this family. If your wife is weak, she's weak. She needed drastic therapy. There are many people in this high-powered, get-rich-quick world who are incapable of facing the pressures and privileges that are handed them. They have to escape from their fears. When your wife is able to adjust to her situation, I am certain she will be all right. Until then, I have only relieved her, and, I may say, you, also, of the realities she is not ready to face."

"I think it would be better if you go into general practice," said Fergus. "The studio does not need to maintain an office here for you anymore."

"I was going to suggest it myself," said Wolfrum. "It is limiting for me to belong to one studio."

"You can get out tonight," said Fergus.

"I don't think so," said Wolfrum. "I do like to take a little time. I have so many documented files, under lock and key, of course, that contain personal records. You would not wish to have any of them disturbed, I am sure, even though they are duplicated elsewhere."

He crushed his cigarette and turned to Fergus before he left.

"My office will be at Seventh and Broadway," he said, "and I need not tell you what a good doctor I am. Just think of your nose, and of Claudia Barstow. And think of the death certificate I signed for Martha Moses. You will find there are many things in my career for which you should be deeply grateful."

The news spread around the studio that Esther Austin had a breakdown after having her baby. All the secretaries shook their heads and sagely observed that wealth does not always mean happiness. Look at that Moses family, the son dead in the war, the daughter dead, a suicide most likely, it was so hush-hush, and now Esther Moses, so lucky to marry an attractive, hardworking up-and-comer like Fergus Austin, actually in a loony bin in Pasadena. It just shows how lucky you can be not to be a Moses.

6

♦♦♦♦♦♦♦♦

For Fergus, the years following the birth of his son were a time of such personal stress that they were only made bearable by the pressure of work that filled his waking hours.

On Saturdays he dutifully called on his mother at the Hollywood Hotel, more and more concerned with her babbling talk of real estate, and her obsession with the hundreds of thousands of people who, in the years following the population upheavals after World War I, were rushing to Los Angeles to relocate. Once or twice Mary Frances suggested he take a flier in real estate.

"Motion pictures are enough of a flier for me, ma," he said. "A picture has to make a fortune now, for the parent company to remain solvent."

"Don't worry, son," she said. "Maybe I'll take good care of you in your old age."

She certainly wasn't buying a stylish wardrobe with the money he gave her. He wondered if her mind was giving way. It would mean some old-folks' home for her. In that rocking-chair brigade on the hotel veranda, a favored chair would often be empty. The survivors rocked the time away, watching the Hollywood traffic and bragging about their illustrious children. How little they really knew of the lives of their young who had uprooted them to be part of this bogus richness, their hands and minds empty.

"Look, ma," said Fergus, "I'll raise your allowance. Now, for the love of God, go out and get some decent clothes. Don't save your pennies for me. People will think Titan isn't doing well if you dress like that."

She smiled enigmatically.

"My closet is brimming, and everybody knows how successful you are. Why, David and I are going to a matinee today to see one of your movies at the New Taj Mahal, with one of your fancy prologues thrown in!"

"Not mine," said Fergus, "Titan's. Don't mix them up. Pretty soon you will be seeing my name as producer. It's a new title for supervisor, and they put it in the credits on the screen."

"Isn't that nice," said Mary Frances.

"Not particularly," said Fergus. "I've been doing the same work for years. But now, for the price of one, old man Moses has got me wearing two heads. The new title is producer, yet somehow Simon Moses Presents always ends up in bigger letters."

"That *isn't* nice," said Mary Frances.

Fergus went over to the birdcage. The green parakeet pecked at him.

"Nasty little bugger," said Fergus. "Well, I've got to be going. I have to get on to Pasadena to see Esther."

"Say hello for me," said Mary Frances, "if—if she remembers who I am."

Fergus saw a wistful look on his mother's face and realized her loneliness, her only lifeline himself and David.

He brought out her weekly envelope prepared by Miss Foster, and he took out his money clip and peeled off another hundred dollars.

"Here, ma, get yourself something special. I'll have Hori pick you up in the limousine, and you can take David to Mullen and Bluett and get him a nice sweater or something. Have a good time. I—I'm glad you're such buddies."

He put his arms around her and kissed the top of her frizzled hair. As usual, she spoiled the moment, looking up in gratitude and blowing her denture breath into his face. He quickly dropped his arms.

"Oh, thank you, honeybun," she beamed. "You're so good to me!"

He felt guilty. He gave her little time and thought. Money was conscience' payoff.

"Look, are you happy here? Maybe you'd like to have a little house in Hollywood, with that orange grove we used to talk about."

She shook her head. "Oh no! Not with good help as much as fifty dollars a month! And I like to be right here, in the middle of everything."

◆◆◆◆◆◆◆◆

One Monday morning, as she often did, Mary Frances Austin awoke before dawn. She braided her gray hair in a tight loop, pinned it carefully around the slightly bald spot on the crown of her head, slipped into her oldest, most comfortable corset, her laced walking shoes, a flowered silk dress of many summers; she put on her light wool coat and an old navy-blue straw hat.

She stuffed into her shiny reticule half the bills Fergus had given her on his traditional Friday afternoon visit.

She paused to smile and listen to the birds outside in the lush, palm-trimmed garden. The hotel would not allow her a dog or a cat, but there was no law about birds, so she had chosen a parakeet. Mr. Noyes, the night clerk, had suggested, since she couldn't have a dog, she call the bird Fido. So Fido he had become.

She lifted the yard of calico she had fastened into a bag over his cage, and pursed her lips into an almost silent whistle to awaken him. He fluttered his feathers, and his upside-down eyes winked open at her.

She let him crawl across her shoulders while she cleaned his cage. She gave him fresh water, gravel and seed, and she carefully hid two new property deeds under the thickening hoard on the pull-out bottom of his cage.

"First national bank," she said, as she clucked at him, "mamma will be back this afternoon."

Fido twittered sleepily, and she took him gently and deposited him in the cage where he could stare at his reflection in a small mirror and ring a bell at his image.

"I'm sure you won't be lonesome," she said, "with your friend. Bye, bye, pretty boy."

"Pretty boy," he said.

Mary Frances walked quietly down to the lobby. Mr. Noyes was having a quick breakfast in the dining room near the door where he could watch the flash of the switchboard reflected in an angled french door. Actors and actresses received calls from assistant directors and casting agents at ungodly hours.

"Well, what today, Hetty Green?" asked Mr. Noyes, taking a toothpick out of his vest pocket.

"It was my birthday last week," said Mary Frances. "Fergus gave me some extra money. He was too busy to come by, poor boy, he works so hard." She smiled. "He's always after me to get some new clothes. But you know what, Mr. Noyes?"

He shook his head. "What?"

"I'm not going to Coulters. What do I want with such fancy clothes? I'm just going to run down to Hamburger's basement. He'll never notice the difference."

"I'm sure," said Mr. Noyes. "Say, go downtown and get on the bus to Wilshire. My son says a new tract is opening."

"I'm still occupied with the old tract downtown,"

said Mary Frances, "although you mustn't tell anyone. Fergus would be very cross with me."

Noyes knew, as did everyone in the hotel, that Fergus Austin spent from ten minutes to half an hour with his mother once a week, his penance for being born. He paid off his conscience and blew. But this was standard with all the mothers of the well-off and famous.

"Well, time to get on the switchboard," said Mr. Noyes. "My son Robbie says that there's a new trick at the subdivision. It's something those escrow Indians just thought up. Leave it to the real estate sharks. They ring a bell at the tract office at eleven o'clock. Then everyone has a right to grab the flag off his favorite lot, with the number on it, and carry it back to the office. Cash on the line. They line up to grab the sticks off the choice lots. Sometimes they even beat each other up because it's first come, first served."

Mary Frances shook her head. "My company downtown is more refined," she said. "They offer free lunches."

"You're the limit, Mrs. Austin," he said.

"See you tonight."

She caught the trolley, unfolded the *Examiner*, and started to firm up on what was going on in El Pueblo de Nuestra Señora la Reina de los Angeles de Porciuncula, referred to loosely as the City of the Angels.

◆◆◆◆◆◆◆◆

Tourists fresh off the Santa Fe and Southern Pacific loafed around Central Park. It was a meeting place where they could sit and talk with the same sort of folks they were.

Mr. and Mrs. Petersen talked to the nice woman with the brown Hamburger Co. bag in her hands.

"It isn't that we didn't like Colorado," said Mrs. Petersen, who did most of the talking for the two, "heaven knows we had busy boom times in Leadville, but it's just that things weren't the same after the war."

"You were lucky you could afford to come out here," said Mary Frances.

"We had a good little sum saved up, and nowhere to spend it," Mrs. Petersen replied.

"Mary Frances smiled warmly. "Well, you certainly came to a good place. I'm taking a flier in real estate myself. Say, I'm going out to check the possibilities of a lot. The real estate company gives a free tour of the movie houses, and on top of that a free lunch. Why don't you tag along?"

"A free lunch?" said Mr. Petersen, looking up.

"We wouldn't know how to get there," said his wife.

"It's easy as pie," Mary Frances said, smiling assuredly. Her blue eyes were wise and friendly. "The real estate people put you on a bus and give you a tour. Maybe I'll be seeing you at the bus at the corner. Here are some tickets somebody gave me."

"People are real friendly, William," said Mrs. Petersen. "What have we got to lose? They can't hogtie us."

By the time the eleven o'clock bus had left, Mary Frances had worked two opposite sides of Central Park. Sixteen people carried cardboards with her initials on the corners when she got on the bus.

Bertie Sawyer, the spieler, stood at the side of the driver with a megaphone in his hands. As the bus moved along he pointed out various points of interest.

"Here, ladies and gentlemen, is the famous Westlake Park, known to the citizens as Charlie Chaplin's bathtub. On a clear day, which Los Angeles has the most of, you can see the Sennett bathing cuties swimming. But don't let that scare you, ladies, their home studio is out in the San Fernando valley . . . And here, folks, a birthday present given by the multimillionaire Joe Scherck to his beautiful bride, Norma Talmadge. The famous Talmadge Apartments. Each apartment has crystal chandeliers and some have solid gold faucets. And this is Thomas Ince's former home. Jackie Coogan, the millionaire kid star lives behind walls in this mansion, folks, right off Oxford Street. Maybe your kids have more fun playing baseball on the sand lot, but Jackie has more gravel! And this is the famous house where Mary Pickford lived while she was being courted by Douglas Fairbanks. Right on exclusive Fremont Place. Do you pay a big rent, folks? Well, before she hit it big in Pickfair, she stumbled along on a measly eight hundred dollars a month rent here. And this is the house you all saw in the movie when Colleen Moore moved in it from the old, aristocratic society section of Los Angeles. Yes, ladies and gents, real estate gets so valuable here that people move their mansions just like we pack a suitcase . . ."

The bus finally pulled up to a barley and mustard field, where a large circus tent had been set up for an office. Hundreds of pennants fluttered from it. Trestle tables inside held lunches. Everyone was handed a paper plate.

"Excuse me a moment," Mary Frances said to the Petersens. Nice to visit with you folks. Say, I'm going to buy my lot on Orange Avenue. Why don't you do the same, so's we can be neighbors?" She hurried away behind the tent.

"I think you're a chump to take your commission in land," said Bertie Sawyer, eating his lunch. "There won't be sewers here for several years."

Mary Frances waved at a tract salesman who was opening up his ledger at a trestle table.

"I know what I'm doing," she said. "Tomorrow I'm going to investigate out toward Hollywood further. People are moving out that way. There's a new tract where they ring a bell."

"Where they what?" said Bertie, mystified.

"Never mind," Mary Frances said. "I better hurry if I'm going to buy the first lot."

◆◆◆◆◆◆◆◆

Fergus wove through the traffic from Franklin Avenue to Los Feliz. He was irritated, for he remembered when there hadn't been much traffic. He became more and more depressed. How would all the bits and pieces of his family life ever fit together? What kind of a life could he give David when he was so involved with the studio?

He entered the portals of Las Cruces Sanatorium. Beyond the main building, nestled in a lush garden, shuttered little bungalows hid their tragic inmates.

Esther sat in a glider, under a sycamore tree. Her nurse had brushed her hair and tied it with pink ribbons for his visit. She came out of her lethargy to smile at him, and fleetingly he saw all the sweetness and promise she had held as a young girl. But as he savored the bittersweet moment he realized what hell it always was when she came home. She doted on David. He was six now, too old not to be aware of her condition. She watched him in a mindless way, staring at him and shaking her head as if she could not believe this handsome young boy was hers.

Fergus had to install a nurse under the guise of an upstairs maid. One call from her and he would rush home. Esther would be sent back to the sanatorium before she could harm herself, or before her endless weeping be seen by anyone.

Now, after an empty visit, discussing weather and food, how she felt, if she had read any of the magazines he had sent (she had not), and if her radio was working properly (she thought maybe it was), he kissed her cheek and started home. Another weekend.

He was relieved that David's weekends seemed normal. Saturdays, while the Moses family was involved with the sabbath, were Mary Frances's days.

David and Mary Frances would be having their ceremonial lunch at Kathleen's successful restaurant on Hollywood Boulevard where all the important movie people met.

Kathleen often regaled Fergus with stories of how the two enjoyed themselves. Fergus knew she saved the best booth for them. And they were fussed over by all the sycophants who wanted to have an in with the Moses or Austin interests.

David had told him he was used to hearing whispers that he was heir of the Titan studios.

"What does that mean, daddy?" he asked.

"It means," said Fergus, "that you're going to inherit a heap of trouble. You know that fist on the Titan water tower, with the lightning bolts in its fingers?"

"Sure," said David. "What does it mean?"

"It means, watch out!" said Fergus.

But he was inwardly pleased, seeing how little all this meant to David, who was more enthusiastic about the movies he and his grandmother saw. And, like any healthy kid, he was also enthusiastic about the various dishes Kathleen tried out on him before she put them on her menu. Kathleen and Tony told him he was their food tester. Sandwiches were named for the celebrities who preferred them. One triple-decker colossus bore David Austin's name—his first sortie into the propaganda of the notable in Hollywood.

The joke at Kathleen's was that it took a six-year-old kid with a cast-iron stomach inherited from a Fergus Austin, and the guts of a Simon Moses, to eat it.

Sundays belonged mostly to the Moses family. Fergus would take David down the street to their mansion on Hollywood Boulevard. They usually had lunch in the solarium. Fergus and Simon would talk studio policy in a more casual way than in the office. Sometimes Rebecca would take David out to Pasadena. If Esther was not up to it, David would go visiting in homes similar to the Moses estate where grandchildren of the new movie elect were on display. The youngsters usually managed to evade the company of their elders and had fun playing croquet, swimming, learning tennis from a pro, or playing with junior golf clubs on private putting greens.

If he were lucky, David and his father would get up to the Martinez house and join the celebration, with some cousin or another playing the guitar and singing, and the Martinez children, five of them now, running around screaming in rapid Spanish with their cousins from Sonoratown. That was fun and happened much too infrequently for David.

David was not an outgoing child; he seemed to be involved with his inner world. Small wonder, with the confusion in his young life.

Soon the boy would be old enough to attend Black Foxe Military Academy where he'd face the reality of routine and competition with his peers instead of being in a constant tug-of-war between two old women who didn't have enough to do with their time.

Sometimes Fergus felt guilty about his mother's Sundays. But he need not have concerned himself, for Mary Frances looked upon this time as the world she had made for herself with her special friend.

Kathleen was Mary Frances's blessing. She harbored the apostasy of wishing this colleen with her red hair and white skin had been her son's wife.

This Sunday, as always, Kathleen picked her up for early mass in her pearl-gray Marmon.

"These are Tony's mornings to be a paisano," she smiled. "What a guy he is, Mary Frances! He takes the kids to his mother's, they go to church at the old plaza—and then they all stuff on beans and enchiladas to their hearts' content and sit around jabbering in Spanish. Tony's a big celebrity down there. He brings the whole family all the supplies they need for a week, and everybody comes in for a greeting and a handout. But he loves it, and he deserves it."

"You're lucky," said Mary Frances. "He sure works hard."

"You bet," said Kathleen. "He can't wait to get home and start preparing the meal for our guests on his day off. Come on over tonight and have goulash."

"Oh, yes!" said Mary Frances. "Is Fergus coming?"

"No, he has a meeting, and David is having dinner with his grandparents. Poor kid."

They both agreed on that, knowing the stuffiness and sadness of the Moses household.

After church they drove out to the new, flourishing Beverly Hills and had brunch at the Beverly Hills Hotel.

"You know," said Kathleen, "Will Rogers says that Beverly Hills has more real estate men than bootleggers."

They drove beyond the new streets, past dusty bean fields being plowed under, down to the speedway where Barney Oldfield made racing history.

"Maybe I ought to start a new restaurant out here in Beverly Hills," said Kathleen.

"Oh, no, I wouldn't," said Mary Frances. "I think the big bet is around that Rancho La Brea property. I plunged and bought a corner lot for fifty dollars a foot. You couldn't pick it up for three times that today. Let's drive toward town and take a look."

Kathleen smiled. "Does Fergus know it?"

"Heavens, no!" said Mary Frances.

They motored through highways and byways looking at the yellow cuts in the green hills and arroyos, as new streets, sidewalks, and graded lots scarred the caminos and old ranchos.

Even the profitable fields out Pico way were being plowed up; they had given thousands of bellyaching sailors their navy beans during the war. Now, bean fields were making way for airports and factories. In the distance, Signal Hill was beginning to belch out its poisons as the refineries and wells made millions for the midwesterners who had migrated west even before the turn of the century.

Mary Frances had no sentiment about the land rape. She was glad a lot of people were going to use the land, and she only thought about the investment value.

"You ought to buy, too, Kathleen," she said. "If you don't hurry it's going to be too expensive. I'm already beginning to trade some of my single lots for larger pieces of land."

"Listen," Kathleen said, "my money is tied up in my cash-on-the-line restaurant. I don't know about land. But I do know that you can always count on the fact that people get hungry about three times a day."

◆◆◆◆◆◆◆◆

Studio problems were multiple for Fergus. Enthusiasm for the young art of filmmaking was being replaced by criticism. The industry had to get into long pants and forget its carefree youth. The year was 1927.

The tragedies of the past decade in motion-picture society had brought about national concern and censorship. Olive Thomas, a beautiful actress married to Jack Pickford, had taken her life in Paris after a bout with drugs. Handsome Wallace Reid had died at thirty of the same addiction, at the peak of his career. Fatty Arbuckle had been accused of a sordid murder after a wild party in San Francisco.

The unsolved murder of the suave director, William Desmond Taylor, had ended the career of pretty blond Mary Miles Minter, and of piquant Mabel Normand, who was also a victim of drugs.

The public and the press were quick to pounce on the film industry, and the only way out had been to choose an arbiter of morals. Since Will Hays had been made president of the Motion Pictures and Producers' Distributors of America, a shake of his head could end a career.

Fergus tossed and turned in bed every time he thought of how Zukor had been forced to junk two million dollars' worth of Fatty Arbuckle films. With the unruly Barstows on his hands, every time the phone rang at night he dreaded double-trouble. He had learned what palms to grease in the police department and what bouncers to pay off in the speakeasies and nightclubs.

His two major stars had to be protected by any means from the press, thirsty for any juicy new scandal. Yet, Titan needed them desperately.

Throughout Fergus's various and ephemeral escapades in amour these busy years, one little one-night stander, Gracie Boomer, had lasted to move into an area of friendship.

She had been an extra girl, getting her pinches from the front-office hegemony along with standard visiting butter-and-egg men. After Fergus had taken her to dinner, and, as expected, gone to her little apartment on Orchid, she confessed, over a bottle of bathtub gin, that she was sick to death of endless, senseless one-night stands, and she wanted to go legitimate.

Fergus, touched by her honesty, tested her determination. He gave her a chance to work as a mail girl. Gracie kept her nose clean and stuck out the job at the minimal salary, occasionally smiling and waving at Fergus with gratitude.

Finally, he placed her in the growing publicity department as an apprentice to Red Powell, head of publicity. She learned satisfactorily and was Fergus's stalwart supporter in a department composed of ambitious, dedicated cutthroats who leaned toward front-office Moses interests.

Fergus found it necessary to jack up publicity on Claudia's newest epic, *Lucretia*. It was far from memorable, owing to the pedestrian direction of Plimpton and Claudia's obvious lack of chemistry with her handsome leading man, Leslie Charles. The newest rage was the glamorous personal-appearance circuit. The new theater palaces were depots of mass euphoria, as fans fought and queued to see their dream stars in person.

◆◆◆◆◆◆◆◆

Claudia had stayed away from seeing Simon privately. It had been difficult for her as his eyes followed her when she made the required festive appearances at various Titan affairs. Several times she had shaken his hand ceremonially for the benefit of important New York visitors, and of course she had been photographed with him and other Titan stars when the ground had been broken for the new executive offices.

She was disturbed to be near him on such formal terms. She missed the continuity of their relationship; the love she could expect, beyond sexual forays; his personal protection of her pictures; and the camaraderie that had grown since they had helped each other in the simple beginnings.

Fergus was the organizing force of the material side of the studio, but Simon's driving and practical admiration of creative talents and his instinct for what sort of picture would make money were what made Titan pictures illuminate the screen. He was a trend follower, she and Jeffrey had bitched plenty about that, but he had become a powerful showman through the years.

There were more than a score of stars in the company's roster, but she was the special one, for she and Jeffrey had helped build the studio's wealth.

It was surprising for her to get a personal phone call from Simon.

"Claudia, I've got to break the silence between us. Could I see you tomorrow?"

"Oh—Si, it's been so long. How can I face you after what you heard? I don't know."

"Claudia," he said, "it's partly my fault. I must see you."

"Where?" she said.

"Would you mind the casita at the ranch? Do you still have your key?"

A gift from him . . . in a jewel box, a golden replica of the house on the key ring.

"Oh, yes, of course I have the key. What time?"

"How about tomorrow afternoon. Say at two?"

"At two," she said. "I'll be there."

What was the use of getting into it again? The lonely nights, the ridiculous clinging to an older man who was married to a woman he could never leave and occupied with a business that took most of his time.

But she wanted to be with him, to see the warmth of his eyes as he looked at her. She was used to handsome men, men who used their handsomeness in their acting; they had surrounded her all her life—in her family and in her work. But Si was different, so innocently elegant, he didn't strive for effect. How had all that come to a man who had started with a barrow on Doyer Street?

She left her beach house and drove to Saint Monica's, the Catholic church on Seventh Street. It had been a long time since she had lighted a vigil candle. She knew there was no salvation for her in a religion she had abandoned. The thought of ritual and confession eluded her, but prayer was different.

Please God, she prayed silently, let me have this one man in my life, let me love him and care for him as he cared for me. Let there be somehow a love and a growth in me to match his devotion. And let me not disturb his other life, but be satisfied with what I have from him . . .

She left the church disturbed. She would have to seek salvation in her life, not in an empty church with the scent of incense stupefying her reason, a leftover from a childhood fantasy.

The next day she had her cook pack a hamper of tidbits and chilled champagne. She threw riding clothes in a suitcase, hoping she and Si could take horses from the studio stables and ride into the hills, as they had many times. She added a hostess gown and one of her filmiest nightgowns, and she drove off in a state of elation she had not felt for a long time.

How ridiculous to be so eager to meet a man she had lived with for years, who really was far from the most exciting bedmate she'd had.

She entered the house, opened the windows, arranged the champagne, rushed out to the patio and picked a cluster of white daisies, set them in a pewter mug, and turned happily to watch the white curtains rippling in the fragrant breeze. Oh, it was wonderful to be back! The stage was set.

His limousine pulled up. She was surprised to see Timmons, his driver, open the door and then settle down to his *Police Gazette*. Why hadn't Si driven his Pierce Arrow? He was wearing a dark suit and tie. His overnight bag must be in the car, all he carried was a briefcase.

He opened the door and stood looking at her a moment. It was mindful of the time he had come to her apartment, and told her he loved her, asking her to go to Atlantic City with him.

He rushed to her and put his arms around her. And then he held her back and looked.

"Oh, Claudia! Claudia!" His hands trembled even as they had before. And he bent to kiss her, then looked into her eyes. "How beautiful you are!"

She touched his cheek.

"For heaven's sake, Si, take off your coat. Don't be so formal. Let's have a drink."

She took a cigarette, and he rushed to light it. Then he opened the champagne and poured it, but he seemed nervous. What was disturbing him? Of course, they hadn't met for a long time. After what had happened, it couldn't be easy for him, either.

"Claudia—I—I'm in trouble."

"What's happened?" she said.

"The business is in the doldrums. My big movie houses are bleeding me blind. That damned radio is cutting into our family trade."

"Is it really that serious?" she asked.

"Terrible—terrible. I could go broke."

"What about my new picture? Isn't *Lucretia* doing what you expected?"

"I'm sorry, Claudia," he said, "you know the previews in Santa Barbara and Pasadena were lukewarm. And the theater chain isn't doing too well with those flossy prologues. They won't book the picture without you. Now, if you would make a personal-appearance tour with the movie, we'd have to drive 'em away."

"Me!" said Claudia, "you expect me to go out on a junket like that and get pushed around by John Q. Public? Come on, Si, that's asking too much!"

He hung his head.

"I guess it is. I guess you wouldn't do it for me even if you knew I might go broke if we didn't start to hypo our product. It would help get people back in our big-city theaters again. I was always afraid of those colossal movie houses! I knew we were overexpanding. But Abe wouldn't listen—wouldn't listen."

Claudia came to him. It was not like Simon to be scared. She ran her hands along the edge of his graying hair.

"All right, honey," she said, "for you I'll do it. You've done plenty for me. Now, let's settle down. Light the fire, take off that suit, and put on something more comfortable like—like we used to do."

"You will do it?" he said, kissing her neck.

"If you say so," she said.

"Good," he said. "I'll call Red Powell right now, and they can firm up the itinerary. I have a copy for you in my briefcase."

He moved to a vargueno and opened it. There was a phone hidden in it.

"When did you put a phone in here? I thought we promised there'd never be one."

"Well," he apologized, "since I didn't see you—"

As he busied himself on the phone, she looked at him. She had always teased him about being a Shylock. But now she realized that Shylock had become

Caesar, and he was fighting in a very determined way for his empire. Including using her.

When he hung up, she was standing in front of the unlit fire.

He came to her smiling. "Red's delighted. It's going to be great. You'll have the best of everything on the tour, and you know I'll make it up to you."

"About taking off your coat and the lighted fire," she said, annoyed. It was all so preplanned.

He put his arms around her.

"Honey, it'll have to wait. I'm sorry, but I have to get to New York. I could barely take the time to get here to see you—and I wanted to so much."

"I just bet," she said coolly. "Okay, Mr. Moses. I'll protect you. You protected me. I guess you're still angry at me because of what I said at the Hollywood Hotel. You know I wasn't what you'd call true to you. Well, listen, Si, I loved you. So maybe I used you, but I did love you. And now you're not exactly true-blue to me. You're using me as a corporate commodity. I'll go. Sure, I'll go on your lousy tour. It's *my* skin, too. But just get the hell out of my sight. I came here prepared to love you, but you've got what you wanted, so you can go!"

"But Claudia," he said, "I love you. I want to stay, but you don't—you don't know what they're doing to me in New York. It's a fight for life. I ain't got a choice."

"Haven't," she corrected. "Haven't you learned anything? Get out, you've made your point."

She shoved him toward the door, picked up his briefcase and threw it after him, and slammed the door, latching it.

"Claudia—" he said, whispering so the chauffeur couldn't hear.

"Get out!" she screamed. "You son-of-a-bitch. And if you don't, I'll make a scene that'll be heard down at the corral!"

She heard his footsteps as he went to the car.

She sat down, shaking, and then began to laugh at herself. How about that! Claudia Barstow lighting candles in a church and playing the Mary Magdalen bit. And Claudia Barstow being stood up by the man she was condescending to give her life to, even if she just got a small part of his.

She finished the champagne, wrenched open the vargueno, and lifted out the phone. She tried to reach Fergus. At least she'd give him a piece of her mind. The hell with Simon Moses, that was finished.

Fergus was gone to Santa Barbara for the weekend. She opened a cupboard in the kitchen, took out a bottle of scotch, and went out to the patio.

Well, why not go on the road? There would be adulation, admirers, she could show off her new clothes, forget the lukewarm previews. And she certainly was free. She had no commitment, now, and this time, without any sense of anything but fun, she'd let anybody share her bed. After all, what was it Jeffrey had said to her? Oh, yes, she needed a new cast of characters.

◆◆◆◆◆◆◆◆

The whole publicity department had balked at the idea of taking Claudia on tour. Aside from shuffling dozens of trunks, suitcases, wig boxes, makeup cases, and a traveling bar that had to be stocked anew at every hotel, they knew the personal peccadillo of their star.

In desperation, Fergus thought of a way out. He summoned Grace Boomer into his office, complimented her on her work, and poured her a drink. She was overwhelmed. This was not personal, this was business, and she had a sickly mother to support.

"Just think," he said enthusiastically, "you're a real publicist now, Gracie. From errand girl to an important job in one year. I have news. You're getting a promotion. A raise. And that means I think you're ready to do a *very* important job for Titan. Here's where you get your first break. Now that personal appearances are so valuable in the theater palaces, we have decided to send Claudia Barstow on the circuit to promote *Lucretia*. We thought it was a fabulous idea to have you take her. How about that!"

He beamed, and she looked at him big-eyed over her drink.

"The whole U.S.A.," he said, "first-class, all expenses paid."

A twenty-four-year-old novice press agent taking a thirty-five-year-old movie queen on a swing around the country! San Francisco, Seattle, Chicago, Detroit, New Orleans, Dallas, and New York.

Fergus didn't tell her that Red Powell wouldn't do it. Or that Chris Holmes turned down the job, the raise that went with it, and left after five years seniority.

Grace couldn't understand it. You'd meet all the newspapermen. You'd be hostess at a series of parties for a glamorous movie star. You'd make contacts for a lifetime, get to meet the fan club presidents and see how the pulse of the nation beat about the favorites in Titan's stable.

You'd meet politicians and important people who would give you open sesame whenever you came back to these cities. Why didn't Fergus take advantage of his position and go himself?

On the Lark, going to San Francisco, Grace Boomer, with her idea book on interviews, was writing out special publicity material for each town, feeling sharp and executive in her new Broadway-Hollywood suit. When the porter called her in the morning at Palo Alto, she looked out in time to see four college boys, bleary-eyed and drunk, waving good-bye at the window of Claudia Barstow's compartment.

How was it they all knew where she was?

Here was a woman, a performer, who did not exist

if she hadn't an audience. Solitude was anathema to her. But Gracie had not realized it. Why?

Because she was a dope, that's why. And she had tossed off all veiled warnings about liquor, appointments, and luggage. Miss Barstow *liked* her, had been most gracious about her company. And you could learn a lot from being around an exceptional creature like a Barstow. Already Gracie found herself saying *been* instead of *bin* and pursuing graciousness instead of concern with porters and waiters.

She knocked at the door of Claudia's compartment to help her organize her luggage. The train would soon be in San Francisco.

Finally she heard a low-voiced "come in."

Claudia was leaning back on her bed, wearing a lace peignoir. The compartment was a shambles; glasses and empty bottles littered the floor. Butts of endless cigarettes revealed the many visitors who had spent the night.

The train passed Atherton. The porter was asking for luggage to be stowed on the platform.

"You'd better get dressed, Miss Barstow," said Gracie, ignoring her glazed, annoyed glance, "we'll be at the station soon, and we have to get off."

"Let 'em wait," said Claudia. "I've got to pull myself together."

Gracie rang for the porter, bribed him to get coffee on the double. "Let's just try to make it in time. Some members of the press may be there to greet you, and I know your fan club will be on hand. It's a big day for them."

This brightened Claudia considerably. Grace handed her cleaning lotion and makeup. She noted that Claudia applied cosmetics with instinctive genius. It was incredible how she transformed herself into almost immediate loveliness.

Gracie helped her dress. Realizing it was too late to do much about her hair, Claudia pulled on a cloche hat. With amazement, Grace watched her pull a wisp of curl out on each side, making her whole appearance seem ordered perfection.

Claudia took a bromo and belched delicately. She chewed on several cloves, sprayed herself liberally with Jockey Club cologne, and sat back, a portrait of a beautiful, self-possessed woman, eager to meet her adoring public.

Gracie quickly tidied the compartment and packed things helter-skelter. She looked up once to see that Claudia, with the complacency of royalty, was observing the awkward behavior of a serf.

On the station platform, there were indeed several hundred fans, and several policemen who had been alerted by Red Powell, and Claudia was escorted with sirens, for her protection from the people who loved her the most.

Gracie breathed a deep sigh. Well, at least she's a fairly pleasant drunk.

How wrong she was.

After San Francisco, Claudia settled lethargically into sleep. The ride was dull, mostly families traveling, and Gracie kept her out of the club car, blessing Prohibition.

Slowly, her charge became more animated, nervous, and irritable—a wild-eyed maniac by the time they got to the hotel in Chicago.

"Get me some decent liquor and a couple of male companions," Claudia shouted. "Does Si Moses think this whole miserable jaunt is a Sunday-school picnic? I can't meet the press until I've had something to soothe my nerves and some decent male companionship. I'm too goddamned nervous cooped up like this!"

"How can I?" Grace said. "What do I do?"

"Oh, my God," said Claudia. "Why the hell didn't Fergus send Red Powell!"

She snatched a bottle of champagne off the table,

strode across the ornate sitting room to the bedroom, and locked the door.

Gracie heard the cork pop. She knocked on the door. "Miss Barstow, you have to meet the press in an hour."

"Get me a man!" Claudia cried.

It seemed an age before Grace reached Fergus on the phone in Hollywood. While she stood there, holding the receiver, shaking, she heard Claudia raging to herself.

"She's gone crazy," Grace said. "She's in the bedroom yelling her head off, she has to have a man! The press is supposed to meet her in an hour. What'll I do?"

"Call the bell captain," said Fergus. "Slip him a hundred bucks, then explain that our star is nervous and needs companionship. He'll understand. And hold off the press for another hour. Give 'em lots of booze and food. I'll charter Ned Doane's plane and take over."

Grace began to cry. "I'm scared."

"Damn it, get unscared. Grace, you're responsible for a multimillion-dollar business investment. Now look, as I said, call Pete at the bell captain's desk. Tell him 'the treatment'! Wave the money. That's what you've got it for, an emergency. Mention her name. He'll know it. Understand? I'll leave at dawn and get there tomorrow."

Grace called the bell captain's desk. In about ten minutes Pete came up with a handsome Italian bellhop who leered at Gracie. She let them in feeling so dirty she thought she'd never be able to look at herself in the mirror again.

"This is pretty touchy, ma'am," said Pete, "but I'll help you out."

Grace handed him a wad of Titan's money and saw his concern quickly fade.

"Take over," she said, feeling ill. The two men stood at Claudia's door, and Pete began to cajole her into opening up. When Gracie saw the door open slightly, she fled to her room across the hall. She pressed her shaking hands against her sweating forehead and went into the bathroom, where she was sick.

She took a shower, changed into her black dress, her pearls, and her little flowered hat, bought with such stupid excitement, she remembered, just a week—a lifetime—ago.

The press gathered in the elegant Rose Room. A string quartet, like something out of *The Merry Widow,* played behind a screen of fern, and the hotel discreetly served illicit drinks in teacups.

The president of Claudia Barstow's fan club, Helen Crump, a scrawny spinster of forty plus, who wore four strings of red beads and a hat that looked like two hats, met her effusively.

"It must be a thrill traveling with her," she said. "I haven't seen Claudia since she came east to buy clothes. Well, I guess her public will just have to surrender her to us again!"

Grace wondered what Claudia's public was surrendering at the moment, and what she would ever say to the press after an hour, if Claudia didn't show up.

But in about an hour, as planned, the quartet burst into "Velia," and Claudia entered the room.

Even Gracie gasped.

There was Claudia, regenerated and regal in a chiffon gown, pearls glowing at her ivory throat and ears. Her hair was swirled above her neck in a braid that fitted her head like a crown. She seemed to glow in the candlelight, and she gazed at her companions in a dreamy, reflective way which to the romantic seemed close to tears. She extended her hand graciously to each person, recalling some names.

Claudia put her hand gently on the shoulder of the young press representative, as if she were her protégée.

"And now, my dear Gracie, you must relax," she said, in her rich dramatic voice, so the nearby press would hear. "You must be exhausted after those tiring days with me on the train."

"Oh, Miss *Barstow!*" giggled Helen Crump.

Grace retired to the edge of the crowd and gratefully tossed off a scotch and soda out of a teacup.

She busied herself handing out photographs and press releases about Claudia Barstow's new supercolossal Titan picture. She tried not to think, and she found herself smiling with a placating eagerness that would be her trademark while handling stars under varied conditions from that time on.

Claudia, ignoring her, went off on a tour of speakeasies with several members of the press, old buddies who were hearty drinkers.

I hope they do it to her, thought Grace, then this mess will be over until Fergus gets here. She flushed at the ease with which her mind was adjusting to ugliness. She refused several halfhearted invitations from young members of the press, which she figured were made with a promise for some fun after the fun; she gobbled a few limp canapes and went to her room.

Exhausted, she lay in bed, checking the press lists and itemizing the material and photographs she had given out. At least everything would be in order when Fergus arrived.

She fell asleep and was awakened by a pounding at her door. She jumped up, opened it, and confronted Claudia Barstow.

"What the hell kind of service is this!" said Claudia. Her hair was hanging over one ear, and she was drunk, her mouth curved in a thin line of resentment.

So Grace called Pete again.

It was hours before it would be dawn in Hollywood. She wished Fergus Godspeed. At the same time she was furious with him.

The party across the hall lasted all night. She curled up in her bed and pulled the covers over her head.

Damn the Barstow clan. Damn Fergus. And she'd liked him a lot, too. Damn Titan. Damn men.

Fergus would have to get her a raise, at least promote her to senior publicist, and give her an expense account to get her to stay on.

◆◆◆◆◆◆◆◆◆

"All right," said Fergus, as he sat opposite Claudia at breakfast. "Let's out with it. You have a problem, Claudia, and if you're going to stay on with Titan, you've got to face it. What are you going to do?"

"I suppose," said Claudia, raising her eyebrows, "you are referring to my drinking?"

"I suppose you're reading my mind," said Fergus, noting that she was holding her coffee cup with both hands. "Look at you. You're on the verge of dt's. We've come a long way, Claudia. You're a gifted woman. It's a pity."

Claudia strode to the fireplace, lifting one arm up to the marble mantel. She looked beautiful. Even now, mused Fergus, she's going to take stage center.

"Just you look at yourself," said Claudia. "You've come pretty far yourself. If Si hadn't needed you as a go-between, you'd be shuffling roomers in your mother's boardinghouse. Not that you haven't learned your business. But I know who your master is. Power, Fergus, power. And money, of course, which buys power. But remember this, my fine friend, one thing is ambition, another is talent. And all the power and money and ambition in the world can't take the place of talent. Without *us*, you and Si are just lousy businessmen. With us, you have a magic empire. When I work, I work. I do all right on film. I'm there at whatever ungodly hour I'm ordered to be. What I do on my own time is my own. And I pay for it, baby, don't you forget the lonely hours, the rotten impersonal hotel rooms, the drafty stages, the improvised meals, the larceny I face because I'm a movie queen. Do you really think anyone ever really loved me? Believe me, even Simon didn't love me for myself. And don't forget, dear boy, when you were a kid you arranged, right in my own bed, to get me together with Simon Moses. Remember? I was admired and slept with and sought and used because a corporation has me on millions of strips of celluloid."

"Bravo," Fergus said, applauding, "we may use that in one of those pictures you hate, which made you a millionaire."

"No millionaire," said Claudia, "you may be sure. For enough panhandlers knew how to get a lot away from me. Claudia Barstow has to try to buy her way, too. I'm the lonesomest woman in the world. Nobody wants me for me—just for what they think I can give them!"

"Seems to me you need a better business manager," said Fergus. "But you're still avoiding the issue."

"And I'll go on doing it," said Claudia, "which should be a relief to you, since I'm plugging your picture in your picture palaces, and you wouldn't want me to walk out, would you?"

"Not my picture palaces," said Fergus. "I only work here. The Moses picture houses."

"Well, you married into it, didn't you?" she said.

She walked to the window and peered out on a drizzling gray sky.

"Oh, God!" she said, in a voice of such despair that Fergus stopped.

He came to her and put his hands on her shoulders.

"Claudia, I can't help you. We all have to find ourselves. I've tried, and I'm still trying. Not doing a very good job. David's about the only thing I've got going for me."

She looked at him. He'd never seen pity or interest for him in her face before. She touched his cheek.

"Well, we have come a long way," she said, "Fergus, but I wonder if we really knew where we were going?"

"You've given a lot of people happiness," he said. "They forget their own problems when they watch you on film. That should be something."

"I guess it is," she said.

She sat on the sofa near the fire, tapped a cigarette nervously, and he lit a match.

"Just take it easy, Claudia," he said, "and slow down. Maybe you'll be lucky and find someone who really cares for you."

"Not where I stand, old pal," she said. "It's too busy and too late. You know, I guess the only thing I really enjoy is all that fake love and devotion you get while a picture is going. Just find me good stories, good actors to play the words with, a good director to raise my sights, and I'll have a few more years of make-believe. That seems to be the only thing I'm made for."

"It ain't bad." He kissed her cheek. "If I don't get going the plane will leave without me, and I'll miss a board of directors' meeting, at which I'll tell them how great you are and make a better deal when your option comes up, which is soon."

After he left, Claudia walked to a pier glass and looked at her image. The rose peignoir. The hair piled high. The face automatically arranging itself in a charming expression.

"Oh, shit!" she said, sticking out her tongue, "how corny can you get!"

The phone rang. What pest could that be?

"Hello," said a smooth male voice, "I bet you wouldn't know what voice from the past this is—it's Mike Cuneo. Remember your first movie? Well, maybe you didn't know *I* was the bankroll. How about that!"

"Mike!" she said, "for heaven's sake, of course I remember you. The floating crap game. The handsome guy with all the black curly hair. What are you doing in Chicago?"

He laughed. "You haven't heard about me?"

"No," she said, "should I?"

"I—well, I can't talk about it on the phone. But you know about Prohibition, I suppose. How would you like to go out on the town in a bulletproof car? Get the message?"

She laughed. A bonafide gangster, likely bootlegger, rumrunner. That figured, just her speed right now.

"Are you still good-looking?" she asked.

"Better," he said. "Nothing succeeds like success, you know."

"Get your ass over here," she said.

He was not exactly what she expected. He was handsomer, his clothes were flashy but expensive. He really did have a bulletproof limousine. He took her to his clubs, to his warehouses, and showed her with delight what a big shot he was.

But he nixed her drinking of hard liquor.

"It's rotgut," he said, "just for the suckers. With me, honey, you drink wine with your meals. It's healthy."

He loaded her with caviar, took her out on the lake in his fast-running yacht, proudly introduced her to his friends, some equally important, others henchmen.

For a week they traveled fast, drank wine, ate, stayed up late talking, and made love fast, at least for a few hours. He didn't have as much leisure time as she would have expected.

Sometimes he arrived late at night, after innumerable phone calls to keep her from fretting. She learned the wait was worth it. Claudia felt she had finally met a man who was more hedonistic than she.

She did not know how large an invisible kingdom he ruled, but he seemed to live on the brink of danger, and it stimulated her imagination.

A week fled quickly. She began getting urgent phone calls from Fergus.

"Claudia," said Fergus, "I know a phony cough; you haven't got the flu. So don't pull that crap on me. If you don't get back fast, Titan will sue you for damages in holding up your new production. You're a pro, you know better than that."

"Okay, okay," said Claudia, relieved that he hadn't mentioned Mike. Fergus would have been furious. Of all people, Mike Cuneo, his old sidekick, and also, a gangster.

Her compartment on the Chief looked like a seraglio. A cascade of orchids hung from the coat hook. An ermine throw and pillows covered the sofa bed. A basket of caviar, pâté, champagne, and fruit was on the table along with crystal glasses and a silver Tiffany cooler.

Mike stood by, beaming.

"Classy, huh?" he asked. "I bet nobody did you like me."

"Believe me, nobody." She smiled.

"That ain't all," he said. "Close your eyes."

He clasped a wide cuff of diamonds on her wrist. It spelled out in baguettes, like a billboard: MIKE LOVES CLAUDIA.

She was astounded.

"You see how I feel about you," he said.

"You crazy man," she said, kissing him, "it's dazzling!"

"Now," he said, "put on a little fat. I like it. And say hello to that old bastard Fergus for me."

"Why can't you go with me?"

"I've got a big business date in Canada, and that takes precautions. I don't want you to see me next time in a striped suit, they've got lousy tailors, you know. I want to be where I can grab you, baby. Maybe I'll get out to the Coast, or someday we'll make it quick to Europe. How would you like that?"

"I like it, I like it."

She settled back, wishing she could share this snuggery with him. It was sad, somehow, all this bounty alone, after so much excitement and sex. But at least she was going back to the studio feeling like a woman. She laughed at the crazy, extravagant bracelet.

Ah, well, some things in life were better left on a high.

7

Sorties with such personalities as Claudia were a small part of Fergus's expanding life. Progress in filmmaking had created a momentum that swept all the ambitious along a new and frightening path. There was no pause for self-searching, no way to stand by and watch the others.

The age of promotion had taken over. Unheard of luxuries were offered to the common man. He was suddenly promised that he could be a prince. Tastes burgeoned with exposure to a variety of goods hitherto undreamed of.

The effort of the small-time American businessman was swallowed up by the big-time spellbinders in advertising.

Now, theaters belonged to the mother company, the whole merged into one massive operation, making the original concept of just shooting a movie seem like a lark. Titan, now truly a giant, owned and processed the whole operation, and with it, incurred the massive debts.

From the mid-twenties on, America accepted the fact that movie houses must be palaces in which to see their dreams take form. Gilded temples became the meeting place and refuge of middle-class and poorer Americans, suitable shrines for the heroes and heroines on the silver screen who made them believe that all was well with the world and love was ever triumphant. Increasing unrest and shadows of depression were offset by the "gilded tripe" school of picture palaces. Patrons forgot that their shoes were getting thin from pounding the pavements.

One fantasy to lure the public was a twenty-stall ladies room with mother-of-pearl toilet seats and pink velvet lounges. This comfort station was larger than the original Little Diamond Theater.

Fergus smiled ironically, remembering the evening when he had thought Mr. Moses' red-plush Bronx movie house was the most elegant place he'd ever seen. But now, each studio had to keep pace with every gimmick that was introduced to bring the public into theaters.

The new passion for musical scores added to Fergus's problems. No longer did the piano suffice. Thematic music had to be composed to fit feature films. Sentimental themes and "sneaky music" were not enough.

Pipe organs, sometimes costing as much as eighty thousand dollars, rose up from the bowels of movie palace basements. Puccini, Wagner, Brahms, Debussy, Rachmaninoff, and Tchaikovsky were all slaughtered as the organist, a star in his own right, rose up like the Ascension of Holy Mary, the mighty Wurlitzer belching out a "theme song" and dropping vibratos to turn on the sentimental juices of the audiences.

Fergus held an extra grudge against the Russian Revolution when Eisenstein's *Potemkin* opened with a musical score especially orchestrated for it. The Russian director was widely quoted as saying, "The audience must be lashed into a fury and shaken violently by the volume of the sound. This sound can't be strong enough, and should be turned to the limit of the audiences's physical and mental capacity."

Orchestras began to tour with superproductions like Metro's *Big Parade*. In some towns even a men's choir was added, and a sound-effects crew that reproduced the explosive sounds of battle behind the screen. Smaller theaters used an infernal machine called the Alleflex, which could produce everything from the sound of a waterfall to the cry of a baby if the right technician was at the controls.

Fergus convinced Simon that the announcement, "A Simon Moses production, introducing the classical score of Daniele Giacometti," made him indeed a patron of the arts. So Simon sponsored a music department, and, knowing nothing of music, reveled in the overrich scores, believing his hireling, Giacometti, a second-rate conductor from Milan, was not a tune thief, but a genius.

Fergus watched carefully to see if Simon was again going to fall into the arms of Claudia. She was still an important star, garnering top salary and all the fringe benefits a studio could give to a valuable asset. She was beautiful in a time of beautiful people, and her performances were memorable. But something, he knew not what, had soured their liaison. They were at pains to avoid each other. Even Fergus felt her aloofness, although they remained friends. Claudia did not discuss the situation with him, and he decided to ignore it, especially since Claudia was enmeshed more and more in sudden romances and constant drinking, which now, even Simon knew about.

Perhaps Simon's vital juices had dwindled, as he had faced the death of his beloved son David, the tragedy of Martha, and now the illness of Esther.

Fergus often saw Simon's glance on him, and he knew it was filled with hatred. He returned the feeling. Whether they rode in the elevators in the new executive building, looked at rushes with the top brass, or attended board meetings, Fergus could not help but watch Simon with a personal dislike that spun itself into a series of fantasies. In his mind he saw Moses die in so many ways that he was surprised to see him alive the next time they met.

Moses had eliminated Fergus from all New York meetings. Abe was chairman of the board. Abe battled any suggestions that Fergus be granted options on private issues of Titan stock, below the market price. Seymour Sewell, Claudia and Jeffrey Barstow's agent, had been allowed this privilege for his clients to woo them away from competitive companies.

The vagaries of Titan production, distributors putting up financing for a share of the rental releases, the percentage of revenue that Titan got (and Simon's skim-off expense accounts), were a questionable book to Fergus. He owned 2 percent of the original Moses family 50 percent (minus the advances put on each film until it was recouped), but they had compounded new corporations on new corporations, so his ownership was mostly on old, used-up product. Although he had married Esther, he felt he was as much of an outsider as he had been when he was a callow kid in the Bronx.

Simon was no enigma, for Fergus knew the inner workings of Simon's world. Shielded by Fergus, Abe, and his staff, he was placed on a carefully manufactured pedestal as the complete Hollywood mogul.

Fergus resented his impressive facade, his personal charm, his thick head of hair, his dapper moustache, his poetic brown eyes, and his elegance—all unearned assets. The cleverest publicists in the business worked at his speeches, given on ceremonial occasions with great success. He photographed even handsomer than in life.

Fergus knew that Simon had never kept up with the new techniques and advancements of the changing film world. He veered away from any innovation that could add to the overhead, and he had to be argued into improvements before he benignly announced them to the press as his own ideas.

Yet, his instinct sometimes led him beyond his knowledge. His selection of properties and personalities was remarkable. He was in New York often enough to view new plays; he was handed expertly written synopses of good books. His story editor, Laura Gold, a wise woman with dramatic skills, could crack the shell of a promising story and hand him the tempting nutmeat, as she told him the simple theme or intriguing gimmick of a potential property. Practically a nonreader, Simon could analyze best while listening and make flash decisions. Armed with this material and abetted by his funds, Simon could quickly ferret out a property and have it bought before it got into the hands of other studio heads who went through a leisurely gamut of analysts and a stepladder of doubting Thomases.

He was the first to have spies in New York theaters and publishing houses. And he also was the first to look through newspapers at tomato queens, cotton queens, orange queens, football queens, and have them photographed and tested. He also was adept at spotting talent on film. In a film test for a new male matinee idol from Europe, he spotted a young girl sitting in the background and had her tested. She became one of his stars, and the European was never signed.

Having nothing to lose, he dealt serenely with people and situations, then behind closed doors screamingly castigated employees who had to solve his problems without argument to save their own skins. To himself he represented the fulfillment of power. He had no latent ambitions, no unexplored talents, for, like many of his era, film had brought him prestige and worldly gifts, acclaim and attention beyond his wildest dreams. There had been no comparable magic opportunity for a simple, uneducated man in the history of the world.

His fortune proliferated with his theater chain and studio, monstrous Siamese twins feeding on each other's blood. Abe and Fergus, East and West Coast, hatchet men, eliminated the weak and retained the efficient.

◆◆◆◆◆◆◆◆

The moment of intimacy Fergus had shared with Claudia in Chicago was lost. He had hoped it would merge into a close friendship, for he remembered their first trip to California, the first exciting trials of moviemaking, and, of course, the initiation into the rites of man and woman she had so unwittingly given him.

But Claudia's growing world suited her. Never since the times of Poppaea, Cleopatra, and Empress Josephine had hedonistic women come into such a paradise.

Hollywood in the middle and late twenties was a perpetual social circus.

Youth, ambition, and money all seemed to be whirling into a faster and faster vortex, which no one seemed to think might end in a descent into a maelstrom.

Newcomers with newfound prestige found themselves feted, and the stars who had been in the film business from the beginning became the aristocracy.

Everyone of importance had their houses constantly redecorated, bought art and antiques, and had their portraits painted. There was a great emphasis on imaginative pools. It was considered de rigueur to run films privately; some of the elite refused to enter motion-picture palaces, save for premieres, which of course Hollywood society attended en masse.

Out of custom-built limousines, some with both chauffeurs and footmen, stepped dazzling beauties, dripping satins and dragging furs, escorted by handsome heroes, or celluloid Caesars.

Every time a celebrity came to town, Claudia managed, with the help of her staff secretary and the publicity department, to plan a party as elaborate as a picture sequence and to outdo the last party. It was tough competition what with Gloria Swanson's Bastille Day fete for her husband, the Marquis de la Falaise.

Louella Parsons's invitations to meet important visitors were a must. Ouida and Basil Rathbone took over the Victor Hugo restaurant for a party, where several hundred celebrities came dressed as brides and grooms to celebrate a wedding anniversary. The royalty on the hill, Mary Pickford and Douglas Fairbanks, had elegant soirees at Pickfair. If you weren't invited there, you just didn't belong. And the ne plus ultra of the whole society was San Simeon, the 400,000-acre estate of William Randolph Hearst, where people vacationed in baroque villas, dined in a duplicate of a nave in Westminster Abbey, and looked at movies in baronial splendor, but had their luggage frisked in case they brought liquor. Jeffrey said it was too hard on his metabolism and declined for reasons of health. And no one could compete with the birthday parties that Marion Davies gave Hearst at their seventy-room Georgian beach house—a thousand or so were invited. Claudia and Jeffrey were accepted as successful renegades from the stage who were forgiven for making good in the new medium. Claudia loved it all.

Puffed up with social importance, a superstar in a time of superstars, and battling the business world that Fergus represented, when Claudia paid a visit to the studio, she seemed to be deliberately difficult, and Fergus realized that he had an incipient ulcer. He would take several antacid pills, drink milk, and see that Harriet Foster (God help her if she didn't) had Claudia's favorite violet-tipped cigarettes on hand and, if necessary, a ceremonial bottle of chilled champagne to toast whatever disaster had been threatened and averted. If solution was not forthcoming, Claudia would sweep out of the office without a good-bye, and Seymour Sewell would be called into the breach.

This day, as always, she was dressed in full movie-star garb—a chic French silk suit, a cloche hat with a veil over her eyes, and a fox fur slithering over her shoulders.

Fergus dreaded these meetings; they were always a prologue to an unpleasant hassle with Simon. Harriet Foster ushered her in, beaming ecstatically at the presence of a "movie star," especially one who sent her a large bottle of Shalimar every Christmas. Claudia rushed up to Fergus, proffered one cheek, and kissed the air. When Miss Foster withdrew, she threw down her furs, settled into the corner of a sofa, and kicked off her shoes. Fergus lit her cigarette which she screwed into a trumpetlike gold holder.

He knew she would present her grievance after a few puffs. This day was no exception.

"Fergus," she said, so quietly that he knew she was going to take the soft approach, which meant bedrock dealing, "I am not going to pull any crap, darling. I'm speaking for Jeffrey as well as myself, and before Seymour or any lawyers get into it, for old times' sake, I just want you to know from me what it's all about."

"What's your problem?" he asked, trying not to get hot under the collar. The company had just been euchred into spending twenty thousand dollars for a Broadway property for the Barstows. This was a little soon to ask for another moon.

"You know what's wrong," said Claudia, "and I am astonished that I have to come to you. This is something you should have brought to Jeffrey and me long ago. Titan's whole operation is as outdated as the dodo bird."

"We just bought you and Jeffrey the hottest property on Broadway. Don't tell me it's outdated. Or, may I add, the price we paid for it."

"It's the way you're making it," said Claudia. "How

the hell can you do a good drama today without sound? I refuse to do another silent picture."

"Don't think I haven't thought about it," said Fergus, "but Claudia, you're premature. The sound system hasn't been proven yet. The actors stand huddled around a mike hidden in some damned flowerpot. And, most important, sound facilities aren't built into our theaters. Believe me, Claudia, if you knew the expense of converting, you'd see why Titan isn't ready. Business isn't even too good as it is."

"I don't give a damn if you're ready for it," said Claudia, crushing out her cigarette, a danger signal. "You've got the finest theater family, the Barstows, working for you, ready to step into the new medium. The public's tired of seeing Jeffrey's profile on foot after foot of silent film."

In an alcoholic haze, thought Fergus.

"I'll discuss it again with Simon," said Fergus.

"I know what that old bastard will say if it involves a dollar," said Claudia. "But I'll tell you one thing, Fergus, I'm too mature to rely on dumb good-looking leading men like that lavender Leslie Charles. And I'm sick of mugging and pantomime routines. That went out with Mabel Normand."

"What exactly do you want?" asked Fergus.

"One, I want sound. Two, I want a distinguished director. Not some wild-eyed ex-marine or a johnny-jump-up with his cap on backwards like Plimpton. Somebody with a little style, like that charming British stage director, Edwin Crewes."

Fergus's eyebrows went up a bit. He had seen her at the Cocoanut Grove dancing with the Englishman, who had come out to Los Angeles to direct a Christmas pantomime for the exclusive Ebell Club. He found himself, to his surprise, wishing that she were still with Simon. Life would be simpler at the office.

"Somebody who's a gentleman," continued Claudia, "who can move actors across a stage without having them trip over their clodhoppers. And, when the time comes, be prepared. I want someone to write the script who knows enough not to hand us clichés, mixed metaphors, and dangling participles."

"All right," said Fergus, "you're leveling with me. Now I'll level with you. Costs have skyrocketed. We have built up a stable of actors, directors, and writers. We have gone into massive expense to update the musical scores for our pictures. You know how we have hired live talent to add to the glamour of atmospheric prologues to your superproductions."

"That's not enough," said Claudia. "Fergus, that's not movies, it's trimmings. I want somebody important, an exciting pistol of a director–like–like Allan Dwan."

"He's a little busy with Douglas Fairbanks," said Fergus acidly, "but aside from all this bitching, what are you doing for Titan, since you expect it to do so much for you? You know the disaster of your last personal appearance. And vanishing with that gangster Mike Cuneo for a week. If that little caper had hit the papers, it would have been the finish for you and your pictures."

Claudia glanced down, fluttering her lashes.

"I'm sorry," she said, "after all, he was your friend and bankroll–yes, he told me. And he was sweet and kind, wouldn't let me drink hard stuff, and really pampered me. I came home feeling much better about life."

"While you were doing that," said Fergus, "three guys ended up in cement kimonos, and suspicions are on that sweet, kind guy."

"I can't believe it. That's terrible!" She pulled her sleeve higher and flashed the dazzling cuff of diamonds: MIKE LOVES CLAUDIA.

"I guess I'd better not wear this any more. I thought it was kind of cute."

Fergus glanced at it, horrified.

"Oh, God!" he said, "that's all we need, to have the press get onto that!"

He was not too surprised, knowing her, that she shucked any moral implications of her liaison.

"I'm sorry," she said. "I'll put it in my safe-deposit box. I'm really not being a bad girl, Fergus. I was tired. And I had a bad time with Simon. I won't go into it, but it hurt me pretty much."

Her eyes clouded. Fergus had never known a man to affect her so.

"And I had made four pictures in a row. You know that. I was tired and unhappy. I didn't want to go on the road—Simon told me it would save his neck. But you know I can't bear to be alone. And Mike came along, with all his sweetness and generosity, how was I to know what went on behind the scenes? Well, my God, Fergus, I have to have some fun!"

"It's done," said Fergus. "Okay, aside from your private life, taxes, staff, and inventory are eating us up. What you want may be possible next year. But it will take months to gear the Titan holdings for such a big changeover, if and when we feel it is necessary. And as you said, it would take months to rewrite a script into a literary masterpiece even if we converted to sound. And I needn't tell you, you must have heard this—these sound stages have made it necessary for the camera to be imprisoned in a box like a telephone booth. How do you get your action in a setup like that? And the set's a box, too. Nobody can move, because the camera can't move. And let me tell you something else. At Warner's the other day they dragged a fat cameraman out of the booth unconscious. They're keeping it quiet. He almost died. He's still very sick. And did you know that the camera speed has to be doubled with sound? The lights make a sweltering hell out of the stages. Are you ready for that? Are you ready to consider a cut in salary for the enormous cost of rebuilding stages and theaters? Have you talked to Jeffrey about this?"

"I think it's all an excuse," said Claudia, "so you and Simon can go on with your cheap production and your big profits. But you'll see, it won't work. You're going to let Warner's and Vitaphone and Fox and Movietone get ahead of you."

"Look," said Fergus, "just go along with this one, Claudia. I'll talk to Simon about getting a theater-oriented director on a future picture, and we'll get a New York playwright to work when we find a property. Then when we're ready to convert, you will have a perfect production. What else can I do?"

"You can tell Si what I said," she said, slipping into her shoes. "And don't expect us to report to work next week until we have your promises on paper. You can talk to our agent."

She tossed her furs over her shoulder and stood on tiptoe, half closing her thick-lashed eyes. For a moment, she pressed her slender body against him. Claudia's eternal magic overcame him. He put his arms around her. Her total mystery touched him again.

She pulled back, patting him on the cheek. He had to remind himself that she likely had another man on her mind.

"All right, Stilts," she said, "as I told you in Chicago, we've come a long way, and Claudia hasn't forgotten it."

He warmed. But she said, "If you just wouldn't be so bloody stubborn. Tell that selfish old son-of-a-bitch what's what in this great big, fast-moving Hollywood."

She breezed out, throwing him a kiss.

He felt forlorn. He had almost come close to Claudia, to a human, and she had taken it away. She had only come to him, as usual, for privilege.

The bond that had started the whole company—the passion that Simon Moses had for her and her affection—had fallen away these years. Ambition had taken over.

In the hall, Claudia paused, nervously fishing a cigarette out of her purse. Damn it, even Fergus made her nervous, and she could always cope with him.

It was a tough life. She couldn't tell him Jeffrey was on a blind drunk in Ensenada, and she'd had to send Seymour Sewell down to get him out of the local pokey, with a thick wad of bills to buy concealment.

She couldn't tell him that she'd had a personal problem that would have blown sky-high. In a mood of deep loneliness, she'd run off and married Sandy Forbes, a playboy who had appealed to her. They'd eloped in his private plane to his Arizona ranch. But on the wedding night, Sandy hadn't lived up to his lavish expressions of devotion and passion. He was so terrified of the fact that he had married a magnificent beauty, a famous star, that he was impotent.

After a five-day unconsummated honeymoon, embarrassing nights, and much drinking, she had convinced Sandy to buy back all records of their marriage. Humiliated, he had agreed and then had fled to Europe.

God, how could you explain to Fergus, or to Simon (if he cared), that she was lonely, frightened, that she saw the signs of age on her face, that she knew her brother was heading for an alcoholic nose dive, and that she needed every possible benefit Titan could give her to stay afloat.

She wanted to tear off her masquerade of chic Paris clothes. They were all such inadequate cover-ups for her poverty of spirit. She had made a career because she was at the right place at the right time, but she knew that she had not delivered as an actress, and, as a woman, she had failed miserably.

There's only one thing to do, she thought. Get home, take a foaming bath, get into a silk robe, and have a couple of icy-cold martinis as soon as possible.

Fergus looked out to the parking lot and watched her get into her car.

By God, she's right, he realized. That damnable

Barstow instinct is right. Now is the time we have to convert to sound. Otherwise we'll sink.

How will I ever convince the old man?

◆◆◆◆◆◆◆◆

"Let the bastards go!" shouted Simon. "Let them go—go! Release them from their contract. That woman has put me through hell. Now she's trying to destroy me. Every time there's a slump in business some *macher* tries to bring in some expensive gimmick. I wish somebody'd invent a gimmick to get rid of the goddamned actors! Who needs to go bankrupt for ingrates like the Barstows?"

"They're not considered ingrates by the Morgan interests," said Fergus. "They're our principal asset, including all our other stars and properties."

"Who needs Morgan interests!" Simon's hand was shaking.

"Now, take it easy, Mr. Moses. We do. We need Charlie O'Rourke's goodwill. Abe isn't bringing him out here for the ride. We've got to be financed for this massive move. Claudia may have triggered it, but let's be honest. The studio has to convert to sound. Your theaters have to convert to sound. I've already been able to get two thousand surplus army blankets to be hung on our big stage temporarily for the acoustics. It was a coup. Lasky tried to buy them right out from under me."

Simon sat down and clenched his fists.

"I ask you, is it just?" he said. "The Morgan interests put up money to promote sound systems, and yet already we have to put in their systems, and they finance us to do it. Is it just?"

"You know business isn't a matter of what's just," said Fergus. "It's progress. We've come a long way, and we'll go a long way. Sound has changed everything."

"I don't even want to look that banker in the eye,"

said Simon, "after all we've done, all we've done, to go in hock to a bank. Four million dollars!"

"If you didn't have valuable assets they wouldn't lend it to you," Fergus said. "Now, *The Darkening House* company is shooting the scene in front of the mansion in Riverside. We're setting up a picnic lunch in the garden. I'll romance O'Rourke. You just come along and enjoy yourself. It's been a long time since you've visited a location. Everyone knows what a big wheel O'Rourke is on Wall Street, and your appearance will give the whole company a lift."

"I could do without going on that set!"

Fergus glanced at him, surprised. Simon had never made a personal remark to him about the situation with Claudia.

"Let's get going. Oh, by the way, Andrew Reed came out on the same train. He considers Leslie Charles his protégé, you know."

"Yes," said Simon, "I know, only too well—"

Fergus remembered the moment that had launched the young actor's career, when Martha died. He felt sorry for Simon. Life had dealt him a few underhanded blows. And he was bewildered by the recent recession of his business.

"Cheer up," he said. "Red Powell sent over this stuff with the publicity department. It's a quick survey, an interview from Lee de Forest about sound systems and how they work. Now when you talk to Andrew Reed, act as if you invented sound yourself. Don't let him know you're against it. He's sure to quote you in his syndicated columns."

"Damned if I will!" said Simon, crumpling the papers.

"Damned if you won't," said Fergus. "You have no choice."

Smoothing the papers, Simon followed after him in such a docile way that Fergus was concerned.

♦♦♦♦♦♦♦♦

Andrew Reed always relished a trip to the Coast on the Chief. He traded cigars, scotch (carefully packed in flat flasks in pigskin cases), and inner-sanctum motion-picture gossip with important personages who were also on business trips to insanity land.

But the end of his rainbow was his young protégé, Leslie Charles. They would rendezvous at the Riverside Mission Inn in an elegant suite. In his luggage was a magnum of French champagne so rare it was practically holy.

Andrew informed Fergus that he would be on location the next morning, rented a Marmon, and drove out to meet Leslie, his heart beating wildly.

Leslie's handsome beauty, his dramatic gestures, and his luminous eyes heavily fringed with curling lashes was everything Andrew thought the film audience should dream about. But the boy was a nervous wreck and needed help.

After an elegant repast, over their champagne, the sitting room fireplace lit against the chill of the California evening, Leslie opened up, close to tears.

"You don't know what I've gone through. You just can't live as freely as you do in civilized circles in New York; you have to go completely underground for fun, and you have to pretend to be panting over some woman all the time, or your goose is just cooked!"

"How about Claudia?" asked Andrew.

Leslie batted his eyes.

"I—I had to do it with her," he said, "one night on location. It was awful. I threw up later."

"You actually did it?" asked Andrew. "You poor thing!"

As long as it was not a man, it didn't bother him.

"It was just horrible," said Leslie. "I drank a lot."

"Well," said Andrew, "I guess you just have to deliver once in a while. And you mustn't ignore Claudia's value, Leslie, she's a brilliant actress, and her scenes with you have made you look very attractive as a lover. And she's important in other ways."

He lifted an eyebrow. "Don't give her a chance to gossip about you. You could flirt with her—a little." He patted his knee.

Encouraged, Leslie sipped more champagne.

"I—I suppose I could if I had to," he said.

"Well, we must plan a little strategy," said Andrew. "You must be a star, and you must be socially top bracket. My dear boy, you know our world is like an iceberg. There is a great deal more under the surface than on top."

"Don't I know!" said Leslie. "Why even a cowboy star—"

"Let's not discuss that!" said Andrew sharply. "Now, first we must find some lovely young girls, preferably respectable Catholics, who are starting out in pictures. You must escort them to gala affairs like the Mayfair ball. Now dear boy, sandwich these dates between distinguished character actresses, because most of them with good speaking voices will become more and more important in this coming talkie invasion. Thank God you had diction lessons while you were dancing in the Follies."

"Oh, yes," said Leslie, "and I'm working out at the gym as you suggested, and I swim a lot."

"Good idea," said Andrew, "but, boysie, I'd spend more time practicing diction. There is no question, talkies are going to inundate this business. And if you're clever, you'll be one of the first."

He poured more champagne. "Now, you must go to parties given by conservative women with important husbands. It's important for you to get a reputation of being a nice young man who can be trusted. But every once in a while you must seem to break away. Take out a sexy number for effect. Try to select someone who is having a secret affair with an important man, preferably a married executive. This will give you immense publicity as a good cover-up and keep your name going as a beau-about-town. And, my God, avoid tramps like Claudia Barstow. You must always have somebody who is unapproachable for some reason or other, like some secret lesbian star, and show every evidence of being in love with her."

"It's so complicated," said Leslie.

"You know careers are made that way. My column is being syndicated more and more, and I have great hopes for the future."

"Oh, Andy," said Leslie, "what would I do without you! I just dread tomorrow; you've got to be on that set for moral support. I have to do the most awful scenes with Claudia. And I just hate mugging for that vulgar Plimpton."

"Cheer up," said Andrew. "One good thing about sound is that it's going to kill mugging dead and smother pantomime. Dear boy, who knows what the day will bring. Now let's go to bed."

But Andrew's wildest fancies could not have told him that tomorrow would be platinum security for the future—both for himself and his protégé.

◆◆◆◆◆◆◆◆

The set, nestled against the San Bernardino mountains, represented a southern mansion. Claudia in crinolines stood by the veranda. A makeup man blew spray on Leslie's curly hair so it wouldn't fall over his forehead in the rising Santa Ana wind. The hot blast was getting on everyone's nerves.

A violinist and cellist, a screen protecting them from the gusts, were playing "Love's Old Sweet Song" to work Claudia into the mood.

Claudia was not in the mood. Getting up at five on location with a hangover was sheer hell, and she was angry. That was why she had tied one on last night. It had been irritating enough to stay in the gloomy old Mission Inn, and there had been little company.

She had been faced with the sheep's eyes that her

supposed inamorato, Leslie Charles, was casting at his lover, Andrew Reed. They could have had dinner with her, but they obviously wanted to be alone. So she had skipped dinner and, fuming, had had a few drinks instead.

To function this morning, she'd had a prairie oyster, and, when that didn't do the trick, she followed it with a scotch chaser.

And now, Andrew, without asking her permission, had chosen to get as close to the camera as he could to watch his boyfriend emote. The scene almost looked like a three shot. She would have liked him ordered off the set, but his column was too influential to risk his displeasure. All she could do was pretend to be the pansy's best friend, and that irked her, too.

A makeup man rushed up to drop glycerin in her eyes. The reflectors and camera were at the ready, and Plimpton stood, megaphone at hand.

"Okay Claudia?" he asked.

She nodded.

"Action," said Plimpton. "Now Leslie, you rush in. That's a boy. Watch those wrists. Come up behind her. Now kiss her. Kiss her. You haven't seen her for a long time, and you're back from the war."

At this moment, the Moses limousine pulled up. Fergus got out first, handed Simon out, and then O'Rourke, the banker, a robust enthusiastic Irishman who was having his first look at the world of make-believe. The car door slammed.

Claudia looked offstage.

"Cut," said Plimpton. "Folks, let's have a little quiet on the set. Miss Barstow has to get in the mood. Now Leslie, give it a little more punch. My God, you *love* her. Ready?"

"No," said Claudia. "This goddamned wind has dried up my glycerin. You'd better give me more."

The makeup man rushed in, dropped tears in her eyes, and backed out.

"You mean," said O'Rourke to Simon, deeply impressed at being on a set, "that she can't really cry?"

All eyes turned in horror.

Claudia turned on him. "What the hell do you mean I can't cry?" she said. "Who are these people on my set?"

"Oh," said Fergus, "I'm sorry. This is Mr. O'Rourke, from New York."

"Well, Mr. O'Rourke," said Claudia, "you can just bet I can cry. I'm crying for my profits, when this lousy management makes me mug, while everyone else in town is acting with dialogue. Believe me, Titan is run like a Chinese rat race."

Simon stretched his hands toward her. "Claudia, please," he said, "Mr. O'Rourke is from the J. P. Morgan interests."

"I don't care if he's Tom Thumb!" said Claudia.

"Please, Claudia, let me talk to you." Simon turned apologetically to O'Rourke. His face was ashen. "You'll have to forgive these temperamental artists, Claudia—"

"Don't Claudia me," she said, "it's a little late for you to be toadying around. All I get from you is concern about your bankroll. You don't even try to sleep with me anymore. Or maybe you can't."

Fergus stepped forward and took Claudia's arm.

"I think you'd better go to your dressing room," he said.

She pulled her arm away, tearing her dress. Her breast was exposed. He smelled whiskey on her breath.

"And *you* leave me alone," she said. "You're not my lover anymore either."

Compounding her relationship with everyone on the set, Claudia turned to Andrew in her fury.

"And why you have to stare down my tonsils while I and your lily boy Leslie do a so-called love scene, I can't fathom. I should think you'd protect your lover better than that, considering you're trying to build him up as the great cocksman of all time."

O'Rourke, red faced and struck dumb, stood by uncomfortably, not knowing where to look. He finally glanced at Simon, and his expression changed to horror.

The orchestra continued their inappropriate rendition of "Love's Old Sweet Song." In fury, Andrew glanced at O'Rourke and followed his stricken expression.

Simon had opened his mouth, but the words never came out. He stepped over a garden flagstone and tried to grasp one of the pillars of the veranda. There seemed to be an implosion in his mouth. He looked toward Claudia and gasped. Fergus released Claudia's arm and reached out.

"No!" he gasped, pulling away from Fergus.

Claudia put her hands to her face and screamed.

Fergus felt it was like his fantasy but different. Simon grasped the pillar and slowly slid down. All Fergus could think of was that he'd get splinters in his fingers.

Claudia rushed forward and bent over him.

"Oh, Simon," she said, "oh, Si–Si!"

She grasped his hand but he pulled it away, staring at her in revulsion.

Fergus stepped in.

"Get back everybody!" he said. "Call the nurse." An ambulance, doctor, and nurse always stood by on location.

Simon was put on a stretcher and carried to the car.

"Oh, Si, Si, what have I done!" Claudia cried. She ran to Simon on the stretcher, taking his hand.

"Claudia," said Fergus, pulling her away, "for God's sake, don't scare him more!"

This shattered her. She hid her face in his shoulder, sobbing hysterically.

The nurse clamped an oxygen mask over Simon's white face, and the ambulance headed for the Riverside emergency hospital.

Fergus led the hysterical woman to her dressing room. Why, he thought, why do I always get stuck with everything that happens to the Moses family? It seems to be my fate to try to glue it all together.

Claudia threw herself on the small sofa. Fergus noticed that a bottle of scotch and several glasses were more prominent than her makeup.

"Now, Claudia," he said, "I'm just as shaken as you are, so try to calm yourself."

She looked at him through her tears, mascara streaming down her cheeks. He handed her a towel.

"You!" she said, "*you* as shaken as I am! Don't make me laugh, Fergus Austin. You've always hated him. I know how jealous you've always been. So don't give me that crap. Believe it or not, I love Simon Moses. I want to be with him!"

"That's just what he needs," said Fergus. "You triggered this attack, and now you want to have hysterics at his bedside and play your third-act curtain."

He picked up the bottle.

"This is what did it. I told you in Chicago where you were heading. You've got to quit it, Claudia. When you drink you're not in control of yourself."

She nodded. "It's hard to do what I have to do."

"It's hard to do what *I* have to do," he said. "In Chicago, you accused me of being motivated by power. Well, I worked damned hard to get it. And lucky for you I have it. I know more of what goes on than anyone in our studio. They can't do without me, or they'd get rid of me. That's power, baby, and don't you forget it. Right now, with Simon probably in a massive thrombosis—yes, that's it, he has blood pressure higher than a summer thermometer in Death Valley—and Abe Moses in the office right now staring at our lousy returns, you need my power. You know why?"

He saw that he was distracting her. She looked at him quizzically.

"Because I can call this picture off while you go dry

out. I can tell the board that you have nervous exhaustion from your arduous work on location and save your neck while you cost us thousands of dollars. I can tell the press that Simon Moses is suffering from food poisoning. I can shut the mouths of the whole crew—they won't work again if they spill the beans. I can even shut Andy Reed's mouth by bribing him. And this is power, kiddo."

He picked up the whiskey bottle and glasses and threw them in the wastebasket. On second thought, he picked up the basket.

"Now," he said, "clean up your face. I'll have a limousine take you right to Las Cruces Sanatorium. Your maid can pack your things at the Mission Inn."

She wiped her eyes and looked at him.

"Okay, Fergus," she said, "but please, please, let me know how he is, and if it's all right, tell him I'm sorry, oh my God, I'm sorry!"

She began to cry again.

"Knock it off!" said Fergus. "Look, I've got to get over to the hospital. He won't be getting any messages from anyone, Claudia. He'll be fighting for his life if he's lucky. I'll phone you at the sanatorium. Now don't you worry. Just buck up."

She seemed so forlorn and, in her pain, so wistful and feminine that his heart went out to her. Aside from success, she hadn't had too much in life, either.

"I'll try," she whispered. "Oh, Fergus, sometimes, with all the things that are expected of me, I just can't measure up. I'm not that goddess on a pedestal everyone thinks a movie star should be. Everybody's after me for something or other. They all expect more than I can deliver. They bleed me dry."

"Well, you won't replace anything with alcohol," said Fergus. "I've got to go, honey."

She stood up, and he gave her a kiss on the cheek.

"Oh, Fergie," she said bleakly, clinging to him, "oh—Fergie!"

"Look," he said, "I've got to go. I'll keep in touch."

He embraced her a moment. Then he let her go. No use getting emotionally involved with her again.

He carried the wastebasket outside and emptied it in a large trash bin.

He and O'Rourke, who was deeply disturbed, made a brief stop at the emergency hospital. Simon was under sedation. His breathing and heartbeat had stabilized. Fergus called Abe at the studio and made arrangements for Simon to be transferred to the Good Samaritan Hospital in Los Angeles.

As they rode back to Hollywood, Fergus was glad the other man in the limousine could not read his mind. O'Rourke had his own culpable nimbus, for he had triggered the incident with his blundering question.

But Fergus was blanketed with guilt. So many times he had wished Simon Moses out of the way and planned what he would do if he could control the studio. Now that he faced complete responsibility, at least for a while, he looked at things differently. It had all happened in such a shocking manner, poor Moses stricken under the most degrading circumstances.

Without the umbrella of Simon, he knew that all he had worked for, all that he had dreamed and fought and scrapped for all these years was in limbo. This was the worst time for the sickness of a man who was a figurehead of a picture company. Simon Moses was indeed a tycoon. His presence had glued things together through the formative years. He had kept his subordinates in his shadow; even his brother Abe, who managed theaters and real estate in New York, could not project the Titan image as Simon did.

At the studio, Abe was leaning back in his swivel chair, his desk stacked with papers. Fergus felt he already looked like the man in control.

"I called the hospital again," Abe said. "Looks like he'll pull through. The next twenty-four hours will tell. I'll go over and alert Rebecca. I can't tell her on the phone. Fergus, you take care of the press."

"Yes," said Fergus, "and if anybody asks, it's food poisoning. For God's sake keep any rumor of a thrombosis out of the papers."

"You're right," said Abe, "that's all the studio needs now. How long will you close down production on *The Darkening House*?"

"A week ought to do it."

"Are we insured?" asked Abe.

Fergus nodded. "Always," he said.

He was taken aback by Abe's calm, but he remembered how sharp Abe had been when he and David had tried to start FEDA. It figured . . . Abe was a survivor.

Fergus looked up at the Titan tower, and recalled how he had jeered at Titans as a massive, dim-featured race. He had dreamed of breaking the chains like Prometheus and rising up. Now, how far could he rise?

Once in the sanctuary of his office, the wrenching in his stomach caused him to reach for his ever-present antacid pills. He realized how difficult it would be to start business with another Simon Moses even if he could find one. Not only was that breed disappearing, but a studio complex was always changing. Little big things—panchromatic film or orthochromatic, lenses, filters, camera movement, automation of cameras. Moses had always accepted the fact that Fergus worked hand in hand with Jules and his father. He agreed with Fergus's dictum—technical improvements were necessary. Now Fergus would have to carry all decisions by himself.

With salaries soaring and time schedules dominating the studio, outside interference and the resultant time waste would be disaster.

Advertising, promotion, publicity, and distribution, now that Titan was handling all these things, had staffs larger than the whole studio personnel had been several years before.

It took a shock like Simon's attack to make Fergus realize how the studio had grown. A dozen stars. At least thirty contract players. Factories of craftsmen creating clothes, props, sets, and furnishings that could take care of a city, Titan was really the word for it. Titan would have to be a giant to compete with the other giants that were stretching their hands across the land to reach into the temples of cinema and grab the money that poured into the coffers.

He thought of Andrew Reed. His gossip column was sopped up mornings with coffee, he was read more than any other movie writer in the land. His goodwill was invaluable. He was a maker of stars.

Fergus called him.

"Andrew, you always seem to be the one who is around when the Moses family has its heartbreaks. And we're grateful for your understanding. I want you to know *how* grateful—I have arranged to get you a syndication outlet in ten southern newspapers. We're cracking the market for Titan, and I'll give you exclusives on any news we have. And the first scoop is that we are converting to sound. If you would like to come to my house tonight, we'll settle the details. And I'd like to help you with the story you're going to write about Simon Moses and today's events. Of course you understand it was a digestive upset."

He paused a moment to feel him out.

"Of course I understand," said Andrew.

"I'm glad," said Fergus. "As a matter of fact, Claudia must have had the same thing. She's resting for a few days herself. Please tone it all down. I'm counting on you, you're a very valuable man to us."

"Forget that bitch, Claudia Barstow? That's going too far for credibility," said Andrew.

"I understand," said Fergus quickly, "but the most important thing I thought you'd like to know, Leslie Charles's talents will fit very well into our new program. Along with a new and much better contract. This young man has a fine voice and good diction, rare around here."

"Ah, yes," said Andrew. Fergus could see him gesturing to his darling who was undoubtedly standing by. "Well, that is most kind. He is deeply concerned about Mr. Moses, he feels that he is like a father to him."

"The boy has a brilliant future," urged Fergus.

"Good breeding shows," said Andrew. "It's very kind of you to see me under such circumstances. I'll come by."

He turned to Leslie and smiled as he hung up.

"You see," he said, "you never know, do you, boysie."

◆◆◆◆◆◆◆◆

In the history of Hollywood, a studio has never closed down because a leader was ill or died. Simon recuperated at his house in Palm Springs, and Titan marched on.

In due time, the Morgan interests negotiated a multimillion-dollar loan to the Titan studio and theater chain. Sound was to be installed in the theaters. New sound stages and equipment must be built to update the studio.

Jules and his father had the best grapevine in town because of their colleagues throughout the industry, dedicated craftsmen who thought night and day of the great changes in cinema.

"Forget the Vitagraph disc recording," said Jules. "I have some tests to run of the Case Sponable sound track on film. Just listen."

Fergus was in a quandary, but he realized production could not stop, so he accepted their advice and plunged, sometimes sleepless because of the radical decisions he was forced to make. Stages were hung with temporary baffles. Actors sweltered. Following the plan of Paramount, a company often shot at night when there was less noise. And policemen stood outside padded stage doors and blew their brains out with shrill whistles to silence pedestrians or cars that might infringe on the sacrosanct area.

Sound technicians were the cocks of the walk for a short time, telling off actors, directors, and even production chiefs as they twiddled the mysterious dials. Watching their shenanigans, Fergus decided they could be replaced. He had a brainstorm after a conference with the Cadeauxs. They called in experts from Western Electric, and the tyranny was put down. The only despot was sound. Even if actors and crews almost perished as lights were hotter than hell itself, the studio would flourish.

At the same time, careers were ruined. Many actors did not have voices to match their appearance. Directors, used to wheedling their actors into emotion with off-camera direction, were muzzled. Important visitors ruined scenes, and stages were closed, irritating visiting dignitaries who wanted to be in on the new mystery of filmmaking of which they were an economic part. The old backup music, which undid emotions on the set, was ended, and in essence all of Hollywood could hear a pin drop for the first time—or else.

The great German director, Ernst Lubitsch, became more important in spite of his thick accent, while his favored actor, Emil Jannings, received an Oscar for one of the last silents and retired to Germany. All of this led Lubitsch to remark: "the most interesting thing about this changeover to sound is that actors have fallen by the wayside, directors have lost their jobs, writers their careers, but the only group which has remained intact is the producers."

After this sarcastic remark, eyes twinkling, Lubitsch chewed on his cigar and laughed. Considering the often illiterate background of many of the moguls, all Hollywood also laughed—nervously.

Eventually, Titan theater palaces across the land

flashed the announcement: THIS THEATER IS WIRED FOR MAGNIFICENT TITANTONE.

◆◆◆◆◆◆◆◆

Jules was delighted with the new panchromatic film. With the aid of the Professor's filters, blue skies that had previously gone white blossomed into dramatic contrasts. Claudia's eyes became a glorious focus for her expressive face, instead of pale pools—a lighting problem that had necessitated her cameramen to hold up a piece of black velvet behind the camera for close-ups, so her pupils would dilate.

"Soon," said Jules, "cameramen will be as valuable as stars. Color is getting better. Some of us will use our cameras as an expression of realism. Other stories will call for romance, shooting through gauzes and diffused lenses—you know, candlelight, silvers, chiffons, and elegance. And you'd better use color. That two-strip process of Dr. Kalmus at Technicolor is going to make mature stars like Claudia and Jeffrey look much better. The skin tone is great."

The Professor agreed, lost in enthusiasm. He labored endlessly, creating lenses and filters that would make other people look more beautiful.

They even experimented with the makeup department, and the most stunning stars of Hollywood looked strange in the new panchromatic makeup, their lips tinted a walnut brown, their faces on the sallow side, but glowing on film.

Already the ravages of brandy clouded the enchantment of Claudia's eyes, and the noble face of Jeffrey was beginning to reveal his long-standing romance with alcohol. These problems called for soft focus and never-ending experiments in Titan laboratories. It was a far cry from the loft on Elm Street in Brooklyn.

Jeffrey, suffering from a hell-born headache, dressed as a member of a Ruritanian royal guard, was photographed at the Professor's suggestion in dark silhouette—the white of his uniform, faint candlelight, and the glow of his eyes the only gleam in a dark scene. The result was one of such handsome mystery that even Jeffrey applauded and said there might be a future in pictures after all.

Titan's laboratory was coming into focus as one of the best in the industry.

Like all the spoiled stars of a more slapdash silent era, Claudia had to study scripts and work with dialogue directors. Now, directors had such personal relationships with leading actors that a picture became almost familial. Longer production schedules brought about personality clashes, arguments about interpretation, and, quite often, flashing love affairs that could turn to hate in one scene if a director related too enthusiastically to another character in preference to his star. And Claudia had never been too popular with directors because she was willful and because her long-standing relationship with the head of the studio alerted ambitious men that to mess around with her could court professional disaster.

Fergus, spending more and more time in the camera and laboratory departments, sometimes envied Jules and his father. Jules had fallen in love with a young cutter, Georgia Collins, a dedicated girl who thought he was the most wonderful man in the world. He gently taught her French during the cutting sessions. Often, late at night, while father and son still labored happily on some new problem or technique, the freckle-faced slim young woman brought them food and drink, watching them work, intrigued by their expanding world. She talked to them in their native language. Fergus noted the Professor's glow as he sat in the shadows, happy in this family scene.

Fergus also saw that Georgia paid no heed to the Professor's skull face and scars. The three of them were deeply content in this microcosm of a world.

"I'm taking a little time off after this picture is finished," said Jules. "Georgia and I are going to be married and drive down the coast for a few days. Would you consider being my best man? My father's giving her away."

Fergus was touched. He realized how alone he was and how few of his employees had ever asked him to be part of their private lives. Of all the people he had known through the years in this business, these three had the best of it. No social pretensions, no overweening ambitions, only the solid pleasures of pursuing their skills in an expanding world.

Various forms of automation were taking over the film empire. In Simon's absence, he realized he must subtly delegate authority, find the best of the new breed, and tie them up contractually. He encouraged story editors, directors, associate producers, and key staff members to prepare for the great new take-over. He learned as he worked with writers that the written word and the spoken word could be quite different. He developed a talent school, and had young hopefuls run through scripts. It was important to know how the scenes would read before they were imprisoned forever on the sound track. More than ever, he roamed about the studio, staying away from the dull mechanics of his office.

One late afternoon he got a call from Abe Moses in the East who had tracked him down in the lab.

"What in hell," said Abe, "are you doing on the back lot all the time. I've tried to reach you four times in your office. You want to get a card as a cameraman, be my guest."

"What the hell are *you* talking about?" said Fergus. "I have worked my balls off getting this studio geared to exist with some pretty stiff competition. I'm sick of formula pictures; we've got to stop assembly-lining. Look, I'm educating five of our best writers to bird-dog sound production. I've got a new breed of semi-literate producers to understand what's happening. If we don't keep up on the new techniques we'll be out of date before we pay off our loan. Another thing, we've got to break up into individual units, we aren't just a sausage factory any more. Face it, Abe, Simon is getting a free ride in Palm Springs at a time of imminent peril, and I'm carrying the changing world on my back."

"So I'll send out a couple of boys from New York," said Abe. "Maybe you need help."

Fergus caught the sarcasm.

"Listen," he said, "just come out and take a free turkish bath in the miserable stages we're using until we get geared for sound. I don't know how the actors can stand it. Claudia's lost ten pounds and looks haggard, and Jeffrey sweats right out of his wardrobe."

"Hundred proof, of course," said Abe.

"Just give me time," said Fergus. "I guarantee forty sound pictures in a year, good ones, instead of the old picture-a-week crap we delivered when nobody knew anything about quality. Forty, that is, plus westerns. That means we need people who can speak the King's English—more star names among other things. And I've got to have control if you're counting on me—none of your men flying out from New York to poke their heads into a business they haven't the faintest clue about. How do you think we fill your theaters?"

"It's not in my hands," said Abe. "Don't blame me, just think of the money boys, they don't give a shit about whether actors sweat. And right now, follow the current trends. No experimental crap. That's for more prosperous times."

"If you want to help," said Fergus, "get a story department going back there to line me up some good properties and a few intelligent writers to write good dialogue. Production and casting I'll work out here—but stories, stories are king."

"We'll see if we can discuss it at our next board meeting."

"Oh, that's not necessary," said Fergus acidly. "You just forget about it, and I'll drop everything and come look at some Broadway plays myself. Then you'll see what happens out here."

Fergus was seething.

With a sick wife who couldn't help him fight his social battles, he had little clout as a son-in-law. And his interests in Titan plus his personal savings were way under the million-dollar mark he felt he would need before he dared cut away and set up his own productions. A few years ago it might have been possible, but costs had spiraled, and he knew too well, having seen it happen with others, that if he left the Moses company it was more than likely he would get a freeze-out at any bank if he requested financing.

His plans were also shadowed by geographical changes of power. Now that the Morgan interests and Wall Street had an important say in the expenditures, he learned what it meant to be kicked upstairs.

He was appointed vice-president in charge of production, but his budgets were controlled by New York. Simon was still titular president, but Abe was chairman of the board. Fergus suspected rightly that Abe was working hand in hand with O'Rourke. The rumor was spread around by vulgar studio wags that if anyone shaved O'Rourke's ass, Abe would get his chin cut.

The telephone line to the East became a strangling umbilical cord; every step of his progress and every innovation was queried and discussed and analyzed by a board of directors which seemed to him to be the most negative group of men ever assembled to set the course of a big business.

New departments, technicians, bookkeepers, and specialized personnel were needed. Gone was the enthusiastic group of young people who got together with a simple crank camera and a handful of onlookers who became participants to grind out instant action and comedy, ad-libbed from several pages of pocket notes. It was a long way from 1913 to 1928.

His escape hatch was always the lab. In the late hours Fergus would join Jules and the Professor in their new, modern building, and over coffee and cognac hold forth on his grievances. Jules, always puttering, answered his comments phlegmatically or seemed not to hear them. But his insight into the changing techniques in the laboratories about town was invaluable.

Improvements were continued. Sound booms were dangled over actors' heads. When the brilliant young Armenian director, Rouben Mamoulian, discovered there could be two booms, actors were liberated, and speech and action became more than a wrestling match with a microphone hidden in a flowerpot.

When Frank Capra smothered his camera in blankets, instead of having his cameraman roast in a booth and shoot through a glass window, Jules designed what was practically a custom-made soundproof tuxedo for the Titan cameras. When Eastman came out with a fast emulsion, Jules was the first to experiment with it. When Mitchell came up with a silent camera, Jules rejoiced as if the slaves had been freed. He created banks of lighting, spots and "gobos" whose leafy shadows created an imaginative world with a single camera lens.

And then Fergus received word from New York. The laboratory was too expensive. Either Fergus would have to cut down, or the studio would process at a lab like Horsley's where most films were sent.

In despair Fergus talked to the Cadeauxs. Jules had a pipeline to some independent operators. So Fergus, in partnership with his two Titan employees, processed film on the side, split the profits, used their time and the excellent equipment provided by Titan, and lessened expenses. None of them felt any guilt, for the Titan product was improved, and they planned for the future.

Process plates, worked on by the technicians in the laboratory, were perhaps the most important discovery in film techniques. Actors could be shot against a background of black on a stage, and any action involving crowds, or faraway places were introduced, in a "double exposure" on a background. Thus, Claudia could be transformed from a Hollywood barn, to what seemed to be the Rue de la Paix, or on board a ship at sea, any place the clever craftsmen could choose to put her. Locations were often replaced. The studio, with this improvement, was now able to turn out almost a picture a week, if westerns and quick comedies were included. The specials, of course, were more expensive, more time consuming, and called for a higher type of production. Gone the corny subtitles of a more innocent day.

Finally, Fergus asked for high-priced writers who invaded the Coast, armed with a supercilious knowledge of books and plays, all craftsmen from another field, looking with disdain on the antics of crazytown and writing home about the high salaries they received tossing off scripts. They arrived with insatiable appetites for liquor and women, slaked their thirsts, lied about their output, and then in a flurry produced pages which were often, like bakery goods, used while they were hot off the machine. A few good hacks stayed on, working meticulously.

New directors, most of them foreign-born, actors and actresses from the stage, technicians, who with their college educations elbowed aside the robust adventurers who had joined up in the new gold rush—all were programmed to spoil the fun.

But the group that took the worst drubbing in this new world of sound were the actors. They were pressed into doing one film after another; and the fussy dialogue directors, the temperamental sound men who stopped the action if a dial jumped, the meticulous directors, and the carefully clocked time schedule all confounded them. One sneeze could kill a scene.

Some of the favorite stars whose diction did not match their physical attributes disappeared, the rich into their palatial mansions in Beverly Hills, others to a limbo far from the high company and gaiety of easier days.

On the horizon, Fergus knew, was the threat of change, for the four horsemen—radio, sound, color, and bank take-over—were threatening figures, riding more swiftly than the old-fashioned studios realized.

Fergus secretly gloated at the thought that Claudia and Jeffrey and their cronies could no longer debauch all night and then mug through the next day's work.

Both of them emerged more valuable stars. He should have known, he thought, that this challenge would make them rise to a performance. Silent pictures had been too easy for them.

The timbre and elegance of Jeffrey's voice minimized the lines in his face and his slightly hunched shoulders which had been a cause for studio concern.

Claudia's brisk, husky voice gave her a dimension that would lead her into drama—of more value to Titan than the flibbertigibbet flapper or voluptuous vamp of an earlier time.

It became necessary for the studio to hire a male companion for Jeffrey. Stolid ex-football player Bud Regan was the solution. Ostensibly, he was a masseur and gymnast, but he kept Jeffrey from drinking while on a picture, saw that his scripts were in his hands to study at night, and generally made him wretched.

All in all, Jeffrey had more respect for the written word than for action, talkies were a challenge. Still, he was not content with the values of the new cinematic world.

◆◆◆◆◆◆◆◆

Simon recovered slowly. When the dazzling winter months in Palm Springs lengthened into summer heat, he returned to Hollywood. He and Rebecca decided to abandon the mansion on Hollywood Boulevard.

The rooms still had poignant memories of Martha, now dead, and of Esther, who now was usually in a sanatorium. Salons, once a gathering place for Titan's most important social and business events, were now empty.

They selected a rambling one-story Italian house in the growing community of Beverly Hills. The estate was comfortable for a man recovering from a coronary, yet suitable for Simon's position in the community.

He returned to work. A special elevator to his suite was installed in the executive building. Each morning a studio doctor called on him, checked his pulse and blood pressure, and gave him a vitamin shot. This was becoming the status symbol of the aging mighty midgets of Hollywood.

Simon was more of a figurehead than ever. He was more liable to look at rough cuts than to sweat through rushes and make minute decisions. Sound and color pictures baffled him; things moved so quickly. He tried to pace himself without revealing his confusion. But he had lost faith in himself. Decisions were hard for him to make, and he lived in fear. He had cast approval, but he rarely inaugurated casting. He was involved in company-indoctrinated policies after they had been screened by Abe in the East and Fergus in the West. Laura Gold was warned not to tell him stories with violence or too much suspense.

Any property involving Claudia should be discussed in detail away from him and eventually presented very smoothly by Fergus. If Simon liked the story and thought it would be good for her as a Titan star, he nodded a nervous approval. If not, he said he'd think about it.

It almost seemed as if his personal life with Claudia

had been forgotten. But one day Fergus had come into his office unseen and had watched Simon standing at the window. A crowd had come out of the commissary on the street below. As they melted away Simon still stood, peering through the venetian blind, separating the slats with his hands, and Fergus also saw Claudia, alone, walking down the street to her dressing room. Simon peered at her until she was gone, and Fergus saw his hands shake as he lifted them slowly from the blind.

Fergus left quickly and made a new entrance. He could almost pity Simon. He was a man who was stripped of his laurel wreath in the sanctum of his kingdom. As a totem elder he was treated kindly, allowed to pose for empty honors.

But he was still Caesar in the eyes of the world, and no one dared pass on a policy without his approval. He had power of veto. He could buy any property he wanted. He also could bestow favors and contracts on anyone he chose.

Fergus enjoyed his dividends of power that came from Simon's semiretirement. He learned to scrap with the East and relish the battle. This seemed to quiet his ulcer.

His share in Titan was over two hundred thousand dollars in the booming market. He was so intrigued with the stock market that he had a ticker tape installed in his office. Mass production, and America's love for such marvelous luxury items as radios, electric refrigerators, and new cars made corporate profits rise. It seemed foolish to put money in savings when you could earn 20 to 30 percent with the aid of a reliable brokerage firm. And in a rich factory like Titan, everyone was always swapping hot market tips.

It was a big bull market. Fergus plunged on the advice of his brokers, Jackson, Constant, and Kenwith, who had done a magnificent job for many of the private fortunes of Hollywood. Harry Cohn, at Columbia, was reputed to have cleared ten thousand a day.

Stocks could be bought for a marginal down payment of 10 percent. His Titan stock was his collateral. With a little application he could have a million tucked away soon, without even touching his escalating salary, which was put into savings-and-loan companies, after his running expenses, for a special slush fund for David. After all, he could not have all the kid's money come from the Moses family; he was indeed no pauper.

Fergus felt it was time to expand his private life. The traffic was getting heavy on Hollywood Boulevard, and his house, as elegant as it was, was an empty shell to him.

One summer he bought a large Spanish house at the foot of the palm-edged palisades in Santa Monica. The surf beat a soothing rhythm a few yards away from the walled garden. Tycoons and stars were moving toward the ocean, a comfortable drive from the studios in Culver City and Hollywood since Wilshire Boulevard and other roads had improved.

The area became known as the Gold Coast. Claudia had been one of the first to recognize its charm with her pretty bungalow.

It was a time to savor the rewards of work and creativity; California was a beautiful place to live, fine climate, blue skies, and a full schedule of work to make it all merge into an expanding life.

8

In the last days of October 1929 the sky came tumbling down. All the plans that men had made had to be unmade. No more personal prosperity, no more future plans on carefully hoarded money.

Fergus sat in his office, the phone ringing madly. One call after another told of disaster. The panic on Wall Street now reached across the land. For the first time, California with its network of communication, was linked to the East, no more a haven all its own.

After hearing of several of his New York associates taking their lives and listening to panic calls from Abe in the New York offices, Fergus called Simon at home.

"Are you all right?" he asked.

"I am," said Simon. "Of course I've lost a fortune on paper, but I didn't plunge like some of you fellows. Becky says I shouldn't talk about it, my blood pressure's gone up. So I think I'll just stay home and not even listen to the radio."

"It's a good idea."

"Are you okay?"

"I'll let you know," said Fergus.

He hung up, wondering how he was going to keep the news from the studio that he had no more Titan stock. The bank had sold him out to cover his margin on stocks.

He knew that a man in Hollywood without a fortune behind him was in a position of complete serfdom to a studio who owned him. And this was no time to even think of going to another company. Everyone was panicked.

From what he gathered from Abe, the studio might continue to function. The Morgan interests would likely bail them out, as they had managed to keep their product going in these changing times. He knew that Monday morning quarterbacking and criticism would follow, but now the world was suspended in a state of shock. Nothing made sense.

He decided it was no use to sit around. He might as well go home to the beach. Everyone who called with all sorts of information and cries of disaster really only wanted to know if they still were on salary, and what was going to happen to Titan.

A few people were gathered in clusters by the commissary, talking it over. And beyond, the Titan water tower stood like a sentinel, sending out its powerful message of solidarity.

At home, into the evening, the phone still rang. Abe called to assure him that Titan was definitely not going under; Wall Street interests were manipulating to protect any real assets; they had contracts and commitments; just keep things rolling.

Rolling, thought Fergus. How?

He had a habit of putting poker winnings into a tin cracker box in his desk. It was a hangover from his mother's Irish tea canister, which had belched forth, on occasion, money for simple pleasures—going to the Little Diamond or buying a soda for Esther. He had casually tucked away five one-hundred-dollar bills. He smiled, remembering how he had come to Hollywood with much less. He put the money in his pocket. Then he got to thinking about Claudia. She must be wiped out too. The phone kept ringing as top brass from the studio called to report imminent disaster. He got fed up. He let it ring the next time, then dialed Claudia.

Her phone was busy. That meant she was home. He decided to walk up the beach and call on her. After all, they had started together, and it was only fitting that they meet under these unexpected conditions.

He could see lights inside her house. He climbed over the low bulkhead, past the pool, and knocked on the door.

"Who is it?"

"Fergus. I—I just wanted to see how you were."

"Well, for God's sake," she said, "adversity sure makes strange bedfellows."

She wore a pink terry robe, her hair was combed back and tied in a pink ribbon, her face free of makeup. Fergus noted a nest of newspapers around a telephone, some pillows and a glass of scotch on the floor.

"As you can plainly see," she said gesturing at the telephone, "I've been nesting by the vehicle of doom. May I tell you how many people keep calling to tell me they're busted?"

"Are *you*?" asked Fergus.

He poured himself a drink.

"Busted," she said. "Fergus, do you realize how many, many hardworking days it took to get all that money together?"

He sat on a cushion on the floor next to her. This was a holiday from all the things that had separated them—the studio, her demands, his situation with Simon Moses—they were in limbo together.

He smiled, thinking of all the petty larceny, the manipulating, the striving that had made his fortune. It had been tucked away for a future, for the great story he would find, the picture he would make himself, and the new company he had planned for so long.

"How about Jeffrey?"

"Oh, he's always in hock. Life is a perpetual crash to him," she said. "Are we still going to get a salary?"

"Looks like it," said Fergus. "I talked to Simon. He's okay, and Abe says we owe the Morgan interests too much for them to let us slide. I'd say we'll have a future."

"Then I guess we'll make out. I'm glad Si's okay," she said wistfully, "but it's funny not to have any pocket money in the bank."

Fergus reached in his pocket. He took out his five hundred-dollar bills.

"What does that remind you of?" he said.

She laughed. "I never saw a bankroll before—except once, a helluva long time ago."

"That's all I've got," said Fergus, "at the moment."

She pretended to grab for it. "I'll go to bed with you for it!"

"You'll go to bed with me for free," he said. "You always have!"

"Times have changed!" she said. "This is an emergency!"

She stood up and dropped her robe. She was naked. She always had a way of surprising him; she suddenly dove at him, grabbed the money, and ran up the stairs.

"You'd better hurry," she said laughing, "because if I get paid for it, honey, you're sure going to get your money's worth."

He rushed after her, throwing his clothes off as he went. By the time he reached her bedroom, she was standing on the bed. She had thrown the greenbacks in the air, and they rained on the ruffled white bedspread.

Without pulling the coverlet off, she threw herself down, and held up the bills, dropping them on her breasts, over her stomach, and between her legs.

"Come on, Fergie," she said, "let's live a little!"

She was as beautiful as he remembered, the body more voluptuous, but firm, and she embraced him with a fervor that matched his own excitement.

She made passionate love to him, taking the initiative and titillating him; later, he took her on his own terms. It ended tenderly after the past frenzy. In her transport she said, "Oh, Fergie, Fergie, we're so good together. Oh—oh—I love it—I love it."

He was a little disappointed, for she had not said *love you* . . .

He wondered why she made a more passionate bedmate than any other woman he knew. Perhaps because to have her was so rare.

She touched his hand. "You know, Fergie, one of the saddest things about making love is afterwards. The mission's been accomplished. You have nothing to say. And you feel lonesome, oh so lonesome, with someone you don't really know beside you. You usually want to kick him out, you don't want to see him—afterwards. But I don't feel that way about you."

"Thanks," Fergus said coolly.

She leaned up and kissed his cheek.

"Oh, Fergie, don't get me wrong. I didn't mean you. We'll always have lots to say. Don't think Claudia's forgotten the good things. How you worked as a kid to get me started. How you helped me on the train. How you stood by and suffered when I fell in love with Simon. I know—"

"I got along," said Fergus.

"Oh, dear, I really screwed it up, didn't I. I just wanted to say, I love being with you, I love to talk to you—that is when we're not fighting studio policy. You're the only friend I have aside from Jeffrey, and he doesn't count because he's my brother."

Fergus put his arms around her.

"There's nobody like you, Claudia. Your honesty is sometimes a brickbat, but you're, well, unique, wonderful, and very disturbing."

"How about being disturbed again," she said, rolling on top of him.

"You have the knack," he said, kissing her open, inviting lips.

He fell asleep with her arms around him. He awoke at dawn and looked at the porcelain beauty of her face. She looked like a young girl asleep, a faint dribble of saliva at the corner of her mouth, her tousled hair over her shoulders, a wisp across her face.

She stretched her arms, looked at him sleepily, and then noticed that greenbacks clung to her breast and stomach. She smiled.

"Well," she said, "did you get your money's worth?"

"Yes," he laughed, "now I'll take back my props."

He started to gather them up.

"Wait a minute!" she said. "That's *my* money."

"Claudia," he said, smiling, "I always knew you'd name your price."

He left the room, walked down the stairs, putting on the clothes he had dropped along the way.

It was a dreary day at the beach. Fog was setting in, and as he walked out the gate he glanced up. She was standing in the window, naked; she stuck out her tongue and waved the bills at him.

He laughed. Busted, flat. But he felt fine. Maybe this time, refreshing as it was, Claudia was out of his system for good. It was worth it, even to the last buck.

Oh, that Claudia! She had a contract with Titan for ten thousand a week, and she'd snatched his last five hundred dollars!

Everything, Fergus learned, was comparative. He owned a beautifully situated house in Hollywood, which he could sell. He had a mortgaged beach house. He owed the bank over thirty thousand dollars. His wife's medical bills were astronomical, but he'd die rather than have Simon pay them. He tried to raise money on his trust for David with savings-and-loan investments, but they had crumbled into receivership. David went to an exclusive private school, kept his own horse, was taking tennis and golf lessons, and went to an expensive summer camp at Catalina. And that's the way it was going to continue.

With a salary from Titan he could pay off his debts and not go bankrupt. He was considered exceedingly rich, and indeed he was, considering what was happening to the rest of the country.

Breadlines took the place of theater lines. Some of Fergus's best studio craftsmen lost their homes, their carefully hoarded life's savings and insurance. Some of the day workers, never sure of a living anyway, until they recouped their losses, lived like animals in sewer-pipe cities, in construction areas that were now abandoned like concrete skeletons, along with unfinished houses.

So many people jumped off the Arroyo Seco bridge in Pasadena that it had to be fenced.

As he expected, everyone at the studio was glum, once they realized that the depression was real and their years of luxury a thing of the past.

Sam Goldwyn prophesied that 20 percent of studio talent would never make it after the double disaster of the sound changeover and the depression.

"You would choose this time for us to go into hock for sound," said Simon testily. "We're going to have a hell of a time getting out of this mess."

"Look," said Fergus, "I didn't choose. We had no choice. And this is exactly what's going to save our necks. People are scrounging around with their pennies and dimes to get into our picture palaces—remember that, palaces, Mr. Moses, with the best of thick rugs, comfortable seats, cozy lounges, music, and escape, a place to rest and forget the troubles of the world. And sound, beautiful sound, to blank out their scared minds."

He was right. In the worst times of 1929 and 1930 those who could beg, borrow, or scrape together ticket money came in to see and hear. Silent pictures died aborning.

But Simon was too apprehensive to be experimental. He still ran his studio on an assemblyline; he pulled in to protect what he had left, augmented by the strength that Abe had in the East. Fergus knew it was not going to work in the long run. Too many studios like Paramount and Metro Goldwyn Mayer were making fine pictures—Lubitsch's *Love Parade*, Greta Garbo in *Anna Christie* (Garbo Talks, blared the advertisements), Milestone's moving *All Quiet on the Western Front*, Eddie Robinson in *Little Caesar*, and the romantic John Barrymore in *Moby Dick*.

And Simon copied them all. The minute he smelled a cycle he pursued it. Wall Street thought that was fine—safe and reasonable.

Fergus paced the floor at night, wondering what he was going to do. His despair at Simon's policy was something he could not discuss with anyone. All the people in Hollywood were afraid of their shadows, save those who had entrenched themselves with their names on the screen. And he had always remained in the background.

Nostalgically, he opened up the little battered tin box that had held all his secrets throughout the years. Now it was in a library safe behind a hinged picture.

He took out the picture of himself after the Trust had beaten him up. Then he unfolded a faded letter. It was the one he had received after David's death, the credo of what they had wanted to do:

> It's about time we shoot what's real, and have I seen plenty of that! Let's stop crapping around, and get FEDA started again, and make some honest to God stories about real people, and what people want, and what we're fighting for. . . . Anyway, when I get home let's make good movies, our way!

All the dreams, from a boy who had been dead eleven years. And what had he done during this time? Where was he now? He had front-run for the Moses family, married Esther who could not face his busy life and had only been a handicap, and was rearing a son he only saw on weekends. He had covered the tragedy of Martha's death; he had witnessed the tragic circumstances of Simon's sickness. He had let Claudia trample on anyone she chose, and he had covered for *her*. And now, he was just a salaried man, his youth was past, he was thirty-four. Where did he go from here?

Well, he'd see what the others were doing economically. At least everyone was in the same fix.

At the office he ruthlessly slashed and cut, eliminating luxuries, mercilessly reducing staff—old friends, pioneers, and young hopefuls. It was a matter of survival.

He put his town house up for sale, dismissed the housekeeper, and moved the gardener and his wife in as caretakers.

He kept his Filipino cook, Primo, at the beach and informed him he would do laundry and housekeeping as well as cooking and driving, or else he'd be in the city breadlines.

He went to Kathleen's restaurant after one of his most fatiguing days. One solitary customer was leaving as he came in. Tony left the kitchen and he and Kathleen and Fergus huddled together.

"Well, as you can plainly see," said Kathleen, "we can't go on this way. Why at this rate we'll lose a thousand a month."

"Wouldn't you know," said Tony, "that we have a big mortgage on this place. The bank'll get it."

"No it won't," said Fergus. "What about your house? Can you borrow on it?"

Kathleen laughed. "Our mortgaged house. Come on, Fergus, we're hocked to the gills, five kids—count 'em, in parochial school, and umpteen poor relatives, poor dears; if we didn't feed half of Sonoratown, they'd starve to death. And the stupidity of our overexpansion. As you well know, partner, weren't *we* all the bright ones, buying two flossy new refrigerated catering trucks on time at eight thousand dollars apiece!"

"Knowing you," said Fergus, "and being Irish myself, how much money, not in your busted bank, have you got tucked in some tea canister?"

Kathleen flushed.

"Come on," said Tony, "tell him, sweetheart, I'm on to you."

He looked at Fergus with a toothy smile.

"The old lady's modest," he said. "Just so happened while I was looking for some new shirts one day I came upon a hatbox stuffed with greenbacks. I'd say offhand, about five thousand dollars."

"Well, Kathleen," said Fergus, laughing, "I guess you'll just have to cough it up. It's better than my measly five hundred which it seems I lost the first night I counted it. Looks like I might be selling my town house for cash to an old Pasadena couple who need more space for their two nurses. They haven't even heard there's a depression. If I sell it I'll stake you when your bankroll diminishes, to keep our two wagons and the tavern running. I'll give you ten thousand if you give me papers on your truck farm for security. Now, cut down on the menus and go for plain foods for a while. The idea will catch on; people *will* have to eat you know, after they get over their shock. There are still lots of jobs in this town. Movies aren't dead. People will think it's smart to eat stew in such a classy place."

"He's right!" said Tony. "Cheer up, Kathleen. It wasn't so bad at the cafeteria down the street, now was it?"

Kathleen patted his hand. "Sure. No complaints, darlin'. It'll help the pain for some of the people who can't afford steaks any more."

"Listen," said Fergus, "make a menu like the old one. Kid it. Call your dishes things like depression stew, poor man's chili beans, and hungry hobo's hot dogs."

"Okay," said Tony, "and screw those fancy pastries

with the swans and flowers on them; I'll get back to my chocolate cake and apple pie."

"Then I'll tell you what we'll do," said Fergus. "We'll rig our two fancy catering trucks with hot dogs, chili beans, hamburgers, coffee, and ice cream. Titan's going to do a lot of shoot-em-ups for quick money on second features, and I'll get permits to allow our trucks to go onto the lot at lunchtime and late afternoon. With the profits, I'll buy your produce from the truck farm through our Elite Catering Company. That'll help you with your mortgage payments and your food bills. Everybody's hungry, and if they're working, they'll eat, poor bastards, even if they sleep in alleys."

"And all cash, no credit," said Kathleen.

"My God," said Tony, shaking his head at Fergus, "now I know why the Jews are so scared of you, as well as all of us Mexicans."

"Survival, amigo," said Fergus. "You don't think I'm doing all this for noble purposes? I intend for your restaurant to fill my house larder."

Kathleen poured him more coffee and put a piece of cake in front of him.

"We'll never go hungry, Fergus, with your finagling and Tony's cooking. If worse comes to worst, Tony can open a hot-dog stand on the highway out near the Titan ranch on our truck farm, and David can come live with us. Who would know the difference with one more kid around the house?"

"Don't mention it," said Fergus. "I might lose him."

◆◆◆◆◆◆◆◆

Simon had not bought stocks on margin, and his real estate ventures, the only worthwhile property at this moment, were solid.

He postponed his salary and poured back his percentage of grosses to help Titan out of the doldrums.

"After all," said Simon, "the studio's my lifeblood.

What else have I got? You take care of Esther and David, and there's nobody but Becky and me. Just let my wife have her luxuries and not worry, and we'll keep trying to fulfill our commitments."

"We will," said Fergus. "I've cut to the bone. They had to arrest a guy who was patrolling the gate the other day, waiting to shoot me."

"They'll never get you," said Simon. "You're too tough. It'll take a silver bullet."

Now that Simon was gentled by his illness, Fergus found that he was getting fond of him. They had passed beyond an armed truce into an area of discovery of each other. Fergus could tell him about his dreams of making pictures based on good stories, with a realistic approach, instead of the sugarcoated good-guys-versus-bad-guys of earlier days. To his surprise, he saw that Simon felt the same way. Perhaps, Fergus thought, he had smothered it in his quest for power and wealth. Now that these two goals were not uppermost in his mind, Simon revealed a part of himself, which, Fergus also thought, was what Claudia had known and loved.

"Just let Becky live her life like she wants," said Simon. "I messed it up enough for her for a few years."

And that was the only reference he made about Claudia.

Rebecca did as much as she could with the few joys that were left to her in her mid-fifties, a time when she should have been surrounded with her children and many grandchildren.

Sometimes she took David to visit Esther, when the hospital reported she was well enough. And after that, she'd drive him home to the beach.

Simon was either at the studio or resting, staying the prophecy that doctors had given him, trying to adjust to the moving film scene, reading reports, and looking for new properties with the concern of a man who seemed to hear a time clock ticking in his head.

But Rebecca and David were too far apart in age

and interests to be really close. She wanted to do anything that would make them chums. She'd take off her high-heeled shoes and try to walk in the sand with him, but her Achilles tendons would pull, and her wide white feet seemed shamefully naked alongside the slim tanned legs of David. He was going to be a tall boy, and he was handsome.

One summer afternoon she realized that these uncomfortable walks on the sand were impossible.

"You just run along," she said. "I'll sit on the glider near the pool and have a cup of coffee. Come back before it gets dark."

"I'll take a little dip," said David, "and I'll come out when the first star is out."

"Oh, dear, do be careful," she said, staring out to sea.

David laughed. "Grandmother, it's a millpond. There aren't even breakers. And there are several people swimming, see!"

David plunged in and swam easily out along the soft swells. He spluttered under and came up with a long shining piece of seaweed. Flinging it over his shoulder and watching the spray cascade in diamonds from the last sunrays, he laughed.

Alongside him a man laughed also. It was a rich laugh, from a joyous sharing of nature's bounty.

"Hi," said David.

"Hi," said the man. "I haven't swum so far out in ages. I should have known I'd meet a water sprite."

"This is the best time of the day," said David. "I like to swim until the water turns purple and the first star comes out."

The man turned on his back, floating, and flailing out his arms. "Ah, yes," he said, " 'the lengthening shadows wait the first pale stars of twilight.' "

Another man swam up.

"Come on, Mr. Barstow," he said, "it's going to get cold, the sun is going down."

Jeffrey pointedly ignored him.

"Oh, say," said David, "I should have known who you were. I saw your last picture at the studio yesterday."

"You did!" said Jeffrey, cocking an eyebrow. "I haven't even seen it myself."

"I'm sorry," said David. "You were so great. I just know you're going to win the Academy Award!"

Jeffrey put his hand out, and they shook wetly, both submerging a little. "A man of obvious good taste. May I have the honor?"

"I'm David Austin. I think you work for my father."

Jeffrey stared at him.

"I'm sorry," said David. "I didn't mean it that way. I've heard him say sometimes he thinks he works for you."

He laughed. Jeffrey followed and swam around the child, looking at him from all sides.

"Come on, Mr. Barstow," the other swimmer called out.

"Leave me be, Bud," said Jeffrey. "This young man and I are going to run up the beach a bit."

They swam ashore and jogged along the beach towards the Austin house. Jeffrey sometimes stopped to breathe deeply, watching the boy, as he walked backwards, talking to him. He noted his sureness of foot, the joyousness of life which he remembered with a twinge had once been called by critics "the Barstow gait."

They were interrupted by Mrs. Moses.

"David, you'll catch a chill."

"There they go," said David, "taking all the fun out of life. That's my grandmother. Do you know her?"

"I've known all your family a long time," said Jeffrey. "And your lovely mother—"

David gave him a quick glance.

"You knew her?"

"I knew her," said Jeffrey.

"I didn't know anybody really did," said David wistfully.

Jeffrey stopped short. He wanted to weep. Instead he managed a smile.

"Well, I guess I'd better go," said David. "You know how it is."

He put his hand out, and Jeffrey shook it.

"I know how it is," he said.

David walked to the gate.

"Good-bye. Maybe we could swim again sometime, Mr. Barstow."

Jeffrey longed to take this child into his arms, to hold him for a moment, to touch his face, the brow, the hair, the unspoiled perfection, the essence of what his Barstow lineage might be.

My son . . . my son, he thought. Rebecca called out, "David, you come right in the house. You know how your father feels about that Mr. Barstow. He says such wicked things."

"Oh, grandmother," said David, "he didn't say anything wicked to me."

Jeffrey looked over his shoulder. His keeper, Bud Regan, courtesy of Fergus Austin and Titan Films, was watching, waiting for him to come back to the beach club where their car was parked.

Several stars glimmered in the evening sky. Over the low bulkhead he could see David entering the lighted house. Jeffrey watched the flickering of a hearth fire and the silhouette of Fergus as he put his hand on the boy's shoulder and gestured to him to go upstairs. The door was suddenly closed, blocking out the scene.

Lights began to turn on in the garden, against any night intruder. Jeffrey quickly slipped between the houses and onto the sidewalk of the Coast Highway. A quarter mile down the road was Claudia's beach pied-à-terre, always a sanctuary.

◆◆◆◆◆◆◆◆

Several days later it was announced that Jeffrey Barstow was up for an award from the Academy. The industry was thrilled by his elegant performance in *Magnifico.*

The fact that he had come from the stage and used his splendid diction and theater technique successfully on film made quite a few actors in Hollywood nervous.

Red Powell came into Fergus's office.

"We have a very ticklish situation," he said. "I have some pretty straight information that our man Barstow is going to be awarded the dummy. We're in a tough spot. You know what that means to us now. It takes clever handling. You're the only man who can do it."

"You can't find him," said Fergus.

"How did you know?" asked Red.

"You don't have your ear to the rails. Porters at the station get a sawbuck from me if they see anything peculiar going on with our people. Unfortunately, Jeffrey Barstow is our people."

Fergus sat down.

He sure is a nervous bastard, thought Red. I wouldn't want to be Fergus Austin, with all his connections.

"Where do you think he is?" he asked.

"I know where he is," said Fergus. "He visited with my kid at the beach last week. Apparently got away from his keeper, broke into Claudia's house, and got a snootful of gin."

"Where is he?"

"He's in his usual retreat, a colored whorehouse in Saint Louis."

Fergus pushed back from the desk and walked slowly to the window. "We've got to get him back here for the Academy Awards," he said in a calm voice. "Simon Moses is going out socially for the first time since his illness for the event."

"But it's three days away!" said Red.

"I'll take Dr. Wolfrum. Get hold of Pete Doane and his plane and tell him to stand by."

Fergus hated Wolfrum's guts, but he was the only one to be trusted in a deal like this. He didn't dare gossip.

From the Saint Louis airport, they took a cab to a Green Street address and were warmly welcomed by a café-au-lait madam and several enthusiastic ebony girls.

Jeffrey Barstow facilitated the search by appearing at the head of the staircase looking like Michelangelo's *David.* Two naked black girls beside him made his skin seem more alabaster.

He looked down the stairs and saw Fergus and Wolfrum staring up at him.

"Salutations!" he cried, weaving slightly, "my dear friends, I did not know you had such excellent taste. You have discovered my wellspring in the wilderness. Ah, well, a mystic bond of brotherhood makes all men one."

He turned and slapped the girl next to him on the buttocks.

"Is that not true, my black narcissus?"

She giggled.

He moved down the stairs.

"All right, girls," said Fergus.

The two girls saw the bills he fanned out in his hands, and they both grabbed Jeffrey at once. The madam moved in.

"No trouble, mistah. You promised on the phone."

"I promised," said Fergus.

Jeffrey turned blearily to look at the girls. He was unsteady.

"Ah, that deceit should steal such gentle shapes," he said.

He began to weep softly, not at capture, but betrayal.

Wolfrum gave him a hypo, and in an hour, Jeffrey cautiously ensconced in a straitjacket, they were flying over Saint Louis.

They bucketed through the turbulent skies. Fergus spent the last few hours pouring coffee into Jeffrey, rubbing down his puffy face with chunks of ice, and struggling with him when he cursed and flailed against his captivity.

God, thought Fergus, how did life ever ace me into being wet nurse to this insane family?

They landed in Yuma, long enough for Fergus to call ahead for a limousine to meet them at the Los Angeles airport. Also, a wardrobe man with Jeffrey's dinner clothes, and a makeup man.

Ten minutes before the awards, Jeffrey walked into the side door of the Ambassador Hotel banquet room. He was impeccably dressed; his face glowed with the beauty of his famous features and the makeup man's art.

He accepted his prize with a short bow. He seemed overwhelmed. He held up the little golden figure in his hand and swallowed.

"Oh my God," said Fergus to Wolfrum, who stood by his side in the wings, hypodermic needle in his pocket, "he's going to throw up on it."

But Jeffrey held the figurine as if he were proffering it to that dear audience who had given it to him.

"We are the Jasons, we have won the fleece," he said in a voice so quiet it seemed humble.

He walked off the stage during the ovation that followed.

"I'm delighted," said the president of the Academy to Simon at the speaker's table, "there is one gentleman in Hollywood."

While the two men congratulated each other on Hollywood's paragon, Jeffrey handed the statue to Fergus and then vomited privately into a potted palm.

"I'll get the car," said Fergus to Wolfrum. "You hold on to him."

He rushed toward the exit, running into a cluster of studio people gathering around Simon, congratulating him on his star's win. Rebecca, wearing black velvet and a cluster of white orchids, stood by her husband. She rarely attended these affairs, but this was ceremonial.

Pushing through the crowd, a vision in white fox fur and satin, came Claudia. She rushed toward her brother to get in the limelight where a crescent of cameramen stood.

Fergus grabbed Claudia by the arm and whispered fiercely, "For God's sake, Claudia, hold the Oscar, he'll drop it! Get it over with fast. We're trying to get him out of here without disaster striking."

He handed her the Oscar and rushed to get the car. It seemed a hundred flashlights went off as she and her brother smiled beguilingly at the press. Then, Wolfrum led Jeffrey to the door. Claudia strode alongside, blinking because of the flashes. Blinded, she ran straight into Rebecca.

There was a hush.

"I beg your pardon," said Claudia. And then her vision cleared. "Oh, God!" she said, backing up quickly, almost losing her balance.

Simon put out his hand to steady her.

"Claudia, this is Mrs. Moses. You—you know her, of course."

Claudia saw a battery of curious eyes, amused eyes, shocked eyes. She steadied herself and felt into her gut for the Barstow voice. She tried to pretend she was playing a role on the stage. It was the only thing she could do.

"No—" she said throatily, "I have never had the pleasure of being in your home, Mrs. Moses—but here's this Oscar. I shouldn't have it. It belongs to Titan, really, like we all do. May I put it in your keeping until Jeffrey gets it?"

"Thank you," said Rebecca faintly.

Claudia handed Rebecca the Oscar, smiled, and then looked at Simon.

"It's wonderful to see you looking so well, Mr. Moses," she said.

She joined two attractive men, fortunately near at hand, hooking onto their arms so they went along with her. They exited gaily as if they were going to a party.

"Let's tie one on," she said sotto voce. They were delighted, having come stag.

Everyone who saw her said it was the best performance of the year and fitting that she held the Oscar while she started her little scene.

Fergus returned. By this time Simon held the Oscar and was on his way out with Rebecca.

"Thanks, Mr. Moses," he said, "I'll just take this out to Jeffrey."

As Simon stared at him, Fergus realized how he looked. His suit was filthy. He hadn't had the time or place to change. He probably smelled, too.

"I'll keep the Oscar for the time being," said Simon. "I think you'd better get out of here. This is no way to represent Titan Films."

Wondering what was making him so cantankerous under the circumstances, Fergus rushed back to Jeffrey and Wolfrum.

"The car's waiting," he said. "Let's lam out of here fast."

That's what you get, thought Fergus, for expecting Simon Moses to be your friend. And leave it to a Barstow, too, to put you behind the eight ball and then take stage center smelling like a rose.

He and Wolfrum waited while Jeffrey, in a stunned, upright position, posed for more pictures. They turned out to be a collection of portraits of a dignified gentleman.

However, knowing Jeffrey couldn't hold up long, Fergus signaled Wolfrum.

"Very sorry," said Wolfrum, "but Mr. Barstow has a fever. He has the flu—he shouldn't even be here."

"He insisted," said Fergus, smiling at Clarissa Pennock.

She clucked in sympathy, and admiration.

◆◆◆◆◆◆◆◆

On his following Saturday visit to Las Cruces sanatorium, Fergus noted Jeffrey sitting on the veranda of the main building with Claudia, who was also drying out. They both looked pallid and bored.

Fergus compared the two fine profiles, as they sat, wrapped in the cocoon of their beauty.

Jeffrey seemed much younger than his past-fifty mark. He was in league with the devil, thought Fergus.

Claudia was already stamped with the sharp fragility of alcoholism and debauchery.

They seemed enchanted, born to the purple, and out of time, capable of being Hellenic, Roman, or Florentine, instead of the sotted progeny of a line of Irish mountebanks, whose unearned handsomeness had allowed them to compete with the talents of such great families as the Kembles or Barrymores.

Fergus cursed the magic that had chained them to his life and economy. When Claudia smiled at him he could almost forget her perfidy.

Jeffrey saw Fergus first.

"Once, for me, too, this man was my worst foe," he said, turning to his sister.

"You got your statue, didn't you?" said Fergus. "What the hell do you think all those telegrams and congratulations are for, your performance in Saint Louis?"

"Hell is paved with big pretensions," answered Jeffrey.

"Jeffrey, your predicament was no skin off my ass. It only gave me trouble. Now if you'll forget you swallowed Bartlett's *Quotations*, I can stop boring you and go see my wife."

"Wouldn't you know she'd end up here," he heard Claudia say as he marched away.

Fergus was angry at himself for mentioning the fact that Esther was in residence.

The last thing he heard as he turned the corner to Esther's bungalow was Jeffrey's ringing voice.

"I could tell you a tale," he said. "But I won't."

As Fergus looked back, he saw Jeffrey glancing at him with an expression of extreme dislike.

Why should that s.o.b. dislike me? thought Fergus. He resented Jeffrey intensely. He had protected him, helped to build an image that made him a colossus among film stars; he had covered for him, lied about his habits, and escalated his contract to keep him in the Titan stable.

He was a volatile property, too much trouble. His criticisms of scripts were insulting. He could not remember his lines half the time, and the idiot board held up by property men often was not close enough for him to see without glasses. He was hell on the production schedule. An incredible price was paid to help him win the Oscar. Was it worth it? The award was too new for anyone to know.

Fergus even had a feeling as he said good-bye to Esther in the garden that Jeffrey was peering at them. A fleeting instinct warned him that Jeffrey was interested somehow in Esther's reactions.

As he left, he saw a shadowy figure walk down the hall, and he was certain it was Barstow. By God, thought Fergus, artistic triumph or not, one picture of his runs into the red, he's out. I've got to get that bastard off my back.

Esther glanced up, for a shadow had passed between her and the warm afternoon sun.

It seemed to her, as often happened in her half-world, that Jeffrey Barstow himself was standing looking down at her, as he had so long ago when she was pregnant with his child. In memory her lips formed the same words.

"Thank you, Jeffrey," she said and closed her eyes so he would not fade away.

"I am very proud," he said again. But new words came out. "I have seen our son, Esther, and he is beautiful."

"That's so nice," she said, her eyes closed.

Jeffrey looked at her a moment. The lost loveliness, the sweet and guileless surrender was remembered. Under other conditions, this might have been the woman he could have loved. It was unbelievable that she had given him a son—a son who could have enriched his life, and now he could not have.

"I love you, Esther," he said. "I truly love you."

Her face warmed with a soft smile.

"We should have run away from them," he whispered.

Jeffrey was saddened, struck by a pang of what might have been. But then he smiled to himself. Esther was the fortunate one; her mind had protected her from the body blows of life.

As for himself, he was on his way to a cure, and soon he would face another picture and the rock-hard road of career and life.

He walked away with soft footsteps, not looking back. What a fool he was to envision a crazed woman as a Madonna of the Rocks. And anyway, he argued to himself, long ago he had made a vow not to let anything disturb him but a bad performance.

9

It was in the depths of the depression, and large homes with elaborate grounds were a drug on the market. One estate in San Fernando Valley housed a hacienda which was a fine example of Mexican colonial architecture. It had been built by a once-important Mexican family and had remained in peaceful dignity, undisturbed by new city streets and bungalows. Its surrounding jungle proliferated in the valley heat. A meandering stream glistened with watercress.

It was a difficult time in Jeffrey's life. His thought kept returning to the boy he had met in the sea, his natural son, who could have shared with him the life he rarely showed to anyone. To think of his son being reared by Fergus Austin, without the gentle care of poor Esther, disturbed him more than he thought possible.

He bought the property and made it the host of his dreams, the object of his latent poetic nature.

He focused his attentions on it, made it a repository for all his longings. He restored it, sought suitable furnishings and paintings, selected rare books for the study, built a fabled palm-edged swimming pool, and indulged in a small zoo. He dreamed that David would share these delights with him, he knew not how.

After euphoric delight in his new surroundings, fits of deep depression burst into sessions of drinking, debauching, to smother the burning fires of loneliness within him. Servants moved in and out of the house, unable to cope with his ravings and the wild sessions that ended in depression and a return to his only solace: his work.

The agency sent Euphemia Briggs, a young Negro woman, only because she needed a job, and times were hard. She was strong, and she could take it, she told the interviewer.

When she met the sad-faced man who looked at her as a woman, not a black woman, and with whimsical overtones, instead of lecherous undertones, she felt she could help him somehow; she knew she was needed, for he was the most alone man she had ever seen.

And when his sister Claudia came to visit, Euphemia observed that both were surrounded by some spell that encased them in an invisible, untouchable prison.

It was good to work for a movie star. The pay was fine, the chauffeur took her to and from the bus on her days off. There was a bountiful table; after parties the Chinese cook slipped her food to tote home to her two children.

Jeffrey called her Effie, remarking that by the time he finished pronouncing her name, he'd forget what he wanted.

Mr. Barstow made bright jokes about her figure, which was very trim. He likened her, with her straight carriage and handsome face, to the Queen of Sheba. He was often amusing and had a flash of the old charm and wit she had seen in movies as a child.

When he went on drunks, Bud Regan took over. He strong-armed Mr. Barstow effectively, sometimes even locking him up.

Of course, it was part of Effie's job to clean up shattered glasses and bottles, vomit, filthy towels, and soiled garments. But she was young and strong and had plenty of experience with her husband, Tom, who had done the same things without such decent living conditions. When Tom was killed in a brawl in a Central Avenue beer joint, she was secretly relieved.

Grandma Jones, her mother, took care of young Tom and Sam. The repentant tips that Mr. Barstow gave her after his debauches helped the whole family considerably.

Effie had to remember this, sometimes, to keep her stomach strong, when Bud wrestled Mr. Barstow into a bathtub, screaming and cursing, and she had to clean up the diarrhetic filth and urine around a chair where he had sat, stone naked, drinking for a wild, terrifying night.

Sometimes she'd laugh off his obscenities and graphic propositions and skip out of his way, carrying the garbage of his wastrel sessions. Then she'd go off to the incinerator where she burned the trash, weeping secretly, saying to herself, *poor thing . . . poor thing . . .*

When he had been dried out and was ready to face a summons to confer at the studio, he would sally forth smelling of English cologne, the bloat removed by diet and steam, his hair carefully dyed to hide the white streaks, his beautifully built clothes camouflaging the skinny arms, knobby knees, and flabby stomach. He would look like the dynamic Jeffrey Barstow again.

Effie would see him go, sitting next to Bud in the car, a homburg perched on his head.

"Take care!" she would say, beaming with pride at his elegant wardrobe so carefully assembled by her. She would enjoy preparing for his return, laying out his lounge wear, tending the books and magazines so they would be at hand, putting fresh roses where she thought he would enjoy them the most.

He would return several hours later, exhausted, a

script in his hand. He would throw it casually in a corner, while agents and pettifoggers filled the house.

The man of the hour again, needed and wanted by a corporation; he was a commodity, an inventoried item, no matter how much trouble, a very rare and valuable bird.

Even his agent, sharp, toadying little Seymour Sewell, fresh from contractual negotiations with Fergus Austin, would sit up on his hunkers, quiet and courteous, sucking slowly on a long drink and respecting the presence of the only man alive who was more of a rumpot than himself.

Jeffrey, keeping his advantage, would watch the nervous antics of the sycophants, drink ginger ale, and stare at them all, until they paid their respects and left, laughing hollowly at the gibes and insults they had to accept as penalty for his enforced sobriety.

After they departed, Jeffrey would don an old cardigan with leather-patched elbows, left over from backstage service at Drury Lane. He would go down to his zoo, at the back of the estate, and he would return hand in hand with Pansy, his pet chimpanzee.

That always meant more cleaning for Effie. But she liked the chimp. Pansy had lived on Mr. Barstow's schooner, the *Zahma*. Two of her fingers were off at the first joint where she had caught them in the rigging in a fierce blow off Tonga. She was a lovable clown. She would stand on her head to show affection, and when Jeffrey read her parts of a new script, she would applaud, purse her lips, or put her hands over her big ears and somersault.

Depending on her reactions, Jeffrey would either get drunk or study his lines. Everyone on the household staff waited to see how Pansy would take a new script. There was an apocryphal story that Bud Regan called the studio on a private line to report the monkey's reaction.

But when Jeffrey was on a long drunk, and Bud

was off salary because Jeffrey was not making a picture for Titan, women of all types would continuously drift into this valley House of Usher, some so appalled at his awfulness that they fled, others so awful that they even appalled Jeffrey and Pansy and got flung out.

His one constant visitor was Claudia, who would come and look at the current films with him. The two would react vehemently to the make-believe world which was their yardstick of human behavior and achievement. Even as an outsider, Effie soon realized that these two Barstows could sustain a character on film longer than they could sustain a personal relationship outside their own sibling world.

Claudia had been dismayed that she lost her savings in the crash. But so many were in the same fix that she shrugged it off. She had been amused by the *Variety* headline, "Wall Street Lays Egg." But she would have no future problem, at least. The studio had to pay her well to make back money they needed.

Her greatest concern was Simon's film cycle complex. If another studio made a successful gangster film, Titan was immediately embroiled in machine guns and tough characters who talked out of tight lips.

During the early 1930s, the great human-drama films came into ascendancy. Glamour was the placebo of the poor who found their only palaces in the public temples of cinema. "The trend" became the yardstick, and the fear of rejection by the public guided careers. A star was only as good as his last picture, Wall Street informed Abe. Titan was in no position to experiment. New York selected the subjects.

New stars were added to the lists, and young talents were groomed, with a heavy leaning toward youth, music, and glamour.

Claudia and Jeffrey, feeling like elders, scanned all the successful movies from other studios. They knew that whatever they saw would ricochet back in a script a few weeks later. They could almost prophesy what their next characters would be.

"Next time," said Claudia, "they ask me to play Greta Garbo on a tugboat, or Marlene Dietrich, full of feathers in a sleazy café, I'm going to throw my contract, along with a bottle of acid, right in their eyes. Can't they see what we are?"

"Don't fuss," said Jeffrey. "So far I have escaped Gatling guns and foreign legion caps. But study, dear girl. There's a lot to learn, and this is an age of beautiful and talented people."

Claudia looked with concern at the new stars, for she could be labeled old guard. Barbara Stanwyck, Norma Shearer, Marlene Dietrich, Jean Harlow, Joan Bennett, Claudette Colbert, Carole Lombard, even the newcomer, Mae West, were all a threat to her. She screened their films and analyzed the specific characteristics that gave them star quality.

"Now just watch that, Jeffrey," she'd call out, observing a scene. "You can be sure Fergus is looking at this in some projection room. Next week I'll be given some shitty carbon copy and be expected to be better!"

Her brother was the only person she dared to confide in or to share her disturbance with.

Garbo distressed her. In the Olympian quality of her facade—this woman who did not look at man alone, but at all earth's beauty—Claudia found a challenge to her own hedonistic life. After watching a Garbo film she would be deeply dejected, seeking to find a fleeting affinity with the universe and lapsing into a melancholy that Jeffrey tried to medicate with liquor.

Jeffrey enjoyed the performances of such actors as Fredric March, Cary Grant, Edward G. Robinson, Charles Boyer, James Cagney, Leslie Howard, and Spencer Tracy.

He thought they were a splendid stock company,

they were youth, they were vitality, and they were the new images.

Three people bugged him. He knew that Chaplin was such an original that no one could approach his talents, but he felt Chaplin had not plumbed his unfathomed depths in the new medium. And the two Barrymores disturbed him—Lionel, because he did not do enough or care enough to express his qualities, and John, because in him Jeffrey recognized his own pattern of self-destruction.

One night after they had run John Ford's *Arrowsmith,* and sat, shattered by its beauty, Claudia snuffed out her cigarette angrily and jumped up.

"My God—what drama, and what a break for Helen Hayes and Ronald Colman!"

"What a break for Ford to have them," said Jeffrey.

"Well, however you make it, how long are we going to sit by and let Titan shove us around? Do we have any choice of stories? Of course not! Our product is ground out like sausage in a machine."

"True," said Jeffrey. "They've put the ham in the sausage mill. In theater you pull up your audience and you know it because it's there. But we have to conjure up some excitement without really knowing how we do it until we see the rushes. And God knows you can't make sense out of that mosaic until you see what the cutter has done. My dear, a corporate marriage to a studio is just as dull as a marriage to one person. After a little experimentation, I wouldn't have one. Why the hell should I have the other."

"Let's get out of our contract," said Claudia, pouring herself a scotch. "I'm sure we can do better elsewhere."

"Easily said," answered Jeffrey. "Don't think I haven't talked to Seymour about it."

"What did he say?"

"Well, if you really want to know, he said that there was no use to bug Fergus. He really has no power in choosing product. It's Simon Moses who is spellbound by the Morgan interests and will do anything they say. He's the only one who can push the buttons."

"It's hard to believe," said Claudia. "He was so enthusiastic, so willing to take chances when we were together. What has happened to him?"

"*You* happened to him," said Jeffrey laconically.

"I guess I'll have to see him," said Claudia.

"Do me a favor," Jeffrey said, holding his hands out, "it's bad enough as it is. Just stay away from him please. Remember what happened to the poor bastard last time? Only a coronary."

"No, no!" said Claudia. "Our meeting was unexpected, and I'd been tippling, to say the least. We always got along fine, you know that. If I see him, it will be only under the most considerate conditions. You know, Jeff, I really miss him; I wish he were still in my life. I'd behave, really I would."

"That word is not in our vocabulary," said Jeffrey. "And you also forget the sands of time run fine, and very slowly, but they do run. Your ardent swain of yesteryear has probably lost many of the vital juices—he must be somewhere around sixty."

"What has that to do with it?" said Claudia. "Remember the mess our father got in at sixty-five?"

"We weren't discussing Barstows," said Jeff. "Look, let it be."

But he knew she wasn't listening. He had seen that glazed look on her face before, when she was intent on something. Poor Simon, he thought.

◆◆◆◆◆◆◆◆

"Now," said Claudia, as her brother drove her to the Guadalupe ranch, "I've got it all worked out, Jeff. You just let me meet him at the casita and talk to him for half an hour. Then you saunter in, and we'll tie things up. I know it will work."

"I think we should go in together."

"No," said Claudia, "it was difficult enough to get him to come see me at all. Let me break the ice."

Jeffrey let her out of his car at the entrance to the gates. She wore a simple white dress, and her black hair shone as she tossed it back in the warmth of the day. She saw that Simon's limousine was parked in front, and she signaled to Jeffrey that all was well, smiling.

How beautiful she is, thought Jeffrey. She's really excited about seeing him . . . what a strange animal is this love. He parked his car and picked up his copy of the *New Yorker*. He'd been longing to catch up on what was happening on Broadway.

He looked over the shimmering lake at the curve of straw-colored hills beyond. No wonder Claudia loved it. It had been a quiet haven in her life. Simon had been a haven too. Simon . . . and that brought back the thought of Esther. How incredible that the Moses family had brought such affections to the emotionally peripatetic Barstows. He wondered if David ever came here with his grandfather. He could see his son swimming in the lake, imagine him riding.

A group of horsemen in the distance came racing down the hill. A camera car followed after them. He was amused at himself for his bucolic dreams. Thundering toward the lake was one of Fergus's cheap western companies. Wouldn't you know. Irritated, he opened the magazine, and tried to close his ears to the sounds of the loudspeakers as a director barked out instructions.

Claudia opened the door. There was no need to knock, Simon was expecting her.

He walked toward her, holding out his arms.

"Oh, Claudia!" he said.

She let him embrace her, not expecting to; it just happened. She put her head on his shoulder and then looked up into his face.

"Now, now," she said, "no tears."

"No tears," said Simon, trying to smile, his eyes moist. "Oh, Claudia, I've missed you so!"

She pulled away, and led him to the sofa.

"Let me look at you," she said. "Oh, you—you look fine."

He had thinned, and his hair was whiter. But he was tanned, and his brown eyes and fine brows against the dark complexion were arresting.

"You're handsomer than Ronnie Colman," she said.

"And you're as lovely as Claudia Barstow," he said.

Their fingers entwined. They smiled with their eyes.

"Do you think we could possibly pick up the pieces?" he said. "Who knows what life is going to give us, Claudia. Who knows? But we still love each other, don't we?"

"Oh, darling, we do!" she said.

He put his arms around her and kissed her. She clung to him.

"Claudia," he said, "oh, Claudia, love me."

"I want to."

Time had telescoped. They wanted each other. The past seemed to be washed away. And this time he ordered her.

She found herself being led into the bedroom. Again the white curtains were blowing in the faint breeze. The Spanish bed had been waiting for them, it seemed.

She disrobed, to find him waiting, naked on the bed. She came to him.

"Dare we?" she asked.

"We should, my love, we should," he whispered. She put her hands on him.

"Now you must let me do it, Si, I want you to close your eyes and lie back, and I'm going to love you my way, to gentle you and kiss you, and when you are ready, then I'll take care of you, and it will be like it used to be."

"Like it is always when I even think of you," he whispered. "I can't believe it."

"You can believe it," she said as she caressed him and kissed him. She knew when it was time for him to enter her. And as he did, it was as fulfilling as it had ever been in the most frenzied moment of passion she had known.

She cried out with pleasure.

"My Claudia!" he whispered at the moment of their complete surrender to each other. "Oh, beautiful—beautiful!"

He let out a breath. It seemed like an implosion.

And then she realized his weight was heavy on her. He was gasping; his face was turning cyanotic. She lifted his arm away from her side. It was immobile.

She pulled away from under him, moved him over, stared at him, and then started to scream.

He was dead.

◆◆◆◆◆◆◆◆

By the time Fergus arrived, the Guadalupe ranch fire department had abandoned first aid. They stood by while the studio doctor, the terrified chauffeur, the director of the western, two assistants, and Jeffrey sat in the living room.

The company had been dismissed, after running to see what was happening as they heard the bloodcurdling shrieks. Claudia had rushed outside naked, holding a towel over her face. Jeffrey had reached the scene first, dragged his sister back in the house, and managed to alert the director and his assistants to summon the fire department and the studio doctor.

Everything had been tried from artificial respiration to Adrenalin. But it was too late. On Simon's chest was a great bruise where his heart had, literally, exploded.

Claudia rested in the guest bedroom after the doctor had sedated her. Jeffrey took Fergus into the kitchen. Jeffrey's mouth was dry, and he poured himself a glass of water from the tap.

"This shows," he said, drinking it, "what shock I'm in. What in hell are we going to do?"

In the distance, a police siren was heard.

"Oh, God," said Fergus, "here they come. We'll have to make a police report. You'd better stay out of it, Jeffrey. How in hell did you get involved?"

"I was holding the lantern," said Jeffrey.

Fergus looked at him in disgust.

"Can't you be serious at a time like this! Do you know what this is going to do to the studio and a few careers?"

"God knows what led them into this sudden madness; they couldn't have been in there more than twenty minutes," said Jeffrey.

"Long enough," said Fergus. "The only thing that bothers me is that goddamned movie company. They dispersed before I could get to them, and you can't buy off that many people—"

He took a large roll of bills out of his pocket.

"This'll take care of the chauffeur, the fire department, and the doctor. Of course he signed the death certificate, but Christ, Jeffrey, somebody will be on the honker right now, spilling the beans to some member of the press for a goodly sum! Why in hell did Claudia have to come screaming out of the house naked?"

"Well, she did have a towel over her face," said Jeffrey. "She was so scared that she didn't want to see."

"That was a help," said Fergus. "Good God, I've got to tell Rebecca. And Abe—and eventually, my wife."

Jeffrey looked down. "And David," he said.

"Thoughtful of you," said Fergus.

The phone in the vargueno rang. Fergus looked around and finally discovered it.

His grimace showed that answering it was a mistake.

"Andy," he said, "how are you, and where are you?"

"Don't give me that bullshit. You don't care how I am," said Andrew. "I'm in New York. I've just had a telephone call. My informant tells me that Simon Moses dropped dead at the ranch, with an interesting companion, that bitch, Claudia Barstow, and that it happened at a most inappropriate, or should I say, appropriate moment. Is that true?"

"It is true," said Fergus, "that Simon Moses is dead. It was what we had always feared; he had been horseback riding and it was too much for his heart."

"The hell you say," said Andrew. "Don't try to gull me, Fergus, we know what filly he was riding. If he had to go, I'd say, from his past track record, that was the way he would have chosen."

"Don't embarrass me," said Fergus. "This is a most sad thing for Titan Films. They haven't even taken his body away yet."

"Let me know if he still has an erection," said Andrew.

"Listen, you son-of-a-bitch," Fergus said hotly, "I will not discuss this matter further. You may consider that our association is at an end."

He hung up and looked at Jeffrey.

"Nobody has a right to be such a bastard," he said, "but God knows what he'll write now."

"Whatever it is," said Jeffrey, "at least Simon won't worry about it."

Andrew Reed told the whole story in all his syndicated columns in such a veiled way that he could not be prosecuted, but everyone who knew anything about Hollywood realized exactly who was involved, and how.

◆◆◆◆◆◆◆◆

Simon's funeral was one of the most splendid the film colony had ever seen. Rebecca leaned on the arms of Fergus and David. All the moguls, the people who had seen him through his career, and those who had ridden on the tail of his comet sent massive floral tributes. The interment was at the Jewish cemetery on Gower, not far from the little red barn that had been the start of his enormous studio.

Titan closed down for the morning. Fergus, after seeing Rebecca home and in the protection of Abe and important board members, drove to the studio in the afternoon. He went to Simon's suite.

He stood by the desk for a moment, looking at the things that belonged to Simon, pictures of his family in fine silver frames, honors and trophies, an oil painting of the first studio, and a sheaf of scripts bound in red morocco with Simon's name on them. These cherished possessions would soon be replaced by the clutter of someone else's life, until they too were dethroned either by company decree or by destiny.

Remembering the past, and the constant exasperation with Simon, both with Claudia and in work, Fergus realized how Simon had toughened his fiber and fashioned his life. Now he felt empty, missing him deeply, needing his challenge.

Poor Simon, he thought, poor Simon, you wanted Claudia so much that you bought death. All the cheap wisecracks by those who never loved as you did, discussing the way you died. But you did at the last what you wanted, which is more than most people do, and you bought yourself a final moment of heaven. And what you left for all of us is likely hell. To be practical, now that you're dead and buried, if Titan studio's in the basement today—tomorrow it's liable to be in the gutter.

Simon's secretary, Miss Mosby, came in from her long coffee break, fluttering. She hadn't expected a visitor.

"I'm sorry, Mr. Austin," she said, "but Abe Moses told me not to let anyone in the office. It's to be locked tight until he comes to inventory things tomorrow."

"That figures," said Fergus.

He went downstairs to his own office. Angrily he sat at his desk and lit a cigarette, fully realizing how precarious his position was. Simon had protected him from the New York buzzards by needing him. And Abe would be delighted to throw him out.

"Miss Barstow is here to see you," buzzed Harriet.

He was astonished. Of course, Claudia had not dared come to the funeral. Neither had Jeffrey. He had seen a heart of white gardenias at the foot of the casket, and Red Powell had told him someone had been bribed to put it there. Red, eyebrows lifted, murmured that it was obviously from Claudia. His attitude had implied that, considering how Simon had perished, a white heart from Claudia was in bad taste.

"Send her in," said Fergus.

Claudia was dressed in a black suit, a cloche hat hiding most of her hair. She looked fragile, her face pale and her eyes ringed by pain and tears.

She sat opposite Fergus and started to cry. "I hoped you'd be here. I went to my dressing room to get some personal things. Si's picture on my dressing table—you know—oh, Fergus, it's so terrible. I wasn't even allowed to say good-bye to him. What can I do?—What can I do now?"

She wept into her handkerchief, and Fergus could see that she was not playacting.

"Claudia," he said, "I can't get you out of this one. I—I don't know. I guess this will be such a scandal that you'll have to go away—for a while, at least. Damn Andy Reed."

"I don't care about that," she said. "It's just—just Si. What have I done!"

"It had to happen," said Fergus. "He never got over missing you. I knew that. Maybe it's a blessing that you gave him the joy you did, at last, when he loved you so much. I think he'd have done exactly what he did even if he knew what would happen."

"You really think that?" she said. She glanced up, almost eagerly.

Fergus nodded.

"I guess I'll go away," she said, "and I suppose Jeffrey will, too."

"Likely," said Fergus. "Too bad he was there when it happened. But you know how the Hays office is. I wasn't going to tell you today, but we've already had over a hundred wires from the Bible Belt canceling your pictures. And of course, there goes your contract."

"It figures," said Claudia. "Just like it figures that this whole day of Simon's funeral, nobody called me. Not one." She paused, thoughtfully. "But what can you expect? No one dares to miss the boss's funeral in this town."

Fergus was surprised. He thought of all the people who owed her favors. Makeup men who had become heads of departments, assistants who had become directors, famous dress designers she had started in business, actors and actresses who had worked their way up, currying favors throughout the glamorous years, bringing her gifts on holidays, planning elaborate celebrations on her birthdays, and making her feel every bit the queen. Where were they all at a time like this?

Claudia fished in her purse.

"Hello, here I am, Typhoid Mary," she said. "Oh, Fergie, you know how I dread being alone."

"Now, now, Claudia," said Fergus, "it will pass. I've had my bumps, too. We manage to go on living. We had good days—they were, weren't they?"

She nodded, her eyes filled with tears, still seeking something in her purse.

"Here," said Fergus, "you'd better use a man-sized handkerchief."

"Oh, no, thanks," she said, "I have my own. I'm just looking for something I—I wanted you to have."

She handed him a little package.

"You can open it later." She stood up.

"You have too much talent to get lost," he said, rising to meet her. "Remember that. There's only one Claudia."

He put his arms around her. For a moment she was limp, crying into the shoulder of his dark suit. Then she pulled away and looked up through her tears.

"Can I drive you home," he asked, "or maybe you'd like to come to my house for dinner?"

She patted his hand.

"Thank you, Fergie," she said, "but believe it or not, tonight I just want to be alone. I have a lot of memories to put away."

She wiped her eyes, shifted the veil of her hat to cover the dark circles, which he noticed made her eyes seem even bluer, rimmed with her thick lashes. He swallowed, feeling inadequate. What could anyone say? He, too, felt suddenly bereft. They'd both gone a long road with Simon.

"Thank you again," she said, "for everything."

Fergus sat back in his swivel chair, put his arms behind his head, and looked out the window; he, too, was close to tears.

He watched her get into her car in the parking lot. Her chauffeur closed the door, saluted grandly, and she drove off the Titan lot in style, perhaps, he thought, for the last time.

Fergus noted that the cop on duty, who had usually greeted her so effusively from his little booth, had his back turned and was busy while she went through.

In his mind he could see the fans who stood in rain or shine at the gate to get her autograph or cherish her smile. He thought of all the people who had made her working life seem so full, with their lip service. The parking lot would be full if they all were there.

Sic transit gloria mundi, little movie star.

He stared at the small package on the desk. Finally, he opened it.

In it was a gold money clip, modeled after the little red barn. And in the clip were five one-hundred-dollar bills.

In the three days since Simon had died in her arms, she had known she was through. She'd had the clip made by Gershgorn jewelers, quickly; anything could be done if you paid double. So she had seen the writing on the wall. He did not have to tell her.

The next week Fergus Austin and the Barstows mutually and officially accepted the dropping of their upcoming option. The two seneschals to the legal divorce of the corporate marriage were Fergus Austin, and Seymour Sewell, who had tried to act as a buffer between the Barstows and the press and had failed.

Will Hays outdid himself. He shook his head once, and it seemed he ended two careers.

A month later, Fergus faced the noon stillness in his office, knowing full well what it meant. When the phone stops ringing and quiet descends in an executive office, there is an alarm, not unlike the stagnant silence that hits before a hurricane begins to destroy everything.

It was a time of change for the whole town. Schulberg and Lasky were out of Paramount, David Selznick had left RKO, conservators were examining the books of all the studios. Sound stages were empty; and executives and high-salaried personnel were resigning by invitation. For the first time, the pioneers who had fought their way through the boom days were being replaced by more businesslike individuals, many from New York. And retirement even with a personal fortune was unthinkable to the old tigers whose lives were enhanced by the constant adulation of all the people they might help up the ladder to fame and fortune with the vast power at their command.

There had been distant rumbles that there was a stockholders' meeting in New York. Fergus was likely to be dropped for mismanagement, for that's what being in the red was called, no matter what the reason.

Fergus did not have to read Andrew Reed's intimations or Clarissa Pennock's blind item to know he was about to be replaced. Stocks were being unloaded, proxies collected, and there was going to be a big shake-up.

The studio and the product lacked vitality and originality in a difficult time. Everyone noted that the innovators were Metro, Fox, and Paramount, and no question, with Simon Moses gone, Titan's blood would thin to an anemic trickle.

This commentary irritated him most of all, knowing how he had plotted and planned to help create the image of Simon Moses, and then had fought the old man's policy at the end, hoping to make more original pictures so the fortunes of the Moses empire would flourish, and his fortunes along with them.

He wondered how he could manage to exist without this panorama. He had supervised the building of the lot from that first ramshackle red barn. He had bought up acreage for pennies. The narrow, dirt streets had become busy thoroughfares. Life without this studio seemed impossible. What would he do? His lawyer would be as busy as a surgeon separating his nerve system from Titan's bloodstream. In this time of panic, everyone was hanging on to jobs with fang and claw. No other studio would want him.

He had told Miss Foster not to put any calls through. Not having received any, he was rejecting before being rejected. But his pacing was interrupted by the buzzer. He pushed the intercom.

"Damn it, Harriet," he said, "I told you no—"

"Oh, Mr. Austin," she said. He heard the same panic in her voice he had heard so many years before when she had told him that Martha was dead. "It—it's your mother. Mrs. Austin—"

◆◆◆◆◆◆◆◆

There was nothing more impersonal than the death of an old woman in a hotel room.

She lay, covered with a sheet, until the wagon would come to take what was left away. Her dentures were in a glass in the bathroom on the edge of the sink. Her cotton underwear was draped over the shower rod. Her rayon dress was hung on the bathroom door. A bargain-sized jar of cold cream and a comb with a few teeth missing perched on the toilet water tank.

He was appalled that she had not improved her way of living. The bathroom had all the home-laundry sour smells of the boardinghouse in the Bronx.

He went to the dresser and pulled open a drawer. There were the boxes of birthday and Christmas gifts. He opened one. There was an initialed scarf, the tissue paper still pristine, the card, "To Grandma from David, love," still in place.

The desk had a few insurance papers in a folder, her wedding certificate, some postcards from people in the East, and the usual clutter of pictures—of himself, of David, old sepia prints of her and his father when they were young at Coney Island, one of Esther looking absolutely bereft with the little boy on a forgotten day at the beach, and a picture of himself and Esther at their wedding, the Moses family and Mary Frances beaming fixedly in the background.

At the bedside was her Bible, a rosary, and an alarm clock that had rung until its bell had run down. She had died in her sleep. He was a little surprised to see that the alarm had been set for half-past six. What in hell did she get up so early for? She had nothing to do with her time.

He looked around the room, and he marveled that she had seemed so busy and chipper the times he had neglected her and talked on the phone, or had dropped by to leave her money.

He wondered if David would really miss her, or if he had been as secretly bored as he had been by her company.

There was a knock at the door.

Two hearse attendants came in and gently and efficiently lifted the inert body on a stretcher. The hotel manager, Mr. Grieves, came to him and shook his hand.

"She was such a nice lady, Mr. Austin, never caused us trouble. What can we do. Deepest sympathy."

A tear glistened in his eye.

My God, thought Fergus, he cares more than I do. What the hell's wrong with me?

"Would you care to go over her effects? We'll clean out the room as soon as you say. No charge, of course, for a few extra days."

"Thank you very much," said Fergus, "I'll have my secretary come over and pack."

He looked out to Highland where the hearse door was being closed. Finish. Period. That's it.

"Just one thing," said Mr. Grieves, "that parrakeet. We can't look after the little pet, you know."

"Oh," he said, "I'll take it home. I guess my son will look after it."

One of the bellhops was hovering around.

"Would you please call my driver to come get the cage?"

"Sure thing, Mr. Austin," said the bellhop. "Now don't you worry."

Expecting a fat tip, he bustled off. Fergus peeled off a bill thinking how casually people expected large tips from tycoons. Tycoons! How would it be in this town to be a has-been?

The bird was put in David's room.

That night, while Fergus was reading in the study, David entered.

"Father," he said, his eyes wide, "I think you'd better look at these papers I found in Fido's cage. I almost threw them out."

The top papers were marked with bird dung, splattered water drops, and a few seeds fell out as Fergus shuffled through.

"My God!" he said after a few moments.

The properties were in his name.

David looked at him. He suddenly noticed that the boy's eyes were red-rimmed. He did care. He really did.

Included in the deeds was a clipping Mary Frances had cut out of the *Los Angeles Examiner*. Fergus read that the area recently referred to as the Wilshire Boulevard Center was renamed the Miracle Mile. This was the area where his mother had traded, bargained, and amassed her largest frontage. Spot zoning, the increase in automobiles, and the widening of Wilshire Boulevard as a stylish passageway clear to the ocean made the land incredibly valuable. Forty corners in the Miracle Mile stretch showed an annual value increase of 744 percent.

Although the stock market was deflated, valuable land had appreciated. Fergus knew he could sell off a piece of land to a large corporation. And he thought he knew just the man who might be interested. He'd call Mike Cuneo in Chicago. A big shot in the liquor business, now that Prohibition was ended, was always looking for someplace to diversify his cash.

"Well, David," he said, "it looks like your grandmother has taken care of our old age."

"That's what she said she'd do," said David. "She and Aunt Kathleen used to take me driving. She pointed out all that land and said it was hers. I didn't believe her."

"You can believe her," said Fergus.

He thought of the market price of Titan stock, and for the first time rejoiced that it had dropped. It was worth the plunge. Power was always worth a risk.

This day, the day of the death of his mother, was the luckiest day of his life.

III

THE CHANGE:

1934—1947

1

Like many stars and artists, Claudia and Jeffrey traveled and moved without cash in hand. A corporation had always been their fairy godmother, waving the magic wand. Seymour Sewell kept them from raw exposure to the facts of economy for a few weeks, but even he had to warn them it was time to cut down.

Titan no longer protected them from the press. The scandal of Simon's death enlarged with gossip. It had been rumored around town that Jeffrey had been watching when Simon died in the bedroom at the Guadalupe ranch.

Whatever the rumor was, they seemed unemployable in Hollywood. And, since the crash was only several years past, they had not built up a fortune, with their willful expenditures.

Claudia led a solitary life for a few months, getting over the sadness and shock of Simon's death. Finally, she drifted from her beach house to Jeffrey's yacht.

"It's a waiting game," she said, as they lounged on the *Zahma*. "You know, I don't think anyone's going to hire us. Let's get out of town. And if they want us they'll have to look for us."

"Brilliant," said Jeffrey. "We'll take the *Zahma* and meander down the west coast of Mexico and through the Panama Canal. I've always wanted to dive around the Amazon estuary. And you can believe Seymour will flush us out of wherever we are. Any worthwhile ten-percenter can find a client if he has to cross the River Styx."

Sewell agreed it was just as well they leave town. He talked it over with Claudia at her beach house.

"I'm not a pessimist," he said, "but you've got to face it. You're on a blacklist. Maybe it'll blow over. I'd conserve my assets if I were you."

"What assets?" said Claudia. "You know the depression blitzed me. I had to mortgage my house and sell almost everything to get out. And expenses kind of ganged up on me. I was in about two hundred thousand."

"What about all that jewelry you've got stashed away?"

"I sold most of it to meet the margin on my stocks. I do have a few pieces."

"Well, turn them into cash, and I'll get some client to rent this house; you know how they sail in and out of Hollywood loaded on these one picture deals. Somebody always wants a place."

"Okay," said Claudia, "just let me keep part of the servants' quarters over the garage to store my junk."

"Get rid of as much as you can," said Seymour. "It's very cold out."

"Of course," said Claudia, "but naturally I'll keep a few things with me. After all, I have to know I existed here!"

She looked up at the portrait Augustus John had made of her at the peak of her beauty. She had sat for it on rainy days in New York when she was doing a film on location. She had been irritated at the time she wasted sitting when she could have been having fun. Thank God she did.

"You could get a nice chunk for that," said Seymour.

"This one I keep. That's me," she said, sighing, "at least what I might have been. You can ship it to me wherever I land."

"Okay," said Seymour. "I know you, Claudia, but you have to remember no studio is paying excess freight for twenty trunks and thirty pieces of hand luggage. So try to cut down. Too bad that your option was almost finished. You'll only end up with about enough cash to clear your debts and taxes and get started someplace else. I hear that half the people in town have taken a 50 percent cut, rather than lose their jobs."

"What's with Fergus?" she asked.

"Well, he's lucky," said Seymour. "I hear he's sold a whole block on Wilshire. Land is the best asset today. That gangster from Chicago, Mike Cuneo, has gone legit and is using his bootlegging money to start up a clearing house for California wines."

"That son-of-a-bitch, Fergus!" said Claudia. "I'm going right over to his house and give him a piece of my mind!"

"Oh, no you're not," said Seymour. "He's in New York. I hear he's just about cornered the market on Titan stock. What's it to you anyway?"

"Nothing, really," said Claudia, "except people can get so frigging moral when it comes to me, but if they want a break, all of a sudden, ex-bootleggers are grand to do business with."

"I didn't know you knew Cuneo," said Seymour.

"I'll show you," said Claudia.

She ran upstairs and came down with the diamond bracelet.

"Read that!"

"Mike loves Claudia," he read. "My God, Claudia, it looks like the news flasher on Times Square! Here's your passport to a vacation. How about that?"

"Yeah, how about it," said Claudia. "Well, I guess this just about winds up my jewelry, save for one item."

"What's that, and what's it worth?"

"It's not for sale," said Claudia. "It has sentimental value to me."

"Now I've heard everything," said Seymour, pouring himself a drink.

Claudia touched the slender diamond bracelet that Simon had given her on his first visit to Hollywood.

"Well, that ain't much of a blockbuster," said Seymour.

"It seemed so at the time," said Claudia wistfully, remembering the pride with which Si had given it to her that evening at the Hollywood Hotel.

"I guess you really mean it," said Seymour. "I'll get in touch with some connections I have, and we can break down that Cuneo bracelet and get a little chunk of change. I'd say maybe twenty thousand."

"Great! But no 10 percent, you Shylock," she said. "*Twenty thousand*, huh?"

He looked at her and grinned. "You must be pretty good in the feathers."

"I am," said Claudia modestly. "I am."

◆◆◆◆◆◆◆◆

By the time the *Zahma* had anchored for several days in Mazatlán to provision and refuel, Claudia was ready to leave. Two bullfighters, three gallons of tequila, little food save for enough limes to prevent beriberi, a busted-up shore boat, and two local *policía* did it.

"If you ever hear from Seymour again," she said acidly, "you can reach me in Mayfair. A journey through that sweltering Panama Canal is not my idea of a ball. Really, ducks, the *Mauretania* is more my style. I haven't had more than a fleeting glimpse of London these last years. I think I'll establish some digs at the Cavendish and catch up to the people who had enough sense to stay in the theater."

Jeffrey was relieved. From time to time he needed solitude. His bookcases were brimming with books he hadn't had time to read. His mind was becoming unfogged. It would be good to have relationships that would last only dockside to dockside. He would clock his life by brilliant dawns, observe the verdant land through binoculars, and chart his course by the Southern Cross. If he chose, time would stand still, and his cosmos would be, with God's will, of his own making.

⬥⬥⬥⬥⬥⬥⬥⬥

Claudia had worked hard, and now she was going to play hard, and the hell with Hollywood.

She took the forty-eight-hour combination train and air trip to New York. The plane had lightweight wicker seats.

"I'll have a waffle-fanny the rest of my life!" she complained. "Why did I choose this torture rack!"

But the flying speed of almost a hundred miles an hour would be a conversation piece, the handsome pilot informed her.

In her compartment on the night train (for planes would not fly by night) she settled down and let out a sigh of relief. She could do without air travel until it got better.

In New York, she stayed at the Algonquin for a few days. Her arrival was heralded in the gossip columns. Friends, admirers, past comrades of the theater, and the usual wealthy young playboys tossed up by the turmoils of the industrial revolution and sudden wealth joined her in a glittering parabola. Why had she ever bothered to work so hard in that dull Hollywood! Life was going to be a ball!

The night before she boarded the *Mauretania*, she returned to the Algonquin. It was filled with late-night revelers. As she entered the lobby, she passed out and slid to the floor, a puddle of satin and osprey. The night clerk, quick on the draw, ordered a wheelchair and covered her face with a large dinner napkin, so fellow occupants of the elevator would not recognize her.

The next day, friends and sycophants poured into

the bridal suite of the ocean liner. It had cost a fortune, but movie stars had to travel in luxury, and, after all, she was moving into a new world.

When the crowd had left and the stewards had tidied up, she took off her feather toque, ran her fingers through her hair, and kicked off her shoes. The cabin was filled with flowers, baskets of delicacies, hardly needed on such a luxury liner, and the latest books in elegant carrying cases. She opened the cards, sad to be leaving, and trying to convince herself that these gifts were a tribute to something that would happen again. She should be gay—it was going to be fun! But she wanted to cry. Nobody, just nobody really cared.

There was one great basket of red roses, and attached to the card was a small package. She tore open the envelope.

The card read, "I always pay my debts, bon voyage and as always love, Fergus."

She opened the little Tiffany box. In it was a C-shaped platinum moneyclip set with a diamond. It was holding five crisp hundred-dollar bills.

By the time the boat docked, the Barstow family photographer, an aesthetic gentleman named Orville, accompanied by two pale young men, Cupcake and Lollypop, found her in her suite lying in a bubble bath in a sequin gown that had melted to a soggy mass of glue. Orville told the ship's reporters that she had gone ashore in a private launch. They cleaned her up, dressed her, packed her luggage with the aid of a hysterical stewardess, and got her on the boat train. They fortified her with strong tea and toast and spirited her after innumerable arrangements past a vast mob of fans at Paddington Station. She was smuggled out of town to a nursing home in Kent. There she stayed, watching a cabbage grow on a thatched roof, trying to remember who she was, where she was, and wondering why she kept waking up screaming at night, dreaming about Simon, who arose alive and happy after they had made love.

One day, pale Kentish sunlight beckoned her, and she began to think of London and her chums, and she read up on the theater in magazines Orville brought her. Hollywood and her life there was fading.

"You're lucky to be back, ducks," he said. "This is a golden age of theater. Some of your peers have been bright enough to realize the limitations of films, even if one is a bloody success like you, bewitched by your own legend. And here nobody gives a damn about any scandal—it only makes you more interesting. There's a certain style and freedom on the stage. It's a truly lively art, and ever changing. How can you find excitement in that mosaic world of cinema?"

"I can find it," said Claudia. "Do you know how much they pay?"

"How much do you have left on that solid-gold carrousel you've been riding, dearie? All you have, so far as I can see, is the lead ring."

"Well, you can blame the market crash for some of my dilemma," she said, "but offers will come in. How about a portrait sitting?"

Orville lifted his sapphire-ringed hand and pushed a lock of her hair from her cheek.

"My dear Claudia, I have photographed you, your brother, your grandfather, and various relatives for ages. But at this moment I couldn't photograph you through a silk stocking. You look like hell. Get back in shape. I know a divine facial woman who will *wrap* you in herbs and balsams from Peru. You must eat decently, sleep, and of course a little fornicating will bring bloom to your cheeks."

"You have a point," said Claudia, smiling.

Back in form, she settled in a suite at the stylish Cavendish. Her sorrow lessened, and she fell more and more comfortably into the exciting pace of London. The city was happily abuzz. A beautiful and supposedly rich film star, no matter what cloud chased her from Hollywood, was exciting company. She caught up with old friends and made new ones. In no time it was Harry, Noel, Edith, Larry, Leslie, Mickey, Cedric, and Cathleen. A time for elegant gowns and furs and jewels, men in white tie, or smart underdone country clothes. Candlelight dinners, jazz bands, supper clubs, weekends at country estates. The elegancies of glittering gatherings, theater doormen stylishly saying to chauffeurs, "carriages at eleven."

Adults and children payed her homage wherever she went. Some even stood on Jermyn Street in rain or shine to see her come out of the hotel.

It was difficult in such a world to realize a year of this and she'd be down to bedrock.

One afternoon when she and Orville were shopping for crystal at the open-air Caledonian market a young boy followed her, close on her heels. Orville took hold of her arm.

"Take care," he said. "The little bastard will likely pick your pocket."

He nudged her, and the stemmed glass she was holding fell to the pavement and shattered. The boy looked up at her in fear, his face paling. He turned to run, but she took hold of his arm. He was almost ready to wrench away from her when she smiled.

"Now, now, it's not your fault. And it's only a glass. They still make them, you know."

The boy still stared.

"Bug off," said Orville. "Leave Miss Barstow alone. Don't stare like that!"

But the boy was spellbound. Claudia was pleased. She reached in her purse and took out half a crown.

"Here," she said, "go buy yourself a sweet."

The boy took the coin, looked at it, tipped his cap, and handed it back to her.

"No, mum," he said, "no charity from you, Miss Barstow."

He ducked away through the crowd, and Claudia was inexplicably embarrassed.

"Well," said Orville, "now I've seen everything."

"Interesting face," said Claudia, "those wide-set eyes and that dimple on his chin."

"It must be a bore," said Orville, "having people like that staring at you like the Second Coming. It would give me the fantods. You have absolutely no privacy."

"If you're a movie star," said Claudia, "the day they stop doing that, you're in trouble."

The next day the bell captain rang her room.

"There's a young boy here Miss Barstow, says he has a package for you. Says it's personal."

"Send him up," said Claudia, puzzled.

It was the boy from the market. His hair was glued fast to his head, he wore a seedy tweed suit and a tie that had been badly sponged.

"Well, well, it's you," she said. "What's your name?" She put a finger on his dimpled chin. He flushed.

"John Graves," he said, pronouncing it *Grives.*

"Spell it."

He did.

"John," she said, "with that fetching chin and those eyes you may be quite a handsome chap someday. But it really won't do you the good it should with that cockney accent."

He flushed even more, tongue-tied. He handed her the package, carefully wrapped in creased white tissue.

She opened it. It was a Waterford crystal glass, like the one she had dropped.

"Wherever did you get it?"

He examined his cap, twirling it in his hands.

"All right," she said, "I won't ask. How much do I owe you?"

He looked up at her resentfully, his blue eyes flashing.

"It's a gift, Miss Barstow," he said.

"Well, thank you. I didn't mean to be rude. Couldn't I give you some little thing?"

"A photo," he said, "a photo with writing on it to me. I see all your pictures. I never miss one. Never."

"Well, you just go on seeing them," she said. "And while you're looking at films, since they talk now, listen, and learn. Remember, you can be as fine as your voice."

She went to her desk, pulled out a picture, and scrawled on it, "To John Graves, who may be a star himself when his voice and his looks get together, Claudia Barstow."

When she handed it to him he stared at it, stunned by his good fortune.

"I must be going out," she said. "You'll have to forgive me."

"*Forgive* you," he said, and he let out a gasp of astonishment as he clutched the picture, "blimey!"

She opened the door and watched him walk down the hall, engrossed in what she had written. It seemed to have removed her from his memory, the possession of it being so much more important to him.

She sat at her desk autographing a dozen more photographs to important people or their relatives. No one knew where such trails could lead. It was time to think of making money—getting a new film out or setting foot on the boards again.

Every Sunday, that strange little cockney boy with the intense eyes dropped by with another Waterford glass. And by the end of a dozen of them he had claimed a dozen different poses of her.

"He must be using them for wallpaper," she said to Orville at a portrait sitting.

Orville shook his head.

"You're bonkers," he said, "at what I charge for these pictures. God knows who he shows them off to."

She smiled. He caught it. It was the best portrait he

had ever made of her, in spite of the sharpness that age was giving her throat and eyes. For there was a tenderness about it that Claudia had not had in her early days of arrogant beauty.

Looking at the picture later, she realized with a start that she seemed to have found a happiness and life in her that had been lost since Si had died.

The next time John Graves brought his gift, she had him stay to tea. Imagine, Claudia Barstow eating watercress sandwiches and tea with a gangling lad. But his slicked-down hair, his eager, adoring look, and his efforts to set the spoon in the saucer properly touched her.

"Now, John," she said, "you have some spark in you. Let it become a flame. But it won't do you a bloody bit of good if you don't learn the King's English. I'm going to take you to see a play. It's done by a group of amateurs, and it was written before you were born. But I think it will start you thinking, and from there we'll see what can be done about you."

They went to the Queen's Theater on Shaftesbury.

"This is a Sunday show," she said. "It's the Arts and Drama Club putting it on. Someday you'll get a chance, like all the newcomers—Henry Wilcoxon, Larry Olivier—that's how you start, John."

His eyes opened wide. It seemed a dozen people fussed over her, kissed her, and welcomed her, ignoring him as if he were just another fan standing by for an autograph. But his bliss was complete when she sat him on the aisle seat.

As the lights went down she bent to whisper, "Now for God's sake, John, sit on your cap and stop twiddling with it. And don't try to read the program in the dark. You can take it home and study it later. Just relax and listen to what the actors are saying. That's why you're here."

It was an opening of the portals of paradise. Next to him sat his ideal, the most beautiful woman in the world, the woman he had adored on film since he was a little tyke. And she nudged him and pointed out subtleties in the play until his head spun. It was the beginning of his life.

The play was *Pygmalion.*

⧫⧫⧫⧫⧫⧫⧫⧫

Months passed pleasantly for Jeffrey on the *Zahma.* Sometimes, to his surprise, he went for days without anything but a sip of wine. Other times he debauched with the intimates of dark waterfront dives, drinking and sleeping with companions whose faces he did not recognize by the light of day.

His passage through the locks of the Panama Canal was fascinating. It signaled a new chapter in his adventure. The whole journey seemed an odyssey to him, a break with the banal, and a chance few men have to live a dream.

Finally, the morning of a perfect dawn, he realized his fantasy. Off the island of Marazo, at the ocean inlet of the Amazon, he was lowered into the warm waters in his diving gear.

Slowly he settled on the bottom, nesting himself on a sunken log. He waited in the magnificent silence. Gradually, a kaleidoscope of tiny fishes moved about him. One little golden striped holocanthus diacanthus wriggled delicately up to his faceplate and peered in, eyes popping, as if intrigued to see what sort of freak was imprisoned inside.

Jeffrey chuckled. How wonderful to be sitting in this disassociated world, surrounded by fearless and curious creatures as beautiful as jewels in the slanting deep-sea sunlight. But as he rejoiced, the log moved. He pulled away as quickly as he could, for his perch was a gigantic crocodile. As he thrashed to the surface, feeling that the water was working against him like molasses, he glimpsed the green white of its belly as it circled. He never would have believed that a man could break into a cold sweat in warm waters.

After he recorded the incident in his log, he took one of the *Zahma* postcards from its rack and wrote a note.

Dear David,
Thought you would be interested in my adventures this day. Sat on a crocodile in an underwater dreamland, and I almost ended up Long John Silver. Wish you could have shared the good part of it. Your loving father,

Jeffrey

Then, as he knew he would, he lit a match to it and watched it curl into ashes. He felt sad, trying to recall David's voice, his look, his firm step, so—so Barstow.

The shore boat was standing by. He called his deckhand and was taken through the oily black waters of the harbor. How much more beautiful and promising a waterfront looks from the sea.

Comforting himself with the administrations of several café-au-lait girls and a lonesome flamenco dancer who smoked cigars, he dallied for several weeks, enforcing his moral obligations to himself with constant libations.

In time, in the port of Pará, cables found him. From Seymour Sewell, of course. No offer of a job, only an alert. He'd been away four months. Which securities did he want to cash in to face his compounding debts?

The hell with obligations. Why shouldn't he have his *wanderjahr*? Sell everything. Keep the hacienda, that was all. Stocks and bonds had no importance. They could be replaced. Sell. Just send money, that's all.

In Nassau, months later, Seymour himself caught up with him. No doubt about it, both he and Claudia were on movie czar Will Hays's lousy blacklist. Sure, the studios were flourishing, crawling out of the doldrums, but pictures were ornamented with studio-puffed talent; unfortunately, the Barstows were unemployable at the moment.

"It's a rotten police state!" said Jeffrey. "Talent should not be measured by anything but performance. They've made plenty on us."

"Not in the last pictures, unfortunately. You were canceled out," said Seymour. "I'm afraid Claudia's come to a cruel thump, too."

"What's wrong with her?" asked Jeffrey, concerned.

"You egomaniac actors are going to have to learn that the star system is not conceived in altruism. And Claudia did the worst thing she could do in London. It could shorten her acting life ten years."

"My God," said Jeffrey, "what could that be? She's committed everything but mayhem with everything that stood still—I should say, moved. What is it?"

"She scraped together all her annuities and assets to make a quick picture, which ran way over budget. She put up the finishing bond without telling me. I'd never have let her. She played a role much too young for, shall I say, her mature personality, and it bombed out. Disaster, economically and professionally. Now she's lucky if someone wants her to play Granny Goose in a Christmas pantomime."

Jeffrey shook his head.

"How could she not know that talent never pays for itself. Why no takers elsewhere?"

"The takers were at Leicester Square when she fell down on the stage on opening night of a play last month. You didn't hear about that?"

"All I've been interested in is marine weather forecasts, and I am happy to say the only bore that bothered me was the tidal bore off the Amazon estuary."

"Nice if you can afford it. Come now, Jeffrey, aren't you waking a little earlier each day, wondering what you're going to do about your God-given talent? None of the Barstows ever quit until time or bad habits caught up with them. And you look quite fit."

"You've just been telling me that I have the professional pox. Now, pray tell, what is really up your craw? You didn't come here for my excellent rum collins."

"Well, it so happens that there are always wildcatters in pictures. They don't give a damn about an unwritten blacklist. And if they're old enough, they still think you're a top star and remember when you were a brilliant actor."

"I thank you," said Jeffrey dryly. "*All* Barstows thank you for your fucking trust."

"Don't get miffed," said Seymour. "You can't afford it. There's an oilman from Texas who has the hots for a girl, redhead from Earl Carroll's lineup. You could play opposite her for a good chunk of money. And not a bad script, something Dan Hendricks had in his trunk. And although you're so goddamned sensitive about the facts of life, it's a choice between that and losing your mortgaged boat and house."

Jeffrey stared at him a moment.

"I shall consider the alternatives," he said. "Meanwhile, shall we examine a slice of life on the waterfront?"

◆◆◆◆◆◆◆◆

A few months later, at the beginning of production, the girl, a rambunctious redhead, felt she needed more personal empathy with her leading man. Jeffrey was not disinterested. But it seemed the Texan had a twenty-four-hour watch on his lady. The picture and the girl were canceled. Jeffrey now had the distinction of being on a double blacklist. Both Hollywood and Texas were out-of-bounds.

Eventually, the yacht was lost. Fortunately, a young European director, Max Ziska, rented the hacienda at a good price. Somehow the romantic, dreaming part of Jeffrey was kept alive with the knowledge that he still had his own home. Effie stayed on and wrote him that his things were safe and cared for.

He became a wandering minstrel. Sometimes he thought of the nursery rhyme pounded into him by his critical father when things for the Barstow clan had been too rich and too easy.

"Son," the elder Barstow had said, "do not ever feel that you have a leg up in the world when you are adored for the moment. Remember how artists were shunted about and used throughout history and then thrown the bones at banquets. Listen to this:

> Hark, hark, the dogs do bark,
> The beggars are coming to town,
> Some in tags and some in rags
> And one in a velvet gown.

And that's where we end up the morning after the moonbeams are dispelled."

How quickly corporate privileges were lost. How sudden the descent. Broadway was courted and lost—bad script, bad theater, and too many drinks on the desperate opening night. Winter stock in second-rate cities, the ghosts of failure pursuing Jeffrey like an unseen chorus in a Greek tragedy. Quick summer stock for money. And long waits in between. A few fliers in the growing radio craze. More summer stock in areas where his name was still magic. And even this was almost scotched when Andrew Reed, summering at Ogunquit, wrote, "Seeing Jeffrey Barstow's shticks in the sticks is one of the more painful events of a mosquito-ridden bad summer-stock season."

And so it went—each year with less money, poorer lodgings, fewer fans. The worst of it was having to consort with second-rate sycophants. He had been used to the best.

For a man who had lived in the lush golden times of theater and films, 1939 was not a good year. To him the new world affairs and his diminishing assets were all a pattern of confusion and depression. It was the summer of Hitler's insatiable grab for lebensraum.

Luxurious gaiety and abandon had hit New York. Café society and bird-brained doings heralded the insecurity and despair before the inevitable emergence of a world bloodbath.

Jeffrey, bogged down in alcoholic lapses, found himself at odds. The whole world seemed to be interested in what was to come, not what had been.

The greatest blow was when he got a letter from Seymour Sewell's assistant, Harry Clune. It was sent to him at the Algonquin where he had the smallest of suites, near a creaking elevator, and even that out of the charity of the kind host, Frank Case, who had known him when.

Dear Jeffrey:

I am sorry to tell you that Seymour is in a sanatorium, where he is recovering from pneumonia. He was taken off the *Empress* in bad condition, after a prolonged diet of fruit juice and gin.

His agency has been taken over by Star Lists, a new agency based in New York as well as Hollywood, London, Paris, and Rome.

We discover that Seymour had paid you moneys out of the firm's accounts. We will have to present you a bill, since we are under inventory, and also inform you that the expenses of your house upkeep, plumbing, wiring, a new furnace, and a filter system for the pool have added up to a great deal more than your tenant's rent. We are billing you for the whole and no longer can handle your financial affairs as much as we would like to because of our long association. But since Seymour is no longer in the picture, or able to take care of his own affairs, much less yours, I am writing you this personal letter as a friend.

There is a potential bright spot in this bad news. A client of Star Lists, Gustav Jones, has a play which a moneyman from Cleveland is interested in. You may have heard of him, Bertrand Cosgrove. He has always been an ardent fan of yours and says you are the only one in the world who can play Kerry Morgan, the starring role.

If you will call our offices in New York, an interview can be arranged.

I am sorry to send you these bills, but they are necessary to our audit. Perhaps you are not interested in having property in San Fernando Valley anymore, but if you are, I hope you will get this play cracking and be the old smashing Jeffrey Barstow again.

Best regards as always,

Harry

Enclosed were bills totaling $4,220.

At first Jeffrey threw them in the wastebasket. Then he retrieved them and sat thinking. His house, his hacienda, the place where he had kept his dreams, where someday David might see what treasures he had collected. The house was the best of Jeffrey Barstow. Anyone who walked into it would know what he was. Why even now, his tenant, the gifted Max Ziska, a busy director, took time to write him occasionally of the bounty he had discovered in Jeffrey's library. It would be a tour de force if he could step back on the stage and achieve success again.

He admired Gustav Jones. Perhaps he might just call and at least read the script. With superhuman effort, he ordered a simple meal and ignored the bottle. The next morning, feeling fit, he called the Star Lists agency, and, with his best Barstow voice, arranged to have the script sent to him.

The next day he closeted himself and read it. In the evening, he walked among the Broadway crowds. He watched people standing, awaiting curtain time in theaters where he had played. He thought of the play, of Gustav Jones, and of himself, holding control over an audience again, and then he laughed at himself, unnoticed in a theater throng that once had idolized him. Was it Mack Sennett who had said the joke of life is the fall from dignity?

He went to the nearest bar.

But the next day, with a tearing headache, he was

called by Bert Cosgrove. The man's voice was trembling with emotion.

"Really, Mr. Barstow, to *think* you are in New York. I *must* meet you at once. What do you think of the play? Would you consider it?"

"I'll meet you tomorrow at the Colony at one," said Jeffrey. "Sorry I can't today, I have appointments. It's a fine play. I—I'm quite interested."

He got out of bed and looked at his furred tongue and bloodshot eyes.

"Look Jeffrey," he said, "don't corrupt your talent with your inadequacies."

After coffee and aspirin, he called the switchboard and discovered that Gustav Jones was in Connecticut. He called him.

"Gustav," he said, "this is a voice from the dead—Jeffrey Barstow."

"That voice could never be from the dead," said Gustav. "Do you like the play?"

"Like?" said Jeffrey. "You bastard, you wrote *me*."

The brief silence convinced him it was true.

"You double bastard," said Jeffrey. "But tell me, how does Cosgrove dare take a chance on me?"

"You know," said Gustav, laughing, "he's so rich it wouldn't matter what happened. There are dozens of grown-up millionaire boys and girls without talent, whose fondest dream is to find a star in some sort of a bind who will welcome an opportunity to orbit with them."

"Thank you, you son-of-a-bitch," said Jeffrey.

"Not at all," said Gustav brightly. "The making of Bert Cosgrove to himself will be to have a play open that will read 'Bertram Cosgrove presents Jeffrey Barstow in *April in the Flesh,* written and directed by Gustav Jones.' Now, what can *I* do to make it come off? I need a new furnace; it's cold here."

"You rich phony, get your ass into New York," said Jeffrey, "and read lines with me. It seems we have the same problems. I'm trying to keep the old homestead in San Fernando Valley. And, I might as well level with you, since this is likely to be Custer's Last Stand, for God's sake, help me, by getting hold of Bud Regan in Los Angeles. He's my jailer, and I'll need him."

"You really mean it?" said Gustav. "Hold on, throw the bottle down the elevator shaft, and I'll be right there."

Cosgrove was everything Jeffrey knew he would be. A bright-eyed entrepreneur, who carried a sapphire-topped cane and a homely rich wife as security blankets. Jeffrey sold him at a drinkless lunch so easily that he was ashamed of himself. He spoke of the script brightly, with the insight of a few hours' work with Gustav Jones.

He expressed his demands in what he considered horrifying requests. Five thousand cash on signing, agents to arrange details, and his trainer to come from Hollywood at Cosgrove's expense. Cosgrove eagerly agreed, so Jeffrey threw in a limousine and a deluxe suite at the Algonquin. When it was all arranged, he said good-bye, was recognized by several matrons as he left the Colony, which made him feel sprightly, and walked across town, wondering if by any chance it could be his again.

Rehearsals were hell. Withdrawal from liquor was painful, even though he was constantly complimented on how great he looked. But he was surly and depressed. Often it seemed as if all the bright lines went stale, as if all the stuffing were out of him. He did his role only from a platform of technique. Out of the side of his eye he could see Gustav suffering, trying to get the talent out of him.

Once, Gustav came to him in his dressing room.

"Damn it, Jeffrey, it's getting cold in Connecticut. My wife has been in Pendleton woolens for so long that I've forgotten what she looks like, and the kids run around with icicles on their noses. For God's sake

I know the prodigious creativity that can come out of you. I'm taking a hell of a chance on you, too."

"All right," said Jeffrey. "I'll get on with it."

He idly picked up *Town and Country* magazine and, opening it, paused. It pictured a golf match at Del Monte Lodge. And there was David . . . his David. Young and leggy with a clear-cut cameo profile that could have been his own. His heart leaped.

"Anything wrong?" said Gustav.

Jeffrey gave Gustav a dazzling smile.

"Nothing at all," he said. "And as I mentioned, I'll get on with it."

That evening, he conjured forth his own unique talent. He gained strength, overcame the theatrical, and merged into the human reality of the play. He was afraid of the excitement he saw in Gustav's eyes.

At the opening, Jeffrey soon knew that the monster in the dark, the audience, had decided to be a friendly beast. As the final curtain fell, the audience was entranced with the spectacle of a hero saving himself single-handed from old age, alcoholism, gossip, motion pictures, in other words, disaster.

Jeffrey fled to his dressing room, locked it, and picked up the picture of David he had ripped out of the magazine. Somehow the boy would hear about his success . . . somehow.

When Gustav Jones's *April in the Flesh* was bought by Abe Moses and the New York board of directors, it was a coup for the studio which was in need of prestige products. And part of the prestige was Jeffrey Barstow. He went with the package. Suddenly the memory of a scandal was forgotten. Success was the catalyst. He was brought back to the Coast by his new agency, Star Lists, with an astronomical contract for six pictures in five years and fringe benefits that even allowed him time off at his choice in case of "arthritic attacks."

While a young agent, Peter Pruitt, from Star Lists

worked out his contract with him at the Algonquin, he sat down with a notepad and planned all the details with which he chose to punish the studio. And they had no choice, for Metro Goldwyn Mayer, Paramount, and Warner Brothers were all hot to buy the play and to sign him along with it.

"Why do you insist on going back to Titan?" asked Pruitt.

"Because I want to personally piss on them," said Jeffrey, "and one way to do it is to turn in the most magnificent job I've ever done. Also, there's a young person out there who's going to amount to something some day, and I want him to see what real acting is all about."

Pruitt glanced at him in slight shock, noticing a gleam of deep hatred on his face. When Pruitt went back to the offices of Star Lists, he announced that he was very glad he worked in New York and didn't have to handle Jeffrey Barstow and Titan together, it was going to be TNT. He spoke too soon. Star Lists sent him west to look after the affairs of their new and valuable client.

2

Two pictures for the price of one, free dishes, keno, screeno, bingo, door prizes, contests . . . constant juggling with the psyches of new stars, an era of directors' growing importance and writers' peccadilloes . . . The Laocoon acrobatics of the moguls wrestling with the celluloid serpent strips of color processes—it was all a montage in the filmic sense to Fergus.

Sometimes he wondered, as time had slipped by faster in the grim late thirties, why he had not just sat back with his portfolio of real estate holdings and become a rich man. Instead, he had bought every share of Titan stock he could get in the depressed market. Now he realized that his contest had not been to own the studio; he had wanted to best Simon Moses, and now that Simon was gone, it didn't matter so much. He was caught in a treadmill and it was going too fast for him to jump off.

Often, after an impassioned battle on the perpetual war line, the telephone to the New York offices, that left him wringing wet and angry, smoking furiously and taking antacid pills, he would stride to the picture window in the office that had once belonged to Simon.

People going about their various chores would look up and see him grimly staring below. He would note their quickened pace and almost hear some of them frame the words, "There is the old son-of-a-bitch."

The day he was forty-two, he was angry. Time seemed to be hurrying him toward middle age. Many on his staff were now much younger than he.

Many people worked for him whose names and occupations he did not even know. The payroll was staggering. He watched some of them wandering to the coffee shop. The bastards were all going in for coffee and gossip on Titan time. He might station a security guard on the premises and clock in some of them, especially writers who took coffee breaks six or seven times a day. They should be alerted that they were abusing a privilege, and if they continued they could be dropped from the roster. He began adding up facts and figures of wasted time in his head. It was astronomical.

It had been a rocky time to be in charge of the studio. He was second in Titan ownership. Rebecca was the prime stockholder, now that Simon was dead. She did not interfere with policy and was amenable to anything he advised, but the responsibility on his shoulders was immense.

It seemed incredible to him that a stagehand's strike could close down all the studios in Hollywood, but it happened. Talent began to split into guilds, each with its own bargaining power. Unions orbited salaries. Only payoff kept Willie Bioff from getting more and more wage boosts for the International Alliance of Theatrical Stage Employees. Fergus, along with other management chiefs, was alerted when Herb Sorrel organized AFL unions into the Federated Motion Picture Crafts and obtained a 15 percent wage increase and arbitration rights. Once a contract was signed between a studio and a local union, he knew it was the first rung of an endless ladder of rising costs and studio problems.

But what was the use of worrying? A battery of lawyers would fight it out.

He knew he was getting too introspective. As a young punk, he was so busy that he hadn't had time to do anything but live. That, for the love of God, was when he had turned twenty. Where did all the time go?

It had gone down there, he thought, into the most expensive fantasy in the history of man. And every single picture as much of a gamble as the slot machines had been on the Carnero boys' gambling ships anchored off Redondo. Even more so.

He decided to see what went on in the various departments when they weren't expecting him. He'd end up with Jules and the Professor, see their tests of the new Kalmus three-color Technicolor process, and discuss its possibilities over a cup of coffee and cognac.

On the way out of his office, he could tell by Harriet Foster's nervous smile that a surprise party and all its trimmings were in the air. Irritated, he left his suite, wondering how much she planned his life in her own orbit, and what she canceled out that he knew nothing about.

Disgruntled and feeling older than his years, he walked down the studio street relishing the flurry of a cluster of his writers who quickly got out of sight when they saw him approaching.

In front of the wardrobe department, he saw Niles Conrad, one of his top designers, a dress folded over his arm, stamping his slim alligator shoe in fury at a young girl.

The young woman shook her head vehemently, tossing her glistening copper-colored hair.

Fergus wondered, if she were an actress, why he didn't know about her. She had the most perfect figure he had seen on the lot. Or off it, he thought. Her small waist was girdled by a wide patent-leather belt. She wore a pleated skirt that only emphasized her slim hips and long legs. A white blouse with a pullover jersey did not conceal her high, jutting breasts.

She didn't notice Fergus.

"It just won't work for the scene," she said, "believe me, Mr. Conrad, you can't dress a gorgeous sexpot in tweed and have her come out sexy. I don't care if it is an English country scene. The star's got to have sex."

"Well, Miss Klopfinger—" Conrad said testily.

God, thought Fergus. Klopfinger . . . she certainly isn't an actress!

Conrad continued, "I suppose you'd dress her in satin. For a breakfast scene."

"Not at all," said the girl. "Jersey—clinging jersey. Haven't you ever really seen a woman's body. Look at me!"

She swung around, and her jersey skirt clung to her legs. Fergus felt he had never seen such sexuality.

"Miss Klopfinger," said Conrad, "if I need another stylist, I'll hire one, but since you're a typist, I suggest you return to the typing pool."

He swung off in anger.

The girl turned and came face-to-face with Fergus. She recognized him but did not seem embarrassed.

"Well, Mr. Austin," she said, "I am right. He just doesn't know what a woman is—I'll go collect my things."

She disappeared into the building.

Instead of going to the lab, Fergus went back to his office. He called the typing pool himself and asked for Miss Klopfinger to come up for a special typing job.

She appeared clutching her secretarial pad and her employment record. She had a shorthand record of 120 words per minute and she typed 60 words a minute.

"You have the skills, Miss Klopfinger," he said.

"Jessica."

"What about the sex you mentioned. Do you know what a woman is for?"

Her gray-green eyes gazed at him calmly. For a second she said nothing. He thought he had confounded her.

"I have the skills," she said.

He looked at the deliberate thrust of her flawless young body. The surge of his manhood clouded his thoughts. He knew what was going to happen in the private room behind his office.

So did she.

She set her pad and pencil down, he took her hand, and she followed him. He locked the doors, ordered the staff to close up for the day, and switched off the phone.

Harriet Foster was disturbed that the birthday celebration was canceled, but she meekly said nothing, locked up the office, and left.

Fifteen minutes after Jessica had first walked in Fergus's office, he was penetrating her.

◆◆◆◆◆◆◆◆

Jessica was immediately promoted to executive secretary and she became Fergus's mistress.

The first week she was given a studio car. That Friday, after the usual late-afternoon weekly rushes, the exodus of directors, producers, and cutters, and after a quick dinner sent in from the commissary, Fergus ran film again, Jessica sat by his side taking notes, her flashlight pen twinkling.

Only the night watchman was on duty when they said good-night to the projectionist.

"Oh, my God," Fergus said, "I forgot to call Hori. Jessica, drive me to the beach. Esther's home from Las Cruces for a few days."

He looked so unhappy that Jessica pitied him. She didn't dare take his hand. Who knew what janitor peered out from a darkened room.

"Of course," she said, not knowing that she was setting a pattern.

They drove to the Gold Coast area, where the moguls had built their castles on the sand. He directed her to pull up in front of his house, and he peered out into lighted windows that shone in the dark.

"I can't go in," he said. "Esther's still awake. That means there'll be tears and recriminations. Let's drive."

She drove up the coast toward Malibu. They parked at the side of the road facing the waves. He fondled her, telling her how well made she was, like school kids did in parked cars.

When he was aroused she made quick, oral love to him. He apologized that it had happened in such an unsatisfactory way for her, but after the relief she had given him, he slouched on the seat of the car and talked on and on about his problems as if, she felt, he had never done it before. She listened, held his hand, and sympathized.

When they drove back to his house, the upstairs lights were off. He kissed her quickly. She drove away while he was still fitting the key into his front door.

She drove back to her apartment, frustrated, trying to hide her humiliation at the way the evening had gone, yet in a turmoil about the sudden turn her life had taken. She was glad it was not someone else who had given service to his desires. He excited her in a way no man had. Perhaps someday Esther would be back in her sanatorium permanently.

She wondered how she could be so concerned about a man who so early in their relationship let her drive home alone after she had satisfied him in the most subservient way. Yet she knew why.

He was the key to a life better than that of the dozens of women who worked in the studio. Without him, she'd be going out as she had for several years with young actors, middle-aged writers, and old directors, and she'd be doing the same things on a short-term basis for all of them until they spread the word, and someone else would try. And Fergus Austin had let down the barriers of his importance and had needed her. As time passed, she accepted the conditions of their liaison.

And so did he. Never before had a woman been available to him on conditions that suited him so well. Her working hours meshed with his; she was deeply involved with his interests both in business and personally. His passion could be assuaged on his terms with complete privacy. She had no way not to be available, and she was always eager for his lovemaking. They had a lasting desire for each other's bodies—rare in a town of sudden change and whim, and Fergus, without realizing it, allowed her to become the most important person in his life outside David.

He felt no compunction about having her come to the house on a Sunday if the need came for dictation, or an important meeting was held. Here she was the perfect secretary, and even those who knew them both did not suspect their intimacy. And Esther's mental condition when she was in residence made Jessica, the sympathetic employee, seem doubly valuable.

If Jessica had been a star, she could have sported the finest mink coat or new custom-built car, but as Fergus's secretary, she could only have the fringe benefits of their relationship.

She lived in the smallest apartment at Wilshire Palms, a chic address. She had the latest perfumes and colognes; a standing order of fresh-cut flowers from a florist who billed them to the studio; a persian-lamb trotteur, which could pass for an executive secretary's extravagance. Her car was from the studio pool—a Chrysler convertible, exchanged for a newer model once a year, but never in her name.

For pocket money, she got anonymous cash handouts on poker winnings. If Fergus had a dry spell, and she hinted pointedly at something she wanted, he would invent poker winnings and give her cash.

Her refrigerator always held champagne, paté,

caviar, and smoked turkey and ham at Christmas, loot purchased through the studio commissary, all delivered to Fergus's office, with no sign of its eventual destination. Her bar held a case of Fergus's favorite scotch, as well as mixes, but assorted drinks for any other guest was her own problem.

Every time she ordered pearls or diamonds for a special gift for Esther, who often wore them in her sanatorium rooms, the jeweler was ordered to throw in a gold pin or simple bracelet or earrings which were added to the cost of the large items for Mrs. Austin.

Once a year she received a generous stock bonus, which was entered in the books as a deductible gift to a secretary.

Jessica also took the power that a bright executive secretary/mistress could use. She could blight competition at the source. Eager actresses, bright, handsome young women writers, socialite sex careerists were all carefully jettisoned before they took Fergus's time and interest.

Twice she had received personal letters from Claudia to Fergus. One asked him to read a script; another was a note asking him to let her know if he were well and happy and to call her sometime. Both of these were answered personally by Jessica, informing Claudia that Mr. Austin sent best regards as always and was occupied with pressing business problems.

To be certain that there was no record of the letters, Jessica destroyed them and her answers. There was no use, she thought, to bother him with a woman who, she had heard, had caused nothing but trouble and loss to Titan.

Jessica forgave her own duplicity by convincing herself that she was saving Fergus distress and concern.

And so she built up an invisible wall of protection around him, and at the same time around herself, by keeping the world away from him as much as she could.

Sometimes when Esther called, Jessica listened to her babblings with a sympathetic ear and kept this from him, too. Why should he be bothered by a woman she well knew was unstable and could break his heart?

Sometimes, in the dark, Jessica's body reminded Fergus of Claudia—Claudia who had long been in England, but was often in his thoughts. He could never look out on the streets of the studio without expecting to see her. He knew that no one would stimulate him as Claudia had, but he had been permitted to be in her bed only five times all through the years, and each time was fraught with drama. It hurt him that she never bothered to drop him a line.

However, this one woman, Jessica, seemed to have a deep affection for him. Sometimes she would put her arms protectively about him and hold him for a silent moment. Then, she would glance at him, and he felt as if she pitied him. If he asked her what was on her mind, she would just smile and tell him not to be foolish.

That was the leavening that kept him to her, believing that she truly, in this hard-core world, adored him, no matter how he used her. It satisfied him, not knowing that it was indeed pity that shone in her eyes.

For she often remembered that crazy Sunday afternoon, when they had been together a few months and the Austin world was new to her. Esther, during one of her rare sojourns at home, had put her thin, pale hand on Jessica's arm, and said, "Let's get away from them."

It was a hot day at the beach, and the men were going through their dreary routine of afternoon poker and gin rummy. Abe Moses, Charlie O'Rourke, both in from New York, and producer Mark Fremont, the "in" group, were playing cards in the air-conditioned cardroom, designed to ignore the fact that the house was on the shore of the beautiful Pacific Ocean.

Several young stock actresses, and some of the younger wives were sitting out by the pool, exchanging gossip and killing time. Any woman who would have thought of interfering with this top priority card game would have been drummed out of the human race by the menfolk. To get in the game was tantamount to a seven-year contract at Titan.

Jessica was puzzled when Mrs. Austin asked her to come with her to her enormous bathroom. She was certain that Esther didn't have any idea of the relationship between her and Fergus. She most likely wanted to talk about David, who at the age of seventeen had a driver's license and had motored up to Malibu for the day in his first car.

Esther locked the door of the mirror-lined room. It was horrible. You couldn't even sit on the john without seeing yourself reflected everywhere, including the ceiling. The shelves were lined with bottles of perfume. Jessica, at loss for conversation, admired them.

"They're just filled with colored water," said Esther, her big blue eyes wide. "Everyone gives them to me instead of throwing them away, and my maid fills them."

It's like her life, thought Jessica. Expensive bottles filled with colored water. She had an uneasy feeling. Was this woman insane enough to be violent?

"I thought we'd get away from them," Esther whispered as if they were in league. "This is the room where I really live."

She moved to a large massage table and pressed a button. The table vibrated.

"You see," she said, "I lie on it and it puts me to sleep. Now look, dear, you try this."

An electric bicycle, on a stationary stand, with straps on the pedals, was in front of one of the double marble sinks. Jessica obligingly got on it. Esther put on a switch, and Jessica found herself bucketing along, her feet pumping, as if on a steed.

"That's good after that heavy kosher lunch," said Esther.

She went to a wall and switched on a radio. The hearty call of "Hi-ho, Silver—" came over it.

"Well, really—" said Jessica, feeling trapped as the machine gathered momentum.

"Now," said Esther, "it'll do you good, with that fine figure of yours. I'll just rest a minute myself."

She got on the massage table and closed her eyes.

She could kill me, thought Jessica, and nobody'd ever know with that goddamned horse whinnying on the radio and these mechanical monsters going.

"Don't you think my David is handsome?" asked Esther.

"He certainly is, Mrs. Austin."

"Well, he ought to be," said Esther, "with Jeffrey Barstow as a father."

Jessica took a moment to absorb the name. Her feet went whirling a whole circle before it sank in.

She smiled.

"You mean Fergus Austin, Mrs. Austin," she said.

"Oh, no," said Esther. "We were up at Arrowhead Springs. You know, on location—only Claudia Barstow was there. And Jeffrey in his suite across the hall. I thought it was a bit much when I caught Fergus with Claudia. Right under my eyes. The door unlocked. They didn't expect me. And that Jeffrey, he was a nice man, no matter what they say. He found me walking in the corridor, and I was crying, I guess. I'll never forget. He said, 'Ah, tears such as angels weep,' and he took me out of my loneliness. He took off my coat and cuddled me and gave me some brandy, and then he took off all my clothes, on the sofa, there in front of the fire, and he loved me all over, while I cried more, and then he made love to me again. Believe me, I stopped crying."

She sighed.

Jessica's feet almost tangled in the pedals.

"Mrs. Austin," she said, "you shouldn't—"

"Yes," said Esther. Her blond hair had unfastened as the table vibrated, and a long coil of it fell, trembling like a serpent, over the edge. "Yes, you're right, I shouldn't. I knew it when I did. This man was wonderful. He made love to me once, and we sat up and drank some more, and he caressed me again and said I was all soft and lovely. You know, he took his time; he lived fully in those moments, he didn't just relieve himself like—you know."

Oh, God, thought Jessica, like Fergus. She knows; she knows . . .

"Well," continued Esther, "he loved me again, deep, deep, slow and warm, oh, it was beautiful—and that is why my David is so handsome."

"I—I'd better get down," said Jessica. "You really shouldn't talk about these things."

"Oh, I never do, but it happened—I guess I'll always love him. I keep the little notes he wrote me under my handkerchiefs—I look at them every day—but it's just that since you're with Fergus so much, you should know."

"Please—" said Jessica. She managed to pull her foot out of one of the straps, and balanced crazily, while the other foot swung in its arc until she reached the button and switched off the exercycle.

"When I found out I was pregnant," said Esther dreamily, "I had such a hard time getting Fergus to sleep with me so he wouldn't know. But I managed to vamp him, with my Claudia Barstow hostess gown and my hairdo. Ah, Jessica, sometimes men are so blind. He thinks David looks just like him."

Esther smiled affectionately. "It didn't work out too badly. Fergus is wild about the boy. Of course, Mr. Barstow has some bad habits. It wouldn't have really worked out, would it, although I often think of it when I see his pictures. What a lovely man—well, anyway, I have a fine son."

Jessica's hands were sweating. She went to the sink and washed them and turned around.

Hi-ho Silver was still racketing away. Esther Austin had closed her wild blue eyes and was asleep, as the gentle vibration of the reducing table soothed her.

Jessica unlocked the door, got out of the terrible room, and sat for a moment in a pink moiré chair in the overdecorated bedroom with its glaring picture window, looking out over the waters of Santa Monica Bay. It was like being on the bridge of a ship going nowhere.

She went to the hall to pick up her wrap, hoping she would not have to face Fergus. The door to the cardroom was ajar, and she heard Abe Moses' loud voice.

"So there's your morality," he was saying. "The bastard gets the critics' award, the play wins everything in New York, and that kook Bert Cosgrove won't sell it without Barstow. What happens? Success, the great whitewasher, makes moral turpitude and all that crap go out the window. Jesus, Fergus, let's keep that trainer Bud Regan glued to Jeffrey's side. This picture's worth too much to us right now. Hang on to him."

"Pain in the ass," said Fergus. "I wonder if I'll ever get rid of Barstows."

There was knowledgeable laughter at this.

"Anyway," said Abe, "we've lost Claudia. I heard she was off with some maharaja in his palace in India. He loaded her with rubies. I hear tell she called him Sambo, which he thought was kind of cute until someone tipped him off that it meant nigger. He sent her a message to leave his palace and return his jewels at once. She sent him back the classic message that since he couldn't take back his fucking, she'd keep the rubies."

"That should have set her up," said Mark Fremont.

"She's hocked them to produce a play," said Abe. "The same old pattern again. Bombed. Down to scratch. That's Barstow for you."

"Hardly," said Fergus wryly. "Her brother's in the chips again. You should know, you wrote his contract. I didn't send for him. You New York boys one-upped me on that, don't you forget it!"

Jessica cautiously opened the front door and escaped.

She verified the sad tale in the family files, meticulously documented, as befits a dynasty composed of the Moses and Austin families. The blood types didn't match; couldn't. She thought about the notes in Esther's bureau drawer under the handkerchiefs.

She cross-checked company insurance papers on Jeffrey Barstow. It could be true. It could.

And so her pity reached out to Fergus Austin. For David was the one person in the man's busy life that sustained him. And every time Jessica looked at the boy, who often popped into the office on little errands or stopped to admire her and chat with her when she was at his home on business, she noted the profile and the peaked hairline that had been familiar to her in all the years she had watched Jeffrey Barstow on film.

Somehow the studio, with its new players, did not have the impact on the public that the Moses star system had nurtured. Jeffrey Barstow, with all his private problems, was a valuable commodity; the studio needed him for the very luster it had built before he was thrown out.

As Abe Moses had said, Jeffrey's national acclaim on Broadway had whitewashed previous moral lapses. And the public enjoyed setting him in an upright position; in some future caper, he could be toppled again in the giant bowling alley of publicity, the lifeblood of newspapers.

Meanwhile, with Jeffrey back, Jessica wondered if

the similarity between the two would be observed, or if society would just think he resembled the long-forgotten blond beauty of Esther, who now was never seen in public.

3

Perhaps the most ardent of Claudia's fans in London during the next years was young John Graves. He awoke to her pictures on his wall. He did not linger in his little alcove bedroom, for his mother wanted him out of the house so she could entertain gentlemen.

The flagship of his flotilla of dreams was the portrait on which Claudia had written "To John Graves, who may be a star himself when his voice and his looks get together."

His first realization that he was not just a pale, cockney boy, as thin as a herring, was when she had touched his chin and remarked that he was attractive. And, as she had said, he could be as fine as his voice.

Although she was usually unavailable when he called with his gifts of trinkets, effort and perseverance paid off occasionally.

Several times she had him to tea and, seeing his eagerness, gave him books to study. Histories of the theater, the complete works of Shakespeare, books of classic plays, Shaw, Ibsen, Barrie, and O'Neill.

"These are just exercises in judgment," she said, "judgment in reading the written word and understanding what it could be. You won't truly realize a play until you see it on the stage. The spoken word and interpretation makes the pages you are reading look like a road map as against the actual scenery.

When you first perform in front of an audience, you'll know what I mean."

He stared at her, wide-eyed.

"I wonder if I ever can," he said.

She sighed.

"What's up, mum?" he said, "did I say something wrong?"

"Oh, no," said Claudia. "It's just that I'm teaching you so many things I didn't do myself. But it's not too late for you. And don't call me mum, call me Miss Barstow, and when you win your spurs perhaps I'll let you call me Claudia. Meantime, dear boy, pinch any pennies you can, and get to the theater. Sit in the balcony, stand, do anything, but go."

"Yes'm—Miss Barstow," he said.

"And if you don't understand what they're doing, go again and again until you do."

"I will," he said, juggling with his teacup, spoon, and a scone.

"Practice with your dishware and silver as I taught you, John. I don't want you to be handicapped by improper dining habits. Also, go to the talking pictures, study all the Barrymores, look at Eric Charrel's *Congress Dances,* watch Clark Gable in *It Happened One Night.*"

"Oh I will, Miss Barstow!" he said, secretly wondering how he could manage.

She fished in her purse and took out a five-pound note.

"I'm not as flush as I was once, but I want you to stretch this, dear boy, and get the cheapest seats for as many plays and films as you can. Use your spare time well now. You may not always have it."

He gasped as she handed it to him.

"Oh, thank you, but I—"

"Look," she said, "who knows how you got all the crystal you keep bringing me? But you gave it to me. So I shall say this is a loan that you can start paying back on your first job on the stage. And may I remind you of something?"

He looked quizzical.

"There is a lot of drama to study that isn't on the stage. Follow people and see what makes them tick. File it all away. And don't neglect some of our greatest actors who are on the world stage right now—Roosevelt, Mussolini, Hitler, Chamberlain, Farouk, Churchill, to name a few. These are the great character actors. Look, John, if you're an actor at heart you can't walk down the street without learning your craft."

When he left, a copy of Terry Ramsey's *A Million and One Nights* under his arm, Claudia sat staring into her fireless fireplace, wondering where she was going to get her next five hundred pounds.

Her British film was a disaster. She had done a play, and fallen down inebriated in front of a glittering West End audience. Now she would likely follow the sad pattern of many actresses—play in Christmas pantomimes, go out into the provinces in revivals if anyone would have her, and abandon the thought of trying to be a film star.

She realized that she had left Hollywood in a time that was perilous for the whole industry. The tragic years following the crash had left America lean and hungry. It was no time to go back.

Perhaps she could get in on the booming voice that was heard over the land, the British Broadcasting Company. Ah, well, she thought, talent will always out . . . and as for that boy, he really had something. He studied and he never gave up. She had thought about a few things herself while she was talking to him. If worse came to worst, she could teach.

As he grew older, not knowing of Claudia's qualms about herself, John Graves spun his dreams, believing that Claudia Barstow would be his sponsor when he was ready, though several years passed and he did not see her. Sometimes she played the provinces and other times was away with any swain or group who would pay her way. Their paths separated.

But he did not despair. When he became famous, he would bring her back into films again. Great people often had rotten breaks. But they rose up with greater success; literature and films proved that. For her he had to be better than a barrow boy. He haunted the Leicester Square theater palaces and playhouses, studying the manners and voices of any man worthy of her, while he made a living in the barrows and junk shops around Nottinghill Gate and practiced diction learned from films.

He discovered he had a memory for any scene that pleased him, and he also developed a pitch to imitate any voice he chose. One week he would be Leslie Howard or Ronald Colman. Another, Gable or Cooper.

When he read Claudia's name in connection with various men, he decided that they were not worthy of her. He must become the best at something and bowl her over when he was grown.

As he was old enough for desire as well as dreams, he put his hands on himself, mad with excitement as he looked at her picture, on his pillow for the moment.

Time passed, the Cavendish, like Claudia, became less stylish. But she maintained digs there, though they changed from a suite to a single room as her fortunes declined.

After the fall of France the Blitz began and John, too young for the forces, volunteered to help with the fish industry in Norfolk.

He called to see her before he left, but she was in a stock company at Newcastle on Tyne.

He wanted to do something for her, but he couldn't mail a crystal goblet to a theatrical company. After having seen so many clever comedies, he decided that to be witty was the way out. He put a chunk of coal in a box and mailed it with a little note: "Dear Miss Barstow, I'm sending you a coal to Newcastle. If you keep it a million years I hear it will become a diamond, ever yours, John."

And he went on his way, wherever he was going, without a word from her. He found himself up to his elbows at Yarmouth, packing slippery herring into the crans for Billingsgate consumption in London. It was a stinking cold job which he loathed, until the bright-cheeked itinerant Scotch girls migrated southward, pursuing the herring shoals, to perform their ritual function of curing the fish, creating the tasty Yarmouth bloaters.

John knew at last he had a chance to rise above the crowd. His voice would be his weapon. There were men taller than he, men more handsome and more mature, but by using the Gary Cooper approach, a strong but gentle voice, lowered blue eyes, and the fascination that the cleft in his chin seemed to have with some women, he did well. He discovered the delights of the pursuit of selected females. Most of all, he was pleased that no woman seemed to realize he was only sixteen. He had grown inches; he felt time was approaching to see Claudia, man to woman.

He sought out the company of a widower, a retired navy man, Admiral Marks. The old man was a fixture along the waterfront, where he hobbled about with a cane on his strolls. Two of his four sons and three of his six grandsons were in the navy. He lived in a cottage which was a cluttered depot for books, navy memorabilia, treasures from the seven seas, and old correspondence. He had a sharp mind that assuaged the infirmity of his age. His alert ear heard John's diction, and he annexed him, as a boy with whom he could talk in this intellectually arid Norfolk town, at the moment no vacationland, but only a depository of farmers, soldiers, sailors, fishermen, and itinerant refugees from London.

He dismissed John's occasional lapses into cockney and helped him correct his speech. When the weather bound the fishing fleet in, he held classes in his study. He had a patience born of loneliness and a kindness distilled from the fact that he had been beached as obsolete by his country and his children years ago.

In his innocent way, he tried to aid talent. If a young boy sketched well he lent him a book of Alma Tadema's sketches; if a lad whistled a tune, he played a wheezy record of Handel's *Water Music* on an ancient phonograph.

One night while they were whiling away time during a storm he gave the young group *Quality Street* to read aloud.

He sat back with amazement as John brought forth a Leslie Howard voice and dominated the reading.

Over cocoa and biscuits, the old man sat in his rocking chair, his arthritic hands tucked in the sleeves of his worn sweater.

"I really think you should be an actor, John," he said. "You have a knack. I don't know quite how to tell you to go about it. Now, of course, there's Ibsen. His speech is natural, you could do that. Barrie is always a winner. Oscar Wilde is a bit—ah—baroque, I think. And of course there's that American, O'Neill, he's vigorous. I couldn't possibly help you unravel the Bard."

He scratched at his pinkish bald pate.

"I say, I have an old connection in London, who is trying out people for this new ENSA thing." His eyes twinkled. "You see, in my gay dog days, I was more, ahem, interested in actresses' parts than the parts of actresses!"

Having expressed this oblique comment, he settled back to see if John would get it. He did.

"What is ENSA?" asked John.

The admiral reached behind him and unscrambled

a stack of letters on the small captain's desk. He peered through bifocals and fished one out.

"Since the theaters are closed, Drury Lane is its headquarters," he said. "It's the Entertainment National Service Association. The navy, army, and air force have sponsored some mobile units out on tour. They perform, show movies, do musicals, concerts, and variety. Edith Evans, Robert Donat, John Gielgud, John Clements, Constance Cummings, Gertie Lawrence, and my friend Claudia Barstow, led off by Basil Deane, are entertaining all the poor bastards who are lumped up as we are."

"Claudia Barstow!" John turned cold. He could feel his hands sweating. He felt giddy.

The admiral nodded and continued. He seemed to have no idea that he had shaken John's world.

"They've even given concerts in coal mines. They're spreading out wherever the war forces are. They must be valuable for the morale. They say they're getting a budget of two million quid a year."

"Claudia Barstow," John said.

"You said that," said the admiral.

"Well," said John, "you won't believe me, sir. I know the lady."

"You do!" said the admiral, astonished.

"She met me at the Caledonian market and was kind to me. That's why you said I might be an actor. She helped me."

"Why didn't you tell me before?" said the admiral.

"Well, I didn't think you'd believe me. But I'll show you. I'll bring her pictures and the books she gave me. They're in my footlocker. Do you think ENSA might come here?"

"They are coming," said the admiral. "Here's the letter. I informed her that England doesn't finish at Aldershot; there are still some poor buggers sitting it out in Norfolk. When she shows up we'll get you together, and we'll find out if she thinks you're doing well with your reading."

John felt ill. He wasn't ready. His dreams were one thing, reality another. His shabby clothes. When he was a kid in London it was forgivable. But now he was a man. He looked in the mirror and even his lean face, the dimpled chin and sensitive mouth which seemed such a target for women, looked wrong with his bad haircut. And the stark wartime setting of Norfolk after the glamour of London, why did it have to be this place? He was in a turmoil. He finally came to the admiral.

"Please sir," he said, "if I'm working when she comes in, don't let her see me on the dock with all those smelly fish. I'd rather meet her cleaned up."

The admiral valiantly hid his amusement and slapped him on the shoulder.

"Of course," he said. "I think you are absolutely correct. One wouldn't want to shake Claudia Barstow's hand all fishy, would one?"

"I knew you'd understand," said John, flushing.

"I shall arrange it. Don't worry."

◆◆◆◆◆◆◆◆

"Oh, God," said Claudia as she stepped off the train, "I never thought ENSA would lead me up to my ass in kippers."

The platforms were silvered with crans of herring that were to be transported to London.

Behind her clambered a sad-eyed, seasick ex-Tiller girl, who managed to play the violin while dancing on her toes; a red-haired tenor, a human souvenir of the invasion into England of Eric the Red, who was to sing, "The Last Time I Saw Paris," while he juggled empty champagne bottles; a projectionist with a portable projection machine, a screen, and a print of Lana Turner, Artie Shaw, and Ann Rutherford in *Dancing Co-eds.*

Claudia was a sort of den mother, to see if her troupe could take it, and to fill in with proper readings, after analyzing the caliber of the audience.

"It isn't exactly the Old Vic," said the admiral, "but we're mighty glad to see you, Claudia."

She embraced the old man.

"Darling Basil, you make even the station seem a gala," she said. "This is a bit draftier than our last performance in a Welsh coalpit, and it does stink more. Let's move off."

John, his cap pulled over his eyes, hid behind the crans he was stacking. His heart beat fast; he could peer through the slats and see her, his Claudia. She looked the same to him, beautiful and mysterious, even though she was wrapped in a tweed greatcoat, her hair tied in a chiffon scarf, and her nose pinched red from the biting wind. It was dreadful not to speak to her, but looking at his slimy hands, and seeing the fish scales and filth on his apron, he could not bear to be exposed to her obloquy.

"Come up to the cottage," said the admiral, "and I'll give you a whiskey, and you can get all the fresh air you can use for the rest of your life. That's about all that's going on in Yarmouth these days."

"Oh, love," said Claudia, "I vowed not to touch a drop of anything but off the vine, until Hitler is under the sod. Of course, if by a miracle of fate you should have some wine or brandy, that's not off limits."

The admiral took her arm firmly and bent close; she was such a little woman.

"I have some bubbly for you," he said.

"Oh, Admiral Marks," she said, "this is Lucille la Valle, and Frank Ryers, and Mr. Whistler, who runs the film. Where are our digs?"

They shook hands all around.

"I feel woozy," said Miss la Valle in a piping voice.

"You're all billeted at my cottage," said the admiral, "in a rugged row of sons' rooms. Tea is waiting up there and a coal fire and a decent dinner. Managed to get some Whitstable oysters, some sole and tinned asparagus. We shall live rather high on the hog. I don't often have lovely female houseguests!"

They picked their way along the platform.

John thought fast. He would get himself cleaned up, bring flowers to the admiral's digs, and take his chance. His voice, his manner, and a cache of daffodils he had seen on a slope would do it for him. She would be surprised, and he hoped impressed; he had changed.

As John dressed, the noise of the other boys irritated him. No matter where he had gone, the pictures of Claudia had ended up in his footlocker. If they only knew . . . but they were all such beastly chaps he knew that the pictures would be tossed about and snatched to pieces.

"I say," said his friend Coxie, "did you see that dish, that la Valle? 'Ear she dances on the end of 'er toes."

"Not arf!" said another boy, " 'er feet are so 'uge, she'd be six feet tall."

"Claudia Barstow's the real star," blurted John. "I've seen every movie she's made."

"Go on! She's older'n yer mother," said a boy. "You ain't got the 'ots for her?"

"Why not?" said Coxie. "Everybody's boffed 'er."

John lunged at him and smacked him across the nose.

In a moment they were rolling on the floor, pummeling each other. The boys stood about until Old Bert, who supervised them, rushed in and broke it up.

"That's enough, lads," he said.

He looked at John.

"Gawd," he said.

John's eye was swelling, and a trickle of blood was streaming down his face. Coxie had a pulpy nose.

"Well," he said, "you're a great masher for this evenin' ain't yer!"

They put cold compresses on his face, and he

bathed and shaved, holding a witch-hazel pad on his eyelid.

Old Bert whispered conspiratorially, "'Ear the guy invited you up to his digs to meet the actors, seein' as 'ow yor so good at that stuff. Goin'?"

John looked in the mirror. His eye was a fright. He shook his head.

"Tough luck, old chap," said Old Bert. "Gonna stay 'ere?"

"Guess I am," said John.

"Yer can sneak in the back of the 'all after it's dark and see the show," he said. "Got a throbber?"

"A real throbber," said John, "but I won't miss the show."

John sent a message up to the cottage; he regretted that he had been called on extra duty; a new catch had come in and had to be shipped. Compliments to Miss Barstow.

After the hall had darkened, John watched the show. Miss la Valle was alive and warm—that was about all you could say for her. The red-haired tenor should have brained himself with his champagne bottles before he butchered "The Last Time I Saw Paris."

After all his dreams, the sleepless night anticipating meeting her, he was heartsick. The show seemed interminable. He had a feeling Claudia wouldn't recommend any of them for further ENSA duty. And the movie also seemed endless, for his only aim was to see her. It was a typical Hollywood product dedicated to the vogue of Lana Turner, Artie Shaw's horn, and clean-cut juvenile sex. He resented all their good looks, fashionable clothes, glib manner; nothing ever seemed to go wrong with whatever they did, they just seemed to glide through life.

At last it ended, and after an introduction by the admiral, Claudia came on the stage. After applause (not enough, thought John), she bowed, a vision in a blue gown. She smiled at the audience and then announced her selections. She read from *The Taming of the Shrew*, from Shaw's *Saint Joan* and some poems of Edna St. Vincent Millay. John was deeply stirred. He had never seen her on stage before, and the beauty of her face in emotion and the power of her voice thrilled him. In spite of his pulsing eye, he forgot himself when she ended her reading with the words of Rupert Brooke:

If I should die, think only this of me:
  That there's some corner of a foreign field
That is forever England. There shall be
  In that rich earth a richer dust concealed:
A dust whom England bore, shaped, made aware,
  Gave, once, her flowers to love, her ways to roam,
A body of England's, breathing English air,
  Washed by the rivers, blessed by suns of home.

And think this heart, all evil shed away,
  A pulse in the eternal mind, no less
Gives back somewhere the thoughts by England given,
  Her sights and sounds; dreams happy as her day;
And laughter, learnt of friends; and gentleness,
  In hearts at peace, under an English heaven.

There was a moment of silence, as fisherfolk, sailors, soldiers, citizens, and homesick London children sat choked at the beauty of her words. A whistling wind was beating against the hall. Dimly, in the background, they could hear enemy bombers passing over the coast on their way to batter the industrial midlands.

These all joined to make Claudia's words more poignant.

She bowed her head for a moment. Then she looked up slowly, and her dazzling eyes captured the audience. John ached with love and longing.

Even though he knew it was a planned dramatic effect, his heart beat stronger. Claudia Barstow had made him love England more. Oh, to be able to do that to an audience. This was the living theater. This was where he belonged.

The simple people stood up and sang "God Save the King," tears in their throats.

Cursing his purple eye and thick nose, John went off to his bunk, thinking of the conviviality that would be going on in the admiral's cottage, high up on the chalk cliffs, comfortably nestled over the sea.

He could not sleep, thinking that she was near, and he had missed the opportunity to see her, to show her how he had learned what she had suggested.

The next day he was up early and about his work. When the group arrived, he peered at them between baskets. They seemed forlorn, none of the tinsel of the theater clinging to them as they left; Claudia stumbled as she walked toward the train, her ruglike coat wrapped about her against the sharp wind. Her face looked thin and bloodless, and John saw that she, like all of them, was suffering the cold and misery of the war.

He watched, his heart sinking, as the train moved away from the platform. Soon it became a speck, no different because of its passenger than any other vehicle fighting the seemingly endless war against Germany.

After the day's work, he walked along the front and found the admiral puttering about his shell-lined walk, tending his roses.

The old man stood up, arched his tired back as best he could, and then looked at John.

"Oh, Lord, your black eye!" he said. "No wonder you didn't come. I knew jolly well you weren't working. Whatever happened?"

"Someone insulted a lady."

"Well, we can't have chaps insulting ladies. I hope the other fellow looks as fierce."

"I heard her. She was wonderful. It must be something to move a whole audience. Did she know I was here?"

"No," he said. "Since you didn't appear I thought it wasn't provident."

"Thank you," said John.

Noting the underplay of the admiral's affection for her, he resented the old man. He was a gentleman. He had *been*, and he didn't shout about it. But it showed. Voice wasn't enough, you had to have a proper manner to go with it. He'd watch the admiral, and he'd match him someday. Hand in the pocket, oh, so casually. When a gentleman moves, even in shabby clothes, the economy of motion means something.

As he walked down the hill, he practiced. He didn't thrash about or jerk his head like Coxie. He tried to feel like a man who had lived in a big world and was now content to study a cowslip in a garden. That was a gentleman. That was the admiral. And that was what Claudia Barstow would like.

◆◆◆◆◆◆◆◆

The weeks that followed were momentous. Manpower was short. Dunkirk was a tragic blow. John, with the bigger boys, went out with the fishing fleet.

One morning, while the fleet lay with the nets cast out, a raid of German Heinkels buzzed them. They expected attack. In the distance they could see puffs of smoke as targets were hit. The muffled explosions traveled across the flat sunstruck sea to pound their ears.

There was nothing they could do but haul up their catch and go about their business. It was all anyone did in war.

When they returned, John walked along to the admiral's cottage. There was a smoking ruin where it had been. The garden was blown to bits, and a pall of white dust had fallen over everything.

The old man sat on the stub of a stone bench. He bent over, picking up fragments of his seashell border, and stared in surprise at an ant, which somehow had survived the holocaust and was crawling over his dust-covered brogan.

"Admiral, sir," said John, "are you all right?"

"I don't quite know," he said, in a crumpled voice. "I always knew my family would grow up and go away, but I never thought my *things*," he said it as if they were people, "would not always be mine—"

He gestured at the yawning hole where his cluttered study had been. "I saw those buzzards flying over your fishing fleet. I went down to see if you were going to get home safe. I fancy that's what saved my life."

The old man savagely trampled the ant as if enraged it should outlive his books.

⬥⬥⬥⬥⬥⬥⬥⬥

John received word that his father had gone down on the *Cape Queen* off the Newfoundland Banks, and, the next week, he heard that his mother was injured by shrapnel during an air raid.

She had been working, as she wrote, "beating my arse off serving tea to those poor blokes off a mobile canteen. Meet nice chaps, though. Never a dull mo'."

"More likely on 'er beat," whispered Coxie quietly so John would not bash his nose over on the other side of his cheeky face.

John petitioned for time to go home. Since he was practically an adult, and now the man of the family, it was granted.

He sought out the admiral, presumably to say goodbye, but as he confronted him, he knew what had been perking in the back of his mind.

"Do you think I could call on Miss Barstow," he said, "and tell her you're all right? She must have heard rumors that you were bombed out."

"That's a capital idea," said the admiral. "Go to the Drury Lane Theater. Give her my best. And here's a pound for a treat. Enjoy yourself and get back safe. It's frightfully dangerous to go, but one must do one's duty."

John traveled up on a fish train, snatched a few kippers as a treat for his mum, and walked from the station back to his old haunts.

There was little use to sympathize with his mother about his father. She had hated him. She seemed much older to John, limping from her shrapnel wound, bent over her spirit lamp brewing tea, her tatty knit shawl on her shoulders.

"Poor pa," said John, not remembering him well at all, but it seemed the proper thing.

"Just don't be a soft bastard like 'im. 'E was the kind would sink even in peacetime."

"I won't sink, mum," he said. "I'm doin' real good. Got a date to see Claudia Barstow over at Drury Lane."

"*That* Claudia Barstow!" said mum, her eyes wide. "One whose pictures you always had when you were a tad?"

"That one," said John. "The ENSA come up with a show. We 'ave it good up there. Wot would you say if yours truly was an actor?"

He strutted a little.

"Well," said mum, "good luck. Just remember, ducks, it's high society. Drop the old mopsy a compliment or two, and get out fast before yer get flung out."

John stood in front of the Drury Lane Theater.

Traffic had been detoured away from its smoking ruins. It was a victim of incendiary bombing. A demolition squad was dragging wood and charred furnishings out of its dust-belching depths. Everything was smoke black and smelled of fire, the rank putrefaction of wormy wood and ancient timbers. Beams stood like upended bones.

An old man wearing an air-raid warden's helmet wiped soot out of his eyes and stood blinking for a moment. John came up to him. He smiled, revealing yellowed false teeth in the black face.

"I say," he said, "I must look like a bad provincial Othello. Just fancy, the old girl caught an incendiary."

"Jolly good thing they closed these theaters," said John, using his cultivated voice. "I suppose it's a total disaster."

"Never! I know this place like a book. You know this site was burned to the ground to get rid of the brothels in the early 1660s; that's why the theater is here. It was closed for the plague in 1665; opened and burned down again in 1672. As a matter of fact, they used gunpowder to stop the fire and did in a loitering actor. Mind you, lad, that's history; born out of the ashes of burning brothels, closed by plagues, burned in 1809 again and rebuilt. Kean brought it back to glory. The old phoenix will rise again."

"You certainly know your history," said John.

The man looked at him. "Certainly. I'm an actor. You one? You don't look it, but of course everyone's a ragbag these days."

John almost winced. He had thought he was rather well put together. He illuminated his face with a sad smile. "No. This wasn't my theater—yet. But I have friends—"

"Shades of Peg Woffington, Sheridan, Kean—Barstow," mused the man.

"Barstow—Claudia Barstow is one of my friends."

He turned to the old man, suddenly alarmed, "Oh, my God! Don't tell me she was here when—"

"Oh, no!" said the old man. "It was at night. Thank God nobody was here. You'll likely find her at the Cavendish."

"I know," said John. "I'd better run."

The old man stared at the ruined facade of the theater.

"Shocking—shocking—" he said. "Well, good luck, boy. Give her my best."

John nodded and ran off and later realized he didn't have the faintest clue who the man was, if he did see Claudia.

On the way to the Covent Garden tube station he decided to phone her and speak as if he had not met her. At least he had a reason, a message from the admiral. That would likely get him through. He phoned, using the Ronald Colman voice. It got him through.

"Miss Barstow," he said, "I'm a friend of the admiral's from Great Yarmouth. He's bombed out, but all right. I came in to see you about getting some books together for him."

"Oh, dear," she said, "is he hurt?"

"Not at all. May I drop by?"

"Come on up," she said. "I'll get something together for poor old Basil."

He realized that he must do something to impress her. Of course champagne would be proper, but he didn't have enough money. The admiral's pound was his bounty.

He passed a vendor selling hot chestnuts, but he knew they wouldn't do. On an instinct he detoured onto Charing Cross Road and browsed through a front rack at a bookstall, with a special half-crown section. Most of the windows were boarded up, people were scurrying for home or work, and it was likely that there would be bombing during the night. He'd better run. If he were lucky, he'd be at the Cavendish before the sirens went.

He was in luck. First he found a watermarked warped book, *Shakespearean Comedy*, for the admiral, a tarnished copy like one the old man had owned, and then he came upon the treasure.

A silverfish-nibbled red and gilt book, it was large and pretentious. It had gone through bad days, but it must have been Victorian, and it was handsomely entitled, *Great Scenes at Drury Lane* (*Theater Royal*).

He flipped through. Toward the end was a page of text facing two etchings.

One was a robust gentleman with a walrus moustache. He was posed with shoulders hunched. The caption read, "This is Peter Barstow, playing the sweet, near-to-nature Old Shepherd in Shakespeare's *The Winter's Tale.*" The other, of a weak-chinned dimpled beauty, read, "Another member of the noted Barstow clan, Phoebe Barstow, portrays Helen in *All's Well That Ends Well.*"

He bought both books. But now that the Drury Lane book was his, he looked at it with sudden misgivings.

He passed a boarded-up wine and spirits shop. On a hunch he walked around into the alley. Sure enough, the proprietor was there, fishing bottles out of a large bin of soaked straw.

"I say," said John, "I know you aren't open, but I just got in from Norfolk. My girl has a terrible weakness. Wine. I have a weakness, too. Not much money."

The man pulled himself up. He leaned on a crutch.

John held out the remainder of his money. It all rattled.

The man looked at him sympathetically.

"Well," he said, "mostly chaps want gin. But I tell you I have some wretched bottles here and a little problem. Labels got rinsed off during the blitz last night in a flooded basement. You can 'ave one cheap. It ain't amontillado of course, but it's kissed the ass of sunny Spain."

He plucked an unlabeled green bottle out of the collection. It was at least corked tight.

"Good enough," said John.

He stepped into the toilet closet in back of the shop, adjusted his tie in the cracked glass, slicked down his hair, tried not to look nervous, and left.

He marched into the Cavendish and announced his appointment with Miss Barstow.

"First floor, front right," said the desk clerk, not even glancing up.

Claudia let him in, and he tried not to show his panic.

The place was not as elegant, but the war had mottled all of London. Tables covered with Spanish shawls, with silver-framed pictures of celebrities, cluttered the room. A comfortable faded sofa contained a cargo of embroidered pillows, and a slightly yellowing ermine throw. Dominating the room, as always, was the Augustus John portrait of Claudia. But, to John, it seemed overpowering in its elegance and sophistication.

Using his best voice, he blurted out, "I know this isn't what you're used to, but it's the best I could get."

He awkwardly shoved the bottle at her.

She took it and looked at him curiously. She seemed disturbed. Her hair was pulled back from her pale face, and her powder did not hide the dark circles under her eyes.

"That's very kind," she said.

He was flattered that as she scanned him there was no recognition in her face. It made hin feel like a man. He looked at the bar set up on a table. And he saw five of the glasses he had sent her so long ago. He smiled.

"What's so amusing?" she said.

"I see you have five of them left," he said.

She walked around him and gasped.

"Good God!" she said. "You're the boy!"

Feeling like a Noel Coward hero, he nodded and smiled.

"I'm the boy."

She touched his chin.

"I should have known. A chin like that is not usual. It was on my brother, and on Cary Grant. And a little toff I saw at a barrow on Caledonian market day."

She smiled.

"How can anyone change so much in several years?"

He felt he was blushing, seeing the open admiration in her face.

"Well, my boy—"

"I—I missed you at the admiral's bash."

"So," she said, "*you're* the young hopeful that got bashed in the eye! I heard!"

He nodded. "I—I wanted to see you before I get shipped out."

"You—shipped out?" she gasped. "You're just a baby!"

"I'm old enough to die for my country." He tried not to overemphasize the drama. And he felt he wasn't exactly lying. The herring fleet did go out to sea.

"So," she said, smiling, "if you're old enough to go to war, I think you're old enough to uncork this bottle."

She handed him a fancy corkscrew, and while he figured it out she fetched two of his crystal glasses.

"Who would ever believe," she said, "that I would toast with you as a young man. I adored these glasses. Sorry that some were victims to time and life."

"Ah," he said, "there is always good Waterford to be had."

He used his best Clark Gable voice.

"Well, where did that come from?" she said.

"I go to the cinema as you advised," he said. "I'm going to be an actor."

"Perhaps you are," she said, appraising him.

He handed her one of the books.

"Here's a gift," he said. She took the book, looking at him with amusement, and went to the window. He could tell she needed glasses; she squinted.

"My God!" she said, "the two idiot Barstows on one page. Great-uncle Peter and Cousin Phoebe. The ones you don't hear about; they were the worst actors of the clan."

"Oh, then I don't feel too badly," said John. "The book only cost half a crown."

"You were robbed!" she said.

She closed the cover and looked at the gilt imprint of the Drury Lane Theater. Her eyes filled with unexpected tears, and to his surprise, she turned away, so he wouldn't see them spill.

"I'm sorry," he said, "very sorry. I went over there to find you. It was terrible."

"Excuse me," she said. "I don't usually fall apart. But Drury Lane got to me today. I think everyone I ever cared for was part of it. And yesterday, I filed a thousand papers in my desk there, locked it, and walked out."

Her white teeth flashed through her tears.

"That's likely why I'm so cross with those blitzing bastards. I spent the whole damned day putting things in order. You couldn't know what it means, John. To have been a movie star, to have the world at your feet—the premieres, the clothes, the elegant houses, the seeking lovers, the whims fulfilled. And then you come back home and you try—try to do your bit and be part of the human race, and it all gets blown to eternity in spite of all your attempts at regeneration and nobility. It just doesn't work—oh, hell, let's have a blast!"

He poured the drinks, hoping she wouldn't notice the little floats of cork. He'd have to get more expert with a corkscrew.

"Here's to you, John Graves. May your name be in lights. That's a good name. You won't have to change it. You know, you're quite a lad. Lost your cockney pretty well until you said Graves. Somehow it came out a bit *Grives*. Watch out for the familiar words, old boy. The unusual ones always come out all right. Just watch for simple Judas words tumbling out. Take it slow."

"Thank you," he said.

"Cheers." She tasted the drink. "Where did you get this?"

He felt sick. It was likely slop.

"Best I could do," he said.

"Best!" she said. "John, this is as good brandy as I've had since in a dog's age. How did you manage?"

He took a swallow. The liquid almost scorched his throat. "The man said it had kissed the ass of sunny Spain."

She laughed. It thrilled him. Her voice rippled.

"You're a bit of all right," she said. "What service will you enter?"

"My father went down last week," he said. "I guess the best I could do is seaman's apprentice."

She glanced at him, almost sadly, and poured herself another drink.

In the twilight he could see what she had been when he watched her at the cinema as a boy. Her hair was curled in soft dark tendrils and her neck was a slim column against her white lace collar. Her high breasts swelled, cleaving their little valley as she bent forward. Her aristocratic Barstow nose, the arched eyebrows, and her pale brow reflected a wistful picture of not quite lost loveliness to him.

"You're all so young—so young," she said.

"You're a beautiful woman," he said. "Age has nothing to do with—with—" he halted lamely, almost afraid of what he had insinuated.

"And I daresay you'd like to be 'friendly' with me," she said.

He half rose.

She put her hand out, palm towards him.

"No, boy," she said, "tonight I'm older than God. And you're just too, too damned young. Maybe it's Drury Lane. I was weaned there, and did my first walk-on, and got laid in one of the boxes to get a job from a son of a bitch who couldn't give it to me; the last time I saw my father, he was there in his greasepaint in his dressing room. He was furious that I was going to the United States. When I could get away from Titan studio for a breather I came back several times and felt guilty because I wasn't treading the boards where I belonged."

She poured another drink. He did the same.

"And even now, I look at you, a kid, and think that we could still make love or whatever you call it to expiate the death and destruction around us. Yes, I see your look—you're a man, the war has done that fast. Yes, one more orgasm for me in a long line of such, no matter how ridiculous."

He was so astonished he could hardly breathe. But he realized he was only a sounding board. She was deeply disturbed.

"Strange, boy, that we die from the head up. Our bodies, even in middle age, aren't too bad from the waist down. I feel just as fully, perhaps more eagerly than I did before. I could teach you a lot. But tonight I won't, you know why?"

"Because I'm too young?" he whispered, "but, I've, I've—"

"You've done it, of course," she said. "No. That isn't it. God, almost thirty years ago I took the cherry of a man who is now, to my thinking, older than God, even if he runs a studio. And then he was about your age. It isn't that, John, and for God's sake, don't think it's because I'm moral. It's just that my theater's just gone up in flame, and my life was so involved in it. Even these last few months, as I worked at Drury Lane with ENSA, at my silly little desk, I thought, well old girl, here you are right where you started, but doing something that makes sense for a change.

"But did it make sense, boy, did it? All those pissing little papers I filed for all those people who wanted to give of themselves, which meant they were performers and wanted to spill their special guts out. Half of them will never think that they may be lost on paper in my ruined water-soaked desk, and they'll go sulking about because we don't call them. So what, John, is it all about? What's left? What's left?"

"It's like the admiral," said John, "his books and bits and pieces all gone. Several of his grandsons, and a son, and I think he grieves more for his books."

She smiled sadly. They heard the howl of an air-raid siren.

"Well, it looks like the tube," she said.

She moved to a closet and took out a satchel. In it she expertly fitted the remnants of the bottle of brandy and an electric torch. She pulled on the same tweed coat he had seen in Great Yarmouth, tied a scarf on her head, and snatched up a blanket.

"Come on, lover," she said, "damned glad you brought brandy—I promised not to touch anything but the offshoot of the grape till they get that bastard Hitler."

An explosion ripped across their ears. She snatched up a packet of books tied with string.

"This may not be here when we get back, so let's take these for the admiral."

People were huddled in the shelter. Families, strangers, all bound by the necessity to live.

"This looks possible," said Claudia.

They encamped in front of a padlocked door. The sign, Gentlemen's Lavatory, had been criss-crossed by a pasted sticker, OUT OF ORDER. There must have been fifty people grouped along the subway platform.

Strange place to spend the night with Claudia Barstow, thought John. She plumped up her satchel for a pillow, spread the blanket, and poured brandy into two small metal cups.

"Settle down," she said. "When one is tired, this is as good as the Savoy. And anyway, bub, nobody's there right about now."

He drank the fiery liquid. Fancy, Claudia Barstow's head against his shoulder as she snuggled down. He thought wistfully of the hope he'd had for a moment at the Cavendish that he might have been between white sheets with her, he might have felt her naked body against his skin, he might . . .

There was the roar of a bomb up above. The lights flickered. She sat up, sharply, and without a word poured each of them another drink. A child cried in the distance. Snoring and wheezing stopped dead. The world stopped.

Then there was another roar. The earth seemed to heave, then vibrate, and the lights went out. There was a sound of hissing, as dust and dirt seeped all about them, a dry waterfall. John's eyes smarted. He reached his hand back toward the door. It had been blown open. There was another great roaring thump, and a screaming cry in the distance, "Oh God, oh God, oh God–oh–"

Another roar.

Then deep silence.

The earth sifted to a stop.

Claudia fumbled with the satchel. In a moment she found the torch and lit it. They had been walled in from the others by earth. The lavatory door was knocked flat.

Claudia pulled herself on top of it, away from the dirt. She dragged her possessions with her as if she were on a raft and then flashed the torch in his face. He could hear the rasp of her breath as she tried to control her panic.

"I'm okay," he said. "Are you?"

"For now," she said.

He took the torch. His hand was shaking.

"We'd better save it."

As he flicked off the light, he touched her hand; her fingers felt icy. In the dead silence, he realized she was shivering.

Almost to protect himself from loneliness, he put his arm about her. And finding her frail, he held her close. It seemed for a long time.

"There's nothing we can do," he said, "but wait. I think we could do with a nip."

This time, the bottle found their mouths. Somehow as it coursed down his throat he felt better.

"Now, now," he said, "Miss Barstow, you just stop trembling." His mouth found hers, and they forgot their fear.

There was a flash of light. He squinted up into an electric torch, held by a man with stout boots tucked into combat pants. He was an air-raid warden. A door to the rear of the lavatory sent out shafts of light.

"Good God!" said the man, "'ere I go interruptin' something again. Jesus, you all want to fuck when you think yer going to perish. When you chaps finish, you can get out through the loo."

The man stepped over them and examined the damage beyond without further ado.

"I'm sorry," said John. "He didn't understand—"

Claudia smiled at him.

"Too bad," she said. "The name without the game."

They settled down until the raid was ended. She put her head on his shoulder and fell asleep, snoring slightly.

When the all clear was sounded they gathered their things like two old chums after a portable tea at Hyde Park and left, crawling over upended urinals.

She wiped the saliva and dirt away from the corners of her mouth and took out her lipstick. "God, I must look dreadful."

"Never," he said gallantly.

They found the street not too badly damaged. The Cavendish was still there, and, therefore, what was left of her existed.

"Well, thank you, John Graves," she said, "you're quite a chap you know."

She touched the cleft of his chin, reaching up and kissing it.

"Thank you, Miss Barstow," he said. "Can I come up to your room?"

She began to laugh, and so did he.

"You never give up, do you, boy? No, but I think you earned calling me Claudia even if you aren't on the stage yet," she said. "And if we survive all this, I'll help you if I'm still at the old stall. God help you, you're going to be an actor."

4

◆◆◆◆◆◆◆◆

It was the winter of 1940.

Hollywood, the eternal egotist, faced war in Europe in its usual hedonistic fashion.

Fergus's main concern, like other people's, was that the European market was cut off. Foreign funds were frozen as currency was blocked, and Titan again had to pull in its economic belt.

Paris was occupied. London, Liverpool, Coventry, and Plymouth were being smashed by Germany's massive air bombardment. British shipping was fighting a desperate battle to deliver munitions and food to the homeland's shattered shores.

Rumania and Greece had fallen into Hitler's hands. British forces were mustering to battle in the eastern Mediterranean.

Throughout the United States, the sad voice of Gabriel Heatter called forth on the nation's radios his lugubrious laments, and Americans wept with sentimental abandon about the city most of them had never seen, when Hammerstein and Kern's "The Last Time I Saw Paris" pulsed on the ether.

Fergus thought of David Moses and was glad that his own son, David, was so far from the theater of war.

David would soon graduate from Stanford. All he

needed for his B.A. was his corrected thesis to be typed before he got his diploma in June.

He was planning to stay over at Stanford a few days into the Christmas holiday when he could have the library stacks to himself, go over his material, and get his gear crated for his return to Hollywood.

Fergus was disappointed that David was more interested in anthropology and archaeology than the wonderful microcosm of films he could have probed during his holidays; for David would eventually come into full ownership of Titan studios.

Thinking of how the young Irving Thalberg had poured his creative "plasma" into Metro Goldwyn Mayer, Fergus dreamed of David using his splendid potentials and coming to his aid to jack up the flagging spirits of the studio, which was overladen with aging stars and expensive properties moldering on the shelves for want of some brilliant catalyst to pull them all together.

"Perhaps," he had argued, "you might enjoy analyzing the studio as a sociological study."

"It's too unstable," David answered. "It's not a true society. An ethnologist would go mad trying to analyze a socioeconomic system based on New York boards of directors and a fluctuating economy." David tried to keep a straight face. He loved to see his father steam over his comments.

"Listen, squirt," said Fergus, "all you young iconoclasts sit on your prats up there at college protected by the economy of your folks' sweat, argue about lofty subjects like was Bacon really Shakespeare, and all that crap, while serious moviemakers are turning out such classics as *Gone with the Wind, Wuthering Heights*, and *Ninotchka*."

"True," said David, "but out of the combined efforts of a massive industry, you can only mention a few. I admit, it's a changing medium. You've gone far from the nostril angles of Feyder, Granowsky, Pudovkin, and Eisentein. But you settled for the spit on the nipples of Harlow. One era was highbrow magic rabbitin-a-hat tricks; the other is lowbrow *in transitu* sex images."

"It's not that simple," said Fergus. "Whatever we do, we try to create a reality. We prefer good stories, good actors, good production. We are improving our techniques all the time, trying to adapt natural things through machinery to a dramatic art. Christ, do you young whippersnappers sit around and bitch the theater like this?"

"What did you bitch at when you were my age, dad?" David grinned. "From what I hear, it was grandfather. You and Simon Moses never really saw eye to eye."

Fergus flushed. "Well, someday you'll own the studio, thanks to him, and to me, don't forget. And don't forget brilliant directors like Max Ziska, and talents, no matter what trouble, like Jeffrey Barstow. They'll add luster to our industry as long as they don't burn film for the silver nitrate in it. And if you want someday you can make pictures like the Conquest of Mexico, or the life of an amoeba, or anything you choose, if you can dramatize it right."

"If the board allows," said David genuflecting.

Fergus looked at his son. How far he was from the scrawny young man he himself had been when he came out to California doing Simon Moses' dirty work for him. It still made Fergus sore to think how he had been put on the train to take the rap in case anything happened to Claudia, while Simon stayed safe in New York.

It hardly seemed possible that they had arrived in California two years before there was even a cross-continental telephone.

David's casual elegance, even in his moleskins and crew-necked sweater, impressed Fergus. This mixture of himself and Esther had been good, no matter what had gone wrong with their private lives. At the same time, the perpetual battle between critical youth and proffering parent irritated him. Kids expected everything on a silver platter.

"Look, buddy," he said, "I'm glad you got to play polo, instead of cat-on-the-rock in the streets of New York; I'm glad that you fish for marlin off Catalina, instead of hanging on a bridge at Throgg's Neck; but be prepared to step into your grandfather's shoes, and mine, without a sneer on your face. You'll find your knocks aplenty bucking your Uncle Abe and all the boys in the blue suits."

But David, even with his supercilious attitude, made Fergus proud. This was a son to cherish. He ought to be with him more, now that he was a man. Let him meet some of the pretty girls under contract. Let him fling a little.

He wondered if David had got the message about himself and Jessica Klopfinger. Jessica was just a couple of years older than David. It wouldn't do for David to think his dad was tied down to a secretary, no matter how pretty and smart she was. Of course the kid understood, he must, that with his mother away, Fergus had a man's life on the side. Perhaps he'd better spread himself around a little, be more of a man-about-town.

"I might just get up to Stanford before you pull up stakes," Fergus said. "I'll call you as usual on Friday."

◆◆◆◆◆◆◆◆

Fergus ran *London Bridge* twice in the executive projection room.

"For God's sake, Fergus, it's okay. We've got to ship the print," said Mark Fremont, his producer.

"I know," said Fergus, "but we've got to preview it away from Hollywood. I'm sick of their smart-ass preview cards. Let's go up to San Jose and run it in a small-town atmosphere."

Oh Christ, thought everyone—Fremont, two cutters, June McCleod, the head of the cutting department, and Jessica Klopfinger. That means he wants to visit David again and has to have an excuse.

"I want my boy to see it," said Fergus, echoing

their suspicions. "David has such a good young audience reaction to the product."

They all groaned inwardly. Some of them remembered when David was fourteen and had suggested that a picture be shot in France, and the whole company was shipped out, instead of doing it on the Paris streets on the back lot. Fergus had hoped that he and David would have a wonderful father-son holiday in Europe. Not that you could blame the old man; after all, it was tough having your wife in a loony bin most of the time. But David had chosen to go fishing with some school buddies on the Rogue River.

"I'll order the Lark to put on the private car," said Jessica.

"That isn't necessary," said Fergus. "I'm not going to take a whole goddamn army. I'll just run myself. Mark can meet me there with the film."

Jessica wondered if anyone in the room knew that she was being dusted. There had been a time when Fergus had ordered that private car so she could be with him. They had traveled through the dark, charged with the excitement of the night and the glimmer of the ocean and beach, as they made wild and uninhibited love.

Those train trips had always engendered wilder lovemaking than on the nights he spent at her apartment, or the times they had made love furtively in Palm Springs during weekend conferences, or the countless times he had taken her into his private room and, without removing their clothes, they had coupled in a passion of release, sometimes walking from their unorthodox postures straight back into a world of work . . .

They left the projection room and went back to the office. Jessica followed. Fergus spoke without looking up as he sat behind his desk.

"I won't need you, Jessica," he said. "You can run along."

"Of course, Mr. Austin," she said.

They always talked like this in front of people.

Jessica felt it made the relationship more exciting. In five minutes he could have her on the floor behind that door. Jessica felt her heart thump. He excited her. He was the only man who ever really had. For over three years she had told herself that she mustn't fall in love with him. It was too good. No woman she knew was as fortunate. She had held the interest of a very busy and important man, and he had treated her wonderfully well, with much more dignity than such a carnal relationship usually found. It should have terminated after a few months. But it clung. She fornicated with him, and she worked with him. It was remarkable.

As usual she went to her office and turned on the intercom. When Fremont left, the red light would go on, and he'd say, "Get in here, you bitch!" and she'd begin to be hot and breathless.

She listened. The intercom switch was on, and he didn't know it.

"Don't you want me to run up north with you?" said Fremont.

"No," said Fergus, "I don't want anybody. I just want to be alone with my son. It's his birthday. I'm getting sick of people around all the time. Sometimes it's a tightrope act."

"No cutter, no Jessica?" said Fremont.

"No nobody," said Fergus. "I'll meet you at the theater."

Jessica heard him strike a match. He was puffing one of his endless cork-tipped cigarettes.

"I think I'm going to get out the broom and sweep clean," he said, "Jessica and all. Have you noticed how women move in on you when they think they're indispensable?"

"It would be pretty tough on her," said Fremont.

"That's just why," said Fergus. "I don't want to be tough on anyone. It's just another goddamn responsibility. I have enough troubles at home. Well, think I'll get down to the beach."

He's saying that to bug me, thought Jessica, smiling.

She heard Fremont leave at the side door, and in a few moments a door closed again. She waited, and then she had the feeling that she was in the suite alone. She walked into his office. The door to the dressing room was ajar. He was gone.

She went back to her desk, got her coat, walked out, saying good-night to Hank, the night policeman, and went to her car in the stall marked with her name.

She drove toward the gate. A company limousine pulled up to the dressing room building ahead of her. She parked at the curb, unnoticed among a group that came filing out of the music building.

She saw Fergus get out of the car and heard his footsteps go up the stairs. Her methodical mind went to work. There had been orders to refurnish Suzy Derain's suite a few days ago. She had been exciting in her supporting role in *London Bridge*. Fergus had sent memos congratulating her, and Jessica had typed up the memo to New York, raving about the girl's star potential.

She heard the laughter of the French girl and the drone of Fergus's voice. A venetian blind was flicked. A light dimmed. This was not the first time. It was his method. Move in fast. Mow down. She could imagine everything that was happening. The girl would do anything he asked. The pattern took form. She could recall the memos. It was just that he had never been so careless. Almost as if—he wanted her to know.

God, if he dumped her, it would be terrible. She suspected some people must know now. At least among the men.

She hadn't slept around for a long time. That is, if you didn't count that crazy French actor who came swinging in and out of town and popped in her apartment one defenseless rainy night. And of course, there was the writer she had helped, who had stayed several nights, and had been so terribly grateful, and discreet, because his wife was coming out from New York if he sold his script, which he did.

I hope that French broad gives him a dose of clap, she thought, recalling the rumor that the lady had left a chain of gold keys and the French disease to a distinguished group of top brass in the town.

Jessica went home. Fergus hadn't told her where he was going. That was a tip-off that he wasn't going by himself. He would probably stay at the Santa Barbara Biltmore and drive on from there in the morning. He would likely detour for lunch at Del Monte Lodge, get in on Saturday for the preview, and have Sunday with David, all this with that French bitch.

Jessica poured herself a stiff scotch. If she had thought of someone who was new and exciting, who would be glad to be called, she would have made quite a night of it, but she only thought of rejects, or people who would know that something had gone wrong, and that wouldn't do.

Her phone rang. It was the switchboard at the studio. There was a telegram for Fergus Austin. She was expected to take it and find him, wherever he was. It was read to her from Western Union. Rebecca Moses, David's grandmother, had died of a stroke while on a visit to Miami. Please inform her companion, Miss Maude Perkins, what should be done.

Jessica swung into action. She reached Maude Perkins, made plans to ship the body to California, and called the family lawyer, Sam Unger, in New York. Abe Moses was on a junket to South America, where he was jacking up what was left of the foreign market. Jessica informed the lawyer she would cable him.

"That David Austin's a lucky young man," said Unger. "He gets all his grandmother's stock on his twenty-first birthday. And do you know when that is?"

"It's tomorrow," she said.

"Right," said Unger.

"Mr. Austin is on his way to see him now," said Jessica. "I'll get right up there and tell him, Mr. Unger. Don't you worry. Everything will be taken care of."

"Good," said Unger. "Since you've got it under control, tell him I'll fly in Monday. I have to go to Washington over the weekend."

Jessica hung up, glad that Fergus hadn't told her where he was going to be. She had every reason to say that she didn't know how to reach him.

She threw an overnight bag on her bed and packed it quickly. She would get to Stanford before he did, break the news to David, be waiting, and show him how efficiently she could take care of a crisis—the first important one which had happened since she had been his mistress.

Everything was tied up in a sweet, neat bundle for David Austin, she thought. Son and heir of Titan studio. Bright, intelligent, charming. And now, incredibly rich. What would happen to the handsome kid from here on in—no wonder he was so handsome, with such a sire? Good God, what would ever happen to Fergus's muscle-bound ego if he ever knew David was not his son?

Armed with the secret that had been locked in her mind these three years, she drove toward Palo Alto, the windshield wiper click-clacking like the rhythm of Esther's awful mechanical bicycle.

She rapped on the door of David's little house in the woods behind the campus. After a moment, the door was flung open.

"For Pete's sake, Pete," said a sleepy voice, "do you have to—"

She stepped in and saw that David was standing naked in the doorway. His eyes widened.

"Oh, my God—" he said, "Jessica!"

He fled from the room and came back a moment later wearing a terry robe. She stirred up the ashes in the fireplace.

"Quite a build, Dave, you should have let me know."

"I always sleep in the buff. I thought it was—"

"Pete?" she said.

"Yeah—pal who works at the Hoover memorial—gets tanked and comes over for a bull session in the wee hours. But, what the hell. What are you doing here?"

"Dave," she said, "first, I need a drink."

"Oh, sorry, what a lousy host. I got some applejack from a farmer up in Los Gatos. Okay?"

"Okay."

While he went to the kitchen, she peeled off her polo coat, and kicked off her shoes. She suddenly realized that she was with the richest young man in California, only he didn't know it. She smiled, thinking of the handsomeness of his tanned, wide-shouldered body. Jeffrey Barstow must have looked like that in his golden youth.

What a pity to break the news to David.

He came back smiling. "How come I'm honored? Where's the old boy?"

"Do I have to come with him?"

He handed her the applejack. She took a sip and sat back in a worn leather chair.

"Wow!" she said. "Jersey lightning! Is this what you seduce co-eds with!"

He took a big swallow and smiled.

"My feet are freezing!" she said.

She pulled the scarf off her head, and her hair fell over her shoulders. She undid the top buttons of her cashmere sweater and leaned forward to rub her foot.

"Oh, come on, let old Doc Austin do it."

He took her foot in his hands and chafed it.

"Oh, boy," she said. "Worth the trip."

"What pretty little feet," he said. He looked at them and then up at her. She leaned back, the sweater clinging to her breasts and revealing the cleavage.

He took another drink.

"How come you're not out at some bash at the Mark or something?" she said. "You're letting down my humble working girl's opinion of the high life of the idle rich."

"Not so idle. I'm correcting my thesis before it goes to the typist. Ten straight hours. Greasy grind, you know."

She took a sip of her drink.

"David, you're going to get me loaded."

"No such luck."

He'd always thought she was stunning. And she couldn't have been very much older than he was.

"You didn't answer my question. What are you doing here?"

"You know," she said, "it's almost morning."

She stood up. He was tall. She lifted her arms up and put them around his neck.

"It's your birthday," she said, "and I want to be the first to wish you happy birthday."

His robe had fallen open. She put her arms under it, next to his tanned skin, and she looked up at him. Their mouths joined in a full, open kiss. Her tongue touched his; then she pulled back.

"Oh my," she said, "what will you think of me!"

She pulled away and took another drink. She saw how much he had been disturbed before he fastened his robe. He flushed.

"Now, now, Jessica," he said, "I think I'm very flattered. You must have read my mind a couple of times around the pool in Santa Monica. Boy, you have a more beautiful body than any star at the studio."

She hung her head, noticing that he had drained his drink.

"Thanks, Dave, but I don't go on that basis. If I did, I'd have been an actress."

"I know you could. Where's the old shoe?"

"I'm afraid he's a little tied up with an actress at the Santa Barbara Biltmore. I doubt if you'll see him until the preview in San Jose tomorrow night. And I knew you'd be wanting to celebrate your birthday. So I thought, why don't I run up and take him to San Francisco. We could do the Wharf and Chinatown and have a little fun. You know, I think about you a lot."

He looked into her eyes.

"Jessica—"

"Why couldn't I have been a co-ed?" she said. "Why couldn't I have been your date—"

"You are my date."

He poured two more drinks.

"So he won't show up until tomorrow night—" he said, "that is, tonight—it's into Saturday."

He seemed saddened. She put her hand out, touching his cheek.

"Don't think of it. Please, Dave, I want you to be happy—"

He drank, and she drank along with him.

"I don't care what you think of me, David. You're twenty-one. You're a man."

"And you're a woman."

He took her hand and led her to the little bedroom. It was a tumbled mess. He took off her sweater, bending to kiss her breasts as she tugged at his robe. They sank into the bed, and, as she felt his smooth flesh against hers, he peeled off the rest of her clothes. She exulted in the fact that he was who he was, that she knew more about him than he or Fergus Austin did; but all these things left her mind as he loved her with eagerness and joyous pleasure in her supple body.

She had never known anything like the quickening she felt in his arms. She cried out with pleasure at the abandoned moment of their ultimate fusion. And when she lay exhausted and astonished at the pulsation still beating in her body, he made love to her again, even more deeply, in the warm moistness that his first possession had given her.

For a brief moment, her mind flashed back to the story Esther had told her of Jeffrey loving her twice, the second time, "deep, slow, and warm," and the very thought of it forced her into an orgasm, which made him cry out "wait, wait!" and it happened to her again quickly along with him. She was glad he could not see the surprise in her eyes as they lay in the dark. It all seemed so natural to him, as if it were just a thing that happened. She found herself resenting unknown girls who had been on this bed with him, and she wondered for a moment if she rather than he were the victim.

But he held her in his arms tenderly, erasing any thoughts other than his presence.

The soft thumping of rain against the shingle roof embraced them in a private world of shelter and coziness. They fell into a warm, fatigued sleep.

In the morning, he turned her into his arms, rolled her up on to him, and in a moment he had pinioned her and made love, holding her up above him, cupping her breasts in his hands.

"You're wild!" he gasped.

When he finished, he rolled her gently back to the bed, and she hid her face in his shoulder.

"Oh David, I must be crazy. You're the wild one."

He put his hand over her mouth.

"Shut up!"

He hung over her face, kissing her. He held her hair like ribbons in his hand. She started to speak.

"Shut up!" he said again. "I'm no virgin, Jessica. But you make me crazy. It's never been like this. Never! What have you done to me?"

"I've done to *you*! We've got to get up. Someone might come here."

She went to the kitchen. He followed her. There was some coffee, a package of cereal, a half bottle of milk, and some stale bread and marmalade.

"Bachelor digs," he said.

They sat naked at the little wooden table and ate everything.

"Are you going to let me buy your birthday lunch?" she asked.

He stared at her and reached to softly caress her nipple, which hardened under his stroke.

"I'm going to take you through the Portola redwoods and up the skyline drive, if I ever let you out of my bed."

She laughed and evaded him, running to the bathroom.

She turned on the shower and stepped in. He was after her quickly. She soaped her back and neck, and his arms were about her, so she rubbed suds on him and reached down, to find he was hard against her.

"Oh, now, David! This has got to stop!"

Laughing, he pulled her down on the tile floor, and they made love, gasping, the water flowing across their faces, and into their mouths, and between their legs, until the hot gush of their passion was cooled by the running water.

"Let me out before I drown!" she said.

They dressed and she twined her wet hair in her scarf and rushed out the front door.

The sun was out, bleaching the muddy roads and rain-spangled trees.

David put the top down on her convertible, and they started up the winding roads, past country and meadow to Portola. A little white adobe church lay nestled against dark green clustered trees.

"Stop," he said.

They got out of the car.

A meadowlark let out his jubilant, throat-bursting song.

"Now, you didn't have to go to all that trouble for my birthday," he said.

She looked up at him through a glaze of happiness. His neck and bronzed face were a cameo, his light hair limned stroke by stroke by the gilding sunlight, his blue eyes narrowed protectively against the sun.

He kissed her as reverently as if he had never touched her.

Hand in hand they went into the little church. A young priest came from the sacristy door.

"Welcome," he said.

"Hi, Padre," said David. "We're shopping."

"Glad to see it, lots of young people shop here. Let me know if I can sell you the goods."

"We'll be back," said David. "This young lady and I, well, we might just fix to get married here."

"David!" said Jessica.

She rushed out of the church, her eyes filling with unexpected tears.

He came up to her and put his arms around her.

"Jessica—"

"You shouldn't have said that just because we slept together."

"I mean it, I want you always, Jessica."

"I'm older—"

"Two, three years. It doesn't matter. It's how we feel. I was never like this before—it's you!"

Jessica looked at him. Could this be, could this be?

"Your father'd hate it."

"Of course, but I'm marrying you. Remember, Jess, I'm twenty-one. It's our choice."

"We haven't got a license."

"We'll get one. Let's go right now."

She looked at him, and she was tempted. Even if he had been anyone—she was touched. He offered himself, without reservation. She had never felt this way in her life. She couldn't do it. He'd never forgive her when he found out about his grandmother's death. She should have told him at once.

"David, I can't do it this way. I have to do it right. For keeps. With or without permission, but not behind everyone's backs."

"I should have known you'd say that."

The priest came to the door.

"We'll be back, Father," David said.

They drove off, and he parked under the flickering shadow of a sycamore tree.

"You will marry me?" he said. "Right now?"

"David, I'd marry you right now," she said, "but I can't just yet. I didn't tell you. I couldn't, it all—all happened so fast. But I didn't want to spoil your birthday at first, and then this—this happened—"

"I don't care what you tell me, Jess, I love you. The hell with lunch. Let's go back to bed."

He smiled at her.

"David, I really came up to tell you—your grandmother just died in Miami."

He looked at her swiftly. "That's why you came!"

"That's not why I stayed. I hate to give you bad news now. Do you despise me?"

He hung his head.

"Poor gran, poor gran. Dying in that faraway place, with just a paid companion."

"You're angry," she said. "I don't blame you. But if I'd told you, you'd never have loved me. Guilt would have taken it away."

"Then I'm glad I didn't know."

"David, I'm going to do something for us. I'm going back to Hollywood. I don't want to face that—that French actress and your father on your birthday. You tell your dad I called you and gave you the news. And then you come down after the preview, and we'll make our plans after—after the funeral. I won't press you—"

"Press me! Jess, I won't let you go."

"Don't you see, Fer—your father will get it all mixed up in his mind with your grandmother. You know, you're going to be very rich. He might—"

"I don't give a damn what he thinks; what has he thought about me? He's been so busy all these years."

"Don't say that—"

He put his hands at each side of her head. "You're right, it doesn't matter. Oh, Jess, I love you more. Poor gran. But she lived her life. We have ours."

"Please, do as I say. We won't be apart again."

They drove back.

As they walked into the living room, he threw a log on the fire while she gathered her things.

"I'm supposed to grieve. I can't feel it. I'm too happy." He put his arms around her. "What if you'd told me. It might not have happened."

"Now I'm guilty," she said. "David, please, for me,

don't say I was here. Just go with your father, think of us, and come to me on Monday. Now, not a word, don't spill it, it's going to be very hard."

"Hard for us to do anything?" he said. "Never."

All the way home she tried to reason. What couldn't happen had happened to her.

When she got home she fell across her bed. It was no use to call David. He'd be at the preview, then late supper and a long bull session with Fergus. Her pulse quickened. Oh, God, what would happen if he told his father . . .

◆◆◆◆◆◆◆◆

All day long there was no word from Fergus.

Sunday was limbo, a hell-time, in which she reviewed every stick of furniture in David's cottage, every line of his body, every erotic moment, so that she found herself ready for love and empty without him.

After a sleepless night, on Monday she dressed for the studio with care and realized with relief that this might be the last time she would do it. Even her own apartment seemed strange, a stagnant stage setting. As she clutched the chain of office keys that had rested with such familiarity in her hands all these years, she stared at them as if they were a token of an unfamiliar world.

The day was filled with trivia. Still, thank God, no Fergus.

She finally locked her desk. The last few hours had been a prison sentence, composed of fear and nervousness at the thought of confrontation with Fergus.

The studio was buzzing with Christmas excitement. Stores delivered parcels. Secretaries wandered from office to office, bearing expensive, overwrapped gifts—the careful measure of prestige, each assayed to the penny in proportion to the significance of the donor and the importance of the receiver. Max Ziska was finishing his superproduction with the all-star cast, *Crown Imperial.* Jeffrey Barstow was doing the last scene.

Red Powell and Grace Boomer had both called last week, asking her to see that Mr. Austin got to the set. And Ziska himself had paused to pinch her cheek and tell her that he was looking forward to the Christmas party as the traditional day that directors seduced secretaries. She smiled at the compliment, for Ziska was a vital man with considerable finesse, she had heard.

The death of an old woman meant little to the Christmas pleasures of the hundreds who worked at the studio. This gigantic bash would provide them with fun and scandal to last all year, as well as gifts from staff superiors and a bonus check to take home.

But now, to Jessica, the Christmas gaiety meant nothing. She wanted to get away, as fast as she could, grateful for the amenities of poor old Rebecca Moses' demise, which had likely kept Fergus with Esther all day.

Soon, she could flee from all this with David. Her body ached for him, and her mind kept reminding her that in every way he was perfect—young, handsome, virile, and rich—and a complete revenge for Fergus's treatment of her.

So Jeffrey Barstow would be on the Ziska set! She had been to his house several times at conferences with Fergus these last few months. She had appraised him in her mind, admiring his decadent, handsome elegance.

What a muck-up he had made of his life and his talents. She had little use for him as a man, but now she wanted to see him because he belonged to David. How sad he did not know he had such a son.

She smiled thinking of the interoffice memo she had filed. Fergus Austin had been forced by the New York brass to give Jeffrey Barstow a new contract. In spite of his drinking bouts, his talent was money in the till. He'd had the best from the studio—care, protection—and now he was to get more money than any star in the Titan stable.

She knew it annoyed Fergus, but he had followed the dictum of the money boys. Max Ziska, the most talented of the star makers, had directed his genius toward Jeffrey in *Crown Imperial*, and the rushes proved the vehicle and the talent.

Softened by her new love, she thought of the old man. He must have once been wonderful in his wild way. Esther Austin had never forgotten her one night with him. Perhaps he had been as wonderful in love, passion, and tenderness as David was to her. If she never had another night with David, what she had known would be something to remember all her life.

Love made a woman so defenseless! She felt like a bride, awaiting her groom's embrace, and she felt her groin weaken with longing. What a reprieve from what her life had been! She was grateful that she had the skills of love and the experience; she would use it for one man. To have this and youth and wealth was too much. It giddied the imagination. And wouldn't everyone be amazed!

Her reverie was disturbed by a buzzer.

What was Fergus doing in the office?

She had no choice. She flipped the intercom lever, astonished at the natural sound of her voice. She hoped the panic didn't show.

"Yes, Mr. Austin?"

"Come in, you bitch," he said.

She switched off the lever. Oh, God! It was what he said when—when.

She picked up her pad and pencil and marched through the corridor and into the office. His desk seemed a block away. He sat there, staring at her. His face was sallow.

"Well?" he said. He got up slowly.

She stared. Had David said anything?

He opened the door to his private quarters.

"Miss me?" he said.

She stopped.

"Well, as a matter of fact, I—"

"Shut up, I missed you. Yes, very much."

She moved automatically toward the door. Then she paused.

"What's the matter with you, Jessica?"

He pulled her into the room. With his usual gesture he pushed her onto the couch and opened his zipper.

"Oh, but no—" she said. She pulled away.

"Why Jessica, whatever is wrong with you? My willing, loving Jessie—"

With his usual quick movement, he reached under her skirt. He pulled down her lightweight girdle, and, as she put her hands up, he was upon her quickly. There was nothing she could do. It was too sudden, and too usual.

In a frenzy, he pulled her skirts above her waist, leaving her half-naked; his face, full of angry passion, looked down at her as he forced himself into her. There had never been such rapine in him. She turned her head upward trying to pull up her knee to fight him off.

She looked up into the face of David. He had been ushered in, she realized, by arrangement, through the side door.

She gasped.

Fergus arose, himself exposed.

David stood, paralyzed.

"I told you," said Fergus, "you wouldn't believe me. So see it with your own eyes. She's been my mistress for four years."

She stared at David, her mouth working. There were no words.

David shook himself from the apathy that captured him. He paled under his tan. He walked out of the room. The door to the outer hall slammed after him.

Jessica bent over and slowly pulled up her girdle. She looked at Fergus. He stood, zipping his trousers, and stared down at her. His face was a study of hatred.

"You lousy slut," he said. "My son!"

She smoothed her skirt. At his words, the blood seemed to flow back into her head after the blanched emptiness that had been there.

"Oh, no," she said.

How could he have entrapped himself so fast. She had the opening; now for the zinger.

"Not your son, Mr. Austin."

"What stupid remark is that?" he said, adjusting his tie and sticking his chin out slightly, as if he were fighting a noose. She'd seen him do that a thousand times in business conferences when things weren't going along his prescribed path.

"I never intended to tell you," she said, "but look in Dr. Wolfrum's medical files. Blood types A and B cannot have a type-O son. Incredible that nobody spotted it before."

"What are you talking about?"

"Ask your wife, and look at the little notes she keeps hidden under her handkerchiefs. She had an affair with Jeffrey Barstow the night she caught you with Claudia at Arrowhead Springs Hotel. Or didn't you know she walked in and saw you?"

Fergus's pale skin turned paler. These were facts. He reached for a cigarette. Jessica had the feeling that he and she were pinioned in this room, sealed together in hatred.

He had just wrecked her life. She was still numb. She knew the pain would trickle through later. And all she could think of was to deal him a mortal wound.

"Jeffrey Barstow!" he said, "I don't believe it."

"Type O," said Jessica. "Check that, too, Mr. Austin."

"That paretic old bastard couldn't have a child."

Fergus stood before an angelic Paul Clemens portrait of Esther with David as a little boy, their two golden heads nimbused in a madonna-and-child attitude.

"That's not what Mrs. Austin told me." She picked up her notebook and pen. "Ask her, if you dare."

"Get out of here," said Fergus, "and don't come back on this lot, ever. Don't ever let me see you again."

Jessica turned at the door. There was a glossy eight-by-ten framed snapshot of David in his polo helmet, grinning, triumphant and young on the Stanford polo team. She remembered his sickened face as he had stared at her and Fergus.

"The record is not in your file," said Jessica. "I hid it to protect you. But you will find a copy in the mail tomorrow, if you don't believe me. And look for the notes in Mrs. Austin's handkerchief drawer. Merry Christmas, Mr. Austin."

She went to her desk, threw her key in the wastebasket, put on her coat, and started out the door.

Hank, the night cop, winked at her, and two tipsy secretaries who were sharing his paper cup of scotch called out "Merry Christmas!" and giggled at each other.

She paused at the hall doors.

She knew there would be a directive that she'd never come on the lot again. She'd seen it happen to a director who had married a big shot's mistress, a new actress from New York who had spit in a tycoon's face when he ripped the buttons off her blouse in his office, and others. Fergus would be on the phone to Blackie, the chief cop, right now.

Why not go on the Ziska set on her way out? What did she have to lose. Maybe Jeffrey Barstow would be there. She wanted to look at him, to see what she could fathom from his face and bone structure.

She pushed open the heavy doors to stage five. Baroque rooms and scenic vistas had transformed the large barnlike stage into a dream of old Vienna, save that it was harshly lit by work lights.

The party was almost over.

A large bar was wet with spilled drinks and melting ice; emptied bottles had been abandoned by the crew who had gone home to their wives and broads with their gift bottles of scotch and bonus checks in their pockets.

Max Ziska was sitting in his set-office, gathering up an assortment of gifts and cards. He was a handsome man, his sparkling black eyes, high coloring, and unruly dark hair only an indication of his vitality and deep curiosity about the world and the people in it.

"Ah, my lovely," he said, "I am so glad you came. There is always time for a toast to friendship in our cardboard world."

Ziska's welcoming smile bored a little warmth into the terrible shield of cold that had formed these last minutes about her body.

"Nice of you to ask me, Mr. Ziska. Looks like the party's over."

"Not with you here!"

He moved forward and held her arms out, looking at the slender column of her body.

"My God," he said, "you are a Venus."

He took out a packet of black Balkan Sobranie cigarettes and offered one with a courtly gesture.

She lit it while he poured them each a glass of champagne.

"Cheers," she said.

"To you."

They sipped the chilled drink, and he leaned back.

"Oh, God, I'm weary. That Jeffrey Barstow is a load when he's successful. I liked him much better when he was down."

"You knew him?" asked Jessica.

"In a way," said Ziska. "I rented his house and knew his books and paintings. Because of them, we became friends. Why?"

"Just curious," said Jessica.

She downed her champagne. Max poured more.

"How did you get away from Augustus Caesar?" he asked.

The words triggered a flood, which had been waiting for release. She felt tears on her cheeks.

"Now, now," he said, "my dear child, what is it?"

The set was deserted. Someone had left on a record of Ravel's *La Valse*. The disturbing music seemed to pound into her head.

"I'm in such deep trouble."

He patted her hand.

"Sometimes what we think of as trouble is the change we must go through to find our own path, and you have youth and a verve about you. I am sure it cannot be so truly tragic."

"Tragic! Mr. Ziska, I'm finished!"

He bent over and touched her cheek, felt the tear on it, and brushed it away. Comforting her, he held her and kissed her forehead. She responded pressing against him.

The beat of the music had smothered the whoomp of the stage door. She looked over Max's head to the livid face of Fergus. Behind him stood Hank, the night cop, his jaw slack with surprise.

"All right," said Fergus, "out, both you sons of bitches. You've both seen your last day in this town. Hank, they're trespassing and committing an immoral act on my property."

Max turned to him. "What do you mean? There's nothing wrong here."

Jessica saw the startled faces of Red Powell and Grace Boomer as they rushed to the door.

"You fornicating bitch, get out," said Fergus.

"Get out of my private office, you bastard," said Max. "This is my set, and you are invading my privacy."

"Get out of my studio," said Fergus.

"You'd better get going, Ziska," said Red Powell's pale voice.

"I shall leave when I am ready," said Max, enraged. "You will please leave!"

Fergus turned to the policeman. "Hank, throw the bums out."

He turned to Jessica. "Hell will freeze before you two set foot in a studio in Hollywood again."

Jessica quickly snatched up her purse and pushed

out of the room. She heard a scuffle and the slamming of Max's flimsy office door, as he struggled against manhandling.

She got out into the darkening alley, took a deep breath, and clutched her purse, grateful that her car keys were in her possession. Then she remembered that even her car belonged to the studio.

It was not cold, but Jessica stood shivering in the evening air.

The gaiety of the late afternoon had gone with the celebrants. Tonight there would be no showings; it was the one time of the year that cutting rooms, recording stages, even random rendezvous were not in session. Everyone was either headed for home or had found a more comfortable place to celebrate.

Only someone involved in disaster like herself would be wandering about the sterile sound stages.

She saw a lone figure walking toward her, the old cop, Smiley, coming back from the location lot across the road.

So she veered through a small garden and found her way into the maze of alleys, decorated with phony Spanish streetlamps and trimmed with shrubs, that dressed the front of the star dressing rooms.

They were almost all vacated. A janitor swept up in unit A.

As she moved along she saw lights in one dressing room. The blinds were slatted open. She saw a man sitting dejectedly in a chair. It was Jeffrey Barstow. He was looking at the *Hollywood Reporter* in a sodden sort of way, and Bud Regan was packing his suitcases, for the picture was finished. There he was, Mr. Jackpot, the one chance she had. Money, fame, and—the one man who could devastate Fergus Austin—if . . .

She watched for a moment and then walked in.

"Merry Christmas, Mr. Barstow."

Jeffrey cocked an eyebrow. Even though he was weary and sober, he always had an eye for a beauty.

"Miss Klop—Klop—" he said.

"Jessica."

She turned sweetly to Bud.

"Bud," she said, "Mr. Austin's been looking for you. He has a present for Mr. Barstow. Could you get it?"

Bud looked at her suspiciously. "I'm not supposed to leave him alone."

"I think he had a little bonus check for the good job you've done, too," she said. "You know, end of picture, and all. I'll stay with Mr. Barstow."

"Oh, *well*–" said Bud.

After he was gone, she turned to Jeffrey.

"You know, that was just a dodge. I think it's terrible the way they lock you up. You're a great man. I know the janitor, and we could get into any of the dressing rooms, where they have some booze, and have a little party."

Jeffrey's eyes widened.

"Am I going too fast for you, Mr. Barstow? Wouldn't want to shock you. I just thought we ought to ball it up a little. Life's too short."

"Why me?" he asked, blinking at her.

"Why you! The most attractive man in the world!" She put her hand on his leg and moved it caressingly upward. "Just let's have a little fun and talk it over. Is there anything you wish? Gin? I'll get the keys."

He shook his head in disbelief.

"Just–procure the vicar to stay for me at church twixt twelve and one–" he quoted. "Where have *you* been?"

She smiled as she left. Leslie Charles had a well-stocked bar next door, and she could get the key.

It was twixt twelve and one in Tijuana that they were wed. It took two witnesses to hold up the groom. The bride held her own.

5

♦♦♦♦♦♦♦♦

The event was headlined in the morning paper, as the bride had personally called Clarissa Pennock from Baja California, broken the startling news, and apologized for not putting the groom on the wire as he was busy signing the registry papers. The article was read apprehensively by the kitchen staff at the Barstow hacienda.

The bride was not what anyone would have expected (including the groom, as the gossip said). Effie had talked to her many times when she ran Fergus Austin's office at Titan. As a matter of fact, she had come out to the house several times for script conferences.

Jessica came down the stairs at ten o'clock the morning after the wedding in Tijuana. She was clad in a black dress with a white collar and patent pumps on her slender, aristocratic feet. Effie, who was polishing banisters on the main staircase when she appeared, thought she had the most beautiful figure she had ever seen. And the coldest face.

"Get Bud up here, please, Effie," the bride said crisply. "Mr. Barstow is trying to climb the wall. And clean the bathroom before Dr. Wolfrum arrives. He's on his way. Are there any pajamas in this house?"

"We've tried, ma'am," said Effie, "but Mr. Barstow sleeps raw. But he's got lots of robes."

When Dr. Wolfrum arrived, Jeffrey had been

momentarily bludgeoned into donning a satin, monogrammed robe, a relic of a love affair with a producer's wife who had been *very* grateful. Later, he tore the robe off, ruining it, but it didn't matter, because the groom then was put into a straitjacket and taken off in an ambulance to Las Cruces Sanatorium.

When the cure was finished, Jeffrey came home to find his house immaculate. There had been a change of staff after Jessica went over the household accounts. But Effie remained. Jessica noted her willingness to serve, clean, protect, and keep her mouth shut. Since Bud Regan had a link with the studio, he stayed on, too. But it was no rumor that the studio was angry at him for leaving Mr. Barstow alone long enough to elope with Jessica.

It was also noted that Mrs. Barstow, although she had been a big-wheel secretary at Titan Films, never went back there, even when there was a preview. She seemed to have shut some door when she married Mr. Barstow. It was odd, very odd.

It could hardly be said that the newlyweds led a gay social life. Several sorties into the outer world where conditions could not be controlled ended in disaster.

Some evenings at home were quite pleasant; the amenities of candlelight dinners with a few friends, mostly business connections. Jeffrey drank sparkling apple cider, while the others had wine. Movies in the projection room, with Jessica on one side of him and Bud on the other, so that even in the dark, with the help of some old drinking pal like Seymour Sewell, Jeffrey couldn't slip down a drink.

Sometimes, Effie felt that she saw Jeffrey looking at his placid bride with a gleaming eye and an upturned brow, as if he were waiting for the moment to leap at her.

Pansy, poor creature, was exiled to the zoo. But when Jessica went to the beauty parlor, or to see Herb Weiss, the business manager, Jeffrey would bring her into the house, and Effie would quickly clean if Pansy had slipped up.

Nobody could really complain about Mrs. Barstow. She ran the house and the people in it as she had run Fergus Austin's office. She always listened with a patient smile to Mr. Barstow's anecdotes. She never interrupted and never had any conflicting ideas or arguments with him. She seemed to be trying hard. And one doctor after another came to the house with needles and nostrums, attempting to restore the ruined frame that was once the handsome talented Jeffrey Barstow, last male of the great acting clan of theater and films.

Jessica had decided that it was necessary to fulfill the reason for her marriage, the justification for her life with Jeffrey, the revenge that motivated it.

She had gone to the best gynecologists and gland specialists in Beverly Hills, Wilshire Boulevard, and Westwood. She had absorbed hormones in every known way, had innumerable examinations and tests, had taken lemon douches, gone on alkaline diets, had her tubes blown, and even discussed artificial insemination—bringing up the subject casually to Jeffrey one Sunday morning on the terrace, the excuse being an article in the *American Weekly*.

Jeffrey exploded. "Are you insinuating that after fifty years of getting women in trouble, beginning at the age of twelve with my mother's Irish parlormaid, anyone would be audacious enough to suggest that I have some sort of a machine do my inseminating?"

"I was just discussing the process," she said blandly. "Hardly a problem with us."

"I doubt if my withered loins maintain one little sperm with enough vitality left to swim upstream," said Jeffrey. "My seed, shall we say, has been scattered."

"Well, my prince," answered Jessica coolly, over her coffee cup, "I have no complaints. I have you."

He wondered how much acid was in her words. Her eyes were cast down. At twenty-four, she had a lot of mileage on her, he knew, but only where it didn't show. Oh, she was good! She seemed to have a little sailor boy inside her that took hold of him as if he were a rope, and pulled him up hand by hand until he went soaring off into a sensual sea and exploded. He had known it in many lands, by many names—in Italy, succubus; in Mexico, dog—and it was a little disconcerting that it was in his own house; in his—God knows how—wife.

She was an expert, and he should know. He'd had all kinds and colors for three erotic generations. Jessica could almost have been his granddaughter. He had never felt her falter or make an error in passion. That would have been much more exciting than perfection, for it might have been true.

Effie came out on the terrace. "Dr. Wolfrum is here, madam."

"Let's get our shots, pops," said Jessica, smiling.

Jeffrey appraised her transparent beauty and opaque larceny quizzically.

"Are you certain," he said, "that these are vitamin shots? I have a sharp suspicion that the leftover hormones of stunt men are being pumped into my groin."

Dr. Wolfrum came out on the terrace. Jeffrey, making a grimace, lifted his robe, revealing an oyster-white, withered backside. "It's all yours, doc," he said. "At least what Jessica's left. Never marry a young wife."

Wolfrum smiled. "Surely you can't be complaining," he said, gesturing toward Mrs. Barstow, who looked better in a white bathing suit and a tan than all the accumulated actresses he had been snapping out of Nembutal with Dexedrine, or vice versa.

"Not I," said Jeffrey. "I love sex. Especially when I'm able."

And so the happy couple had their vitamins.

However, Jeffrey's vitamin shots were pure Dr. Voronoff out of Steinach, and, Wolfrum thought, if this batch worked, he indeed had a real commodity. It should have changed a eunuch into Errol Flynn.

Well, Jessica Barstow must know what she wanted. She had not only suggested the experiment but had privately handed him ten crisp one-hundred-dollar tax-free bills, cut neatly in half, and told him that the missing parts would be given him the day she was technically informed she was pregnant.

Another shot, vaguely related to tincture of cantharis, and the good doctor left with the hope that his patients had no social obligations for the next twenty-four hours and that the servants had the weekend off.

Packing his handsome leather medicine valise, fashioned in Paris (the grateful gift of a homosexual South American plantation owner, forced to wed a president's daughter in commemoration of their one and only heir), the doctor said adieu. He wondered what in God's name this beautiful young woman wanted with the long-hung parts of this paretic old sot.

What will happen, mused Wolfrum, if alcohol mixes with this brew? In spite of the doctor's varied experience, he was puzzled. This pattern did not fit any jigsaw puzzle he had ever worked, and he thought he knew them all.

◆◆◆◆◆◆◆◆

The cozy projection room in the Barstow house had not exactly been designed for legal concupiscence. It took Jessica to recognize the potential.

At the back of the room, where even the projectionist couldn't peek, was an eighteen-foot sofa. At one side was a self-contained bar, and the armrests were rigged to fold into the upholstered back for lounging and allied purposes.

Jessica had never fathomed the creative and poetic side of Jeffrey. She knew that looking at himself in youthful beauty triggered his gonads. But she did not know that he was attempting to turn back the clock to a time when his vitality and joy in life was more constant. She believed he wanted to see himself forever in the glory and beauty of his youth.

To Jeffrey, the films were the opposite of Dorian Gray's portrait in the attic. He could close out the world, forget his veins and wrinkles, the corded neck, the receding hairline, and the skinny body. He could see himself as a perpetual Childe Harold.

He knew that in his youth females had made themselves the target of his selective penis. He had used it in his mind like the bow of Achilles, the unsheathed sword of Arthur, to slay the doubts that lay within him. He had mastered his craft, but never his life, and so he deprecated himself.

"I'm just a tired old fart, stuck together with canned hormones, who has nothing left but his prick and his hair, and very little of them."

But his eyes begged his listener to argue, and seeing himself in youth and beauty often stirred the dormant bird in its nest.

Recalling this, Jessica planned her strategy.

After the hormone shots, she arranged a light dinner.

There seemed to have been an error, he was served champagne instead of apple cider. This was followed by French 75's in the projection room. By this time, his suspicion was blurred.

His wife wore a beautiful hostess gown, cut very low. The unseen projectionist ran *Love in the Sun*, costarring Jeffrey Barstow and four beautiful women, with special attention to the love scenes in reels two and three. If the operator received a buzz, he was to run the reels over again, as many times as she buzzed.

She paid the projectionist ahead of time, gave him a bonus, and told him he did not have to check out when he left. Baffled by her generosity and wondering what was up, the projectionist did just what she ordered.

The next morning Effie came to the projection room to hang fresh towels. Something was strange.

The hall door was open. Effie went into the bathroom. There was a heavy smell of sickness, urine, vomit, and most of all, a primitive scent, all animal.

The projection room door was open. She peered in. There in a muddle of velvet pillows and cast-off clothes on the great divan against the wall lay three creatures.

Jeffrey was in the middle, asleep, and nude, an empty brandy bottle clutched to his bosom. Mrs. Barstow, on her stomach, hand pressed to her head, lay to his right, in a noisy sodden sleep. Her naked body was striped with red welts.

On the other side of Jeffrey, Pansy sprawled. The chimpanzee had one arm around Jeffrey. As Effie stifled her shocked gasp, Pansy heard her and careened up on one elbow. It took Effie only a second to see that the monkey was drunk. Pansy let out a belch, lifted her long hairy hand to her forehead, and began to chitter.

The noise woke Jeffrey. He rose up slowly. His bloodshot gaze wandered to Jessica, and he froze for a moment, memory jogging him.

He signaled to Effie to be quiet. Her towels on her arm, she backed into the adjacent bathroom. He followed her. He was like a crazed man, the pagan rites of the drugs carrying over in the brandy fumes of which he stank.

Crowding Effie, he pushed her farther into the bathroom.

"Oh, Mr. Barstow!" she cried.

He put his hand across her mouth. "Quiet, me beauty, you wouldn't want her to hear us would you? You just wouldn't do that to me, Sheba."

Silent and panicked, Effie was borne to the floor. Lying in a welter of towels, Jeffrey took her in a violent frenzy.

"I've wanted this," whispered Jeffrey, getting up.

Effie, holding back her terrified sobs, straightened her uniform and stood there, shaking. To her horror, Pansy stood watching.

Jeffrey began to cry. Long, racking sobs like a wounded animal.

"Oh, my God," Effie whispered, "forgive me, dear God, forgive me!"

He stared at her, his ravaged face crumpled through his tears. "Get out," he said quietly, "and forget it."

He sat on the toilet, wailing noisily. Effie slipped out the hall door. She heard the buzzer ringing in the servants' hall. No one else was up. She rushed out and picked up the kitchen phone. Mrs. Barstow was now in her bedroom.

"Effie, for God's sake, bring me a bromo," she said. "I'm dying."

◆◆◆◆◆◆◆◆

For a month, Jeffrey stayed away from Jessica. He remained in his study, made phone calls to Wolfrum, told him never to come near the house again, discovered the nature of the drugs that had induced such insane passion, and looked at Effie with apologies in his eyes and no words in his mouth.

Since his marriage, there had been no direct contact with Titan Films, save through the publicity department. Fergus Austin, as he had figured, would never talk to him again. Likely because of Jessica. But Jeffrey began to wonder if that was all there was to it. A Borgia like Jessica with her potions and her plans did not come along every day. And if she could have seduced him with her hormone shots, God knows, she may have had some inner reason for marrying him in spite of her cushy berth with Fergus Austin.

It puzzled him, but he did not really care. Now all he wanted to do was get rid of this succubus. He wished to God that Claudia was not in London. His guilts about sitting it out in so-called luxury during the European holocaust were only alleviated by the random thought that in his condition, the enemy would probably pay to get him to go to London.

His film had been finished the day he was abducted

to Tijuana. He sometimes felt like the unsung groom of the black widow spider. As much as Jessica had been after him to keep his health, stay sober, and bed her, now, as far as she was concerned, he seemed to be on an orbit of his own.

If he chose to sit in a chair in his study and drink all night while he read poems aloud, she merely stayed away from him and let Effie clean up the filth. Somehow, in his bout with Doc Wolfrum's hormones and aphrodisiacs, his wife had devoured him, squeezed him of his overripe manhood, and now, obviously, he was finished.

There was no makeup man to observe the findings of liver decomposition, the red capillary webs on his face, arms, and neck, and the jaundiced dullness of his eyeballs. There was no wardrobe man with tape measure to note the swelling of parotid glands, the gathering fluid in his belly, or the edema of his lower legs. There was no director to report his occasional slurring speech and vacant stare; no reader to see the worsening of his handwriting, no woman to notice the sweetish fetor of his breath.

One morning Effie found him in the garden, doubled in a fetal position. Jessica was shopping. Effie and the Japanese chauffeur got him to his bathroom. When he tried to climb the honeysuckle wall in the bathroom to get away from the ants, the usual emergency calls were made, and he was straitjacketed back to La Cruces. After a long battle, he defeated the ants.

On his way back to sanity he sat in the library, trying to relate to the world. There seemed little connection with anything he cared about. He had managed these last few years to hoard enough, owing to a clever business manager, to keep him going for more time than he was interested in. With a pang, he occasionally read gossip about David in Europe. David, who belonged to the OSS. David, who for some reason seemed as much embittered with life as anyone, even Jeffrey himself at the same age.

He picked up the paper, folded at the picture and stage news page, and there he read it. The bannered news in Clarissa Pennock's saccharine column was that Jeffrey Barstow was going to be a father. The lovely Jessica Barstow, former executive secretary to Fergus Austin, had phoned in the gladsome news, informing her favorite columnist. The Barstow line would continue.

◆◆◆◆◆◆◆◆

Belinda Barstow, weighing seven pounds and two ounces, met the break of night on a December evening—three days before Pearl Harbor, a time of prosperity in Hollywood. Most of the local ostriches, in the wave of successful picturemaking, were ignoring the implications of the ruckus in Europe. For this reason, the press had space to get sentimental. Here was a new member of the Barstow clan, a fifth generation who might appear on the American stage. It didn't matter who or what her mother was. The public knew that she would grow up, be beautiful, get in trouble, have talent, throw it down the drain, and arise again like all Barstows, filling their empty lives with reams of newspaper copy that would make life much more interesting.

Clarissa Pennock was again euphoric. She was happy to announce that in the sunset of his life, a child would carry on the dramatic tradition of a great family, to bless Jeffrey's union with a girl of great charm.

Jessica read the article at the Queen of Angels hospital, uncomfortable because her breasts hurt and she was trying to dry them up before the nipples darkened. She was surrounded by masses of flowers, and she set about cataloging them as she had done at many studio weddings, christenings, and funerals, jotting down the description and the probable cost on the back of each. The Barstow name still had pull, and she would see that it continued.

And Fergus . . . Fergus . . . wasn't it ironic that his name was linked as her former boss in the birth announcement. He may run a studio, he may own all the stock, he may have any woman in his studio any way he wants, but this baby will shake him up more than anything that ever happened to him. I bet Dr. Wolfrum is giving Fergus Austin a shot right now. Right in the ass.

The great Fergus Austin always worked things out his way. All but this. It serves him right. She wondered what he had thought when he read the papers. It could almost have been his child, and he also knew it could almost have been David's. But most of all, she had proven to Fergus that Jeffrey could father a child.

At the hospital, Jeffrey looked through the nursery window and stared at the little bundle that was his daughter. It seemed incredible to him that one day she would hold his hand, smile at him, say his name. His substance, his flesh, his blood. He tried to ridicule himself, for having high hopes at his age, but emotion tore at him in spite of what he considered his built-in iconoclasm. Perhaps, because he had yearned to know David and had been denied, this child could be his salvation.

Above all, he must live to protect her from the coldness of Jessica. He watched her in the hospital room, busier on the phone than with the infant who had been put in her arms by the nurse. Why—why had she wanted this child?

After the baby was home, Jeffrey checked into Scripps Metabolic Clinic at La Jolla. He suffered every treatment possible for his liver condition and fought depression as he realized what little chance he had to watch his child mature.

"She must be named Belinda," he insisted. "Her great-grandmother, Belinda Pierce Barstow, was considered the most effective Juliet of the eighteenth century."

"Eighteenth!" exclaimed Jessica.

"Eighteenth," insisted Jeffrey, "and into the nineteenth. Do you realize *I* am a relic of the nineteenth century? God knows what in the name of fate ever allowed me to conjure a child out of my loins who will be my age in the year two thousand. It's obscene."

He managed to hold himself together regally for the christening. Dozens of pictures of him were snapped in the garden holding the infant in an elaborate embroidered robe which Jessica informed the press had been ordered for this auspicious event the day she knew she was pregnant. Which she did not inform me, thought Jeffrey.

After the last guest had left, save for Seymour Sewell, now retired, the two went to the study.

"What have I done?" said Jeffrey, suddenly depressed.

"I'd say you've performed a miracle," said Seymour. "Are you sure the kid is yours?"

"Sure!" said Jeffrey. "My dear friend, I still ache. That bitch got me shot so full of hormones, I wouldn't have been surprised if the sofa got pregnant—but what have I done!"

"What do you mean, you've still got a lot of time to live and enjoy that child."

"Don't jest," said Jeffrey. "You know bloody well my clock is running down. I'll never know what Belinda is, or what her life will be. What good is one more Barstow going to be?"

"Maybe she'll be a great beauty," said Seymour. "She ought to. And most likely she'll be a star, and I'll come back and be her agent."

Jeffrey smiled wanly.

"The day of miracles is past."

Seymour was dismayed. He had never seen Jeffrey so depressed.

It seemed to Effie that Mr. Barstow was fading into senility. Occasionally, like a crazed grandfather who has been hidden in a back bedroom, he would burst forth in a debauch.

He caused the flight of Belinda's first nurse, an English nanny, when he appeared in the nursery in nothing but a red sash and a gold earring, a bottle in his hand, and announced that he was the Pirate King of Penzance.

Effie was put in charge of the child. It was easier that way, Jessica figured. She could control Effie, she could save money, and she knew that Effie would become a slave to Belinda, which of course would give Jessica more and more free time.

Several weeks later when Effie was holding Belinda in her arms, brushing back the little fuzz of golden hair with a tender hand, she looked up to see Mr. Barstow standing at the nursery door. Mrs. Barstow was away at Elizabeth Arden's Maine Chance, getting her figure in shape again. There was an expression of incredible affection on the face of Mr. Barstow as he looked at Effie. She turned away, shaken. And when she peeked back, half-fearfully, he was gone.

But she could never take care of Pansy again. She told the Italian gardener she was afraid the monkey would bite her. So he took over.

As Belinda got older and sunned in the garden in her carriage, Effie sitting by, the chimpanzee screamed and raged, shaking the bars of her cage. The whole household was afraid her great jealousy might cause the baby harm.

So, Mrs. Barstow gave Pansy to the Griffith Park Zoo. The plaque on her cage read "Pansy, chimpanzee (*Anthropopithecus*), Gift of Mr. and Mrs. Jeffrey Barstow."

Pansy became a tax deduction.

◆◆◆◆◆◆◆◆

In London, in the days of the blitz, it was sometimes more dangerous to be working at Number

Twenty Grosvenor Square than to be parachuting into an occupied country.

Lieutenant David Austin of the Office of Strategic Services and his buddy, Wing Commander Sidney Keyes of the RAF, did both. They were deeply involved in the manufacturing of propaganda films, and propaganda was found where you sought it.

Sidney tugged at his distinctively air force handlebar moustache and pondered on the fact that David was the most devil-may-care son-of-a-bitch of all the extrovert lot he knew, and he knew them all. It was a paradox that a multimillionaire owner of a motion-picture studio would rather hitch a plane ride to join in a commando raid than use his considerable skills in coordinating training films in London.

David seemed to be using the war as his own purge; he was his own whipping boy. None of the basic needs of man seemed to involve him—food was a necessity, shelter and rest immaterial, and sex a random exercise.

When Sidney fell in love with one of the most beautiful of the Windmill girls, David stood up with him at their wedding. But Sidney had the impression that he looked at his bride Jennifer with a sardonic lift of the eyebrow.

The ladies' steam room at the Dorchester, of all places, was a likely refuge from bombing when one was in the neighborhood. One night, after being rousted from the bar, Sidney and David stumbled down to the shelter in company with military personnel and civilians.

The rumor spread that the Café de Paris a few blocks away had got it. Soon after there was a roar and the usual fall of plaster.

"That's a close one," said Sidney. "My God, I hope Jennifer didn't stay in the mews. She was supposed to meet me here at the bar."

"Nobody's meeting anybody on schedule," said David. "Let's just sit it out."

Someone passed around a bottle snatched from the bar upstairs.

The door opened and a very young man walked in with a woman. She was holding her hands over her head, which was liberally powdered with plaster. She obviously was tipsy.

"Good God, John," she said, "I've gone white."

He laughed at her and brushed off her hair.

David glanced up sharply. He knew that voice.

"Well, it's all in a day's work. I wonder if the Cavendish is still there."

"It always is, Claudia," said the young man.

David snuffed out his cigarette and took a swig from the bottle in his hand.

Sidney took it and offered it gallantly to the woman.

"Madam," he said, "be our guest."

She lifted the bottle in a dramatic gesture.

"Here's to my niece, Belinda Barstow," she said. "I got the word today. Can you believe my brother Jeffrey Barstow's wife Jessica whelped him a girl!"

Several people looked up, recognizing the name, and cheered.

"Well," said Sidney, "David, don't you know him? Isn't he—"

David had turned pale. He went to the door, getting away from Claudia.

"What's up?" said Sidney. "I say, did I do anything—"

He caught up with him.

"Come on, wingco," said David. "Let's get over to the mews."

"You know we can't get out until the all clear."

"I know how," said David. "For God's sake, let's get away."

Sidney, puzzled, followed him.

They found their way to a freight elevator and into an alley that led into Audley Street.

He and David rushed through the mews alley, tearing debris away. It looked like a direct hit. The all clear had barely sounded.

"Oh, God," said Sidney, "she couldn't have been there!"

Up the broken stairway, the room was a shambles of plaster and broken lath. Every time they moved a board, dust rose in the air. Fire was crackling nearby.

Sidney's young wife hadn't bothered with the air-raid warning. She had been too busy. She was naked, lying under Sidney's commanding officer. His shoes, tunic, trousers, and skivvies were on the floor. He hadn't bothered to take off his shirt or tie, and their stolen, erotic moment had been frozen. They were both dead as mackerels.

Sidney stood, staring in horror, until he realized David was pulling at his arm.

"Come along, old boy," said David. "There's no use to try to kill the dead."

He pulled him away from the crackling fire and got him to a pub. The weeks that followed and the many sessions of pub-crawling were a haze to Sidney. But, as he recovered, he looked at his friend with a different eye. He realized that David, for some reason, hadn't been able to heal the scars that someone had given him. Men in those war-weary days often ranted in a drunken sleep. And the name Sidney often heard was uncommon: Jessica.

Somehow, he felt, David was not only very young, but his maturity had been stultified. His girls had to be off the street or strangers picked up in a crowd. And it ended there unless they were paid companions and kept their places. He gave of himself in his work, his friendship, and in dogged integrity in all he did. But in certain areas the door was shut, and no one ever saw through the keyhole.

◆◆◆◆◆◆◆◆

Fergus realized, as well he should, that Jessica had arranged the whole marriage and parenthood to prove to him that Jeffrey was indeed the father of David.

Tormenting himself, at Las Cruces Sanatorium one Saturday when Esther was in one of her lucid moments, he brought up Jeffrey's name and watched to see her reaction.

"I'm thinking of using our new teen-ager, Martha Ralston, with Jeffrey Barstow," he said. "What do you think, Esther, of having Jeffrey play a father? Would the public like it?"

Esther smiled at him. He noticed that her face was eternally young; no wrinkle marred it. No thought, save gentle melancholy or a smile about David, seemed to touch her.

"Oh, Jeffrey," she said, almost as if her voice was in an echo chamber. "Yes, such a nice man. So gentle—"

She picked up one of her ever-present fan magazines.

"What do you think of the idea?" pressed Fergus.

"I think Martha Ralston is a pretty child," she said, "but is she aristocratic enough to be a Barstow? I think Barstows are very special people."

"You admire Jeffrey that much? That old drunk?"

"He is a gentleman," said Esther. Her face clouded. "You never show me any of his movies anymore."

Fergus wondered how much she thought that she never said. He was afraid to confront her with more.

But as he drove home, he thought of the little girl in the Barstow house, and of Jessica and her revenge, and he grasped the steering wheel until his knuckles were white. The loss of David embittered his every hour. Fergus despised him and hoped he wouldn't have to deal with him again. When the war was over it would be a good idea for him to run the European theater of Titan affairs. David had already signified his desire to stay on. That was fine with Fergus, considering their last meeting—when David had seen him with Jessica in his office.

His pride turned to bitterness. To find such treachery with Esther where he least expected it. He tried to bury the thought of David, but it was impossible. For the only thing that had mattered in life had been taken away from him.

This meeting with Esther triggered his anger. He went to Esther's room, kept for her occasional return home. And there, under a lavender sachet in her handkerchief drawer, was the yellowed piece of Arrowhead Springs stationery and the words, "Thank you forever, J.B." Along with it was a florist's card, from when David was born: "I share your happiness, J.B."

He wanted to tear them up. But he didn't dare. The slightest deviation from her pattern could send her into a deep depression. And he knew he had looked deeper into the secret, sad life of his wife than anyone should ever do. He sat in her room, noticing for the first time how devoid it was of anything personal. For the short time he had lived with Esther, he had never really seen her. He pitied her loneliness.

In a gush of remorse he realized that it all had been triggered by the fact that he had been with Claudia, fornicating on the floor in that rare sensual coupling. How incredible, he thought, that in the space of several hours, two chance sexual encounters with the Barstows could have caused so much heartbreak, trouble, and permanent tragedy.

6

In the winter that followed Claudia's promise to help him, John became a seaman's apprentice. The overall portrait of war reserved for civilian rumination was false. No one could read about it.

He froze. He sweated. He saw death. He escaped it. But when he was not on duty, when suspense hung as heavy as treacle, when seconds, hours, and days ticked by, he found a solitude among the sweating men he was forced to live with, and his escape was in the books Claudia had given him.

He began to form a dream. He studied how he would advance himself and what his progression would be. Analyzing the careers of the men ahead of him in theater, he knew the wise way would be to get in the Royal Academy of Dramatic Arts, if he could. After that would come, most reasonably, carrying a spear at the Old Vic, so he could watch the professionals and learn the proper vocabulary of the theater. After that he would join a rep company; then, if he were fortunate, perhaps the Malvern Festival. And if he did not find that he was moving along quickly enough, he would look for a suitable original play or screenplay, manage somehow or other to get it put on, and have control. If he worked hard enough, using his prodigious memory, and corrected the faults of his beginnings, he knew he would make it. And if he did, there would be a place for Claudia—oh, yes, that was his touchstone, the luck in his life, and he would be her luck.

Sometimes, as he witnessed the fearful din of chained, man-made lightning and the death and destruction about him, he felt little of the amazement of the great holocaust, because he knew he had a destiny beyond it.

Other times, when a man vomited his lifeblood, or died in a wretched heap, or if a man got a letter that blotted out a life he knew, John saw war in its personal aspects. And it triggered him more to spend the rest of his life doing what he wanted. He dreamed of the theater and the great world, and he related everything that happened to him with the image he someday would be.

From time to time he came up to London. He attached himself to a pretty barmaid who had a room in the tavern where she worked. He knew the pleasantness of sleeping the night through, flank to naked flank, with a woman.

He learned that comfort sometimes had its cost in the selection of a bedmate. This was not always the answer, nor was the fleeting moment of fornication in peril the solution to the way of a man with a maid.

Claudia was the goddess who had peered out into the darkened theater, thirty feet tall; she was the melting excitement of woman. She was never a tired, middle-aged woman with brandy-tainted breath who had lain terrified with him on the door of a gentlemen's lavatory, while it seemed death would be the imminent climax.

At sea, in cramped quarters, he dropped her a note occasionally; and one summer evening when he was on leave, his heart in his mouth, he bought champagne and streetside daffodils and called on her by appointment. He planned to expiate his dream by sleeping with her; he would show her what he really knew of himself and of women.

She, too, waited for this.

Her room was sprayed with old Paris cologne. She wore a brocade gown that smelled of a chemical spotting. Her hair was done in a pyramid of blue-black dyed tresses, and her makeup had been applied carefully.

"I managed some potted shrimp," she said. The Waterford glasses were prominently displayed and polished for the event. But as he brought forth his bottle it was ordained that there would be nothing. The champagne was corked. The attempts at naturalness somehow seemed faltering, excitement was gone like bubbles in the sour drink.

They toasted, anyway, and the smell of the potted shrimp seemed to rise up like a dead aroma in a besieged city. She had the grace to turn away from him and be real.

"Here is a book by Stanislavski," she said, "*An Actor Prepares*. Not that he is the living answer. It's the old Russian realism. You can't go the whole stuffy old theater route when this war has ended. You have too many gaps in education like all your sad generation. So you will have to find another way to catch up. This self realization will likely do it. You have to be an authority on something, ducks. It will have to be yourself. So be interesting."

She looked at him wistfully.

"Anything wrong?" he asked.

"I just wondered—" she said.

"Maybe—" he murmured, moving toward her, smiling in what he considered a sophisticated manner, his arms out, to embrace her.

"Oh, no," she said, holding out her expressive hands, "it doesn't always just happen like that. You must learn timing, my boy. You don't do it that way."

She moved to the sofa and sat tapping at a cigarette with elegance. Suddenly, she terrified him, for he remembered that she was the great movie star, the first and only goddess in his life, and by some miracle, he was confronting her, man to woman. He found manners enough to light her cigarette. He knew if there hadn't been a war, he would never have found the chance to be sponsored by Claudia Barstow. This, indeed, was a time of opportunity, and he mustn't muff it.

He tried not to be awkward, but he realized that any experience he'd had with females so far, no matter how youthful or pretty, was as nothing when facing a woman of Claudia's substance, style, and glamour.

Eagerness and youth were his only assets. He'd almost burned his fingers lighting her cigarette and playing the gent. He noted how graceful her gestures were; she could see through his inadequacies. However, he would have to plunge. It was now, or not at all.

"You did say you'd help me with my training when this war is over. Without your advice, I—I wouldn't know how to go about it."

He looked at her appealingly, abashed at his own revelation of his fears.

"I promised," she said in her deep voice.

Her face became alight with an affectionate glance. The moment seemed eternal. He dared not even look at her, despising his earlier presumption. He walked to the window and looked out on the crowded street, swallowing to keep from choking with emotion.

She had handed him a world. And that was what came of that meeting.

◆◆◆◆◆◆◆◆

From time to time, she mailed him a book, to help him on his way.

His mother went off to Hammersmith to live with her brother over his pub, the Blue Falcon. John returned from the Mediterranean to discover the pub blown to bits. It shattered him again to realize how the civilians were taking it on the chin while the forces were away.

It was difficult to think of his mother or his Uncle

Horace dead, and it was more incredible to find that the magic carpet of circumstance was still swirling him to giddy heights. He was awarded war damages, as he was the only heir. He was to get 2½ percent per annum after five years, as well as the value of the property. And he was going to be Claudia Barstow's protégé.

When the war ended, Claudia, as he had dreamed, helped him with his audition for the Royal Academy.

"Now look, dear boy, don't get into any particular dramatic rut at this time. You see, you're such a phony that you're imitating imitation gentlemen. That is not necessary. It's more than possible that people will enjoy an Elephant and Castle vowel proponent after all the grand Oxford and Eton boys. They say it takes two hundred years to create a gentleman, and your family hasn't even started. So you'll have to take a shortcut. You must search for your individual reality."

"I'd find it fast enough if you'd just step into bed." He pretended to leer at her.

She waved him off.

"Sometimes you remind me of myself when I was young and fresh," she said, "but bug off. It takes one to know one. You're faking, and, being a sort of male whore, you might perform out of gratitude, but it wouldn't be real, and I can assure you, Claudia would know the difference. Forget it. I should have one legitimate protégé, so you might as well be it. I've been associated with you so long, I haven't the time left to do it all over again with someone else."

"You aren't going to give me a chance to brag?" he smiled.

"Reminds me of the old story Lubitsch, bless him, loves to tell," said Claudia. "This actor was in a Hungarian road company with a famous star. He pestered her to death. Every time they embraced in the play, he would whisper in her ear fiercely, 'When! When!' He seemed to be dying of love for her.

"Finally, he bothered her so much that in spite of

the fact that she really wasn't too interested, she decided to grant him her favors.

"So she told him to appear at her bedroom that night. She let him in, he tore his clothes off, fell on her, and it was over in a moment. Before she could sit up, he was leaping into his clothes.

" 'What are you doing?' she asked.

" 'Getting dressed,' he said.

" 'Where are you going in such a hurry?'

" 'To the tavern.'

" 'But why?' she asked.

" 'To tell,' he answered."

Claudia looked at him impishly. He grinned.

"Are you going to say you did?" Claudia asked.

"Why, of course," said John. "Aren't you?"

"I have already," said Claudia. "You don't think I'd ruin my reputation. Now get the hell out of here before I seduce you."

He kissed her quickly and let her go. He was disturbed, looking into her eyes, she was so glamorous, so provocative. He could never think of her in terms of age.

But he was glad that she had released him. This was no time to be touched emotionally by a woman. He shouldn't be anything but free in this new world of opportunity. He had war compensations coming to him. His tuition was paid. He had total recall, memorization would be easy for him. The theater was coming into full life. The great prewar caste system had broken down. London was in such ruins that no one asked where anyone lived. It was a world made for opportunists. Since housing was so wretched, any place of public performance was the place to be. Films were being made all over the world. By the time his apprenticeship was finished, he would be ready.

It was also a time of lost manpower. The flower of English youth had been thinned out. There were dozens of lush women begging for the companionship of a personable man. Their bodies and minds were ready for any liaison. It was a wonderful and privileged time to be alive.

John followed in determined pursuit of his career. He performed the chores expected after Claudia helped him enter the Royal Academy. He pretended a calm acceptance of the training demanded of him, but he knew he was not on top of the curriculum as much as it seemed. Away from curious eyes, he studied more than anyone would believe, to cover his lapses of education and background.

His aloofness was interpreted as dedication. His memory aided him in overcoming chasms of ignorance. And if he ever retrogressed into a mispronunciation, he followed it with a burst of cockney that won him a reputation as a very amusing chap, brilliant with dialect.

He rebelled against academic training and pursued the Stanislavskian school. Then he abandoned theories for reality. He studied talent and enshrined it, no matter what its background. His heroes were John Gielgud, Noel Coward, John Huston, Laurence Olivier, Ingmar Bergman, Brendan Behan, Sergei Eisenstein, and so he called himself ecumenical in his taste.

He apprenticed in Bristol Old Vic, joined a Kensingtonian experimental theater group, relished playing the title role in *Othello,* the only white man among a group of Nigerian students. The play was an artistic triumph and caused comment in flamboyant circles.

It seemed his life would flow as he planned. He began getting more and more offers.

But he had no idea, when an original screenplay fell into his hands by way of a young writer, Victor Epps, what would happen.

Victor Epps was a thin, pale young man who did ambiguous chores for British Broadcasting Company. He loitered hours over endless cups of tea, or gin and bitters, as actors held forth at the Magic Carpet on King's Road. He was a good audience for John and laughed at his cockney stories and admired the behavior of the young hopefuls of the theater, who found him a satisfactory audience for their peacocking.

One evening after a performance John had gone as usual to the Magic Carpet for a pink gin and a quick bite. He planned to phone for a rendezvous with a girl he had just met who would be at her digs after she finished performing at the Windmill.

Epps joined him, clutching a script. His chin jutting out more than usual, and, fixing John with what he intended as a penetrating glance of his brown eyes behind his glasses, he announced in an unusual voice, "John, I am now ready."

"Be my guest," said John. "How about a pink gin with me?"

"No, not that," said Epps. "I mean this."

He cautiously wiped crumbs off the table with his tweed sleeve and set down the pristine script.

"It's ready," he said. "Fresh off my machine. I've done it over six times. But it's here, and you're the first one to read it."

"What is it?" asked John, cautiously. He had been handed so many rattily written manuscripts that he was ever suspicious.

"It's a picture script," said Epps. "I've been studying them all. And I think this is a good one. It tells the story—"

John held up his hand.

"Stop right now. Don't tell me. You'll spoil it. Let me find it out for myself."

He glanced at the eager, nervous face of Epps, staring at him.

"Look," said John, "I can't read this with you looking at me like a hungry hound, waiting for a bone. I'll take it home."

"Of course," said Epps. "But don't tell anyone the plot, promise?"

John smiled at him. Having been in the theater a year or so, he felt sorry for the naïveté of amateurs. "You authors are all alike. You act like I'm smuggling your fortune and might lose it." He flipped open the title page. "*Quest for a Key*. That's a good title."

"Part of it happened to my aunt," Epps said, "during the war."

"I'll take it home right now," said John, "before you insist on blabbing the plot."

He signaled the barmaid to take his money, and, while he was waiting for the change, he flipped open the first page. Then he turned to the second, and the third. He looked at Epps, in surprise, picked up his change, and tipped the girl.

"I'll give you a ring when I've finished it, Vic," John said.

"My phone's on the title page," said Epps.

John nodded; already he had altered his plans for the evening.

He returned to his digs off King's Road overlooking a bombed-out crater. Industrious neighbors had planted a pretty little garden, gathered broken bits of rubble, made neat borders for the paths, and built a bench and chairs of stones and cement with homemade wooden seats. A streetlamp shone down on it.

Between one and three John read the script with growing excitement. He forced himself to brew some tea and dig into a Huntley and Palmer biscuit tin to keep himself going. He read it again, more slowly. At dawn, he stretched and looked out on the bomb crater with its little garden. It was ideal for the first set of this picture.

When it was light enough, he walked in the streets to clear his head, and he wondered if he was fooling himself. Everywhere he went, he saw Victor Epps's screenplay. It was written for this time and this place and these conditions. Bombed-out, valiant London. These very people who were now going to their chores, out of their wretched lodgings in their tacky clothes, fed poorly, queuing with their ration coupons, all of them trailing an unspoken legend of courage, laughter, and tears.

At eight o'clock he called Claudia.

She answered sleepily.

"I'm coming to see you. I'm sorry if I disturbed you, Claudia."

"Who is this? I'm asleep. Are you mad!"

"It's John. I have to see you."

"You must have been up all night."

"I was."

"Well, go back to bed," she said. She hung up.

He rang her again.

"I'm coming over," he ordered. "Get up, put on the teapot, and let me in."

As he hung up, the phone rang. The reedy voice of Victor Epps came on.

"I—I don't suppose you've read it," said Epps, "but I wanted to tell you—"

"Don't tell me anything," said John. "Yes, I've read it. I like it. I'm taking it to someone, and, for God's sake, don't show it to anybody, *anybody*. You promise?"

There was a pause, Victor Epps was recovering.

"Hello," said John, "are you there?"

"I'm there," said Epps faintly.

"Well, stand by," said John. "I'll call you. Okay?"

"Okay," said Epps. John had the feeling that wherever he was, or in whatever position, he was going to remain frozen until that phone rang again. And John hoped he would.

Claudia sat in her wrapper, the teapot in a cozy between them, while John read, with many gestures and growing excitement. The first five minutes with her had been a scene of irritation, anger, and annoyance; he was an ingrate, he only came to see her when it suited him, he spent all his time with whores, and now he appeared at an ungodly hour. What kind of manners did he have?

But she saw a new John Graves when he answered.

"Just be quiet for once, Claudia," he said. "It's happened faster than I thought, and it's smacked me right in the face. Nobody else would understand it. I rather imagine it's not unlike the way you started in films—that's how it must be."

"You couldn't possibly know, but what's it all about, now that you've got me up?"

An hour later she leaned forward, her hands under her chin. Her hair was pinned back, and the light makeup she had put on before he arrived seemed nonexistent.

"So it's made for you," he said, "and that bastard Victor Epps has caught my pretentions, my cockney lapses, my phoniness—yet I'm willing to do it."

"You're willing!" she said. "It's a star maker. Imagine being an actor, a toff, a pickpocket, and a man who sacrifices himself all in one film. But you're asking me to be myself. A fading demimondaine, a woman whose whole economy and future lies in finding a key that opens up all the ducal jewels she could never admit owning. An ex-mistress, a passé actress, a failure, a hand-to-mouth war victim."

"That's bad?" said John. "Who was it I heard raving about Anna Magnani in *Open City*. Well?"

"That wasn't quite so biographical," she said. "Read me that scene where they climb through the rubble and go up the staircase hanging on the wall, that baroque mirror where her drawing room once existed. That's fabulously dramatic."

"I like the scene where they get in the warehouse and the rats climb all over them," he said.

"You can get a double for that!" she said.

He ignored her. "It has to be neorealistic. It has to be a bombed-out city. We'll only need one sound stage—for her bedroom, for the jail cell, and for the drawing room. And look, Claudia, another reason you have to play it is because we can sneak in that theater in Bermondsey that does all your reruns and get stock of you as the star. As the character, Helena, looking at the film, you suddenly realize that the key to your hidden vault in the ruins is in that same purse you used in the film."

"Looking ratty, of course," she said, "then finding

you pickpocketing at the Caledonian market and collaring you to help find the purse. You, with all your muscles bulging, oozing sex to the female tourists. Wouldn't you just!"

He smiled and bent over to kiss her on the cheek. "Can I help it if you taught me all those things? Come on, Claudia."

"My dear innocent," she said, "do you know how much it would cost, even to wing a picture. We've got sound to worry about, and if we shoot real locations around London, we have to dub the sound, and that's expensive. And permits for all that. Then you have major labor unions to deal with; you have to go through the Association of Cinematographers and Allied Technicians on Soho Square. Proper salaries and working conditions are necessary. Think of all the expenses, even if you and I and your Victor Epps defer everything. We've got laboratory work, prints to be made, mechanics and opticals to be gone through. We have to find a releasing organization."

"How do you know all this?" he said, surprised at her knowledge.

"Because," she said, "when I first came to London after my slight lapse in Hollywood, I was stupid enough to get into a tea-and-crumpet comedy with a great deal of my money involved. Why do you think I live like a second-rate rep character actress; didn't it ever enter your mind?"

"I think it's beautiful," he said. "It's full of wonderful things."

He gestured at the Augustus John portrait. "That's enough to make any room beautiful."

She smiled. "You obviously haven't been around, yet. Just wait until you are, and you'll see how shabby this place is. One of the saddest things about a has-been like me is that a few ghosts haunt me, like that portrait. It's almost as bad as watching yourself in old movies." She sighed. "But anyway, who could we get to bankroll us? I haven't any connections, have you?"

He shook his head. "If anyone bankrolls us, we lose

our creative control. Claudia, I *know* what I want to do. I can make it. I must direct it. And I can play my scenes, too. I know how to catch all the glory, all the despair, and the heart of London. A war's a terrible thing. But what happens afterwards in the lives of people is even more dramatic. It's how they cope. I know it's too soon for me to float it. But I do have a few benefits put away I could dig out. Say, a thousand pounds."

"You have that?"

"War benefits. I have not lived high on the hog," he said.

"My income from California is based on my house being leased," she said, "and I get nailed with repairs, painting, new furnaces, and such, not to mention an ugly little thing, thriving beautifully in California, called property tax. I barely make it."

"No family jewels?" he asked.

"No more," she said, "save one cigarette case, in hock until my next check comes from the States, and a bracelet which is to be buried with me. Now you know."

John took her hand and kissed it. "You're valiant, Claudia. You're so much like Helena in the story."

"If you tell anybody, I'll sue you," she said.

She went to the window.

"I'm sorry you even brought the screenplay," she said, rubbing her arm. "Oh, John, it's been so long since anything's really given me gooseflesh—It's impossible. It's a wonderful script. Too bad, because it's too late for Claudia. And too early for you."

"Not at all," he said, jutting out his chin.

◆◆◆◆◆◆◆◆

One Augustus John oil painting 50 by 37½ inches in fine gold frame: subject, Claudia Barstow; masterly portrait of a beautiful young woman; asset, fine painting; handicap, subject too well known, better in the market if subject unknown. Two Sisley sketches. One James Montgomery Flagg pen-and-ink portrait. One gold and ruby cigarette case, inscribed "To Claudia, Happy Birthday, Sambo." One delicate diamond bracelet, fine diamonds, platinum filigree setting, circa 1914. Ladies' beaded dresses and jackets of the 1925 period. Six fine beaded and embroidered handbags. One ivory and silver dressing-table set, initialed C.B. One leopard coat. One lynx trotteur. One silver-fox cape. One white fox jacket. One sable stole. One mink coat with cuffs and shawl collar. (All in moderate condition.) Two Spanish shawls. Six assorted gold bangle bracelets. One ermine bed throw in yellowed condition. Six sets French paste costume jewelry. Total fetching, in both auction or pawn, £6,245.

One bank account of £1,250 6s. One lot, former site of Blue Falcon Pub, £1,560. One gold gift watch with band, £40; loan on insurance policy, £220. Total fetch: £2,070 6s.

One loan from Victor Epps, £500. Sale of encyclopedia set and various books and assorted lithographs, £45 6d. Loan against family property in Hammersmith, £250. Sale of one motorbike, £30. Total fetch: £825 6d.

Total funds raised: £9,140 6s. 6d. Immediate future potential: $1200 from American investments, £50 from performances on BBC, £30 from appearance of male lead in Kensington Theater, £20 from writing chores at BBC, all to be contributed by three principals in Quest Productions.

Random notes, after Quest Corporation conference. Principals: Managing Director, Claudia Barstow; Directors, John Graves and Victor Epps.

"Necessaries: permits; check Wardour Street. One DeVry camera, used by Signal Corps in war films; one Eyemo camera, both can be hand held. (Hand held will be okay, cinema verité and the subject of *Quest for a Key* allows it.) Black and white film. Triple X Eastman film to be used for special effect in theater. It will be grainy, but we'll call it style. One rubber-tire dolly rented for three days. Lenses: long focus, K3 heavy amber filter. Spray machine for fog effects. Small studio at Beaconsfield, sound stage 24 by 49, can squeeze sets and spray paint and dress for various effects. Smallest crew possible includes assistant, cameraman, operator, gaffer, electricians, props, sound technician, clapper boy, makeup, cutter. No wardrobe. Keep it neorealistic. Pattern: *Open City*. Laboratory fees. Raw film. By using natural sets can save. Everyone says our project will cost at least £15,000. We will make it for ten. (Or else!)"

Claudia, John, and Victor sat in her room.

"You see," said Claudia, "this really *is* a great deal like our pioneering days. The difference is, then it was the Trust. Here, it's the bloody unions telling us who we have to hire."

"I think," said Victor, "I could hold the Eyemo while you and Claudia do some of our scenes in preproduction. That ought to save a lot."

"Of course," said Claudia. "We'll take that shot climbing up those outdoor steps and some of those scenes among the ruins, and I don't know why we can't get those pictures of me looking at my old film."

"No," said John, "I need all the expertise of a cameraman to get your face in light reflected from the screen. I was talking to Henry Graf. He had lots of experience filming in the war. He's getting hold of some supersensitive film that the Americans used to film nighttime rocket launching for your friend David Austin."

"Not my friend," said Claudia. "He was just a kid the few times I met him on the lot. No favors, please. Besides, I read he's about to go to India, setting up new studios for Titan."

"Too bad," said John. "You might have talked him into a deal."

"Not so easy, if he's like his father," said Claudia.

"We do have to have a release," said Victor.

"Let's make the picture first," said Claudia. "We

never asked why we were making a picture, or who was going to buy it. We just did it. Now let's go over our lists of locations."

"I found a good one," said John, "near Saint Paul's down by the waterfront. There is an incredible warehouse, intact in the middle of a disaster area. I can rent it for a couple of pounds for a day. We can get in there in the morning, swing the great door open, and the sun will flood the place. It's full of packing crates. Great for the scene where you're trying to find the box you hope has your purse in it."

"Whatever we do," said Claudia, "we have to gear our locations so we can get from one spot to another in record time. We do this whole show in three weeks, or we're dead."

◆◆◆◆◆◆◆◆

The pewter dawn caught itself in a reflection of rainwater in the pit where once had stood a private home.

A staircase clung to the building, which had been sliced in half. At the third floor, a crazy door swung out into the void, revealing a salon, one side fallen away. Strangely, a large baroque mirror still hung on the wall, solitary sentinel of past grandeur. Victor admitted to John that this was what had triggered his imagination.

John had entered the building by a ladder from the opposite side, and stood in his picture wardrobe, tight-fitting trousers and a striped turtleneck sweater, a flat cap rakishly over one ear. He bent down to gesture to the frightened woman, dressed in a shabby tweed dress and sweater, but wearing white gloves and a wisp of veiled hat on her curled raven locks. Her feet were clad in the stylish ankle-strapped high-heeled slippers of another era. Her face was pale, her lips slashed with crimson.

Cautiously she stepped onto the steps that stuck

out of the wall like fish bones with no banister or railing for her to hold.

In the building across the chasm of ruin, Victor Epps braced himself on a fire escape, holding the Eyemo camera, a friend hanging onto his waist so he would not topple off.

"No matter what, keep grinding, Vic," yelled John across the void. "We can do it again, but it'd be better the first time. Okay, ready, Claudia?"

"Ready," she said. "I'm terrified of heights. For God's sake give me a hand when I get up there."

"I'll haul you up," he shouted. "Just look up at me, don't look down, okay, sweetheart?"

"Okay."

"Camera, Vic. Rolling!"

In spite of the early hour, a group of onlookers had gathered on the street.

Victor panned the camera as he had practiced.

"Holy God," Claudia complained, "how was I stupid enough to pay to get into this ridiculous situation!"

"Just shut up," said John. "We'll dub later, but there might be some lip-readers in the audience. Watch your language and remember your role. You're Helena . . . Helena . . . Your whole future depends on this moment. Come on, Helena, come on, you can do it!"

Claudia climbed the dizzying staircase, sometimes catching hold of the next step with her gloved hands, her handbag dangling on a chain. She pulled herself up to the first landing, took the turn, moved one flight further, and stopped once, leaning against the wall, her eyes closed.

"I can't go on!" she said. "I just can't!"

"Come on, Helena!" said John. "I've seen some of your first pictures perched atop Castle Rock in California. It can't be worse."

"I was thirty years younger, you bastard!" she said.

He laughed at her, and she crawled up the last steps.

He held his arms out.

There was a scream from the crowd as she reached up to him.

The staircase toppled away from the wall. There was a roar of falling masonry. John bent down and took her hand just as the support broke away. For a second, she dangled in space with one hand clutching his, the white gloves and ornate purse ridiculous, as death seemed to approach. But John braced himself against the doorjamb, reached down, caught her other hand, and pulled her to safety as she fainted dead away.

◆◆◆◆◆◆◆◆

"Well," said the laboratory technician, as they looked at the rushes, "I have never seen anything like this in my life! How did you ever do it?"

"We don't reveal our secrets," said John.

"I ought to cosh you," said Claudia. "I can't bear to look at it. I noticed *you* got into that room by a safe ladder. You never told me nobody had tried that staircase, you son-of-a-bitch!"

"It's a marvel," said John, waving her silent in his excitement as he watched the incredible slip of her hand, just as he braced himself and grabbed both her hands. "God bless Victor. Look at what he did with that camera!"

Victor had shot the scene to the point where she had fainted and was held safely in John's arms. Then he had panned to the cluster of observers who stood horror stricken on the sidewalk. One woman held her hands over her eyes, one was shrieking, or would be when they put in the sound track, and one man had dropped a parcel of groceries.

"And bless the citizens of London, too," said John. "They're what the film is all about."

The gray silhouette of the city, dreary dwellings, traffic-burdened streets, cobblestone squares rimmed with stalls and barrows, and drab crowds all became a fiber of the story of two people of disparate backgrounds who shared one adventure in a world of chaos.

They had a spate of good weather. In inclement weather they could photograph at the small sound stage in Beaconsfield where they could indulge in close-ups and dialogue.

The last day of exteriors, they chose to shoot at the warehouse, a complicated traveling shot from exterior to interior—the most dramatic photographic experiment in the picture. For some reason Claudia feared that scene. She was afraid of the musty reaches of the old storeroom.

The day before John went to Nottinghill Gate. There he gathered around him several urchins of the same sort he had been. They spoke the same language, and after a show of half crowns, they scurried off, bent on their errand. They knew exactly where to go, and what to do.

It was bright enough in the early morning for the fog machine to come into use and curl knee-high wisps of mist.

Claudia, in a linen sheath, carrying a purse, and wearing the ever-present white gloves, was to enter the warehouse with John, who was to force open the door after back-twisting effort. They were to throw aside cartons, rush to a packing box labeled "Helena Fielding, 20 Sloane Square," find it torn open, turn it on its side, and fish among masses of salvaged debris, searching for the purse with the key to a fortune in it.

It was to be a daring one shot, dollying from exterior to interior, and it required complicated planning.

"I don't see how I can spend ten quid on a rubber-tire dolly," said John. "I'm going over budget now, and we have that wretched set to dress in Beaconsfield."

Graf lifted his hand. "I was going to talk to you about that; you see I've had a little makeshift experience in the recent unpleasantness shooting for the

RAF. Believe it or not, I did this in Paris to show a dawn takeoff. We'll borrow my son's pram, use a couple of supports, and dolly in our camera on it. It will work just as well as rented equipment, I can assure you."

So it was arranged. Tracks were laid over the doorsill into the building so the run would be smooth.

"I can't believe this is the last exterior," said Claudia. "I don't care how crappy that sound stage is, it's going to be great to be between four walls, instead of perching on street corners with ragamuffins breathing down my neck. Who are those little bastards hanging around the set giggling?"

"Chums of mine," said John, "doing a little atmospheric work."

Graf's operator wheeled in the pram. It looked ridiculous, with a ruffle and ribbon around its edge and the camera set up on a makeshift platform on it. Claudia laughed.

"I know two dear old men in Hollywood who would delight in this. They set up our lab way back with stolen cameras, filched film, and a lot of love."

"This has a lot of love in it," said Graf, "unless we return it to my little woman with the ruffles ripped. Let's get cracking."

"All right," said John. "Claudia, while I'm wrenching open the lock, you turn to see if we are being watched. Then when we get in, I'll throw the cartons aside. Pay no attention to me, be intent on what you're doing. Then when you see your carton, throw it on its side so we can scramble for the contents. When you come up with the paisley purse, I don't need to tell you what to do. And Graf, just keep on shooting whatever happens until we run out of film."

"What extravagance!" cried Claudia.

The reflectors were put into place; she had a feeling of exhilaration; it brought back sharply to mind the day so long ago when the Trust had broken up Fergus's picture on Coney Island. She suddenly realized that Fergus had been even younger than John, and so had she. She wished time could go back and she could see Fergus and Simon cheering her on. In a strange way they seemed to be there, for they were part of whatever she was.

"Camera," said John, toeing his mark. "Action."

The scene went smoothly. John broke the lock, shoved and heaved to get the heavy door opened, and they ran into the building. They paused, getting used to the darkness, while the operator cautiously opened the lens on the camera. It followed Claudia as she pulled two boxes down, jumping back to avoid them, then, in desperation, shucking her white gloves and getting into the fray, as John tumbled massive crates on their sides and created a pathway to the box that bore the magic legend, "Helena Fielding." In a panic she saw it had been opened, and turned it over, spilling out the contents.

She let out a piercing scream. Dozens of rats rushed out of it. As she fell on the floor, she had to push some of them away from her face. One rodent climbed on her leg, one over her head, catching its paws in her little veiled hat. She ripped the hat off and threw it away with its squealing burden, crawling on her knees to get away from the terrifying pack. John picked up a stick, batted the scurrying creatures out of the way, and lifted her to her feet. She was breathless with hysteria; her voice came out in cutting gasps; she lashed out madly. He had to hold her to keep her from running in her panic.

In a moment the rats scattered, and she still screamed. Finally he shook her.

"Helena!" he said. "Helena, look! It's here!"

There lay the paisley purse. With a bleeding hand, which was still shaking, Claudia reached down and picked it up. Sobbing, she opened it, took out the contents, and triumphantly held up a glistening key.

The cameraman flashed a small pinpoint torchlight on it. It was the key to a fortune, relief from poverty and pain, a talisman of a life.

Claudia lifted the key up for a moment, looked at

it through her tears, and then, sobbing, closed her eyes and held it against her eyelid, as if to blot out the horror of the rats.

For a moment John held her close, placating her, and then he turned to the camera.

"Cut," he said.

Claudia stifled her wrenching sobs. Then she saw the little boys giggling behind the camera and the open wicker basket.

"You son-of-a-bitch," she said, "you did this to me."

She turned away from him and walked off the set, through the door, and past the warehouse to the street.

For a stunned moment, nobody said anything.

"Why didn't I think of that?" came Victor Epps's reedy voice from the shadows. He was crying.

"I better go find her," said John, disturbed.

He rushed down the crowded street. A few steps away was a pub, the Purple Dragon. He tried the door. Of course it was closed.

God. Poor Claudia! She'll get drunk. We'll never find her. The picture won't be finished. It's my fault. I should have told her about those rats. But I couldn't. It had to work this way.

It was the peak of the morning traffic. A dingy alley led to the waterfront. He saw a gleam of something white that seemed out of place. He rushed toward it.

She was sitting on a piling, wiping off the smudge around her eyes with her handkerchief. As he approached her, he was afraid. She looked at him with a blue-eyed flash of such anger as he'd never seen. Perhaps she wouldn't even finish the picture. He was sick with fear.

She gestured to another piling.

"Sit down, John," she said.

He perched on the piling obediently. Her voice was deep and calm. That disturbed him more than the explosion he expected.

"Why didn't you tell me," she said, "that you had

those rats planted? Were you afraid I wouldn't do it?"

"I wanted the scene to be the way it was," he said. "A thing of complete terror."

She paused a moment.

"I see," she said finally. "Everything I ever taught you, you didn't believe. You thought *you* had to give me my moment of truth, didn't you? I told you the actor must dredge it up himself or it was not good. *You* didn't think I was an actress. You just thought I was a movie star. Is that it?"

"Not recently," he said.

She stood up and closed her purse. She would likely walk out on him. She should, he thought. And it sickened him. She meant more to him than anyone had in his whole life.

"Well, let me tell you something. You also expected me to run off and get drunk and blitz the picture. Don't be stupid. I never misbehave unless I'm bored. Of course I'll never trust you again. But I admire your goddamn guts. Are we going to have to do a retake?"

She straightened her dress and smoothed her hair.

He shook his head. For once he couldn't speak.

"I didn't think so," she said. "Well, the day is young. Let's get over to the theater, my first show goes on at twelve o'clock. We can do the scene where I watch myself on the screen. That'll save a day's pay. Is Graf prepared?"

"He will be," said John, swallowing.

He followed after her. She walked back to the warehouse. The whole crew was standing by. As she came toward them, they all set down what they were doing and applauded.

◆◆◆◆◆◆◆◆◆

The final cut of *Quest for a Key* seemed an anticlimax. Once the opticals were finished and the picture shown, Claudia knew it was time to see about selling it.

"There's one company might be right," she said,

"and I'm not going to have you go through the vapors. I know who it is, and I'm taking it myself."

"Hogging the credit?" said John, grinning.

"Fat chance with you and your rippling sex all over the screen," she said. "And you would add a little chippy or two for the ending."

"It takes all kinds," said John.

"Just deliver the film to this address on Wardour Street," she said, "and I'll call you after the showing. Cross everything! Don't get drunk, wait for me."

Claudia knew she was being audacious to ask for an appointment with David Austin. After all, his father had seen her out of Titan, and he must know what she had done to his grandfather Simon. Maybe he even knew about her and Fergus.

But there was no other way.

As she came into his office, David came around the desk to meet her.

"Miss Barstow," he said, "I'm terribly sorry, I can only give you a moment. I'm on my way to the airport. I've been called to Madrid. Our picture is in trouble, and there's nothing I can do."

He looked at his watch. Distressed, Claudia looked at him. How strange, he did not look like Fergus at all. Well . . . maybe it was Esther, although she could hardly remember how she looked.

But his handsome turn of head, the way his hair grew, the way his ears were set, and the arch of his eyebrows seemed strangely familiar to her. She could not place it, but he had a smoothness, an entity about him that intrigued her. Casting the thought aside, she rushed into her problem.

"You mean you can't see my film?"

"I just can't," he said. "Would you mind terribly if my associate Sidney Keyes looked at it?"

She saw that his mind was on getting out of an embarrassing situation.

"Well—" she said, "I wanted you to see it so much—but—"

She stopped, deflated, overwhelmed at the realization that she had no power any more, no arresting beauty. He was obviously just trying to get away without being rude.

"I'm sorry," he said. "I must go."

She tried to hold back her frustrations. But she faced him angrily.

"Then go," she said, trying to keep her voice steady. "You couldn't possibly know what this picture means to me. You'd have to have gone through what your father and grandfather did to understand. Listen, David Austin, this is the first time in my life I am proud of what's on film, including the biggest blockbuster I did for Titan. This picture is mine. I guess I wanted you to see it first. But it doesn't need you, or Fergus, or Simon Moses, or anybody. So go fuck off. Catch your plane."

He looked at her, surprised, and then he grinned.

"Well, Miss Barstow," he said, "I heard a lot about you, but the original surpasses the legends. Sidney will have to carry on."

He put his hand out and shook hers warmly. She was overcome by his manner, and he puzzled her. He rushed away just as Sidney came in. She stood wondering at him and the way he moved.

Sidney laughed. "That's our David. Perpetual motion. Come on, Miss Barstow. I'm going to see your film with our story editor and one of our legal advisers. Let's get cracking."

As the lights came up, Sidney turned to Claudia.

"Miss Barstow," he said, "it's magnificent. I've never seen anything like it. It's a tour de force all the way round. But you know we can stop you from releasing it."

"What do you mean?" she asked. "It's not immoral. It would pass any code, I'm sure."

"Don't you know why?" he asked. He looked at her. Her face had paled, and her eyes stared at him. "You really mean you didn't think about it when you made it?"

She shook her head.

The two men sitting behind him were straining to hear.

"Would you mind," she said, "privately. In your office?"

She was not there more than five minutes.

She thanked Sidney blindly and left. She didn't spend money on a taxi. She took a bus and walked to the Cavendish. On the way she passed bombed-out lots with flowers pushing through the fences. She dared not look at some of the places they had shot.

Her two partners were waiting. They had divested themselves, as had she, of everything material they had except their talents, and she had allowed it, not realizing how she had unthinkingly led them down the daisy path. For she alone, being the experienced one, should have known better. How could she have been so stupid!

Somehow, John had scrounged a bottle of champagne.

They took one look at her face as she sat down.

"It's no go." She held up her hand. "At least no go here. But I think I have an ace up my sleeve. I am going to fly to the United States with our picture, and I'm coming back with it sold or not at all."

"And what fairy godmother has the money to take you and the film to New York?" asked John.

"The one who is going to buy it," said Claudia.

She went to the mantel where a chipped Staffordshire dog was the only ornament, now that the portrait was gone. Underneath its hollow base was a small box. She opened it. There was a money clip tipped with a diamond, and she took out five hundred-dollar bills.

"My holdout," she said. "I saved it in case the picture ran over budget."

7

◆◆◆◆◆◆◆◆

As Claudia boarded the Constellation at Croyden, she looked at the split-tailed four-engined monster, and thought of the wicker-seated plane that had bucketed her across the country when she had left Hollywood. Now she'd fly over the vast Atlantic in less time than one of those dreadful days. Incredible!

She was certain of one thing. In answer to her urgent wire, Fergus Austin had reached across the years to assure her that since he was going to be in New York on Titan business he would arrange to see her.

She certainly didn't look her fifty-two years. Her eyes with their thick lashes were still her best feature. Her body was supple, and her elegant slim legs and petite feet a blessing in this world of larger, heavy-boned young girls. Her type might be old fashioned, but, like a Rolls Royce, she thought with amusement, she could remain a classic as long as she kept herself up.

With this in mind, she smoothed her carefully tinted hair which still seemed a glossy black counterpart of the original. She wore a simple black dress and jacket salvaged from the days Adrian had dressed her (and his things would never go out of style), white gloves, a small white hat, and Harrod's jewelry-counter Majorca pearls which she hoped could pass for the real thing. As an amusing token, and the only real jewelry she had left, she took the C-shaped diamond money clip Fergus had given her and stuck it on the neckline of her dress as a brooch.

She peered out the window at the fleecy clouds and the shining sea below. It was such a big world, and she had settled into such a small one these last years. Her heart sank. She wandered back to the ladies' room. In the mirror, with the unflattering lights above it, she peered at herself critically. A tired, more than middle-aged woman. A failure, blacklisted, given to alternating fits of depression and euphoria, both bad for the soul. One cheap, runaway grainy film to bolster her hopes, and, in the matrix of its footage, a vital error that could not be removed.

As she put her hand to her throat and patted the skin, she wondered how Fergus would think she looked. She feared the little flicker of his eye; she had seen it lately in men she had known before. They had always enthusiastically said she looked great, then turned to younger women, leaving her with a pasted smile on her face and a drink in her hand. And they wondered why she drank.

She came back to her seat, ordered a double martini, and flipped through a slick magazine. Who were all these new, beautiful people? Another generation of international pets since she had come back to London a dozen years ago.

Martha Ralston, the new Titan beauty. Long taffy-colored hair, a voluptuous body, big tits. That's what they wanted now. Depressed, she ordered another drink. The stewardess informed her that she shouldn't really give it to her, but here was one more if she didn't mention it. So she nursed it and leaned back, dozing as the plane droned on.

If I don't make it . . . her last thought was, I'm going to tie that can of film around my neck and jump in the ocean. There seemed nothing worse than being stranded in a plane that sounded like a Mack truck—a thousand miles between drinks.

◆◆◆◆◆◆◆◆

How different the austere New York offices were from the Hollywood studio.

A taxi driver helped Claudia into the creaky elevator with her heavy film cases. The corridor walls were lined with flossy little polychrome one-sheets advertising new products. Occasionally a larger three-sheet divulged the names and credits of current pictures.

She saw several of Jeffrey, standing giant size among the little figures of minor characters. His newest picture was *Tiger of the South*, and he portrayed a heavily decorated dictator of a mythical country. Leaning voluptuously against him, her blond hair falling over her face, her breasts half exposed, was this same young Martha Ralston she had noted in the magazine, the new sex symbol. Oh . . . thought Claudia, how far they have come. Even if I were young, they don't want my type anymore.

When she reached the executive floor, she pushed the button to hold the elevator. A young receptionist at a desk in the hall asked for her credentials and, when she heard her name, her eyebrows lifted.

I didn't know she was that old . . . thought Claudia.

"You'll have to help me," she said. "I'm afraid these film cans weigh more than I do!"

After a moment, the girl called a messenger boy. He was not too delighted with the job. Claudia was asked to sit down and wait a few moments.

This had never happened to her before. She wanted to run. Then she looked down at the film and thought of John Graves, and she busied herself with the last little pack of her violet cigarettes. They were stale, but looked good.

The phone flashed.

"You may go in now, Miss Barstow." Claudia felt like an antique on exhibit as the girl took in her appearance. In this world there was no place for her black crepe dress and fake pearls.

She was ushered down a long corridor. This was the world she had never thought of, she suddenly realized—the mechanics that made celluloid dreams come alive in theaters throughout the world. Making films was just a prologue for this vast economic machine. It was far removed from the effort she and John had gone through in London. She had come full circle, and she wondered if it would work.

She was received by a secretary in an inner office. The woman, a middle-aged relic of Titan's solidarity, greeted her with gushing enthusiasm.

"Oh, Miss Barstow, it's so great to see you again! You look just marvelous!"

She thanked her, hoping her heartbeat was not showing in her throat. She came face to face with a bronze bust of Simon Moses. She felt sickened, remembering him in life, startled to see his features in the cold austerity of metal. She put her hand protectively at her wrist, but of course the diamond bracelet was not there. It was in a pawnshop in Kensington.

She walked into a large room, overrich with thick rugs, mahogany, accents of antique English brass.

Twenty paces away was Fergus. He left the desk to greet her. He seemed more spare, taller, she thought, or had she shrunk? His red hair was graying at the sides. He took her hands and looked into her eyes.

"Oh, Claudia," he said, "you look the same!"

The boy she had first known gazed out of his eyes. The admiration, the surprise at her beauty. She remembered that somewhere she had heard people always remain the age they were when you first met them.

"The same for you," she said.

He led her to a sofa and sat her down, still staring at her.

"It's all changed, Claudia," he said, "but we had the good days, didn't we?"

"Yes," she said. "Why must we know too late?"

And then to her utter dismay, her eyes filled with tears.

"Now, now," he said, "please, Claudia, please. It'll be all right. You know, whatever your troubles are, I'll help you."

"It isn't that," she said. "It isn't what you think—I—I mean, economic."

"What is it? What can I do?"

She took her handkerchief out and wiped her eyes. "You've got to see my picture, Fergie—"

He stared at her and then started to laugh.

"Oh, Claudia," he said. "All right. I suspect it isn't a comedy."

"So far it's been a heartbreak," she said. "I couldn't even get your son to look at it in London."

Fergus gave her an odd look. Could she possibly know that her brother was David's father? But he saw from her casual glance that she didn't know.

"The hell with him," she said. "I'm afraid I told him to bug off—or worse. Fergus I'm going to say something you never expected to hear from me. All the time I worked in Hollywood I was a fake. I didn't really get into my acting. But this time it's different. I'm the actress I should have been. No youth, no glamour, not even any sex appeal to sustain me. And also, I've developed and discovered a fine talent in a young man, John Graves. I picked him up as a cockney kid and played a reverse Pygmalion. I went right back to where we started. Only this time I fought and scrapped to make it come off. You'll see. It did. And no matter what happens, I'm proud to show it to you."

She began to cry.

Fergus reached for her and put his arms around her.

"Now, Claudia," he said, "you must be tired. Just pull yourself together, honey, and we'll look at it. Would you like a drink?"

To his amazement, through her sniffles she shook her head.

"Okay," he said, "let's go. I know how you feel about empty projection rooms, but come on."

Long ago Claudia had told Fergus that it wasn't fair to view a picture in a projection room with one or two critics watching it. And now her fate depended on this viewing with no audience to create an emotional experience.

As she tried to glance at him without him seeing her, she was sick with apprehension. She couldn't tell whether he was moved or not. The picture changed character to her. It looked dingy, badly lit. She was dreadful, a washed-up woman emoting under cliff-hanging conditions. John Graves was too flamboyant. The young actors they had used for bit roles from the various rep companies seemed wrong. And she waited with a pounding heart for the scene where she watched her own picture as a Titan movie star.

The lights came up. Fergus turned to her and took her hand.

"Well, Claudia," he said, "you really turned in a magnificent performance—and John Graves is a great discovery."

"But—" said Claudia.

"I have to think about it," he said. "By the way, who owns this?"

"My partners and I. That is John Graves, the young man, and the writer, Victor Epps."

"You did it all yourselves? Finance and all?"

She nodded.

"Our everything."

"I'll have to talk to Abe Moses," he said. "I cannot make a unilateral decision."

She stood up. There wouldn't be any more tears. She wouldn't allow it.

"We did it in good faith," she said. "We tried the best we knew. I know what's wrong, Fergus. But it's too late, I'm at your mercy. So I guess I'll just go back to London. I wouldn't want to put you behind the eight ball again with the Moses family."

She started for the door.

He rushed up to her.

"Now wait a minute, Claudia." He looked at his watch. "Could you have dinner with me? I have to stay in my hotel for a call from the studio. Abe's out there."

She had no place to go. He must know it. She nodded.

At the Plaza, while Fergus took calls from Hollywood, Claudia looked down on Manhattan. Even this skyline had changed. The whole world was too much for her. She didn't belong to any place. She thought of her barren room at the Cavendish and of John treading the boards in his little theater in Kensington, nervously wondering if there would be a cable for him when he went back to his digs. And owl-eyed Victor Epps nervously sloshing down pints of tea at the Magic Carpet.

She went to the lavish powder room, freshened herself, and combed her hair, pulling some of the curls over her temples to soften her face. She rouged her mouth carefully, sprayed on a little Tantivy out of a purse flagon, discarded her jacket, and set her pearls so they fitted the hollow of her throat.

She returned to find that Fergus had turned on music and was mixing her a drink.

"It's a pretty far stretch from your old apartment, isn't it?" he said. "I went by for sentimental reasons several years ago. It isn't there any more, Claudia."

"Ancient history!" said Claudia. "But what about the picture? Tell me."

"Claudia, we're not going to speak about it just yet, although I am deeply moved by it. But right now, here's to us."

She took her drink and tried to sip it. She wanted to pour it down her throat, she was so nervous. How long she'd held off heavy drinking because life had given her such responsibilities. But, she thought, there was nothing more boring to a man than an old flame, with as many years between as they remembered: 1913-1947. A third of a century!

"How's Esther?" she asked.

He shook his head.

"That's verboten, too," she agreed.

"You must be hungry. It's been quite a day."

"Yes," she said. "London to New York in twelve hours. Too fast. I'll take a ship any time."

He ordered dinner. The meal was luxurious. She settled down afterwards, sipping brandy. She leaned her head back against the chair and closed her eyes. She was comfortable with Fergus. But it hadn't worked. And she was tired to the bone. How dared she dream of a renaissance? What was the use? She had tried her best, and it was no good. Well, at least John Graves was young; he'd get over it. And so would Victor. They both had talent.

She felt Fergus's lips. How could it be? She opened her mouth slightly. The same excitement once more, so long after they were young. They clung together.

He picked her up, and carried her into the bedroom. Amazed, and almost wearily, she helped him remove her clothes. They embraced tenderly, and he caressed her as she once had caressed him, leading the way for her. When they finally moved in mutual passion, she held him tightly.

"Oh Fergie," she said, "it's so good with us. We fit together."

"You always say that," he whispered. They laughed and embraced each other.

In the morning, he gave her a robe and ordered breakfast while she showered. When the waiter had left they joined in the sitting room, and, as he poured coffee, he took her hand and kissed it.

"Look out," she said, "your cup runneth over."

He set down the coffeepot.

"We're buying your picture. Titan will release it."

She jumped up, almost upsetting the table.

"Fergie!" she said. "Why didn't you tell me before!"

"I thought you might not go to bed with me!"

She rushed to the window. Life was almost too much to hold in one body. How beautiful Manhattan looked. How wonderful the world!

"I think it's because I went to bed you bought it. At

least be a gentleman and say so!" she said, kissing him.

"You lucky, lucky woman," he said. "How could you have been such a fool as to use film from a Titan picture as your plot point? Don't you know that Titan's the only company that can release it?"

"I know," she said. "I realized it when I tried to sell it to Sidney Keyes in London."

"You bitch," he said. "I got second choice!" He seemed oddly disturbed for a second, then changed the subject.

"We'd like to sign John Graves," he said, "and your problems with the Hays office are long forgotten."

"I suspected so," said Claudia, "when you signed Jeffrey. Time and tide—Could I call London? And Jeffrey, and—and you?"

She ran to the bedroom, dropping her robe as she left.

That's my Claudia! thought Fergus, always provocative.

In a moment the bell rang on the sitting-room phone.

"Get in here," said Claudia from the bedroom phone. "You have an appointment with your new star."

◆◆◆◆◆◆◆◆◆

As the Constellation circled over Los Angeles Municipal Airport, Claudia turned to Fergus. "I guess you might say I'm on Titan's magic carpet again. It's a little faster than that first train ride." She glanced down at her new suit, new shoes, and quickly assembled Cartier jewels—all on new charge accounts sponsored by Titan.

Fergus had hardly spoken to her on the plane. His briefcase was bulging with papers, and he utilized his time to the utmost. As fond as she was of him, she realized what a dull bastard he must be to live with day after day. She counted the times she had slept with him in the third of a century they had known each other. Only six times. No wonder it was a festival every time. Maybe it was just as well to keep it that way, although she wasn't certain she could hold out another ten years. Well, there wouldn't be too much time to worry about it. These last few days of press conferences and ecstatic calls to London had proven how quickly things could change. And likely there would be plenty of live ones around again.

She discreetly avoided mentioning Jeffrey's wife, for she remembered the international gossip about Jessica being Fergus's mistress and somehow ending up with Jeffrey. That she couldn't puzzle, but she couldn't wait to see the baby. Baby? She would be six years old! It would be interesting to see if she looked like a Barstow.

"You'll get the full treatment at the airport," said Fergus. "I have to go straight to the office. The company will handle your luggage, and a limousine will drop you off at the Beverly Hills Hotel."

"And I'll meet my brother, I hope," she said.

She noticed the sudden hooded look on Fergus's face, and she could have bitten her tongue. Funny anything could touch him that much. What difference could the loss of Jessica mean? She was as cold as a fiddler's bitch from what chums had told her. She hoped Jeffrey would meet the plane.

But she was disappointed. He was not there. There, believe it or not, was Titan's star, Leslie Charles, holding red roses, flanked by Andrew Reed. Come home. All is forgiven, or should one say, all is forgotten in the great razzle-dazzle, success. From the rumor that had sprung out of the fresh-as-bakery-goods publicity, Claudia not only would be up for an award for playing Helena in *Quest for a Key*, but, somehow or other, she was the managing director of a British film company.

Before them stood a battery of flash artists, along with Gracie Boomer and Red Powell. Both of them were smiling brightly and talking through their teeth, as they had learned through many such an occasion.

"Would you believe," said Gracie, "that we have to cope with her again?"

"Not for long, I'm certain," said Red. "She'll fall on her prat again."

"But she'll surface," said Gracie. "She always does."

They both rushed to kiss her and welcome her home.

"Claudia," said Andrew, pushing forward, "I can't wait to see your picture."

"You'll love it," said Claudia. "It's full of rats."

Leslie interfered quickly. Claudia noted that he was a much more attractive man than the callow actor she had played with so long ago. She decided to give him a break. It wasn't his fault that he was dominated by Andrew. Maybe she could work on that, even an old score, and God knows he'd be a good escort.

"Leslie," she said, with her best throaty voice, "you look absolutely divine. I've enjoyed your films so much. How you have grown as an actor!"

He looked surprised, then drew himself up and smiled. Suddenly, she seemed incredibly attractive to him.

"What a wonderful thing for *you* to say," he said, "of all people. You know you taught me so much, Claudia, and I was too stupid to realize it. I always wanted to write and tell you. I should have."

She linked her arm in his as the battery of flashes went off. She managed to maneuver away from Andrew. Clarissa Pennock, slightly late, rushed in gushingly, and Claudia linked her on the other side as flashlights popped again, thus insuring a Sunday spread. It was all heady; back in again.

"There she goes," said Gracie to Red. "Watch old Andrew Reed get dumped by Leslie. I heard it was in the air, anyway."

"The trouble with the world," whispered Red, "is that all these boys are getting very liberal about sex.

You can never tell these days which way Leslie will jump."

"I can," said Gracie. "His option has been slipping."

Claudia looked around.

"I guess Jeffrey couldn't get away. I'll call him."

"You'd better," said Leslie, now in a position where his know-how could be valuable. "That wife of his has him tied to a pillory, and today they're giving some sort of bash for the child's birthday."

"Well," said Claudia, "we can't miss that, can we? I've got to meet my niece. Want to go?"

"Delighted," said Leslie, glad to get in on it.

They stopped by the gift counter, bought a giant panda, were photographed again, and rushed off, laughing.

◆◆◆◆◆◆◆◆

Jessica used her daughter's birthday as a frame for her social ambitions. Every child with suitable parents in the film colony was invited. The patio was set up with a merry-go-round, a rented pony circus, and a gaily decorated stage for clowns and magicians to perform on. The projection room had been done over in a profusion of animals and flowers to tie in with the newest Disney motion picture, obtained by Jessica by way of a great deal of name-dropping.

An elaborate champagne, caviar, and paté bar was set up for the parents. Ice-cream molds, nestled in a sculptured ice basket, would be wheeled in along with an enormous multicolored butterfly of a cake, with six candles blazing. Each child's chair had a ribbon tied to it, which led to a gift.

Jessica had appraised Jeffrey's medical record and realized that she'd better make an effort at a splash while he was around. Since Belinda was such a beautiful child, this was the time to make contacts with the social world, if she intended to belong to it.

Jeffrey watched the preparations as long as he could.

"This is not a child's birthday," he said. "This is a

Roman saturnalia. My God, what will happen to all these little bastards when they grow up? They're not royalty, you know, they're just the children of mountebanks and opportunists. It isn't the expense that bothers me, it's the vacuity of your mind."

"I know what's good for her future," said Jessica. "I don't want her to end up like all the Barstows, a wandering minstrel, waiting for some sort of handout. You're not getting any younger, you know. You'd better leave the maneuvering up to me as far as her future is concerned."

Jeffrey looked at her, enraged.

"You can say this to me!" he whispered.

"I can say that to you, Jeffrey." She took her list and went to the dining room, dismissing him.

He went to his room, away from the confusion. He sat down, suddenly giddy. She's right, he thought. She's right—what can I do for this child?

Effie knocked. Her teeth flashed in her dark face. "Ready?" she whispered. "I kept your surprise in my room like you said. Oh, B'linda'll be so happy."

"Tell her I'll meet her in the garden," he said. "You hide it where I told you."

Belinda was waiting for him in a cluster of tree ferns by the pool. He thrilled as always at the sight of her. Her flaxen hair, her dark-fringed blue eyes which somehow looked like Claudia's, and the delicacy of her body promised the beauty she was to be.

Look at her . . . pure Barstow, he thought. He couldn't wait for Claudia to meet her.

"And now," he said, "we're going to find a wild beast in the jungle."

"Is it a lion?" she asked.

"Worse," he said. "It's an animal that eats you up—with love."

He kissed her.

"And that is the only way to be devoured," he said, kissing her cheek. "Oh, you're my sweet honeysuckle!"

He took her hand. "Now, look sharp," he said. "Watch out for it, because it's your birthday surprise."

Under the ferns she saw a little basket. It had a closed hamper lid.

"Oh!" said Jeffrey, stepping back in mock fear, "that must be its lair. Oh!"

"Now, daddy," said Belinda, "like mother says, don't put on so much."

He looked at her, slightly pained.

But she rushed to the basket and flipped it open. She let out a squeal of delight, which mended his hurt.

"Oh, daddy!"

She picked up the little bundle of black, soft fur. The button eyes with the astounded gaze of puppyhood looked up at her. It was so tiny she could encircle its body with her two hands.

"What is it, a teddy bear?"

"It's a Yorkshire terrier," he said, "a pedigreed beauty. He won't always be black. He'll grow beautiful long silver and gold hair, as soft as yours, that will fall on each side of his body like a waterfall. He will love and protect you like a dragon. It's happy birthday from me."

Belinda held the puppy tenderly.

"Daddy, you're so *romantic*. He's beautiful, beautiful!"

In the distance they heard Jessica.

"Belinda! Belinda!"

Belinda moved closer to her father and put the puppy in the basket.

"I suppose it's time for me to go meet people." She frowned. "Oh, daddy, I wish we didn't have to go to this dumb party. The same clowns, we know all their tricks, and that tired old pony circus. We see the same things at every party!"

"I wanted to take you on a picnic," he said, "and we could run along the shore with the little dog."

"Well, why don't you?" said a voice.

Claudia stood staring at her niece.

"Claudia!" cried Jeffrey.

His sister stood, transfixed.

"Oh, Jeff, she's beautiful."

"Belinda, this is your Aunt Claudia. She's my best birthday present to you."

"Now I know why I was meant to come home. Oh, Jeff—a new Barstow!"

She rushed to Jeffrey and embraced him.

"Belinda!" came Jessica's voice, "Belinda, I know where you're hiding! Come right here, this minute!"

"Did *she* see you?" Jeffrey asked Claudia.

Claudia shook her head. "I ran into Effie and she whispered to me where you were. I dragged along Leslie Charles, and your wife probably wants Belinda to come in and meet him."

"That's a thrill," said Jeffrey.

Belinda made a face.

"I have to meet everybody," she said. "It's my birthday, I wish I could do what I want!"

"What do you want?" asked Claudia.

"Did you see my puppy?" said Belinda. "Daddy gave it to me, Aunt Claudia. I'd like to run on the beach with it, just us."

"Well, why not?" said Claudia. "I have a limousine waiting."

Belinda's eyes sparkled with mischief. "Dare we?"

Jeffrey put his arm around her.

"It's your birthday," he said. "We dare."

He lifted his brows and flashed his old, debonair glance at his sister. "Let's walk to the gypsy wagon and take off."

They skirted the pool, moved out the back gate past a cluster of camellia bushes. Claudia plucked three blossoms as they passed. She put one behind her ear, one behind Belinda's, and as a last gesture, tucked one over Jeffrey's ear. Belinda giggled and hugged her precious basket tightly as they ran for the driveway.

They jumped in the waiting limousine.

"Take us to the Santa Monica oceanfront," said Claudia, "and don't spare the horses!"

En route, Jeffrey turned to Claudia.

"Tell me," he asked, "do you ever see David Austin in London?"

"Funny you should ask," said Claudia. "He was rather rude to me. They say he's always on the run. Why are you interested?"

She looked at him, and her mouth fell slightly open. There was something so much like the David she had seen, was it possible? He turned, slowly, and stared at her, wordlessly.

For the first time in her life with her brother she smothered her impulse to blurt out what was on her mind.

"You know, Jeff, you don't get to see people all the time like we used to. London isn't the same small town it once was."

"Nothing's the same small town it was," said Jeffrey.

He seemed sad and withdrawn. Claudia looked at him and shivered. He had a gray, empty look. She realized it was an effort for him to bring forth the old Jeffrey charisma, his only drive now was to give his daughter a feeling of joyous companionship. This was no time to go into the complicated, instinctive feeling she had about David. A Barstow could recognize a Barstow anyplace.

They pulled up at the state beach at the bottom of Santa Monica Canyon. They kicked off their shoes and ran down to the tide line. It was a sunstruck day, the waves were gentle, the curve of blue seemed more a bay than an ocean; the tide was low. Belinda lifted the puppy out of the basket. It looked with some surprise at a wavelet, then galloped off, such a tiny thing that it tripped and fell over a seashell.

Belinda picked it up and kissed it on the nose.

Jeffrey grasped Claudia's hand, his knuckles were white, and she winced at his strength.

"Look after her," he said. "She sure as hell is going to need you someday."

His eyes were shiny. Claudia squeezed his hand. Words were suddenly not good enough between them.

A middle-aged couple approached and stared at the three of them with the camellias over their ears.

"Happy birthday!" cried out Jeffrey, picking up a strand of glistening seaweed. He waved it like a flag. "Happy birthday, all Barstows!" He gestured to them to join in.

"Happy birthday, all Barstows!" they shouted.

Belinda took the strand of seaweed from her father, and twirled toward him with it.

She cried, "Dance of the seven veils!"

Jeffrey stopped short. A moment of pain hit him. He remembered the brief moment with his son David, so long ago, as he had made exactly the same gesture.

The spectators stared.

"Hey, who are those crazy people?" asked the man of the woman.

There was a silence, one of those rare low-tide pauses between waves, when time stands still, and the smallest sound floats in the air. The three Barstows stood yellowed in the sunlight—surprised for a second that there was anything else in the world but themselves.

"Didn't you hear?" said the woman. "Barstows, Barstows, of course."

Belinda took her father's hand.

"Daddy," she said, "just exactly what is a Barstow?"

Claudia rushed to the little girl and put her hands over her ears.

"For God's sake," she said, "don't tell her!"